Wrath

Wrath

K'WAN

www.urbanbooks.net

Urban Books, LLC
300 Farmingdale Road, NY-Route 109
Farmingdale, NY 11735

ISBN 13: 978-1-60162-132-0
ISBN 10: 1-60162-132-9

First Trade Paperback Printing September 2019
Printed in the United States of America

10 9 8 7 6 5 4 3 2 1

This is a work of fiction. Any references or similarities to actual events, real people, living or dead, or to real locales are intended to give the novel a sense of reality. Any similarity in other names, characters, places, and incidents is entirely coincidental.

Distributed by Kensington Publishing Corp.
Submit Orders to:
Customer Service
400 Hahn Road
Westminster, MD 21157-4627
Phone: 1-800-733-3000
Fax: 1-800-659-2436

Wrath

by

K'WAN

Prologue

Jonas Rafferty stood in the middle of what he referred to as his "office," but calling it such would've been a compliment. On its best day, the room was little more than a storage space at the top of a storefront that Jonas owned that got too hot in the summer and too cold in winter. Aside from the modest desk and few chairs, it didn't look like much, but that's how Jonas liked things . . . simple and unassuming. He liked to play the role of the small fish in the big pond . . . until you got up close and realized that the fish was a piranha. By then, it was usually too late.

He walked over to the two-way mirror that took up a good portion of the wall. It gave him a bird's-eye view of the room below. It was a large space that he had converted into his own personal rest haven called Sweets. There was a small bar he'd picked up from a home furniture store, a few televisions, and a tiny square of dance floor for occasions where people wanted to get their boogie on. It was more of a clubhouse than an actual lounge. Before Jonas took ownership, it had been a grocery store called Juan's. Juan's was a place where you could get your household needs, loose cigarettes, and even trade in your food stamps for cash. The grocery store had been servicing the neighborhood for longer than Jonas had been alive, which is why it came as a surprise when he wiped all traces of the landmark from existence . . . including the previous owner.

That night was its grand opening, and the turnout hadn't been disappointing at all. The whole hood had come out. The whole place was full, and people were lined up outside hoping to get in. Jonas had announced that he was having the grand opening, and word of the party spread like wildfire, as he had expected. No one even blinked twice when he decided to charge a hundred-dollar cover charge to attend. Jonas Rafferty was the man, and $100 was a small price to pay to stand next to him and his associates on such a special night. Not only was it the grand opening of his social club, but it was also his birthday—twenty years on earth. There was a time when he thought he would never live that long. But he had not only outlived his life expectancy but managed to make a few dollars in the process.

At the stroke of midnight, they had all toasted with the free champagne Jonas had provided to usher in his birthday. Jonas recalled working the crowd, receiving well wishes and celebratory slaps on the back from his guests. From someone on the outside looking in, you'd have thought Jonas was the most loved man in the room, but he knew better. Those same hands celebrating him could be the very same ones plunging knives into his back if they ever caught him slipping. Phony people bothered some, but not Jonas. He had learned a long time ago to separate his personal feelings from business, and with him, it was always *business*. His heart knew no love outside those in his immediate circle. Love could kill you. That was a lesson he had learned from his sister.

Thinking of his sibling drew his attention to the cigarette pinched between his fingers. It was the first one he'd had in almost a month. That was about the time he had promised her that he was going to quit. A promise he was now breaking. Because she was no longer living, it technically freed him of his oath, but he still felt guilty.

He could picture her somewhere in heaven, or possibly hell, waggling an accusatory finger at him for dabbling back into what she always referred to as a "disgusting habit," so he stubbed it out in the ashtray. They said that time healed all wounds, but Jonas could find nothing to validate that theory. She had been gone for more than a month, but the pain of her absence was still fresh in his heart. It likely always would be. She would surely be disappointed that he was smoking, but proud of the man he had made of himself. Jonas had come a long way from the nappy-headed little boy in apartment 5H, but there was still so much further to go.

There was a soft knock at the door, but Jonas's attention remained fixed on the mirror. After a few beats, the door opened, and Tavion stuck his head inside. He was a fresh-faced youth with ripe yellow skin and a thin mustache tracing his top lip. "Yo, Wrath . . ." he began, but a sharp look from Jonas cut him off. "Sorry . . . Jonas. Alex asked me to find you. The car taking you guys to the airport will be here in five minutes. There's a lot of traffic, and she's worried you guys may miss your flight."

Typical Alex. Always punctual. Always organized.

"Tell her I'll be down in a few," Jonas replied and went back to staring through the looking glass.

"You okay?" Tavion asked, but Jonas didn't reply. He had been working under Jonas long enough to gauge his moods. The darkness was on him again. It seemed to visit more frequently lately. With this in mind, he slipped back the way he came and left his friend to his brooding.

Jonas waited for a few minutes until he was sure Tavion had gone before allowing the hints of a grin to touch the corners of his mouth. The youngster probably reasoned that he was angry with him, but he wasn't. Jonas knew better than most how hard it was to break old habits. He had gone by the moniker of *Wrath* for so long that even he had a hard time coming to grips that that part of him was no more. The monster had been put to rest, and he could start getting reacquainted with the man who had been so deeply buried beneath his pain for all those years.

Jonas decided to make his exit a quiet one. There would be no grand farewells, no tearful speeches, and no second thoughts. He would simply slip out the back door without even so much as a farewell to his guests. He owed them nothing. Those in his inner circle knew that he was leaving and why. Those were the only ones he felt any obligations to. The rest could go fuck themselves. In truth, he doubted anyone would even realize that he was gone. They were too busy goring themselves on his hospitality.

A few minutes after Tavion had gone, Jonas made his way downstairs. He bypassed the main area and went through the rear storage area, where they kept all the supplies. Tavion was standing near the back door, while Ace was pacing back and forth, occasionally stopping to exchange words with Tavion. Ace was one of Jonas's closest friends. He and Jonas had come up since kids. Ace and Tavion always argued like an old married couple, so Jonas didn't think much of the exchange. The volatile disputes between the two of them were just one of the many things he wouldn't miss about his old life and affiliations. When they spotted Jonas approaching, the conversation came to an abrupt halt.

"*El Jefe.*" Ace gave Jonas a curt nod. It was something Ace called him when he wanted to get under Jonas's skin.

"As of midnight, that distinction became yours," Jonas reminded him.

"Like his ego wasn't big enough already," Tavion mumbled. He hadn't been in favor of Ace taking over when

Jonas stepped down. He had been hoping it went to Prince. It wasn't that Ace wasn't solid; Prince was just where the popular vote would've gone, had there been one.

"Ace has been with me longer than anybody. He helped me build this thing of ours and deserves this as much as anybody," Jonas told Tavion.

"You don't owe anybody any explanations. It is what it is, and anybody who ain't happy with the new order of things can get swept out with the rest of the trash." Ace was talking to Jonas, but his eyes were on Tavion.

Jonas was about to comment on the obvious tension between the two men when the back door swung open, bringing in with it the winter chill and another of Jonas's running buddies. Willie was huddled in a green army jacket and matching skully. His thick, black beard was its usual mess. The black glass eye in his head seemed to see everything in the room without moving. "Cold as a bitch out there." He stomped his feet to try to get the circulation going in them.

"Then stay your ass inside instead of dipping out every five minutes," Ace suggested.

"Gotta make sure the perimeter is secure," Willie said, sounding every bit the soldier that he was.

"We got a dozen homies armed up and holding it down tonight," Tavion said proudly. He had been in charge of arranging security for the night and was proud of the ensemble he had pieced together.

"And most of them are high, drunk, or have never been in a combat situation," Willie shot back. "Next to the Fourth of July, New Year's Eve is the best night of the year to catch a brother slipping. There's so much noise that no one notices the gunshots. There's something wicked in the air. The eye always knows." He pointed to his glass eye.

"You need to chill, Willie. In addition to my people having the building locked down, I also had Stacey vet everyone who bought tickets. We're good," Tavion assured him.

"I'm sure Malcolm said the same thing when he walked into the ballroom," Willie said.

"Where's Alex?" Jonas asked, noticing he hadn't seen her when he came down.

"Outside, chopping it up with Stacey," Willie told him.

"You left my girl out there to freeze?" Jonas wasn't happy.

"*'It's too fucking hot in here.'* Her words, not mine," Willie added. "Sounds like she's ready to get out of here."

"We'll leave in a few. I need to holla at Prince. Where is he?" Jonas asked. He was the only one of his inner circle who was absent.

"He said he was going to pick up one of his shorties and spin back, but that was like two hours ago," Tavion told him.

This struck Jonas as odd. Of all his people, he'd have thought Prince would've been there to see him off. "Anybody check on him to make sure he's good?" he looked to Willie.

"I ain't his babysitter," Willie said in a tone Jonas wasn't used to hearing. He wore his signature poker face, but you could tell he was unsettled about something.

"I need to speak to him before we leave. I want to make sure everything has been set up with his people. I don't want any hassle when we land on the other side of the pond," Jonas said.

"Instead of worrying about Prince, you need to be worrying about Alex kicking your ass if you miss this flight. Prince will come back eventually. All stray dogs do. I'll see to it personally that all the arrangements have been made by the time you touch down." Ace ushered Jonas toward the door.

Jonas stopped short of the exit as if he had forgotten something. He took a last long around the storage area and thought fondly of all the money they had run through it. With little more than his strength of will and no backup plan, he had turned a cursed existence into a blessed life, not only for himself but for those he loved as well. All the pain and hardships he'd gone through to get where he was were small prices to pay when measured against the joy that swelled in his heart every time he found himself putting his people in positions to do better. That was probably the only thing he would miss about the game.

"It's not too late, you know," Willie caught Jonas's attention. "You could call the whole thing off. I don't think any of us would have a problem going back to business as usual." His good eye went from Jonas to Ace, who looked like he was afraid Jonas might change his mind.

Something passed between Ace and Willie that made the hairs on Jonas's stomach turn. The old feelings came back. He always felt like he was coming down with a touch of the flu just before something bad happened. Part of him wanted to pry into the unspoken dialogue going on between his friends, but he listened to the part of his brain that said his time in the streets was up. It was no longer on him to settle disputes among members of the crew.

"Nah, man, I'm done," Jonas told Willie, which seemed to relieve Ace.

"Then I wish you good fortune in your next life." Willie pushed through doors that led to where the party was going on. You would think that after all the work they had put in together, he'd at least have done Jonas the courtesy of shaking his hand, but he'd left without so much as looking back.

"What's up with him?" Jonas asked.

"Just in his feelings because you're leaving. He'll be okay," Ace assured him, but Jonas looked uncertain.

Tavion's cell phone went off. He listened while the caller spoke, nodding every so often before ending the call with "A'ight, we'll be right out. Your ride is a block away," he told Jonas.

"Now or never." Ace held the door open for Jonas.

When Jonas stepped out into the night air, the cold cut through his thick wool overcoat and settled into his bones. Willie hadn't been lying when he said it was cold, unseasonably cold for September. East Coast winters were something that he would not miss. Two of Tavion's retainers were standing around outside guarding the back door. They were smoking a blunt and talking among themselves, but when they saw Jonas, the weed was tossed, and the men stood at attention.

"At ease, fellas," Jonas said jokingly.

Not far from them, he spotted his lady Alex talking to Stacey. She was wearing the full-length mink coat that he had given her the previous Christmas. It wasn't quite cold enough for it, but Jonas encouraged her to stunt. She looked like a white angel standing there. In a sense, she was. It had been Alex who had opened Jonas's eyes to the potential his life held. He thanked God every day for bringing her back to him. *God . . .* That made him laugh every time he spoke the name. Jonas hadn't been much of a believer in God when he was growing up, but he was becoming more open to the idea of a higher power lately. There was no mistaking the fact that he had truly been blessed.

"About time," Alex greeted him with a kiss. "I was beginning to think that you had changed your mind about running away with me."

"Never that. I'm just mad it took me so long to make the decision," he told her.

"I still can't believe you guys are going through with this," Stacey said. She was a short, thick girl with long, black hair that was always pulled into a tight ponytail.

"Well, believe it, because it's happening," Alex assured her.

"I wish I could say that I was sad to see you go, but that'd be a lie. If any of these hooligans deserve a second chance, it's you, Wrath." Stacey called him by his nickname.

"What did I tell y'all about that?" Jonas checked her.

"Please! You know no matter what, you're always going to be Wrath, my protector and savior." Stacey hugged him. She tried to hold back the tears but couldn't stop herself from crying. Jonas had brought her into the game; gave her a better education than the one she'd gotten in college. He was always the one who made sure nobody fucked with her, and she wasn't sure how she was going to get along without him.

"C'mon, don't start that crying shit. This is hard enough for me as it is. You going to pieces is only going to make it harder." Jonas thumbed her tears away.

"I know, and I'm sorry," Stacey sniffed.

"You know if you need a shoulder to lean on, I'm here for you, baby girl," Tavion said suggestively.

"Boy, you've been trying to get into my panties for years, and your dick is still dirt dry. Why don't you give up already?" Stacey asked.

"Because I ain't no quitter," Tavion laughed.

A pair of lights appeared in the distance, bathing the entire alley. The retainers stepped forward, guns drawn and ready. All they needed was a word, and the fireworks show would start.

"Stand down. It's just the car service," Tavion ordered them, as the sleek black town car pulled to a stop short of where they were standing.

"About freaking time. You know the check-in lines at the airport are going to be long as hell," Alex complained.

"Ain't like we're traveling with any luggage. All of our stuff will be shipped, and I'll buy you whatever you need for the time being," Jonas told her.

"I hope Fashion Nova ships over there. You know that seems like the only thing I can fit since I got all big and fat," Alex said, rubbing her baby bump. She was just starting to show.

"You ain't fat; you're thick." Jonas kissed her cheek.

The older Hispanic man who had been driving the car climbed from behind the wheel to open the back door. He looked to be at least seventy and frail.

"Don't worry about the door, OG. I got it." Jonas stopped him. "Just worry about getting us to the airport in one piece. The snow probably has the roads looking real nasty."

"No worries. You're in good hands, Mr. Wrath," the old man said and got back behind the wheel.

It wasn't until Jonas pulled the back door open for Alex to get in that the warning bell went off in his head. The driver had called him *Mr. Wrath,* instead of *Rafferty.* What proceeded unfolded in what felt like slow motion. "What it do?" a familiar voice came from the backseat of the town car. Instinctively, Jonas pushed Alex to the ground. When he whirled on the car, he caught a glimpse of a familiar face just before the muzzle of the gun flashed.

Part I

*"But if any provide not for his own,
and specifically for those of his own house,
he has denied the faith, and is worse than an infidel."*

—I Timothy 5:8 (KJV)

Chapter One

Six years earlier . . .

Flash . . . squirm . . . flash . . . squirm. This had been their third attempt with the same results.

"Jonas, why can't you sit still?" Anette asked in frustration. She was Jonas's older sister, one of a set of fraternal twins. The sour one they called her because Anette always seemed to be pissed off about something.

"The flash is too bright. It hurts my eyes," Jonas complained, tugging at the clip-on bow tie at his neck. It was Christmas Eve, which meant picture day. Every Christmas Eve, Jonas's mother would dress them up in their best clothes and drag them to Woolworth's department store for a family photo after church. No matter what was going on in their lives, it was a tradition not to be broken. This is what had four of his mother's five kids sitting on the artificial grass in front of the cheap backdrop trying to look like a normal American family.

"Your eyes aren't gonna be the only things hurting if you don't act right so we can get these pictures done!" Janette warned. That was their mother. She was only 30 with five kids but had held together well. Her waist was small, hips wide, and her breasts had only begun to sag ever so slightly. Even with a gang of kids, Janette had no shortage of men looking to get with her, but she only had eyes for one.

Slick, who had been their live-in stepdad for the last two years, was lingering behind the photographer with a look on his face that said he would rather be anywhere but there with his girlfriend and her tribe of kids. He was a pretty boy; high yellow with good hair and two gold caps in his mouth. Women swooned over Slick like he was an R&B star.

"If he's having trouble keeping his ass still, I can offer him some encouragement." Slick tapped a manicured finger against the buckle of his Gucci belt. Slick was easy on the eyes but hard on the soul. This was a fact the Rafferty kids knew all too well.

Jonas gave Slick a dirty look. None of the kids liked their mother's man, but he had a harder time hiding it than the others.

"Something you wanna get off your chest?" Slick asked, hoping the boy would open his mouth so he could slap him.

"Leave him be, Slick. Jonas is only doing what young men do, which is make things difficult for women," Janette joked to try to ease some of the tension.

"That's his problem. He thinks he's too much of a man," Slick said.

"More of a man than you," Jonas mumbled.

"Say it again so I can knock your fucking teeth out!" Slick challenged. Jonas wisely remained silent.

"Come sit by me, Jonas." Jonas's other sister tugged at his shirt and motioned for him to occupy the space beside her. This was Claudette, but they called her Sweets because of her affection for sugar. "You keep yourself still so we can get through this, and there might be a candy bar in it for you," she winked. Sweets was fair skinned and kind of on the chubby side, with a motherly nature.

"I don't see why we have to sit through this and Yvette doesn't." Anette sucked her teeth.

"Because your sister wasn't feeling good," Janette said.

"More like she was smart enough to lie her way out of it," Jonas mumbled.

"You hush that smart mouth of yours, Jonas Rafferty, or we're going to have a problem!" Janette warned him.

"Um, guys . . . if we could just get this done. Other families are waiting," the thin, white kid behind the camera said. He was growing frustrated with the unruly black family.

"Then let they asses wait! We paid our thirty-nine dollars and ninety-five cents same as they did! Now, get your nose out of our shit and back behind that camera before you piss me off, cracker!" Slick barked. Not wanting any problems, the photographer did as he was told. Within ten minutes, he was able to get the shots he needed, much to everyone's relief, especially Slick's. "About damn time. I got shit to do. Let's go."

"Are we going to go to McDonald's now like you promised?" This was 8-year-old Josette, the baby of the family.

"McDonald's? You better thaw out some chopped meat when you get in the house," Slick dashed the little girl's dream.

"But Mama promised." Josette looked to Janette with watery eyes.

Seeing the look of disappointment on her baby girl's face made Janette feel bad. "I don't see why not since it's on the way home."

"We ain't got time. We got people waiting on us, remember?" Slick gave her a look. Everyone now wore long faces, so he came up with a compromise. He took out his bankroll and peeled off a twenty which he shoved into Sweets' hand. "Make sure these kids eat. We'll see y'all at the house later."

"Wait, you're not going to drive us back? It's snowing, and the walk is a fifteen-block walk from here." Sweets looked from the crumpled bill to her mother and Slick who were hustling out of the department store.

"Ain't like you can't use the exercise!" Slick called over his shoulder, and they were gone.

"I hate him!" Jonas remarked, ravenously biting into his McDonald's cheeseburger. He had to be mindful not to nick his fingers when he did. The ten blocks they had walked from Woolworths to get there had intensified his already-mounting hunger.

"What did I tell you about that word, Jonas? There is power in words," Sweets scolded him, plucking Josette from Anette's arms. She had been carrying her the last three blocks and looked like she needed a break. Josette had been complaining of her legs hurting, so the siblings took turns carrying her home.

"Sorry, I mean I don't *like* him," Jonas sheepishly corrected himself. "Why does he have to be so mean all the time?"

"Some people just have the devil in them, is all," Sweets said. She had a way of trying to see the good in people even if there was none.

"The devil isn't all he's going to have in him," Jonas said, trying to sound tough.

"Boy, stop talking like you about to do something," Anette teased him, squeezing a ketchup packet over her fries.

"What? You don't think I will?" Jonas rose to the challenge.

"Only thing you will do is get your head knocked off for getting in Mama's business. Slick is a grown man, and you ain't but a boy. Leave it be," Sweets warned.

"I ain't gonna be a boy forever," Jonas replied.

"I know, little brother . . . I know." Sweets adjusted Josette on her hip to get a better grip. She felt a wince of pain, followed by the hollowed sound of her stomach growling. The twenty dollars hadn't been enough to get all of them meals, so she just made sure her siblings ate.

"You can share my food if you want." Josette offered one of her four chicken nuggets to her big sister.

"I'm fine, Jo-Jo. You eat." Sweets kissed her frozen little cheek. It was the purest act of kindness she'd seen in so long that she had to stop herself from tearing up. Times like those she found comfort in telling herself *struggle don't last forever,* but it sure felt like it would.

McDonald's was only a few blocks from where lived, but the journey felt like a mile. The snow had come down hard over the last two days. The city's idea of removal was pushing all the snow from the streets onto the curb creating giant mounts of piss and exhaust fumes that the pedestrians were forced to either navigate or take their chances walking in the street.

Josette's legs were feeling better, so Sweets let her down, much to the relief of her back. Her sister may have been small, but she was quite solid. Josette's feet had barely touched the ground before she took off running in the direction of one of the filthy mounds. Sweets thought about stopping her for fear of what kinds of germs the girl might pick up but decided against it. Whatever she happened to pick up would be nothing that a trip to the laundry and a good alcohol bath wouldn't cure.

Josette had been complaining about her legs cramping off and on for weeks now. Sweets suggested to her mother that they take her to the doctor, but Janette chalked it up to laziness. She didn't have time to be running back and forth to the clinic for something she insisted a little exercise would cure. Sweets had thought about taking Josette to the doctor on her own, but she was underage, and her showing up at the hospital to try to get Josette treated without a parent might've attracted Social Services.

Sweets rounded the corner of their block, mentally ticking off the list of things she had to do: gifts to wrap, dinner to prepare, the bathroom needed cleaning, etc. As usual, the strip was buzzing. Kids were out running around and playing in the filthy snow with no care for the cold. The dope boys were in their usual spot, huddled in front of the chicken shack slinging poison and drinking. They worked for a dude named Eight-Ball who supplied the neighborhood with cocaine and crack. He had been a running buddy of their father Zeke back in the days. Zeke only dabbled in drug dealing, but Eight-Ball was all in. Over the years, he had managed to build quite the operation.

Sweets shook her head sadly as one of them sold some rocks to a pregnant woman. The dealers never bothered her. She had grown up with them, and some were okay guys under the surface. She just didn't agree with their lifestyle. Sweets understood that there weren't many opportunities for kids in the hood, and you did what you had to do to put food on the table, but she couldn't see the logic in risking years in prison over a few pennies, which is exactly what they were doing. The suppliers made the real money, while the hand-to-hand soldiers fought over scraps. She'd even tried to point this logic out to them once, but they laughed at her and dismissed her as a church girl who didn't know anything, but Sweets had a better understanding of the game than most gave her credit for. She may have been a good girl, but a hustler had also raised her. It was only natural that she picked up a few tricks along the way.

As Sweets was passing with the kids, one of the youngsters made a transaction. It wouldn't have been a big deal, but he did it right in front of Josette. Usually, they tried to put at least a little shade on their doings when the smaller children were about, but this young man had no such shame. Sweets tilted her head and gave him a questioning look. *Where's the respect?* He shrugged his shoulders in the way of a weak apology and went back to what he was doing. Sweets was about to check him, but thankfully, she didn't have to.

"Since when do we do that?" Drew appeared in the doorway of the chicken shack holding a snack box. Eight-Ball supplied the drugs on the block, but it was Drew who ran it. This was 139th, his strip. He was wearing a baggy gray Nike sweat suit with a white bandanna wrapped around his starter-kit cornrows. Drew was on the short side, but handsome with a smooth, brown face and the first signs of a beard beginning to sprout on his chin. His keen eyes rested on the boy who had made the sale, waiting for an explanation.

"Doing what?" the boy asked as if he had no clue what he was talking about.

"Not show the proper respect when it's due." Drew's eyes went to Sweets and her siblings.

"I didn't mean no disrespect," the boy said, now realizing the error of his ways.

"Yet no respect was shown." It was more of an observation than an accusation, but the weight of the statement was felt, nonetheless. "Now might be a good time to make a store run. That goes for all y'all." The young men gathered in front of the chicken spot wasted no time doing as he'd suggested. "Sorry about that," he apologized to Sweets and the kids when the boys had gone.

"No need to be. It's not like it's the first time she's seen something like that." Sweets downplayed it.

"It still doesn't make it right," Drew insisted. "So, where y'all coming from all dressed up?"

"Church and taking pictures," Josette volunteered.

"Most people go to church on New Year's Eve."

Sweets shrugged. "We're just different."

"Yo, those joints are fly!" Jonas said, admiring the gray suede Timbs on Drew's feet.

"Good looking out," Drew said proudly, turning his foot over so that the boy could get a better look. "If you were a good boy this year, maybe Santa will drop a pair under the tree for you tonight. And what about you, Sweets?" he shifted his attention. "You been a good girl this year?"

"She's always good," Anette said spitefully.

"Ain't nothing wrong with that. Bad boys like good girls," Drew replied, giving Sweets the once-over.

Sweets couldn't help but blush, as she always did whenever Drew gave her the time of day. He was popular in the neighborhood and could have any girl he wanted, so she never took him seriously when he flirted. Still, it made her feel good to be noticed.

Drew's eyes shifted to something just beyond Sweets. She turned and found a fiend standing a few feet away. From the pleading look in her eyes, Sweets knew what time it was. "Duty calls," she said, taking Josette by the hand.

"And so, it does." Drew frowned. The crackhead had terrible timing, but he still had a quota to meet. "See y'all later." He started toward the fiend but stopped short. "Y'all selling Christmas dinners again this year?"

"Maybe for a select few people," Sweets teased. "You need your usual?"

"Yeah, but make it two dinners this time."

"You having company?" Sweets asked.

"I hope so." Drew winked at her and walked off with the fiend.

"Looks like Mama's good girl is looking to pick up some bad habits," Anette said slyly.

Sweets was about to walk the kids into the building when she spotted her other sister, Yvette, up on the corner. At first glance, she didn't even recognize her. Yvette's face was made up to an even shade of bronze with gold shadow covering the lids of her sleepy brown eyes. She was also wearing one of their mother's skirts, a tight denim number that showed off her budding curves. She looked more like a grown woman than a 16-year-old girl.

Occupying her space was a much-older Puerto Rican man named Juan. Juan owned the grocery store that everyone in the neighborhood shopped in. At Juan's store, you could get just about anything, including items that weren't necessarily advertised for sale. Juan was one of those cats that you could come to in a pinch, and he'd float you whatever you needed until your food stamps or Social Security checks came in, but, of course, he was going to charge you a ridiculous interest rate. His store made him quite popular in the neighborhood, especially among the ladies. Many of them were struggling single mothers who couldn't make it through the end of the month without Juan's mercies. Word had it that he traded as much in favors as he did goods.

The young girls in the neighborhood loved Juan too because he was always giving them free candy and snacks. Sweets steered clear of him. There was something about the way he looked at Sweets that gave her the creeps. She had thought about mentioning it to her mother but reasoned it wouldn't do any good. If it didn't involve her beloved Slick, she couldn't be bothered with it. It didn't take a rocket scientist to know why Juan was hanging all over her sister. Whatever evil he had planned wouldn't happen on her watch. She left Josette in the care of her siblings and plotted an intercept course.

"If you come outside and forget to put your clothes on, no wonder you got sick." Sweets crashed their conversation. "Ain't you supposed to be in bed?"

"I just came to the store to get some juice." Yvette rolled her eyes.

"We got juice in the house," Sweets reminded her.

"Not the kind I like." She gave Sweets her back, hoping she would get the hint and leave, but had no such luck.

"Don't you look nice today, Sweets," Juan remarked, ogling the little yellow dress she had worn to church.

"Thanks," Sweets said dryly, tugging her coat tighter around her.

"Say, we got in some more of those Entenmann's cakes . . . the ones like the white stores downtown carry. I put one to the side for you because I know how much you like them," Juan told her.

"No, thank you. Mama says I need to cut back on the sugar. She don't want me getting fat," Sweets told him. Her mother was always on her about her weight.

"Ain't nothing wrong with a thick woman." Juan licked his lips.

"Yvette, Mama said you need to help me get dinner started before she gets home." Sweets ignored Juan.

"Let Anette help you. I'll be upstairs in a few." Yvette tried to brush her off.

"You know that girl doesn't know how to clean chicken. I'd just have to go behind her and do it again. I need *you* to do it," Sweets insisted.

Seeing that her sister wasn't going to let it go, she relented. "I gotta go, Juan. I'll be back down to get the juice later on."

"Yeah, the juice will be waiting on you as soon as you're ready for it. As soon as you're ready," Juan said suggestively.

"I don't like him," Sweets said when they were out of earshot of Juan.

"Who? Juan? Girl, he's harmless," Yvette downplayed it.

"He's a pervert, and if you know like I do, you'll stay away from him . . . or else," Sweets insisted.

Yvette stopped and folded her arms defiantly. "Or what? You'll beat my ass? Don't forget who the older sister is, *Claudette*."

"I'll remember who the older sister is when you start acting like it," Sweets shot back. "Would it kill you to help out once in a while instead of running the streets all the time?"

"Why should I? Ain't nothing for me in that house but a bunch of stress and some crying-ass kids that I didn't lay up and have," Yvette snaked her neck.

"They're still our brother and sisters. We're supposed to look out for them."

"Sweets, you can spend the rest of your life cleaning up Janette's messes, but I got other plans. In a year and some change, I'll be 18. That means I can get the fuck out of that nuthouse we live in, and when I leave, I ain't looking back," Yvette said in a matter-of-fact tone.

"You're so freaking selfish." Sweets shook her head sadly.

"I got it honest. Look who my mama is!" Yvette capped and sashayed toward the building.

"You should've punched her," Jonas said, startling Sweets. She hadn't even noticed him standing there.

"Family don't fight with family. Our true enemies live beyond our walls, not within them," Sweets told her little brother.

"I guess sometimes it's hard to tell the difference." Jonas shrugged before heading toward the building.

Chapter Two

The Raffertys lived on the fifth floor of a walk-up tenement building on 139th and Lenox Avenue. It was one of the oldest buildings in the neighborhood and one of the few that hadn't yet been touched by the hand of renovation, but its time was coming. Already, most of the low-income tenants in the neighboring buildings had been pushed out and replaced by residents who could pay triple the rate. The landscape was changing.

As soon as they got inside the apartment, Yvette stormed off to the room she shared with her sisters and slammed the door. She was still angry with Sweets for butting in when she was talking to Juan, but it was for her own good. Though Yvette talked tough and could handle herself in the streets, she was still just a child. Juan was a predator, and Sweets had no illusions about what his plans for her sister were. Whether or not Yvette saw it, Sweets was only trying to protect her. Sweets would try to talk to her again once she had cooled off, but right then, she had work to do.

"Y'all take them good clothes off and let's start getting this house ready for Santa," Sweet instructed the rest of her siblings.

"I hope he brings me my Barbie Dream House this year. I've asked for it three times in a row and still haven't gotten it," Josette pouted.

"I think this year will be different," Sweets winked. She knew this to be true because she had put one on layaway at the department store. It had taken her three months of scraping together money from doing odd jobs around the neighborhood and braiding hair to pay for it, but it would be worth it to see the smile on Josette's face when she opened it. "Now, go get changed so you can help me in the kitchen."

"I don't know why you still pump that girl's head full of fantasy," Jonas said once Josette had gone.

"Because it makes her happy. Don't act like you didn't just stop believing in Santa last year," Sweets reminded him.

"He'd probably still believe if it hadn't been for Slick," Anette added.

This was a sour memory for Jonas. That Christmas there was nothing Jonas wanted more than a BMX bike with the wheel pegs. He didn't care about anything else on his Christmas list but that, and he went out of his way to make sure he'd get it. He stopped mouthing off in school, did his homework, and even helped out with chores around the house. He was a lock to make Santa's Nice List! When Jonas got up on Christmas morning and found that Santa had finally honored his request and gifted him the bike, he was over the moon with joy. He hadn't even bothered to open any of his other gifts before he was out the door to take the bike for a test ride.

Jonas was on top of the world riding the bike up and down the block. Even his mother had roused herself to sit on the stoop and watch him enjoy his gift, which was a feat in itself because Janette rarely rose before noon unless she had to go to court. It was the happiest day of Jonas's life . . . until Slick showed up and ruined it.

It was obvious from the scowl on Slick's face that he was in a pissy mood. He'd probably been out all night gambling and gotten himself trimmed again. Still, it was Christmas, and Jonas wanted him to share in the cheer. "Yo, Slick, check out what Santa brought me!" He showed off the bike proudly.

His mother's boyfriend's drunken eyes glared at the bike as if it were something vile. When he spoke, there was an unmistakable cruelty to his tone. "Li'l nigga, you're too old to still be so naïve. Only white people who come around here are police, and they damn sure don't give a fuck about yo' Christmas."

"But Santa—"

"Ain't real," Slick cut him off. "The only reason you got that stupid bike is because your mama stayed out all night hustling."

Jonas wanted to curse Slick and call him a liar, but the horrified look on his mother's face confirmed it. Jonas was devastated, much to Slick's pleasure.

"Merry fucking Christmas," Slick laughed and shambled into the building. A few weeks later, Slick took the bike out for a ride and never brought it back. He claimed that someone had stolen it while he was inside the store, but the more likely scenario was that he had sold it. It didn't matter. The magic that had once surrounded the bike was gone, along with Jonas's Christmas spirit.

"Evil bastard," Jonas recalled. "I don't know what Mama sees in him."

"You know all the Rafferty women have a thing for bad boys," Anette said slyly, cutting her eyes at Sweets.

"What?" Sweets asked as if she didn't know what Anette was implying.

"I see the way you and Drew look at each other," Anette accused.

"Girl, stop. Ain't nobody thinking about Drew," Sweets
lied.

"Drew got mad girls. Why would he be interested in
Sweets?" Jonas asked, which stung Sweets a bit. He
hadn't said it to be cruel; he was just pointing out the
obvious. Drew did mess with quite a few girls in the
neighborhood, but it still made Sweets feel good when
he flirted with her. She knew nothing would ever come
of it, but a girl could dream, couldn't she?

"As much energy as I put into looking after y'all, I don't
have time for Drew, or anybody else, for that matter!"
Sweets said and stormed off into the kitchen.

Jonas stood there, dumbfounded, wondering what he
had done wrong.

Jonas walked into his bedroom and hung his coat on
the hook on the back of the door. He was the only one,
besides his mother, who had his own room. It was hardly
bigger than a closet, but it was still his—the only place
where he could go to find peace in the house.

His bedroom walls, like bedrooms of most teenagers,
were papered with posters. Some he had torn out of mag-
azines, while others he boosted from stores. Some were
posters of rappers Jonas liked, but most were of football
players. Hanging in a place of honor over his bed was a
large poster of Deion "Prime Time" Sanders from back
in his Atlanta Falcons days. He looked menacing, arms
folded across his chest in his black uniform and a red
bandanna tied snugly about his Jeri curl. Deion's career
was on the decline by the time Jonas had gotten a chance
to see him play, but he would sit for hours watching his
old highlights on the internet. He had it all: the flash,

the charisma, and the skill. Jonas wanted to be just like him. His school didn't have a team, but he played tackle football on the streets with the older kids whenever they organized a game and played defensive back in a peewee league out in Queens when his mother could afford to pay the fees. He wasn't half bad either. Though Deion Sanders was who he molded his game after, it was from a local talent where he drew his motivation.

Hanging beside the poster of Sanders was a picture Jonas had clipped from a magazine. It was of a relatively unknown pro named Willie Green Jr. Jonas had had the pleasure of seeing him record his first and only NFL interception one Thanksgiving while watching the game at his uncle's place. Willie's was a face Jonas recognized from the neighborhood. He wasn't a player in the game, nor was he a spectator. Willie was just a kid from the hood who was good at football. Willie was hardly the superstar that Deion was. In fact, his NFL career was an unremarkable one that lasted only two and a half seasons before he faded into obscurity, but he had made it out! Willie was that one-in-a-million shot that got to see what was behind the curtain of success, even if it was only a brief glance. Willie's story gave Jonas something that was in short supply in the ghetto . . . hope.

Jonas fished around under his bed and slid out a dusty wooden box. He flipped the lid and revealed that it was a record player, once owned by his father. His name had been Ezekiel, but everyone called him Zeke. Someone put a bullet in his head when Jonas was younger. Outside of a few faded memories and some pictures, it was the only connection that remained between Jonas and Zeke.

He'd inherited the record player in a most unusual way. A few months after Zeke's body was found, a woman

showed up at their apartment. She was pulling a shopping cart of things that had belonged to Zeke. Initially,
they thought the woman had been another one of Zeke's
mistresses coming out of the woodwork, but as it turned
out, she had been his landlady. Unbeknownst to Janette,
her man had been renting a room across town for the last
few years. It was where he kept his secrets. The landlady
had found Janette's address on some mail while cleaning
out the room and figured she might want to claim the few
things he had left behind. Janette wanted nothing that
reminded her of Zeke's infidelities and was going to burn
everything, including the record player, but Jonas had
pleaded with her not to. He wasn't sure why he wanted
the record player, other than be something to remember
the man who had given him life.

Reluctantly, Janette had allowed the boy to keep the
record player. Most of the records that had been packed
in with it were either cracked or scratched so badly that
they wouldn't play without skipping, but there was one
that had been kept in relatively good condition: *King of
the Delta Blues Singers*. It had been recorded by a musician named Robert Leroy Johnson who had died in 1938
under questionable circumstances. Rumor had it that
as a young man, Johnson had sold his soul to a demon
in exchange for success. At the height of his career, the
demon had come to collect on the debt. Jonas's favorite
song was a tune that his father liked to listen to whenever
he got drunk: "Cross Road Blues." Jonas could remember
that whenever his father would have too much to drink,
he'd get to humming the tune, so whenever Jonas played
the song, it made him feel like his father was still with
him. He was just about to lower the needle onto the
record and give it a spin when Yvette walked into his
room unannounced.

"Jesus, haven't you ever heard of knocking?" he asked, startled.

"For what? You don't pay no bills in here," Yvette capped. Her eyes then landed on the record player. "I don't know why you're holding on to that old thing." She plucked the record from the player and examined it.

"Be careful with that!" Jonas reached for the record, but Yvette jerked it away.

"Relax; ain't nobody gonna break it. Who the hell is Robert Johnson anyhow? I've never heard of him."

"That's because all you listen to is rap music," Jonas told her.

"Is there any other kind of music?" It was a rhetorical question. She tossed the record like a Frisbee and watched Jonas damn near break his neck making a leaping catch for it.

"Dumb ass," he mumbled, checking the record to make sure she hadn't damaged it. She knew the record meant a lot to Jonas and was being mean to him because she was mad at Sweets. "What do you want, Yvette?"

"Sweets said you gotta clean the bathroom," Yvette informed him.

"I cleaned the bathroom the other day. It's Anette's turn," he said.

"Anette is helping us in the kitchen, so you gotta do it. And hurry up. I don't want to hear her mouth." Yvette was about to leave when Jonas stopped her.

"Did you mean what you said earlier?" he asked.

"What?"

"About leaving us and never looking back."

"It's not like anybody would miss me if I did."

"I'd miss you," Jonas said sincerely.

Yvette took in her little brother. His eyes looked so sad. Jonas was always such a vulgar little spitfire that she often forgot that he was just a kid. Yvette sat on the edge of his bed and placed a reassuring hand on his shoulder. "Sometimes people say things out of anger that they don't really mean. You little shits get on my nerves, but we're still family, and family is all we have in this world, right?"

Jonas simply nodded in answer. He was happy that his family wasn't going to be broken up, at least not yet, but there was also something else on his mind. "She was right, you know."

"Who?"

"Sweets," he explained. "The stuff she was staying about Juan."

"And what do you know about it?" Yvette folded her arms challengingly.

"I know Tat and them Red-T boys from Edgecombe were gonna give him the business when Juan tried to force his way into Tat's little sister Tina's pants." The Red-T boys were a neighborhood gang of dudes. They called them Red-T because every summer they turned somebody's white T-shirt red with blood. They were a small crew but quite vicious.

"Tina's little ass is fast. I don't think it'd take much forcing to get between her legs," Yvette laughed.

"I'm serious, Yvette. You need to stay away from that dude," Jonas said seriously. "If Juan was to ever try something with one of y'all, I'd—"

"You'd *what?* Tell Mom?" She laughed as if the idea of her mother coming to her defense was the most absurd thing she had ever heard. "I appreciate your concern, little brother, but I can take care of myself. You worry about cleaning the piss from under the toilet seat and let me worry about Juan." She patted his cheek and left.

Yvette may not have taken Jonas seriously, but it was only because she didn't understand how much Jonas loved his sisters. He may have been young but not too young to understand that he was the man of the house. Slick may have occupied his mother's bed, but it was on Jonas to protect his family. His sisters were all he had, and there was nothing he wouldn't do to keep them safe. This was something that the Rafferty girls wouldn't learn until much later in life.

Chapter Three

The rest of Jonas's afternoon and evening was spent helping Sweets and the others get the house in order for Christmas, which proved to be a far more difficult task than it should've been. One thing about having over half a dozen people living in cramped quarters was that the house always seemed to be a wreck. This was especially true when the two resident adults were resident addicts and fuckups.

Jonas tackled the bathroom, cleaning the sink, tub, and toilet. He even got on his hands and knees and scrubbed the grout from the corners around the sink and toilet with an old toothbrush. Calling the floor clean enough to eat off would've been a stretch, but it was as clean as it would get. Next, he moved to the living room to tidy it up. Josette was supposed to be helping him, but she mostly got in the way. She kept accidentally tripping over the gifts under the tree, which was one of the oldest tricks in the book. She just wanted to tear the wrapping paper to see what was in them. By the time he was done with the living room, Sweets was calling them to the table to eat. She had spent all afternoon prepping the turkey, cutting the greens, and peeling yams, but that was for Christmas dinner. Their meal for the Eve consisted of fried chicken and French fries. Neither Janette nor Slick were anywhere to be found, so the children ate alone, which they didn't mind. Things were less chaotic when the adults were out.

After dinner, Jonas put Josette to bed and helped
Sweets and Anette wrap the rest of the gifts and put
together Josette's doll house. It was a lot of work because
they didn't have any tools and had to improvise with
butter knives instead of screwdrivers and an old shoe
in place of a hammer, but they managed to get it done.
Yvette was supposed to pitch in, but at some point, she
had snuck out of the house. Jonas thought Sweets was
going to get mad when she found out, but she didn't. She
was too tired to stress over it. Instead of going out to look
for her, as she normally would've, Sweets just went to
bed. She was tired. Mentally and physically, her siblings
were draining her, and it wouldn't be long before the girl
didn't have anything left to leech.

It was after midnight when Jonas finally retired to his
bedroom. He was so beat that he didn't even bother to
take his clothes off before crashing across his bed. He
dropped the needle on his *King of the Delta Blues* record
and drifted to sleep listening to Robert Leroy Johnson
singing about that damn crossroad.

Jonas found his sleep fitful that night. He was plagued
with a series of peculiar dreams. One that stood out was
about his father. In all the years Zeke had been gone,
Jonas had never once dreamed of him; yet, there he was
that night posted up on his favorite corner, 137th and
Seventh. That was the block his dad sold a little coke on
when he was between jobs. Only his father wasn't selling
drugs in the dream. He was perched on a milk crate
with a bass guitar across his lap. His fingers plucked
the cords of "Crossroad Blues," while people passing by
tossed change into the open guitar case. This struck him
as odd because he had never known his father to play an
instrument of any kind.

"Dad?" Jonas called out. Zeke ignored him and continued plucking the strings. Frustrated by his father

ignoring him, Jonas gripped him by the shoulder and forced him to turn around. He recoiled in horror when instead of the inviting brown eyes he remembered, he was confronted with two milky-white orbs. Jonas didn't remember seeing him move, but suddenly, he was standing directly in front of him. Jonas made to step back, but Zeke had grabbed a handful of Jonas's testicles and began to squeeze. His hand felt as if it were made of ice. Zeke's touch was as cold as a December morning, and it sent a numbing sensation through Jonas's face. For a minute, he thought the ghost of his father meant to kill him, and then it spoke.

"The devil is a liar," Zeke said in a whispery tone. His breath stank of whisky and death. Jonas had no idea what he meant, and before he could ask him, the dream was over.

When Jonas awoke, he was lying on his bedroom floor. His nuts were throbbing, and one leg of his pajamas was wet. Apparently, he had overloaded his bladder with that extra glass of soda he'd snuck during dinner and pissed himself. He sat there for a minute reflecting on his dad's message from the dream, *The devil is a liar*. What had he meant? Whatever it was, he wouldn't figure it out sitting on the floor in a puddle of his own urine.

Jonas pushed himself up and made his way toward the bathroom. The house was dark and quiet. He poked his head into his sisters' room to check on them. Anette was nestled into the top bunk fast asleep, while Yvette occupied the bottom. He wasn't sure what time she had crept back into the house, but he was glad she was safe. It seemed like the older Yvette got, she tested more boundaries. Janette had always given her too much rope, and soon, she wouldn't be able to do anything with her. Sharing a twin bed on the other side of the room were Sweets and Josette. Jo-Jo was stretched out, snoring with her leg thrown over her big sister. In a few hours, she would be the first one awake and in the living room tearing open the toys he and his sisters had spent all night wrapping.

All of the sisters seemed to be sleeping soundly except Sweets. Her night was a fitful one, as he imagined most were. She tossed and turned in the corner of the bed that Josette had forced her into, and he could hear her whimpering. Worry lines had begun to take up permanent residence on her face. She was a young girl carrying the weight of a grown woman, and it was beginning to weigh on her.

Next, he went to his mother's room. There was no sign of Janette or Slick, but the dress that she had worn to church earlier was in a crumpled heap on the floor. She must've slipped back into the apartment at some point to change her clothes before heading back out into the streets. He hoped she would at least make it back to watch Josette open her gifts, but that would all depend on the level of the bender she was on. Unlike his siblings, who resented their mother for the life she chose to lead, Jonas had begun to just accept her for who she was. Still, he worried when she went missing like this. Having an addict for a parent was like being married to a cop; every time they left the house, all you could do was pray that they came back.

Turning his attention from his dysfunctional family and back to his soggy pants, he continued to the bathroom. He needed to get himself cleaned up and change his sheets before his sisters woke up. If Yvette and Anette found out he had peed the bed, they would never let him hear the end of it. He flicked on the light and damn near pissed himself a second time when he found a body on the floor. It was his mother! She was dressed in torn stockings, a short skirt, and nothing but her bra. She was leaning in the small space between the toilet and the bathtub with a needle hanging from her arm. His first thought was that she had finally overdosed until she reached up to scratch her neck.

"Mommy!" Jonas rushed to her. She stank of beer and cigarettes. When he knelt to check on her, his knee landed in something wet. Jonas hadn't been the only one to have an accident that night.

Janette's head lolled on her shoulders as he tried to help her up. She managed to force her eyes open enough to look at him. "Zeke, what you doing in my house?" she asked in a sleepy tone.

"It's me, Jonas," he told her while trying to help her up. He wanted to get her out of the bathroom before Josette woke up and saw her in that state.

"Get your damn hands off me, Zeke!" She yanked away from him. "You got the stink of evil on you, and I don't want no parts of it!"

Jonas had no idea what she was talking about. She was clearly out of her head and convinced that he was his father. "Mom, you gotta get up." He continued to try to help her, and she continued to try to fight him.

"What's going on in here?" Sweets appeared in the bathroom doorway. When she noticed her mother on the bathroom floor, all she could do was shake her head. She didn't complain or make a fuss of any kind; she simply helped her brother get their mother off the floor and into the tub. The siblings held their mother under the cold spray of the shower before getting her into some dry clothes and helping her to bed. They did this all in complete silence. What was already understood didn't need to be said.

Chapter Four

Jonas felt like he had just gone back to sleep when he was jarred awake again by squeals of excitement coming from the living room. It was Christmas morning. Reluctantly, he got out of bed and went to join in the festivities.

When he got into the living room, he found his whole family up, including his mother, which was a shock. With the condition she had been in the night before, it was a miracle that she had survived the night, let alone was awake at that hour. Yvette and Anette were sitting on the couch comparing the matching Nautica jackets that were under the tree for them. Sweets stood near the window, sipping a cup of coffee, beaming at her siblings as they went through their gifts. The center of attention was Josette, who was in the middle of the living room doing her *happy dance*. She had discovered her doll house.

"Jonas, look! Santa finally listened to me!" Josette pointed at her doll house excitedly. "Isn't it cool?"

"Very cool," he smiled at her.

"Merry Christmas, baby." Janette broke the tension between mother and son. The look on her face said that she remembered the events of the previous night, at least in part.

"Is it?" he asked. He hadn't meant to be mean. It was just how it came out.

"Jonas, not today. It's Christmas," Sweets checked him. She was right—no sense in ruining things for Josette.

"There's something special under the tree for you too," Janette told him. Instead of waiting for him to find it, she retrieved the oval-shaped, hastily wrapped gift and held it out to him.

"Thanks," Jonas said, not sure what to make of it. He curiously peeled the wrapping paper off and was taken aback by what was inside. It was a football that had been signed by three members of the New York Giants. "Are these real signatures?" His eyes were wide.

"Shit, they better be," Janette said, thinking about what she had to go through to get the signatures. She spent half the night letting the three football players defile her only for Slick to blow most of the money on smack.

"It's the best! Thank you, Mommy!" Jonas jumped into her arms and hugged her.

Janette's heart swelled. The hug alone was enough to make what she had gone through to get the football well worth it. Of course, it didn't take long for Slick to make an appearance and ruin the moment.

He shambled into the living room wearing only his boxers and a tank top. His processed hair was wrapped in a scarf, Aunt Jemima style. His eyes were red, and his mouth twisted. "Hell is with all the noise? Don't y'all know a nigga is trying to sleep?"

"It's Christmas morning. The kids are just excited about their stuff, is all." Janette tried to smooth it over.

"Well, let them do it quietly!" he barked and stormed back into the bedroom. He had been out hustling and getting high all night, so he needed his beauty rest to do it all over again.

Janette gave her kids an apologetic look before going off after Slick. Yvette and Anette went back into their room, and Sweets disappeared into the kitchen. Josette sat on the floor looking up at Jonas with sad eyes. Just as quickly as the spirit of Christmas had come . . . It had gone.

The rest of the morning had been relatively uneventful. Janette hadn't been seen since she disappeared into the bedroom with Slick. At least, she was still in the house and hadn't gone running back into the streets . . . well, not yet. Sweets cooked breakfast for the kids; oatmeal, boiled eggs, and toast. It wasn't a five-star breakfast, but they were good and full. After everyone had eaten, the kids all retreated to their respective corners of the house and left her to clean the kitchen alone.

Wanting to ease some of his sister's burden, Jonas went and started straightening up the living room. He stuffed all discarded wrapping paper into plastic bags and broke the boxes down. He was about to sweep the floor when he heard a familiar voice coming from the window.

"Raf! Ayo, Raf!" *Raf* was short for Rafferty. It was a moniker his friends had given him. He opened the window and stuck his head out to find his buddies Ace and Cal in front of his building.

"Chill with all that noise outside my window!" he shushed them. The last thing he wanted was for Slick to come out and start beefing again.

"You coming out?" Ace shouted up, ignoring the warning.

"Yeah, I'll be down in a few. Now, stop yelling!" Jonas slammed the window closed. He turned around and bumped right into Sweets. She had been hovering the whole time.

"And where are you off to?" she asked.

"Nowhere. Just going to check my friends real quick." He went to grab his coat and hat from his bedroom.

"Jonas, don't you be out there getting into nothing with Ace and that Cal. You know those boys love trouble." Sweets was on his heels.

"Why you sweating me? I'm just going to show them my new football." He snatched his gift and darted for the door.

"And don't leave the block!" Sweets called after him, but Jonas was already gone.

As soon as he was out of his sister's line of vision, he transformed from Jonas to Raf. He rolled his winter cap up along one side and cocked it on his head like he saw dudes wear them in rap videos and then sagged his pants enough to show off the new Tommy Hilfiger boxers he had gotten for Christmas. He ambled out of the building like he was the coolest kid on the block and greeted his boys. "Sup?" he dapped Ace, then Calico.

"Took your ass long enough," Ace started right in. He was a thickly built young man with coco skin who wore his hair in a nappy Afro back in those days. He was the young mastermind of their crew, the one who would come up with most of the crazy things they did for kicks. Ace and Jonas had been down the longest, having always lived two buildings away from each other and gone to the same schools since babies.

"Why you sweating me like we in a relationship?" Jonas went right back at him. "I had to make sure I grabbed my fly new ball before I came outside." He brandished the signed ball.

"Yooo, you got the autographed joint!" Cal pointed out. He was the only Puerto Rican kid Jonas had ever met named Calvin. They all called him Cal or Calico for short. Calico came from the time he had stolen a Calico and was showing it off on the block. Had the police caught Cal with the high-powered Luger, he'd have gotten an asshole full of time. Thankfully, Hector, Cal's older brother, caught him before the cops did, and Cal received a beat-down instead of a jail sentence. Cal sported two black eyes for the next few weeks, but the stunt with the gun boosted his credibility in the hood.

"Hands off. I don't want you smudging the signatures." Jonas snatched the ball out of their reach.

"They probably ain't even real," Ace challenged.

"Are too," Jonas insisted. "My mom got it for me."

"That still don't make it real," Ace shot back.

"You trying to call my mother a liar?" Jonas asked, ready to defend her honor. He stood with his fist balled and at the ready. The whole crew knew how much Jonas enjoyed a good fistfight. Ace did not.

"Forget that ball," Ace waved him off. He dug in his pocket and came out with a loose cigarette that he had gotten from Juan's. His was the only store in the neighborhood where even underage kids could purchase tobacco. He placed the cigarette between his lips and was about to light it until Jonas snatched it from him. "What you doing?"

"You can't light that right here. One of my sisters might see you." Jonas looked up at his window and could've sworn he saw the curtain flutter. "Let's go around the corner."

When they made it around the corner to where his sisters could no longer watch him, he gave Ace the cigarette. The young boy fired it up and inhaled with the skill of someone who had been smoking for years. He took two pulls before handing the cigarette off to Cal. "You wanna roll with us to Central Park?" He exhaled the smoke through his nose.

"What's in Central Park?" Jonas asked.

"Pussy!" Cal informed him. "I know some white chicks from 109th Street that wanna hook up. They live in the building across the street from the park," Cal told him.

"Why can't they come up here?"

"How we look bringing some girls from Central Park West to the ghetto to hang out?" Cal asked as if it were the stupidest question in the world. "We gonna go meet Doug on his block, then jump on the train to go see the chicks. You down or not?"

Jonas was hesitant. Sweets had told him not to leave the block, but he didn't want to miss out on whatever shenanigans Ace, Cal, and Doug were surely about to get into.

"Man, you know Raf's sisters will kick his ass if he moves too far from the stoop," Ace teased him. It was all the prodding Jonas needed to defy his sister.

"Fuck it; I'm in."

It was a nine-block walk to Doug's new hood. He and his family used to live around the corner from Jonas's building but had moved to the St. Nicholas Projects a few years ago. Even though Doug didn't still live on the old block, he and the boys remained tight. They found him standing in front of the Bodega talking to a fiend. From the hushed tones they were speaking, it looked like they were bartering for something. That was Doug's game: buy and sell.

Doug was a year older than the rest of them and a bit more seasoned in the inner workings of the streets. He was the first dude out of their little crew to start getting a little illegal money. Doug had gotten hooked in with some older dudes who had a team of crackheads they used to steal stuff they could resell at a discount. They often used Doug as a go-between because nobody would expect a kid like him to be up to no good. Doug was very bookish looking; always clean-cut with new clothes and sneakers. He came from a two-parent home with a mother and father who both worked to make sure he and his sister were good, which is what made the fact that he still chose to hustle so baffling. It wasn't out of necessity. Doug just loved the thrill of the game.

When Doug spotted the trio walking up, he dismissed the fiend and went to meet them. "What's goodie?" he gave everybody dap.

"Ready to bust this move. You still down?" Ace got right to it.

"Yeah, but I got a small problem," Doug said. Before he could elaborate, his "problem" came walking out of the bodega carrying a Snapple and a bag of chips.

"I know you ain't trying to leave me, Doug. Mom said wherever you go, *I* go," Doug's sister Alex said. She was a sassy young girl with high yellow skin and hair she wore in neat cornrows.

Jonas felt his heart skip a little when he saw her. He'd had the biggest crush on her since he was old enough to understand the difference between boys and girls. When they still lived in the neighborhood, she and Jonas would often go to the park and shoot hoops together. Ever since she was young, Alex had always been just as good as anyone in the park. When she and her family moved away, Jonas felt like he had lost his best friend. He and Alex still saw each other in school because they had classes together, but they weren't as close as they used to be.

"Oh, hell no! How we gonna go meet up with these chicks with your sister hanging around?" Ace threw his hands up in frustration.

"It was the only way my mother would let me out of the house," Doug explained.

"All I know is she better not start cockblocking my action," Ace warned.

"Ace, you ain't got no action. Patrice told me you showed her your 'thing,' and it was super little!" Alex shot back with a roll of her eyes for good measure.

"Patrice is a damn liar!" Ace tried to hide his embarrassment. It had been cold on the day he whipped it out in front of her. "Doug, it's bad you gotta drag her with us. The least you can do is control that smart-ass mouth of hers."

"Alex, be cool, or I'm gonna say to hell with what Mom made me promise and leave you on the block, understand?" Doug was serious.

"Okay, I'll be cool," Alex promised, but really didn't mean it. She didn't like Ace because he was always trying to feel her up when he thought Doug wasn't looking. The only reason she was even making a big deal about going was that she knew Jonas would be there.

Chapter Five

Ace led his gang of teenagers to 125th Street, where they hopped the local C-train and rode the two stops to 110th Street. During the ride, the boys made mischief, writing on the subway posters and talking trash, as boys do. Every so often, Jonas would catch Alex eying him, or she would catch him doing the same. They hadn't said much to each other but had been carrying on a whole dialogue through a series of looks.

By the time they had emerged from the train station, it had started snowing again. It was now coming down in heavy flakes and sticking. Jonas had lived in New York all his life and had never visited Central Park before that. He looked on in admiration at the snow-covered trees and ground that was absent of grass. It was like he had stepped into a winter wonderland that had been hiding just slightly over a mile from him. He couldn't wait until he got home so that he could share what he had discovered with Sweets and Jo-Jo. Then he remembered that he wasn't supposed to have left the block. Knowing Sweets, she had probably already gone outside and made a circuit of the neighborhood and realized that he hadn't listened. She would surely be pissed, but Jonas would cross that bridge when he came to it. He was living in the moment.

As promised, Cal's white girls were waiting for them inside the park; a strawberry blonde and a brunette. What Cal hadn't bothered to mention was that there was only two of them and one was ugly. He quickly jumped on the cute brunette, leaving Doug and Ace to compete for the cubby blonde with the overbite. The group of them ended up walking down to 100th Street and Central Park West. One of the white girls knew somebody who sold weed in the projects across down the street. Doug wasn't about to take his little sister to buy drugs, so she ended up getting left behind while they handled business. Jonas opted to wait with her. Unlike his thirsty friends, he had no interest in the white girls, nor getting high. Besides, he could think of far worse fates than getting left alone with Alex.

"Why didn't you go off with your boys and the white girls?" Alex asked as they strolled through the park, tossing Jonas's football back and forth.

Jonas shrugged. "For what?"

"Didn't you want to get high with the white girls too?"

"I don't smoke weed," he informed her, much to Alex's surprise. She'd always assumed he did everything her brother and the rest of their crew did. "Besides, somebody had to stay behind and make sure you're good."

"I can handle myself." Alex threw the football in a tight spiral into Jonas's chest.

They continued to walk, chucking the ball, and catching up on old times. Their conversation eventually brought them to a small lake in the park. The thick sheet of frost that had formed over the water's surface glistened in the afternoon sun. Jonas stopped to admire it for a time. When Alex came to stand beside him, it became the perfect moment.

"Beautiful," Jonas said.

Alex blushed . . . until she realized he was talking about the lake. "Yeah . . . I guess."

"You trying to tell me you've seen something that'll top this other than on television?" Jonas asked.

"One winter, my parents took us on a trip to Niagara Falls. When the temperature drops enough, everything up there freezes," she recalled.

"How come your mom and dad are always taking you and Doug on trips out of town?" Jonas asked. Even when they still lived on his block, it seemed like they were going somewhere different every other week.

"My dad says it's to help culture us. Some of the places are boring, but for the most part, we have fun on our family vacations," she said.

"My family's version of a vacation is visiting our relatives in Newark for the weekend. Jersey is the farthest I've ever been and probably the farthest I'll ever go," Jonas said, feeling a bit embarrassed.

"Don't think like that, Jonas. You don't know what life has in store for you," she said encouragingly.

"You always did manage to find an upside to everything." He cracked a smile. She returned the gesture. An awkward silence lingered between them. Jonas didn't remember reaching for it, but he was holding Alex's hand. When he felt her close her fingers over his, he knew that the moment was right. The stars had finally lined up between them, but before they could act on it, trouble found them.

"What y'all doing out here, yo?" an older boy approached. He was wearing baggy jeans, an army coat, and Tims. A red bandanna was tied around one of his boots. Trailing him were three more boys, wearing threatening faces. They appeared to range in ages between 15 and 17, older than Jonas and Alex.

"Nothing, just chilling." Jonas casually positioned himself between Alex and the boys.

"Y'all ain't from around here. You know somebody from this neighborhood to be chilling in *our* park?" the boy with the bandanna on his boot pressed.

Jonas could tell from the looks the boys were wearing that they had come into the park seeking trouble. Had the rest of his boys been there, he'd have told the boys to go fuck themselves and squared up to fight, but he was outnumbered. If something went down, Alex might get hurt, and he didn't want that, so he tried the diplomatic approach. "Man, we were just walking through the park. We ain't looking for trouble."

The older boy studied Jonas's face as if he were trying to decide whether to give him a pass—or not. His eyes suddenly landed on the football tucked under Jonas's arm. "Nice ball. Let me see it."

"Chill; this was a Christmas present," Jonas told him. He knew what was about to go down.

"Man, if I wanted to steal your ball, I'd punch you in the face and take it. Now, let me get a quick throw." He stuck his hand out.

Jonas looked over his shoulder at Alex, who motioned for him to give the ball up. It wasn't worth them getting stomped out. Reluctantly, Jonas handed him the ball.

"Good looking." The boy pressed the ball between his palms, testing the pressure. He turned his back and started walking off.

"You can't leave with my ball," Jonas yelled, starting after him.

"It ain't yours no more. You gave it to me, remember?" the boy said over his shoulder without bothering to stop.

"I can't let you leave with my ball!" Jonas insisted. He'd only had it a short time, but the football was already one of his most prized possessions. He couldn't bear to lose it. Jonas jogged ahead of the boy and cut him off. "I need my ball."

"Shorty, is this ball worth getting knocked out for?" The boy looked down at the smaller kid.

"Yes," Jonas said plainly. It became obvious to everyone watching that he was willing to go all-out for his ball.

"Russ, give the little nigga his ball," one of the boys in their group said. He was wearing a black Kangol and a thin gold chain. Until then, he had been quietly watching. He must've been the true leader of their group because the one called Russ didn't argue with him.

"Told you I didn't want this piece of shit. Go long," Russ said before hurling the ball over Jonas's head. It bounced off the grass and slid out onto the frozen lake.

"That was some bullshit, Russ." The kid with the Kangol shook his head.

"Ain't my fault the little nigga can't catch," Russ laughed.

"Asshole," Jonas grumbled and headed toward the lake. His ball hadn't gone out very far. He figured that maybe with a stick he would be able to knock it back toward the shore.

"Jonas, what are you doing?" Alex asked. She nervously watched as he approached the lip of the lake with a stick.

"I gotta get my ball," Jonas told her. He used one toe to test the ice.

"Jonas, that ice isn't going to hold your weight. It's just a ball. You can get another one!" Alex pleaded with him.

Jonas ignored her and started out onto the ice. He crawled on his hands and knees, stretching the stick out to try to get the ball. It didn't reach quite far enough, so he crawled a little farther. The ice groaned beneath him but held. *Just a little farther,* he thought to himself as the stick brushed the tip of the football. Finally, Jonas was able to knock the football close enough to where he could grab it. His hands were so numb from resting on the ice that he could barely feel it, but at least he had managed to rescue his mother's gift to him. Everything was going smoothly . . . until he started scooting back toward dry land and heard the sound of the ice cracking just under his knees. The last thing he heard was Alex scream his name before he went crashing into the lake.

Long before his head followed the rest of him beneath the water, Jonas knew that he was going to die. The water was so cold that it stole the breath that he had been attempting to take before going under. Through the murky water, he could see sunlight shining through the hole he had created in the ice. It seemed so close that he could reach out and touch it, and he tried, but his arms would not cooperate with him. He could never in his life remember being so cold, but the sensation only lasted for a moment before his entire body went numb. The water flooded his nose and mouth before filling his lungs. Jonas had always thought that death by drowning was one of the worst ways a person could go, but it was actually quite peaceful. The numbing cold had passed and filled his body with an almost euphoric feeling. It was like drifting off into a peaceful sleep that he would never wake up from. As he faded from this world and into the next, his last thoughts were of not being about to tell Sweets and Josette about the beautiful park he'd discovered.

Jonas was snatched back to consciousness by a racking cough. His lungs cried out desperately for air that seemed to be having troubling finding it. He could feel himself being rolled over on his side and someone slamming a palm into his back.

"Let it out, kid. Let it out!" an unfamiliar voice urged him.

As if on command, Jonas hacked one hard time and released a spray of water from his nose and mouth. This seemed to help. His chest was still hurting, but his airways were at least clear now. Someone was hovering over him. He was a pale figure with eyes that sparkled a shade of blue that he had never seen before. The sun turned his hair so blond that it appeared white and glowing. It must have been an angel come down to carry him off to heaven . . . only angels didn't wear badges. As Jonas's vision cleared, he realized that it wasn't an angel, but a man. A cop to be more specific.

"Are you okay?" the cop asked in an accent that Jonas couldn't place.

Jonas opened his mouth to speak, but couldn't quite form the words, so he just nodded.

"Don't try to talk. Just sit tight; an ambulance is on the way," the cop told him.

"Yo, Raf, you okay?" Ace appeared next to the cop. Cal was also with him. They were both fighting to get a look and invading the cop's space.

"I'm gonna need you boys to step back," the cop told them.

"Chill out, Officer. That's my homeboy right there. I'm trying to make sure he's good!" Ace snapped.

"Then, where the hell were you when he decided to go for a nature walk on the ice? Get your little ass back!" the officer matched his tone. The boys wisely did as they were told, and the cop turned his attention back to Jonas. "Sit tight. The ambulance will be here soon."

Within ten minutes, there were paramedics on the scene, along with a half dozen more uniformed officers. The officers took statements from Alex about what had happened, while the paramedics got Jonas strapped onto a gurney. He was more worried about Alex than himself. She looked pretty shaken up. He was glad that he hadn't died in front of her. As the paramedics were loading Jonas into the back of the ambulance, the officer who saved him appeared.

"Is he going to be okay?" the cop asked.

"Surprisingly, yes," the paramedic admitted. "He's suffering from hypothermia, and we can't be sure yet if the water's done any long-term damage to the lungs, but other than that, we think he'll be fine. Considering how long he was down there before you pulled him out, I'd say this was nothing short of a genuine Christmas miracle."

"I died," Jonas said just above a whisper. It was more of a statement than a question.

"It would seem that you still have work to do in this life," the cop said as he placed Jonas's signed football on the gurney with him. "Second chances are hard to come by. Don't waste yours."

Part II

*"If a thief be found breaking up, and be smitten
that he die, there shall no blood be shed for him."*

—Exodus 22:2 (KJV)

Chapter Six

Jonas sat in the window of his apartment, gazing long-ingly out the window. Spring was closing in, which meant the weather was starting to break. It hadn't snowed in quite some time, and the biting chill had finally started to taper off. The block was busy that day. The first signs of decent weather always brought the bears out of hibernation.

Just below, he saw Fat Moe from the second floor wheeling his mini-grill out of the building. He was a plump, slovenly man who was missing most of the top teeth in his mouth. His signature nappy wool skully was sitting cocked on his head like a rolled-up condom. Fat Moe was one of those people that would drag his mini-grill out all year-round as long as he had somewhere dry to set it up. He flashed a passing woman a smile, showing off the empty space in the top of his mouth where his teeth used to reside. Fat Moe looked a mess the majority of the time, but despite his appearance, no one could deny the fact that he could cook his ass off. People in the neighborhood often made fun of Fat Moe, but Jonas had love for him. Moe had always been good to the Rafferty children, and whenever he was around, they knew they wouldn't go hungry. It was Fat Moe who had taught Sweets how to cook when they were younger. Fat Moe was like family.

Fat Moe must've felt Jonas's eyes on him because he looked up, shielding his eyes from the afternoon sun.

"Hey, Jonas! I'm about to set up in the park. You want a dog?" he called up.

"Maybe later, Moe," Jonas said sadly. He wanted nothing more than to go downstairs and enjoy not only one of Fat Moe's hot dogs but also some fresh air too. It wasn't happening, though. Ever since the accident in Central Park, Jonas had been on lockdown.

By the time Jonas was rushed into St. Luke's Hospital, news of what had happened to him had already spread through his hood. This was thanks to Ace and Cal telling everyone, including Sweets. She had damn near beaten him to the hospital. They wouldn't let Sweets in to see him because she was a minor, so they had to wait for their mother to show up. Janette arrived about forty minutes after, with Yvette, Anette, and Josette in tow. To Jonas's surprise, Janette managed to look halfway decent. Her clothes were clean, and her hair was brushed back into a ponytail, no doubt in case Social Services showed up, and she had to play the role of a caring mother. One look in her eyes, however, and you could tell she was high, but she was at least functional.

All of the sisters were pretty shaken up by what had happened, especially Josette. She cried until Jonas let her crawl into the hospital bed with him and assured her that he was okay. At one point, she asked him, "Did you see God?" It was an innocent question, but one Jonas wasn't sure how to answer. He was sure he had seen something as he crossed between worlds, but he wasn't sure what. He could remember crossing over, and someone being there to greet him when he arrived in the afterlife, and that's when he heard the small voice: "Not yet," and just like that, he was snatched back to the land of the living.

They kept Jonas overnight for observation and released him the next morning with a follow-up appointment. His stay at the hospital turned out to be almost as eventful as his near-death experience. He shared a room with another boy and his unruly family. From speaking to the boy, he'd learned that his name was Cain. Like Yvette and Anette, he was a twin but looked nothing like his brother Abel. Cain had come in with burns to his face and damage to one of his eyes. According to his mother, the boy had sustained the injuries due to a defective coffeepot that had shattered when she heated it. The story didn't sound right to Jonas. It must've smelled fishy to the doctors too because Social Services were called in, and Cain was taken away during the night. Cain's mother cursed the Social Service workers for taking her kid. Even little Abel tried to fight to keep them from taking his brother, but Cain was silent. He seemed almost happy to be taken away from his mother. Years later, when their paths crossed again, Jonas would learn the truth about Cain's "accident." He had been burned and blinded when his mother's crack pipe exploded in his face.

Things had changed for Jonas after the accident. Whether for the better or worse was still up for debate. When he got home, he found out that he had become somewhat of a local celebrity. All the local news stations were reporting on what was being called a "Christmas Miracle." Apparently, it wasn't every day that little boys spent nearly four minutes at the bottom of frozen lakes and lived to tell the tale. Reporters stalked Jonas and his family, day and night, all wanting to get the exclusive on the boy who had cheated death. They even stalked him at school . . . until the principal had threatened to file harassment charges if the reporters didn't quit.

After a while, Jonas's celebrity status had begun to fade, and this is about the time when *operation lockdown* began. Jonas had always been given a great deal of freedom for a kid his age, but after almost losing him, Janette put him on a short leash. He had to come straight home after school every day and was no longer allowed to run the streets with his friends. On the rare occasions that he was allowed to go outside, he couldn't go any farther than the stoop where Janette could watch him from the window. Of course, he tried to sneak off every chance he got, but he never made it too far for too long before either his mother or one of his sisters tracked him down. Whenever he was caught, Jonas could always expect a good ass whipping to follow. Eventually, he gave up and accepted the fact that he had become a prisoner in his own home.

The one good thing that came from his sentence was the fact that in order to enforce it meant Janette had to be around to do so. She still managed to find time to run the streets but not as much. For the most part, she stayed close to the house. There were those times when Slick dragged her out to handle business, and sometimes she wouldn't come back until the next morning. Those were the times she left Sweets to enforce her rule. Though Janette would never come out and admit it, almost losing her only son had rattled her. Not enough to get her act together but enough to at least pay attention. That period of time was the only one where he could remember Janette actually acting like she gave a fuck about him, and it made Jonas feel good. What child didn't crave the love of their mother?

"What you doing perched in that window like a pigeon?" Janette startled him. He hadn't heard her approach.

"Nothing." Jonas got out of the window and closed it.

"I need you to run up to Juan's and get me a pack of cigarettes and a box of cereal," she told him.

"Okay, give me the money."

"I ain't got it right now, but tell him I'll set him right when I get my stamps tomorrow."

Jonas frowned. "You know I hate asking him for anything."

"You ain't asking. *I* am. Now stop giving me lip and do like I said. And make sure you come right back. If I have to come looking for you, it's gonna be trouble," she warned.

"Whatever," Jonas mumbled under his breath and went to get his coat. When he got outside, he filled his lungs with the fresh air. The sun shone down so brightly that he had to squint. He was like a man recently freed, and it felt good.

When Jonas got inside the store, it was crowded as usual. It was the end of the month, so people whose food stamps had run out were there bartering with Juan to get something to hold them over until the first rolled around. Juan's brother, José, was behind the counter ringing up some chips and a juice for a young man. José looked like a younger, chunkier version of Juan. José was cool. He didn't bother anybody and would sometimes cut people a break even after his brother had refused to do so. José was also heavy into sports. He was one of the few people with whom Jonas could have serious conversations with about football. He was an Eagles fan, while Jonas rode out with the Giants, so they often engaged in heated debates.

"What's up, Raf?" José greeted him when he noticed the boy walk in.

"Chilling."

"Yo, what do you think about the upcoming draft? I think we're finally going to get a quarterback that can take us back to the playoffs," José said.

"You might, but you still gotta get by us, and we know that ain't happening," Jonas replied. "But, yo, I need a solid."

José knew what he meant. He waited until he had finished with the boy making the purchase before waving Jonas over. "What you need?"

"A box of cereal and some smokes. My mom will make it right when she gets her stamps," Jonas promised.

"You know I'm not worried about it. Grab what you need off the shelf, but you're going to have to see my brother about the cigarettes. You know that cheap bastard counts every single loosie that moves out of here. He's in the back."

When Jonas saw José, he had hoped he'd be able to avoid Juan. "A'ight." He walked toward the back of the store.

Juan was leaning against the ATM, drinking a Corona and whispering sweetly to a young girl named Jewels. Jewels was Fat Moe's niece. Jonas had been seeing Jewels around the neighborhood off and on for years, but she had only recently moved there permanently. She and her mom had gotten evicted from their apartment in the Bronx, and they were staying with Fat Moe until she got back on her feet. Jewels was what you would call a wild girl. It seemed like every other week she was getting into a fight. To the other girls in the neighborhood, she was still an outsider, and they were always testing her. One thing Jonas liked about her was, win or lose, she never backed down. She would knuckle up with anyone.

Juan was in the process of trying to convince Jewels to take a sip of his beer when he spotted Jonas standing in the aisle. Briefly, a guilty expression crossed his face, but it was quickly replaced by a sly smile that was mostly teeth and gums. Jonas hated that smile. It reminded him of a snake about to swallow up an unsuspecting field mouse. "What's up, li'l Zeke?"

"Jonas," he corrected him. He hated when people called him li'l Zeke, and Juan knew it, which is why he did it. "Can I talk to you for a minute?"

"Sure thing, kid." Juan whispered something to Jewels, which made her giggle, before dismissing her.

"Hey, Raf," Jewels greeted him on the way out.

"Sup?" Jonas said in an uninterested tone. He wanted to get his mother's cigarettes and get back upstairs before she came outside looking for him and acting a fool.

"So, you going to Ricky's house party this Sat? I hear his parents are going to be out of town," Jewels informed him.

"I might slide through," Jonas lied. He knew damn well his mother wasn't going to let him outside to attend a party.

"Maybe I'll see you there?"

"Maybe," Jonas said without bothering to look at her.

"Okay then," she said awkwardly before leaving.

"Why are you always so mean to that girl? You know she likes you, right?" Juan asked.

"Whatever," Jonas said. He knew Jewels liked him, but Jonas only had eyes for Alex. "My mom needs a pack of cigarettes. She'll pay it back when she gets her stamps."

"You know she's already into me for fifty bucks from the beginning of the month when I looked out for her," Juan told him.

"So, should I tell her you can't do it?"

Juan thought about the question as if he were genuinely struggling with the decision. "Nah, I'll look out for her this one last time. Janette has always been all right with me. Tell José I said you're good."

"Thanks, I'll make sure her tab gets settled," Jonas said as if he had two nickels to rub together.

"I know your mom is a busy woman, so if she doesn't have time to stop by, she can send it by Yvette," Juan said.

Jonas knew what he was suggesting, and Juan knew that he knew, but Jonas didn't allow the man to bait him.

By the time Jonas left the store, he had the box of cereal and cigarettes his mother sent him for and a soda for himself. He wasn't even thirsty; he just felt like taking a little extra from Juan's smug ass. He was about to go back to his building when he spotted Ace and Cal coming up the block. The mischievous smirks on their faces said that they were up to no good, which meant he was right on time. It had been awhile since Jonas got into some mischief with his friends.

"I see they finally let you off lockdown," Ace started in on him.

"What y'all fools into?" Jonas didn't take the bait.

"About to get into some gangsta shit," Cal said, smiling slyly.

"What you talking about?" Jonas asked curiously. Cal looked to Ace, who gave him the nod to spill the beans about whatever it was that they were up to.

"A'ight, but not here. Come around the corner." Cal started off without waiting to see if Jonas was following.

When they got around the corner, the three of them huddled in the doorway of one of the buildings. Cal kept looking up and down the street as if he were about to reveal some secret treasure, and he was. From the pocket of his baggy jeans, he produced a .38. The gun was old and partially rusted, but it was still the most beautiful thing Jonas had ever seen.

"Yo, where'd you get it?" Jonas asked excitedly. He reached out to touch the gun, but Cal tucked it back into his pocket.

"Where do you think I got it? From my brother," Cal told him.

"Didn't you learn your lesson from the last ass whipping you got for taking his shit?" Jonas asked.

"I'll have this back before he even notices it's missing. I only need it for a few hours," Cal said.

"What do you need it for?" Jonas wanted to know.

"To rob a muthafucka, what else?" Ace asked as if the answer should have been obvious. "We're gonna go downtown to like Eighty-something Street and place an order from the Chinese restaurant. We'll tell them we're having a dinner party and to bring change for a hundred. When they show up, we're gonna take the food *and* the money. This shit'll be easy. You down?"

Jonas was hesitant. He and his crew were no strangers to taking things that didn't belong to them, but that was mostly limited to stealing bikes or shoplifting. What Ace was suggesting was armed robbery, which was way out of their league.

"I don't know, man," Jonas said cautiously. "What if something goes wrong?"

"Ain't shit gonna go wrong. When the delivery guy sees this pistol, he's gonna give up his shit without a hassle. My brother and them do this all the time," Cal said as if it were just that simple.

"This nigga is scared," Ace said.

"Ain't nobody scared," Jonas told him.

"Then prove it and roll with us," Ace challenged. "You ain't even gotta do nothing. Just watch our backs while me and Cal get him."

Jonas had a bad feeling about it. He wanted no part of the armed heist his friends were plotting, but he didn't want to seem like a punk either. There was a serious debate going on between the devil on one shoulder and the angel on the other. The angel ended up losing. "Fuck it. I'm in."

"That's my boy!" Ace slapped him proudly on the back.

Jonas and his crew started making their way toward the 2-train station on 135th and Lenox. They had barely made it out of the neighborhood, and his heart was already in his throat. He knew what they were about to do was not only wrong but dangerous too. Still, he had already committed and couldn't back out. They were just about to descend the steps into the subway station when the universe intervened on his behalf.

"And where do you think you're going?" a voice called from behind Jonas. He turned around to find Sweets coming out of the Schomburg Library, but she wasn't alone. Drew was with her.

"Nowhere," Jonas lied. "Mom sent me to the store, and I was just on my way back to the block."

"Good, because I'm going that way, so we can walk together." Sweets saw through his bullshit.

Jonas looked from his waiting sister to his friends, who were eager to go and pull off their heist. He knew that no amount of bullshit he tried to feed Sweets would help him to escape now that she was on him. "I'll catch up with y'all another time," he told his boys.

"Sucker-ass nigga," Ace teased before heading down the stairs with Cal.

Jonas, Sweets, and Drew walked back up Lenox toward their block. Drew and Sweets shot the breeze, but Jonas was quiet. He was still pissed at Sweets for blocking his action. In his mind, he imagined all the things that he could've bought with his share of the robbery money. They stopped at the pharmacy on 136th so Sweets could get some feminine products for her and her sisters. She went inside, leaving Jonas and Drew to wait.

"You can't dance on every record," Drew said to Jonas once Sweets was out of earshot.

"Huh?"

"The move you were about to bust," Drew clarified.

"What makes you think I was about to bust a move?" Jonas asked.

"A man is often judged by the company he keeps," Drew said, sounding older than his 17 years.

"And what's that supposed to mean?"

"It means I know how your boys give it up," Drew told him. "Ace is out here playing, and you look like you're still on the fence about getting into the game."

"What are you, psychic or something?" Jonas asked sarcastically.

"Nah, I was just your age once. I know how loud the streets can whisper into the ear of a young man trying to come up. I can't tell you what to do, but what I can tell you is that unless you're ready to go all in, ride the bench for a time longer."

"How long did you ride the bench before you started hustling for Eight-Ball?" Jonas shot back.

"I don't hustle for Eight-Ball. I buy drugs from him," Drew corrected him.

"Still sounds like a worker to me," Jonas called himself being cute.

Drew laughed. "Spoken just like a spectator to this here sport. Let me break something down to you, shorty. When I first started out, I was moving product for Eight-Ball, but when I got my weight up, I was able to buy my own package. Now I ain't gonna lie. I cop exclusively from Eight-Ball and kick him a little something every month for the privilege to hustle on his strip, but all I sell is all I keep. I sling when I want; I don't punch nobody's clock, like the rest of these dudes."

"How did you manage that?" Jonas asked. He had always been under the impression that everybody who sold drugs on the strip worked for Eight-Ball.

Drew thought about it before answering. "When I started hustling, I asked myself if I wanted to be a worker or a boss and took the necessary steps. Which role do you see yourself in?"

"A boss," Jonas said confidently.

"Then you need to put yourself in position to be that. The first thing a boss understands is not to follow anybody else blindly, kind of like what you do with Ace."

"I don't follow Ace; I just hold him down when he needs me to," Jonas told him.

"I dig it, and I respect it, but at some point, you're going to have to ask yourself: Do I gain more by being loyal to a team, or having a team be loyal to me? You might not understand that right now, but in time, you're going to thank me for that jewel."

For the rest of the walk home, Jonas pondered what Drew had run down to him. His words gave him plenty of food for thought. Ace was usually the one that came up with the plans, but did that qualify him to be the leader of their team? Food for thought, indeed. When they reached the building, Sweets sent Jonas upstairs with the items his mother had sent him to the store for and the bag full of feminine products. She stayed outside with Drew, telling him she'd be along in a few. From the way they were looking at each other, it would probably be longer than that. Something was definitely going on between the hustler and his sister. Jonas was just too young to understand what.

As Jonas sat in the window of his apartment watching the world pass him by and thinking about what he would miss out on from not rolling with Ace, he found himself bitter. He was pissed at Sweets for stopping him from going with his friends, but little did he know at the time, later on, he would be thankful that she had. It would be two days before Jonas would see Ace again and find out that his fears about the robbery had come to fruition. Ace had promised that the robbery would be simple, but things had gone terribly wrong. Instead of the Chinese delivery guy giving up his goods as Cal had predicted, he put up a fight. He ended up taking the gun from the kids and kicking both their asses. Ace got away, but the delivery guy held Cal until the police arrived. Getting arrested for the robbery was bad enough, but the fact that the gun had a body on it made things worse. Cal was the first of Jonas's friends that had to go away to do some time . . . but he wouldn't be the last.

Chapter Seven

By the time spring reared its head, Janette had loosened the yoke around Jonas's neck. He was allowed to ease back into some of his regular routines. She still managed to harass him about his whereabouts when she was sober enough to do so, but for the most part, she left him alone.

Things had changed quite a bit between the time Cal was sent away and Jonas being able to come outside regularly again. For one thing, their original crew of three had become four. Ace, in Jonas's absence, had started running around with a kid from 145th Street named Prince. Jonas knew Prince from school. He was a quiet Jamaican kid that Jonas had taken a liking to. The kids used to give him shit because his parents always made him wear slacks and shoes to school instead of jeans and sneakers like the other kids. They were devout Jehovah's Witnesses. Jonas was surprised to see Prince playing the block as much as he did because he knew how strict his parents were. Ace had given him a taste of the streets, and his nose was now wide open. Jonas liked Prince. He was a cool dude once you got to know him. It was the fourth member of their group, Mula, who gave him pause.

Mula was the youngest of their crew, but he had been in the streets longer than Jonas or Ace. He was barely a hundred pounds soaking wet but had a heart that could be measured in metric tons. His uncle, Fish, ran with the Red-T Boys, and Mula was always trailing behind him when they did dirt. He was like their unofficial mascot. Mula was down to do whatever, whenever, to whoever and loved to play the front lines when it went down. He was young, so the few times he did get arrested for things, he only received a slap on the wrist. He acted like his age gave him a license to break the law, which he did quite well. Once, Mula had gone into an appliance store and came running out with a microwave. It didn't matter to him that it was broad daylight. Mula was reckless like that. There was a rumor that Mula already had a body under his belt, but he would never confirm or deny it.

Something else that had changed was that Ace was now dealing. He had hooked in with someone that Doug knew, and they fronted him some weed. It was only a few ounces and not even the highest grade of weed, but it was a start. The young boys were growing up.

Jonas was supposed to meet up with Ace, Mula, and Prince at 3:00 p.m., so they could catch the 3:45 movie at the Magic Johnson Theater. It was already 3:15, and he was just getting out of the shower. He was running behind schedule because Sweets had sent him to the drugstore to get some children's Tylenol. Jo-Jo had been complaining about her legs aching again. The older she got, the more her legs seemed to trouble her. They had taken her to the Harlem hospital to see what was wrong, but they couldn't find anything out of the ordinary. They gave her an appointment to come back so that they could run some labs, but, of course, her mother had missed it. They just dosed her up with Tylenol and hoped for the best.

When Jonas went into his room to put his clothes on, he was surprised to find Slick there. His back was to the door, and he was fishing around under the bed for something, so he didn't notice Jonas walk in. "You lose something?"

Slick jumped like a man who had just been caught with his hand in the cookie jar. He looked a mess, more so than usual. He had been wearing the same clothes for days, his hair hadn't been combed, and he could stand a shave and a bath. Even though he was an addict, Slick had always done a pretty good job at keeping up his appearance, but lately, he seemed to be letting himself go.

"Yeah, I was looking for my wallet," Slick lied.

"Why would your wallet be under my bed?" Jonas asked suspiciously.

"I thought maybe I dropped it in here when I was cleaning up the other day," Slick said. It was pure bullshit. During the years Slick had been living with them, Jonas hadn't seen him pick up so much as a broom. "Say, your mama wanted to ask if you got a few dollars we could borrow. Just until I can get out and make some moves."

"I ain't got it," Jonas lied. All the money he had was the twenty dollars he had made from sweeping up at the barbershop the previous weekend. That was the money for his ticket and snacks. No way in the hell he was going to break bread with Slick.

Slick's dry lips curled into a frown. "C'mon, man. Don't act like I don't know what you and your boys are up to out in that park every day. Let me hold ten dollars."

"I told you that I don't have it," Jonas insisted.

"Then that makes you a damn fool, if you hang around with Ace and them all day, every day, and ain't getting none of that money they're making. If the police ever run them down, they're gonna take all your little asses. Ain't gonna matter whose drugs they are, so you may as well get yours."

"You done?" Jonas asked. He was ready to be rid of Slick so that he could get dressed.

"Guess so." Slick scratched his chin. He lingered there for a time as if Jonas would change his mind about the money. When it became obvious he wouldn't, Slick left him to get dressed.

Jonas jumped into his clothes in record time. He was wearing a pair of blue jeans, a green polo shirt that he had gotten for Christmas, and Nikes. He wanted to make sure that he looked sharp in case they ran into some honeys at the theater. On his way out, he stopped by the girls' room to check on Jo-Jo. He found her lying in bed with Anette, while her big sister read one of her favorite stories to her. "How you feeling, Jo-Jo?"

"A little better. My legs don't hurt as much, but they're still achy," she told him.

"Don't worry. You'll feel better once the medicine kicks in," Jonas promised, kissing her on the forehead. "Where's Sweets?" he asked Anette. She had been home before he got into the shower but was nowhere to be found now.

"Probably somewhere with her head up Drew's ass," Anette said with an attitude.

"What's up with that?" Jonas had noticed that Sweets and Drew had been spending quite a bit of time together. He had even caught him walking her home from school a few times.

"That's her boyfriend," Josette said.

"What makes you say that?" Jonas asked.

"Because I caught them kissing in the hallway before." Josette mimicked what she had seen.

"Seems like everybody around here has got a life except me," Anette said enviously.

"If you want, I can skip the movies and stay here with Jo-Jo," Jonas offered. He hoped she turned him down because he didn't want to miss the movie.

"You go ahead and enjoy yourself," Anette declined.

"Jonas, can you bring me back some candy from the movies?" Josette asked.

"Sure, anything you want," he agreed.

"Raisinetes, but don't keep them in your pocket. I don't like them when they're all mushy."

"You got it, kid," Jonas winked and headed out.

Jonas arrived at the park to find his crew already waiting for him. All it took was one look to tell him something was wrong. Ace was pacing back and forth while Prince watched him with a worried look on his face. Mula busied himself carving his initials into a wooden bench with a pocketknife.

"Sorry I'm late. Y'all ready to be out to the movies?" Jonas gave each of them dap.

"We're gonna have to catch a later show. Some shit came up that we need to handle," Ace told him.

"What happened?" Jonas asked.

"Doug got jumped."

"Word? What happened?"

"I don't know the details yet. We'll find out everything when we get to his crib. One thing I do know is, we ain't letting this shit ride."

It was Alex who answered the door for the boys when they arrived at their apartment. Her face was flushed, and her eyes and tip of her nose were red. You could tell she had been crying.

"Hey, y'all." Alex allowed them inside.

"You okay?" Jonas asked as if she were the one who had been attacked.

"Yes, thanks. I'm just worried about my brother."

"Don't sweat nothing, Alex. We gonna handle everything," Ace boasted. "Where's my boy?"

"In the bedroom. I'll get him. Y'all have a seat in the living room." Alex disappeared down the hall.

In all the years they had known Alex and Doug, this was the first time Jonas could remember being in their home. Even when they still lived in the neighborhood, they couldn't have guests over. Their parents didn't play that. For it to be a project apartment, it was actually quite nice. It had wall-to-wall carpet, a leather sectional, and a flat-screen television. Dominating one wall was a bookshelf full of literature. Jonas studied the shelves, silently mouthing the titles. There were tons of books, most of them he had never heard of. It reminded him of the library at school.

"You think this is real?" Mula called out. He was holding a golden elephant that he had picked up from the table.

"Put it down," Jonas ordered, already knowing what he was thinking.

"I wasn't gonna take it," Mula lied. He put the elephant down and took a seat on the sectional next to Prince.

After a few minutes, Alex reappeared. She was helping her brother Doug, who seemed to be hobbling. He was in bad shape. His face was bruised, one of his eyes was swollen closed, and a bandage wrapped his head. One of his arms was also in a cast. It looked like whoever had done it to him was trying to take him out.

"Damn, they fucked you up!" Mula said crudely.

"You okay?" Jonas asked.

"Yeah, I'm good. My arm got the worst of it." Doug hoisted the cast. It stretched from his hand to his elbow.

"What happened?" Ace demanded. He was angry, and everyone could see it in his face.

"Alex, go in the room for a minute so the grown folks can talk," Doug told her.

"Y'all ain't grown," she capped.

"Do as I say!" he snapped. It was the first time any of them had ever heard him raise his voice at his little sister. Her eyes watered up, and she stormed off into the bedroom. "Damn," he sighed. He felt bad for yelling at her.

"Tell me who did this to you, so we can get at these niggas," Ace pressed.

"Some dudes from Grant Projects," Doug began. "I came up on some of the new iPhones a few days ago and put word out that I had them for the low. My man Brian is from over there. He said he knew somebody that wanted to cop one. I go over there to make the sale, and they jumped me. Took the phone, my chain, and my bread. They even hit me with a bat," he explained the broken arm. "On the real, I thought they were gonna kill me."

"They're going to wish they had when I get done with them," Ace fumed. All of the boys were close, but he and Doug had a special relationship. It was Doug who had helped him get on his feet when he was running around broke.

"Did you know any of them?" Prince asked.

"Not really. A few of them I've seen around before, but I don't know their names or anything."

"I'll bet Brian knows. He probably set this whole thing up." Mula said what they had all been thinking.

"Nah, man. Me and Brian go back to Summer League when he was the assistant coach of our team. I've known that dude since forever. He wouldn't go out like that," Doug said. He seemed convinced, but Ace wasn't.

"We'll found out soon enough," Ace promised.

Their plotting session was broken up when Doug's parents came in. Doug was the spitting image of Mr. Hightower, only shorter. Mr. Hightower was a handsome man with rich black hair that had begun to gray at the temples. Back in the day, he used to hustle, but for the last fifteen years, he had been living the life of a square working for the Department of Sanitation. Mr. Hightower was easygoing; Mrs. Hightower, however, was a different story.

Mrs. Hightower looked like a darker version of Alex, minus the beautiful smile. She never seemed to smile, at least not that any of them could remember. Unlike Mr. Hightower, who had been raised in the hood, Mrs. Hightower was originally from an affluent neighborhood somewhere on Long Island. She was a little less tolerant of kids from the old neighborhood than her husband was, and it showed in the way she looked at Jonas and his crew when she found them congregating in her living room.

"Hey, Mom, Dad," Doug greeted his parents.

"Douglas, what did we tell you about having guests over when we're not home?" Mrs. Hightower asked in her prim and proper voice. She clearly was not happy to see the boys in her house, but most of her hostility was directed at Ace. There was a rumor that Ace's mom and Mr. Hightower had messed around once. It was never proven, but that didn't stop Mrs. Hightower making Ace the scapegoat.

"The fellas just came to check on me to make sure I was okay," Doug told her.

"We were just leaving," Ace said, not wanting to be around Doug's mother any more than she wanted to be around them. "We'll call you later, Doug."

"Douglas won't be taking any phone calls for the rest of the day. It's bad enough he's up hanging out with the lot of you when the doctor said he should be resting."

"C'mon, Mom. You're embarrassing me in front of my friends." Doug tried to quiet her.

"Are these the same friends you were with when you got your arm broken?" Mrs. Hightower asked. None of the boys were sure what she meant, and it showed on their faces.

"Fellas, maybe you should go. It's time for Doug to take his meds," Mr. Hightower interjected.

"We out," Ace announced and led his group out the door. They were waiting for the elevator when Mr. Hightower came out behind them.

"Hold on a second. I wanna ask you boys something." Mr. Hightower caught up with them. "Any of you care to tell me what really happened to my son?"

They were all quiet for a time, not sure how to answer. It was Ace who eventually broke the silence.

"Whatever Doug told you is what happened," he said.

"What he *told* me was that he was with you guys at a basketball game when some guys from the opposing school started a fight." Mr. Hightower gave them the short version of the story Doug had fed him. "Personally, I think it was bullshit. No disrespect to any of you, but I'm not that long removed from the game to where I can't recognize players." He met each of their gazes. "What happened to my son wasn't about basketball."

"Don't worry about nothing, Mr. Hightower. We got this," Ace promised.

"How? By running out and doing something that'll get you locked up or possibly killed?" Mr. Hightower asked.

"So, you're saying we should let it ride?" Mula asked.

"I'm saying don't make an already-bad situation worse. Make no mistake, I'm pissed over what happened to Doug, but he's trying to play a game that he has no business in. This time, he got lucky and escaped with only a broken arm. I guarantee you that there won't be a next time, not on my watch. I hope what happened to him serves as a lesson to all of you boys. Focus on school and getting girls. Leave that bullshit on the streets alone."

"Whatever," Ace said offhandedly.

"I'm serious. If you've got it in your minds to go out and do something foolish, I can't stop you, but don't do it in the name of my son. All that's going to do is keep this cycle of bullshit going, and I won't have that on me, or my family," Mr. Hightower said seriously.

Mr. Hightower was laying some heavy game on them, but it went in one ear and out the other. He was a square. Who was he to tell them what time it was? Mr. Hightower could tell from the disinterested looks on their faces that he wasn't getting through to them. He had been in their position before . . . young and out to prove himself. He understood that the code they followed wouldn't allow them to let the situation rest, but never let it be said that he hadn't tried.

The elevator arrived, rescuing the boys from the rest of Mr. Hightower's speech. They all piled on, anxious to get away from the preaching adult. As the doors were closing, Mr. Hightower said something that Jonas would carry with him for a long time.

"Love and loyalty are two sides of the same coin. Both will get you killed, but only one is worth dying for. Choose wisely."

"This shit is all fucked up," Jonas said once they were outside.

"I say we get the strap and run up in these niggas' hood on some Rambo shit." Mula was ready to get to it. "We find out who was behind this, hit them, and get out."

"Or get trapped off and killed in the process," Ace said. He wanted to get back at the dudes who had jumped Doug just as badly as any of them, but knew they had to be smart about it. "We gotta plan this one."

"Maybe if we can't go in and get them, we can lure them out," Prince suggested.

"With what? Another phone to steal?" Mula asked sarcastically.

"Nah, I got something better. What's the one thing no young, thirsty nigga can resist?" Prince asked. Seeing that they weren't catching on, he answered his own question. "Pussy. We put a bitch on the ring leader and let *her* set him up."

"You think Alex will help us? Shorty is fine as hell," Mula said. He had been checking Alex out heavy when they were at the house.

"Fuck no, we ain't using Alex!" Jonas said a little more defensively than he intended to. This drew questioning looks from his friends. "I figure with all that's going on, her parents will probably have her on lockdown," he offered in the way of an explanation. It was weak, but it was all he had.

"Raf is right," Ace agreed. "Alex is no good, but I like the angle. We need to find a chick we can trust, but who?"

Jonas thought about it for a while, and then it hit him. "I've got somebody in mind."

Chapter Eight

The next two weeks were spent plotting what the crew affectionately called "Doug's Revenge." Initially, they were going to try to pick off everybody involved with Doug's assault one by one, but that would've taken time and resources they didn't have to spare. After some debate, they had settled on catching the dude Doug had been supposed to be selling the phone to and give him the same treatment they had given Doug. Mula wanted to kill him, but Ace was able to talk him out of it. A simple beat-down would do.

Just as Jonas feared, Doug hadn't been able to have too big of a hand in the revenge plot. His parents had him under constant surveillance. Mr. Hightower hadn't been joking when he said that there wouldn't be a second time on his watch. Things got so crazy that Prince had to stop selling weed with Ace to pick up the slack with the ring of crackhead boosters Doug worked with. Doug didn't seem to mind too much because Prince always made sure to kick him a few dollars when he scored. After getting jumped, Doug's heart hadn't seemed to be much in the game anyhow. Getting beat within an inch of his life had changed him in a way that Jonas wouldn't truly come to understand until he was older and more battle-worn. Ace and the others all felt when he started to pull away, but none of them judged him for it. Regardless of whether Doug was hustling, he was still one of them.

Though Doug might not have had been hands-on in the execution, he still proved instrumental in the planning. The first thing they needed to do was to get a line on Brian, the dude who had brought the sale to Doug in the first place. Doug was initially hesitant to give up Brian's address because he still wasn't convinced that his old assistant coach had been in on it, and he knew that Ace had ill intentions toward all parties involved. He didn't want to carry the guilt of something happening to Brian unnecessarily. It took Ace giving his word that he wouldn't let Mula toss Brian up before Doug relented. Even then, he wouldn't give up an address, but he did put in a phone call to Brian and arranged a meeting.

Within five minutes of talking to Brian, Jonas could tell that something wasn't right with him. He was too . . . *extra,* for lack of a better word. Everything he did or said was an exaggeration, from the way his hands constantly moved when he spoke to the knockoff Gucci sneakers and fake chain he was sporting when they met up. Ace questioned him during the meeting, while Jonas hung back and observed. His story was pretty much the same as the one Doug had told them: dude wanted to buy the iPhone, and when Doug showed, they packed him out. He even showed them the bruise under his eye from where he got snuffed trying to help.

Brian gave a very convincing performance, but Jonas didn't buy it. Something about his story was off. One thing that stood out was that for as much damage as they had done to Doug, they had to have been whipping on him for a while . . . but only hit Brian once? Something else was the fact that he still had his chain. Doug said that along with taking his money, they had snatched his chain. Why let Brian keep his? Granted, it was as fake as a three-dollar bill, but the robbers wouldn't have known that. At least not right off. There was no doubt in his mind that Brian had been in on it somehow.

It didn't take much convincing to incorporate Brian into their scheme. He was far too willing to help Ace and his crew get revenge against the dudes who had been behind the attack on Doug. He ran down their names, addresses, and known associates. If the boy hadn't been so crooked, he could've had a promising career as a detective. There were five of them in total, mostly foot soldiers and dick riders who just saw an opportunity to catch wreck when they set it on Doug. They would get theirs in time, but their target was the one who had been behind it, a kid named Black.

According to Brian, Black ran a drug crew who lived on the Broadway side of the projects. He had made a little name for himself for having shot somebody a few summers before, and because of who his older cousin was. Black's cousin was a dude who they called "Gentleman Jack," because he was always wearing a smile, but Jack was a stone-cold killer. He was currently serving a light bid upstate, which was how Black ended up inheriting the drug operation. Brian suggested that the best time to get at him would be early in the morning since he was usually up and on the block. Ace agreed and told Brian he'd let him know when it was gonna go down so he could be on hand to collect his pound of flesh. As far as Brian knew, the plan was all set. He wouldn't find out until much later that it had all been a lie. The real plan was a far more devious one, which Jonas would have to call in a favor to pull off.

Jonas wasn't quite sure what to expect when he stepped to Jewels and asked her for her help in their scheme, but she was surprisingly receptive to it. Mostly because she was so head over heels for Jonas that she would've done just about anything to get in good with him. That, and the fact that Ace had promised to give her fifty dollars for her time. Once Jonas showed her who Black was, Jewels handled the rest. She arranged a "chance meeting" with him at the bodega across the street from his building. Black took one look at her in her skintight jeans and was all over her, as Jewels knew he would be. They exchanged numbers, and so the courtship began.

They hung out a few times, always in his project. Jewels wasn't stupid enough to ever let him know where she rested her head. Black turned out to be a big trick. They had only been talking for about a week, and he was already giving her gifts: sneakers, a chain, and cash whenever she asked. All they had done so far was kiss and play a game of *stink finger*. Jewels hadn't let him sleep with her, and he was acting like they were exclusive. Black's nose was wide open. Jewels had even jokingly asked Jonas if they could delay their plan for another month or two so she could get a summer wardrobe out of him.

Whenever Jewels and Black hung out, Jonas was always somewhere in the cut watching them. During his observation of the couple, Jonas often found himself getting upset. He knew that Jewels was only doing what he had asked her to do, but it still bothered him to see her with Black. Every time he kissed her, Jonas felt ill. It suddenly dawned on him that he was having his first experience with jealousy. All the time Jewels had been trying to get on Jonas's radar, he hardly gave her a second look, but now seeing her with someone else made him mad. He wasn't sure how much longer he'd be able to watch the show before his emotions caused him to do something stupid.

The day had finally come when they were supposed to spring the trap. Black had been pressuring Jewels for sex, and it was becoming harder to keep making excuses without him becoming suspicious. She finally agreed to let him cross the finish line. Black had a romantic evening planned for them. They were to catch a movie, then grab some food from Red Lobster before going to one of the short-stay motels on 145th to consummate the relationship. That was a nut he would never get to bust.

Jonas could remember waking up that morning filled with a sense of dread. That should've been the first sign that it was going to be a bad day. There was a ball of ice in his stomach that spread through his fingertips and toes. For a minute, he thought he was coming down with something, but when Sweets took his temperature, it was normal. He got up and went to school like any other day, but found that he couldn't concentrate. The feeling that something bad was about to happen continued to linger. He reasoned that it was just his nerves over what they had planned for that night.

When the bell signaling the lunch period had begun, Jonas headed down to the cafeteria. Most of his classes were for gifted and talented students, so he rarely got to see his friends in school outside of the lunch period. That was where they would meet up to plot mischief, play cards, and trade war stories. There was always a gang of them huddled up at the back table in the corner, but their numbers had recently thinned. Since Cal had gotten locked up, and Ace dropped out of school to hustle full time, it was just Jonas, Prince, and a few stragglers who they probably would never keep time with outside of school.

While Jonas was waiting for his gang, he struck up a conversation with a kid they called Sticky. He'd gotten the name because of his sticky fingers. Sticky was always looking to sell hot shit that he had stolen. Normally, Jonas had no use for him, but that day, Sticky approached him with an interesting proposition. Sticky had come up on a pair of brass knuckles that he was looking to let go for the low price of ten dollars. Jonas managed to haggle

him down to seven bucks plus the Salisbury steak from
his lunch tray. After what had happened to Doug, all their
crew had taken to carrying a weapon of some kind. Jonas
wasn't big on knives or guns because of the trouble they
would cause if he were caught with them, but the brass
knuckles suited him just fine.

Prince finally came strolling into the lunchroom. Instead
of slacks and loafers, as was his usual dress, he was
wearing new jeans, a crisp polo, and white Nikes. Since
he had taken over for Doug, Prince had started spending
a little money on clothes. Of course, he usually had to
wait until he was out of the house to change so that
his parents didn't get wise to what he was doing in his
spare time. On his arm was a young, big booty girl, who
normally wouldn't have given Prince the time of day, but
money tended to change things for the better. Jonas saw
the girl slip Prince something, likely her phone number,
before smiling and walking off.

"What up?" Prince gave Jonas dap.

"Waiting on your slow ass," Jonas replied.

"My fault. I was handling something." Prince cast a
glance in the direction the girl had gone.

"She ain't gonna let you fuck," Jonas said with a bit
of envy in his voice. Jonas gave Prince grief, but he was
actually glad that his friend was starting to come out
of his shell. Prince laughed good-naturedly before the
youths continued to their table, where a card game was
already in progress. Jonas had just called "Next" and
settled onto a bench when he spotted Alex come into
the lunchroom. She was looking good in a pair of tight
jeans, high top Nikes, and one of the school's basketball
varsity jackets. She had taken out her braids and was
rocking her hair in a side ponytail with a lollipop tucked
in it like a hairpin. He saw her just about every day
in school, but since her brother had gotten hurt, they
hardly spoke anymore outside of the occasional small

talk. It was like she had been trying to avoid him. He thought about going over to say "Hello," but Alex wasn't alone. She was with her friend Sheila and two dudes named Ryan and Bo. Ryan was a nobody, but Bo played for the school basketball team, so he thought he was hot shit. Jonas couldn't stand Bo. It wasn't because they had ever had an issue, but he noticed Bo had been playing Alex close. Seeing that she was wearing his jacket told him that it was closer than he had thought. As they went to stand in the snack line, he watched from across the room like a sad puppy.

"You, a'ight?" Prince noticed his expression.

"Yeah, I'm good," Jonas lied.

Prince followed his line of vision and laughed. "Damn, that's cold. I thought Alex was your girl," he teased.

"She ain't my girl!" Jonas snapped.

"Then why you sitting here looking like somebody just kicked you in the chest?" Prince asked. Jonas didn't respond. He just kept staring. "Go talk to her."

"I'm good," Jonas said.

"You scared?"

"You know better than that."

"Then prove it and go talk to her," Prince dared him.

Jonas didn't even remember getting up. The next thing he knew, he was on his way across the cafeteria, heading in Alex's direction. Inside his chest, his heart thudded, and his palms were sweating so badly that he had to wipe them on his jeans. He considered turning around and going back to the table like he hadn't even seen her, but it was too late. Sheila spotted Jonas and gave Alex a nudge. Alex turned, and for the briefest moment, he saw a twinkle in her eyes that had always made his heart flutter. When she saw it was him, the light dimmed a bit. Jonas swallowed the lump that had formed in his throat and forced himself to speak.

"Hey, y'all," he greeted the girls, purposely ignoring the boys. Sheila rolled her eyes in response. At one point, Jonas and Sheila had been cool, but that changed when she let Ace sleep with her, and he told the whole school. Jonas hadn't had anything to do with it, but she still held it against him. It was a guilt-by-association situation. "Damn, no love for the kid?" Jonas teased when Alex still hadn't said anything.

"Hi, Jonas," she said awkwardly.

"I'm about to go grab a couple of sodas," Bo cut in. When Alex went to reach into her pocket, he waved her off. "Nah, you know your money ain't no good when you're with me." He bumped Jonas when he passed to get to the snack window.

"So that's your new little boyfriend?" Jonas asked her, shooting daggers at Bo.

"No, Bo and I are just friends. So, what have you been up to lately?" Alex changed the subject.

Jonas shrugged. "Nothing, just hanging. How's your brother? I called him a few times, but your mom always says he's sleeping or can't come to the phone. I don't think she likes me very much," Jonas joked, but Alex didn't laugh.

"Mom has really been on us since he got hurt. The doctors are saying he may have permanent nerve damage in his hand," she said with a hint of sadness in her voice.

"Don't worry about it. Me and the fellas are going to make that right real soon," Jonas said proudly. If he expected Alex to find some comfort in what he had just told her, he was wrong. She just shook her head. "What?"

"Don't y'all ever get tired of gambling with your lives?" Alex asked him.

"Them niggas ain't trying to kill nothing," Jonas downplayed it.

"I'm sure that's the same thing my brother said before he woke up in the E.R. getting staples in his head," she shot back.

"It ain't gonna go like that with us. Ace has a plan," Jonas told her.

"Doesn't he always?" Alex gave a sad chuckle.

Jonas sucked his teeth, getting frustrated. "Look, you can come down off your soapbox. All we're trying to do is look out for y'all."

"How? By getting yourself killed or arrested behind some craziness that Ace cooked up? One of these days, Ace is going to get one of y'all hurt."

"I can take care of myself." Jonas poked his chest out.

"Then why don't you?"

"Huh?"

"Look, Jonas, I know those are your friends, but you aren't like them. You're so smart, and if you could bring yourself to focus even just a little bit, you could be so much more than one of Ace's minions."

"*That's* what you think I am? Some type of flunky?" Her remark had hurt him, and he couldn't hide it.

"I don't mean it like that."

"Alex, I don't even know why you're wasting your time. He ain't no better than the rest of them dumb-ass niggas from Lenox." Sheila rubbed salt in the wound.

"Why don't you mind your own business, bitch?" Jonas snapped. He hadn't meant to call her a bitch, but the word just fell out of his mouth in the heat of the moment.

"*Bitch?* I got your bitch!" Sheila hissed and stormed off in the direction of the snack window. Jonas knew how this was going to play out long before she came back with Ryan and Bo following her. "Yeah, him right there," she pointed to Jonas.

"Yo, what's good with you?" Bo stepped up. It was Ryan who was supposed to be defending Sheila's honor, but Bo wanted to play big man in front of Alex.

"Don't start." Alex tried to defuse the situation. Bo ignored her and got into Jonas's face.

"Nah, I heard he likes to call women out of their names. I wanna see him do that shit with a man." Bo cracked his knuckles. He was obviously spoiling for a fight. Unfortunately for him, so was Jonas.

Jonas never said a word. He dipped his hand into the pocket of his jacket, slipped his fingers through the brass knuckles and fried them at Bo's face with everything he had. Bo may have had a strong game on the court, but his chin was weak. The taller boy folded like a chair and hit the ground. Ryan stood there, looking from his fallen friend to Jonas as if he were unsure what to do, so Jonas helped him decide and socked him too. Three more members of the basketball team appeared with designs on jumping Jonas and were met by Prince and a few of the stragglers who had been watching the exchange. Within minutes, fists, feet, and food were flying, and the cafeteria was thrown into chaos.

It took half the school's security force and two teachers to break up the brawl. Bo was taken to the nurse's office, while Jonas, Prince, and a few others were cuffed. The kids who had seen what had happened cheered Jonas on as he peacocked across the messy cafeteria. He was sure to catch hell for what he had done, but at that moment, it didn't matter. He felt like a celebrity. As he and Prince were hauled out, Jonas took one last look at the mess he had created. Standing in the center of it was Alex, with a look of disappointment on her face.

Chapter Nine

"I can't believe this shit!" Janette fumed. She was pacing back and forth in the living room, sucking the life out of a cigarette.

"It wasn't my fault," Jonas mumbled. He was sitting on the living room couch, staring down at his sneakers. In his hand, he held a plastic bag full of ice that he had been applying to his busted lip. The injury hadn't been a result of the fight he'd gotten into in school, but the one that waited for him afterward.

When Janette had gotten the call from the school informing her that her son was suspended for inciting a riot in the cafeteria, she was none too thrilled. She and Slick had been out hustling all night long, and she had just gone to bed when the call came in. She was tired, and the monkey she carried was beginning to scratch at her back because she hadn't had a chance get a fix before heading out to pick him up.

The whole time Janette sat in with the principal, she gave an Oscar-worthy performance of the concerned parent, occasionally even clutching the fake pearls that hung around her neck. She was appalled at her son's behavior and promised that he would be well reprimanded. She hadn't lied either. She kept up the act until they were a few blocks from the school and then let Jonas have it. It was the first time he could ever remember his mother hitting him with a closed fist. Janette was in a foul mood, partially because she had to go all the way to the school to sign Jonas out, but mostly because when they got back to the apartment, Slick was gone, and he had taken with him the drugs that she'd spent half the night on her knees and back to get.

"I'm getting tired of your shit and your excuses," Janette continued. "I got better things to do than run down to your school in the middle of the day."

"Like what?" he hadn't meant to say it out loud, but he did.

Janette stopped her pacing long enough to tag him again. This time, it was an open hand to the cheek. "You keep testing me, and I'm going to make your little ass sorry!"

Jonas tensed as he thought Janette was going to clock him again, but she got distracted. They heard what sounded like the front door opening. At first, Jonas thought Slick might be crawling out from under whatever rock he'd been hiding, but then he heard giggling. Slick was a lot of things, but a giggler wasn't one of them. A few seconds later, Yvette appeared. She was chatting it up with the two friends she had brought home with her, Doris and Shauna. Doris and Yvette had been friends since middle school, but Shauna had only recently started hanging around them. Shauna was a full year older than Yvette or Doris, but they were in the same grade because she had gotten left back. She was known as a girl of loose principals and wore it like a badge of honor. Yvette might've been testing the fast track, but Shauna was already running laps around it.

When Yvette noticed her mother standing in the middle of the living room, her eyes got as wide as saucers. She hadn't expected her mother to be home. "Oh shit!"

"Shit is right. What are you doing out of school in the middle of the day?" Janette pressed, studying her face. Something was off.

"I-uh . . ." Yvette stuttered, trying to untie her tongue. She was high as a kite and doing a poor job of hiding it.

"We had a half day," Shauna spoke up. The lie rolled off her tongue so fluidly that it almost sounded like the truth.

"Bullshit! You hussies are ditching!" Janette accused. "And what the hell are you wearing?"

None of the girls were wearing uniforms. They were all dressed like women twice their ages, with their faces made up. Yvette was wearing black hot pants and pumps with a cute leather jacket.

"It was a dress-down day," Yvette lied.

"You look like a trio of damn streetwalkers." Janette looked them up and down.

"They're your clothes," Yvette mumbled.

"You trying to get cute?" Janette stared her down. Yvette wisely remained silent.

"Maybe we should go?" Shauna suggested. She had come to Yvette's with the expectation of getting drunk and listening to music, not be lectured by her junkie mother.

"Wait, you don't have to leave. Mom, it's cool if they hang out, right?" Yvette's tone was almost pleading.

"You girls get home safe," Janette replied, giving Shauna a dirty look. She didn't care where they went, but they were getting the hell out of her house.

Shauna was one of the coolest kids at their school. She always had a line on the hippest parties, who had the best weed, and which boys were handling a few dollars. Yvette had been kissing her ass for weeks to try to get next to her, and her mother was threatening to undo all her work.

"It's cool, baby girl," Shauna clicked her gum. "I was once young and still being told what to do, so I get it. Catch you another time." She started for the door and stopped short. "You rolling with me, Doris? Or you on punishment too?"

Doris didn't hesitate to follow Shauna out the door, leaving Yvette to her fate.

"I swear, you always gotta ruin something," Yvette huffed.

"You should be glad I busted up whatever y'all thought you were about to have going on. I keep telling your fast ass that the streets ain't nothing nice," Janette warned.

"Then why are you always in them?" Yvette questioned.

"I'm grown, and I don't have to explain myself to you! It's like you kids keep forgetting who're the children, and who's the parent."

"Then maybe you should try acting like one," Yvette said with a dismissive chuckle.

The room got quiet. It wasn't unusual for Yvette to talk back to their mom, but whatever she had drunk or smoked had her especially brazen that day. Jonas could feel the storm brewing. Things were about to go bad. He scooted a little farther down the couch so he was out of the way of whatever was about to happen but would still have a good view of the action.

"You know, I'm getting a little tired of your funky attitude, Yvette. I'm out here in the streets chasing a dollar to keep a roof over your head and food in your belly. The least your ungrateful ass can do is try to show a little gratitude!" Janette shouted.

"Ha! The only thing you're in the streets chasing is that no-good nigga you lay up with and a blast!" Yvette snarled.

And there it was. The invisible line in the sand had finally been crossed.

Janette went rigid. A stunned look crossed her face as if the words had slapped her into a state of shock. Water formed in the corners of her eyes, and for a second, Jonas thought his mother was going to cry. Instead, she let out a feral yell and attacked.

The sound of the slap resonated through the house like a gunshot. Yvette hadn't even realized she had been hit until she bounced off the rickety china cabinet and broke the glass doors. Yvette righted herself enough to mount a defense. Jonas's eldest sister was nice with her hands, but Janette was seasoned. She had been battle tested from decades of street fights. She rained punches all over her daughter's head and face, busting her nose and spraying the living room with blood. Yvette crumbled to the ground, defenseless, but it didn't stop Janette from pressing her assault. Yvette had stopped fighting, but Janette kept swinging. She was like a woman possessed.

"That's enough!" Jonas shouted, terrified that his mother was going to kill his sister. If Janette heard her son, she gave no sign. She just kept swinging. Finally, Jonas grabbed his mother about the waist and pulled her away. "Mama, enough!"

Janette blinked twice as if she had just awakened from a bad dream. Her shirt was torn, exposing one saggy breast, and the knuckles of her hands were scraped from when they had connected with Yvette's teeth. She looked at her daughter, lying on the floor dazed, and tears welled in her eyes at the sight of what she had done. It was then that Janette let loose the tears that she had been holding back. "I'm sorry." She reached for Yvette, but the girl recoiled. It was from a mixture of fear and disgust.

"Don't touch me," Yvette snapped, pulling herself to her feet. Her legs were shaky, so she almost fell back down, but Jonas grabbed her under the arms and held her up.

"You okay?" he asked. Yvette's nose was bleeding, and a purple bruise appeared under her eye.

"I'm fine; get off me." She pushed him away.

"Let me get you some ice," Janette offered. She felt terrible for losing it on her daughter.

"I don't want shit from you!" Yvette snapped. She collected herself, stormed down the hall to the room she shared with her sisters, and slammed the door.

For a while, Jonas and his mother sat in the living room, neither saying a word. The only sound came from the lighter flicking while Janette chain-smoked. Glass and blood were all over the living room. Janette sat on the couch smoking and rocking back and forth. "I didn't mean to," she finally said. "I would never hurt any of my babies. I know I ain't the best mother, but I love you all. You know that, right?"

"I know, Mama," Jonas assured her. "Let me get this stuff cleaned up. Jo-Jo will be home soon, and she don't need to see this." He was in the kitchen getting the broom to sweep up the glass when he heard a loud crashing sound. At first, Jonas thought his mother and sister were going for round two, but he realized the noise wasn't coming from inside the apartment. He rushed to the front door and snatched it open without thinking. What he saw both startled and amused him.

He found his mother's boyfriend, Slick, clawing his way across the hallway floor. It looked like he had almost made it to the door, but the massive hand clutching his pant leg had stopped him. The hand belonged to Bruiser. He was a local thug who had a reputation as a head buster and general asshole. Bruiser got his kicks from dishing out pain, and from the looks of things, Slick was about to get himself a nice helping. Bruiser was a dog, who attacked on command. The person who usually gave this command was standing near the top of the stairs, looking on gleefully.

Eight-Ball got his name not because of his striking resemblance to an actual eight ball: short, fat, and black with a clean-shaven head and flat nose. Nor had it come from his skill at billiards, though he was quite good at the game. He spent a good chunk of his childhood hanging out around pool halls uptown and in the Bronx, hustling people out of money. This is what led to the incident in which he acquired the moniker. He was about 13 years old at the time. He had made the mistake of trying to cheat a man out of his money and got caught. When the man called him on it and demanded his cash back, Eight-Ball refused. The man had him by at least twenty years and easily that many pounds, but Eight-Ball had heart. Still, he knew he would need an edge, so he used the only thing he had at his disposal: a billiard ball. Eight-Ball slipped the ball into a sock and proceeded to beat the man to death with it. He ended up being sent to a youth detention center until his eighteenth birthday. When he was released to the streets, he worked for a while as hired muscle. This lasted until he had saved up enough money to get himself a package and switched his hustle. He had been selling drugs ever since.

"Where you running to?" Bruiser dragged Slick across the floor.

"Come on, man. Cut me a break!" Slick pleaded.

"I'll cut your fucking throat, is what I'll cut!" Eight-Ball produced a knife. His voice was nasal, sounding like he always had a cold. This came from his nose being broken so many times that his sinuses were permanently damaged. "You picked the wrong nigga to steal from, Slick."

"It's not my fault. If anything, blame the little shit who gave me the package. I'm an addict. What did he expect me to do with it?" Slick tried to reason with him. He hadn't meant to run off with the package he'd been given to sell, but the kid's naiveté and the monkey on his back made it too sweet of an opportunity to pass up.

"You trying to get cute?" Bruiser kicked Slick in his stomach with so much force that he coughed up blood.

As Slick clutched his ribs, trying to suck in air, he realized that his remark wasn't the smartest, but it was the only play he had. There was no doubt in his mind that Eight-Ball was going to let Bruiser kill him unless he figured a way out of the mess he'd gotten himself into. This was about the time when he noticed Jonas standing in the doorway, and it was the one time he had ever been happy to see the boy.

"C'mon, man. Don't do this to me in front of my kid!" Slick pleaded.

When Eight-Ball's beady black eyes landed on Jonas, Jonas felt his bowels shift. There was something about the man's gaze that made him very afraid, with good reason. Eight-Ball had killed quite a few people that he knew of, including kids. Eight-Ball studied him for a time. He was waiting to see if Jonas would try to plead for Slick's life. Whether the plea would move Eight-Ball was still up for debate. Jonas wasn't quite sure why, but something about knowing he could potentially have the power over whether Slick lived or died made him feel giddy. It was an alien feeling, and he found that he rather liked it. Jonas looked down at Slick and thought of all the times he had been a dick to him, or things in the house came up missing, and then he turned and went back in the house leaving Slick to his fate.

"What's going on out there?" Janette asked Jonas.

"Nothing," he lied. Janette didn't buy it. She brushed past Jonas toward the door, and he fell in step behind her.

"Oh my God!" Janette gasped when she saw her blood-ied boyfriend. Bruiser was in the process of dragging him down the stairs. "Let him be!" She rushed to Slick, but Eight-Ball shoved her back.

"Mind your own business, Janette. This nigga took my shit and ain't got my money. He gots to go," Eight-Ball told her.

"Wait . . . just wait." Janette rushed into the apartment. Jonas watched as she clawed through the pile of clothes on the bed until she found her purse. She emptied it and only found twenty-three dollars, some loose tobacco, and an empty dope bag. She darted back into the hallway and offered the crumpled bills to Eight-Ball.

Eight-Ball frowned before slapping the money from her hand. "Bitch, this ain't even half what this nigga owes me."

"Just give me a day or so, and I can get the rest. I swear!" Janette promised.

"Maybe we can take it in trade?" Bruiser eyed Janette hungrily.

Janette then realized that her breast was still exposed through her torn shirt and moved her hand to cover herself. "Eight, how long you known me? If I say I'm gonna get you the money, then I'll get it."

Eight-Ball weighed it. "Janette, you was always nice to me when I was a little nigga out here. On the strength of that, I'm gonna give this pussy that you call a man a pass. I'll be back here tomorrow, and I'm gonna get what's owed to me—one way or another." He stroked her cheek with one of his fat fingers. "We gone." He started down the stairs.

Bruiser gave Slick another kick for good measure, then turned to Janette. "I kinda hope he doesn't come up with the money. I heard you got the best head in the neighborhood," he laughed and followed his boss.

Once the threat had passed, Janette rushed to Slick. She cradled his head in her lap and began to weep softly. "My baby, my beautiful baby. What did they do to you?"

It both hurt and angered Jonas to watch his mother heap the attention onto Slick that she never seemed to have time to show her own children. It was at that moment something occurred to Jonas about Slick. He was weak. A man was supposed to love and protect his family, to set an example for the kids watching him to follow, but Slick did none of these things. He was no example for anyone to follow . . . only a worthless junkie who didn't deserve to live. A part of him wished that Bruiser and Eight-Ball had killed him, and then his mother would finally be free of whatever spell he had cast over her. But knowing Janette, she'd just find another Slick to take his place. Jonas could no longer stand to look at them, so he went into the house and closed the door. He had shit to do.

Chapter Ten

By the time Sweets came home with Jo-Jo, Jonas and Yvette had managed to get the house restored to some sort of normalcy. Of course, Jo-Jo noticed the broken china cabinet and questioned how it had happened. Jonas lied and told her he had tripped and fallen into it. She teased him for the rest of the day about having two left feet. While Jo-Jo might've been easy to fool, Sweets was not.

"What the hell happened here?" Sweets asked Jonas, once she had Jo-Jo settled at the kitchen table doing her homework.

"Mommy and Yvette got into it." Jonas went on to give her the short version of the brawl that had taken place in the living room. He left out the part about him getting suspended because he didn't feel like hearing her mouth.

"I swear that girl is on the fast track to nowhere." Sweets shook her head sadly. Her sister was out of control, and she was seriously starting to worry about her. "Must've been some hell of a fight. I saw the blood in the hallway."

"Oh nah, that isn't Yvette's blood. That's courtesy of Slick," Jonas said with a slight grin.

"Slick?"

"Yeah, your boyfriend's boss came through here and kicked his ass for having sticky fingers. I wish they had killed that muthafucka!" he spat.

"Jonas, you know we don't wish death on anyone, regardless of what they've done," Sweets scolded him. "How much does he owe this time?"

Jonas shrugged. "I don't know. It was enough for Bruiser to beat him damn near to death. Of course, Mama promised to pay him back."

"When is that woman going to learn to stop getting involved in his bullshit?" Sweets wondered aloud.

"When he gets himself, or both of them, killed."

"Jonas!"

"I ain't wishing death, Sweets. I'm just keeping it real. Eight-Ball ain't nothing to fuck with," he said. It was something everybody in the neighborhood knew all too well.

"Maybe I should talk to Drew," Sweets suggested.

"I don't want you taking shit from him. That's what got us into this mess in the first place," Jonas said.

"I'm not talking about taking anything from anybody. I only meant that maybe he could talk to Eight-Ball and see if he can buy Slick some time," Sweets explained.

"You've got more faith in him than I do. Eight-Ball is the one putting money in his pocket. Drew ain't gonna stick his neck out for us, even if he is your boyfriend."

"I wish you would stop saying that. Drew *isn't* my boyfriend; we're just friends." Sweets downplayed their relationship.

"Don't bullshit me, Sweets. You think I haven't noticed y'all creeping around? Him walking you home from school. You always sneaking up to the ave. to hang out with him. You've spent more time in front of that chicken shack in the last few weeks than you have the whole time we've been living on this block."

Sweets wanted to argue, but Jonas had a point. She and Drew had been spending a lot of time together lately. A few days out of the week, he would walk her to and from school, always made sure she had money for snacks and had even taken her to the movies a few nights ago. She wouldn't say they were in a relationship, but they were something. "He's not my boyfriend" was all she could think to say.

"Well, whatever he is, I think it would be a bad idea to involve him," Jonas said. It wasn't that Jonas thought Drew wouldn't help. He knew that he would if it was within his power. Drew was a drug dealer, but he was a good dude. He just didn't want to see the dope boy get his hooks into his sister.

"Raf! Yo, Raf!" Jonas heard someone calling him from the window. He went over and looked out to see Ace and Mula in front of the building. "You ready?"

"I'll be right down," Jonas told him.

"And where are you going?" Sweets asked. Whenever Ace came around to get him, trouble usually followed.

"Outside to chill with my friends for a few." Jonas headed to his room to snatch his coat. Sweets followed him.

"Don't be gone too long. Dinner will be ready in an hour," she said.

"I told you I won't be gone but a few. Just wrap my plate, and I'll heat it when I come in." Jonas shrugged into his coat. He patted the pocket to make sure he had the brass knuckles he'd bought from Sticky earlier that day. He'd tucked them into his underwear when security plucked him from the riot, so they never found them.

Sweets knew her brother better than most. Something wasn't right. "Jonas, I don't know what you're up to, but please promise you'll be careful."

Jonas flashed her his most confident smile. "You know me better than that, Sweets," he said, then darted out the door before she could press him further.

"I do, and that's what has me worried," she whispered to the empty room.

Chapter Eleven

When Jonas got outside, Ace was pacing back and forth impatiently, as he was known to do when something was about to go down. He was wearing black jeans and a black hoodie, with low cut Timberland Chukkas.

Mula was wearing an oversized army-fatigue suit like he was about to go off to war. He leaned on a wooden baseball bat with an anxious look on his face. Everybody was where they were supposed to be except Prince.

"His mom put him on lockdown after that shit y'all pulled at school," Ace answered the question on Jonas's face. "I heard you broke that kid's jaw."

"He got what he had coming," Jonas said as if it were no big deal. In truth, he had been terrified that he was going to go to jail for what he had done to Bo, but surprisingly, Bo refused to press charges. Jonas still didn't like him, but he had a newfound respect for him. "How we gonna do this shit when we're shorthanded? The plan requires four of us."

"Then we're gonna have to improvise." Ace brandished a gun.

"Hold on. We said we were just gonna beat him down," Jonas reminded him.

"Chill, Raf. This is just to scare Black. We ain't gonna blast him," Ace assured him.

"Unless he makes us," Mula snickered.

Jonas was suddenly very unsure of their plan. First, Prince not being able to come, and then Ace bringing a gun . . . Guns hadn't been part of their plan. Men with guns, especially dudes like Ace, were unpredictable. He knew that in the blink of an eye, their planned beat-down could turn into something far more serious. He started to call the whole thing off, and then he thought about Jewels. She was risking her life to help them, and they couldn't just leave her hanging. What if they didn't show up, and Black forced her to make good on her promise to sleep with him? No, that was a risk Jonas wasn't willing to take. They would go through with the plan. He would just have to make sure he paid special attention to Ace and his little toy.

They didn't have to bother with stalking Black. Thanks to Jewels, they already knew every step the couple would take that night. They were going to eat at Red Lobster and then catch the 7:30 p.m. show at the Magic Johnson Theater. The movie would run for at least two hours, so that gave Jonas and the others more than enough time to get into position to spring their trap.

There were several short-stay motels on the strip of 145th Street between Amsterdam and Broadway, but only one that would let you rent a room without having ID, which they were sure Black did not. Dudes like Black never carried identification so that if they were arrested while selling drugs, they could lie about their identity. As it happened, Mula had a plug with the girl who worked the check-in desk. She was an ex-lover of his uncle Fish. Ace and Mula visited her earlier that day and gave her a few dollars to look the other way while they administered the ass whipping. Jonas didn't trust it, but Mula insisted that she wouldn't open her mouth if pressed. For all their sakes, Jonas hoped so.

The original plan was for them to lay in the cut while Jewels and Black went into the motel. She would tie her head scarf on the outside of the door so they would know what room she was in. Mula would play the hall to keep an eye out for signs of trouble, while Jonas, Ace, and Prince went into the room and administered the beating. With Prince out of the picture, they were left with two choices: keep with the plan of going into the room three-deep and leave their backs unguarded, or do it as a duo instead of a trio. Between Jonas and Ace, they should've been able to handle Black, but Jonas wasn't comfortable leaving anything to chance. He had a bad feeling about the whole thing, and that feeling grew the closer they got to the hour of reckoning.

"You up for this?" Ace broke Jonas's train of thought. They were loitering in front of a bodega a half block from where the motel was.

"I wouldn't be here if I wasn't," Jonas said, sounding more confident than he was. That strip was usually busy with people coming and going, so it would've been easy for them to blend in. That night, it was quiet, though. Jonas was sure the three new faces stuck out like sore thumbs to anyone paying close enough attention. "Just remember, before we do anything, we gotta make sure Jewels is clear."

Ace laughed. "Don't worry about Jewels. She can take care of herself. You just make sure you don't freeze when I pop on this nigga."

"There they go," Mula spoke in his whispery voice. A livery cab was pulling to the curb a few yards from where they were standing.

Black was out of the cab first. He was dressed in jeans, fresh Tims, and a button-up shirt. A thick chain hung from around his neck. He went around and opened the door for Jewels like every bit of a gentleman. She looked good that night; a tight blue denim skirt with a matching jacket and a pair of Jordans. Her hair was pulled into a ponytail on top of her head and tied off with a white scarf. She looked over her shoulder warily as he ushered her across the threshold of the motel. Jewels had probably been thinking the same thing Jonas had . . . *I hope this shit goes right.*

They gave them about a five- or six-minute head start before Ace motioned for them to follow. In front of the motel, a man stood shaking his cup and begging for change. He was stooped over and wearing a dusty overcoat with a hood that obscured part of his face. He gave the youngsters a smile, revealing a gold tooth, hoping one of them would do him a kindness. Ace didn't give him a second look, but Mula, for no reason other than to be cruel, slapped the cup out of the man's hand. The man looked on pitifully as his coins crashed to the ground and rolled in every direction.

"That's fucked-up," the homeless man said sadly and went about the business of picking up his money. Jonas made to help him, but a stern look from Ace made him think better of it.

Inside the motel, a brown-skinned girl sat behind a Plexiglas window. Behind her, a television mounted on the wall played some reality television show, while she busied herself flipping through the pages of a magazine. When the boys filed in, she spared them only the briefest glance before going back to her magazine as if she hadn't even seen them. So far, so good.

It took them another five minutes to find the room they were looking for. They hadn't factored in there being so many. They started from the top and worked their way down. The hotel stank of weed, sex, and alcohol. It wasn't the most respectable place, but you could get a relatively clean bed to handle your business for a couple of hours for about fifty or sixty bucks.

Ace spotted the scarf hanging from the door on the second floor. He crept down the hall with Jonas and Mula on his heels. Through the door, they could hear muffled voices. It sounded like Black was trying to get right to it, but Jewels was stalling. They needed to get in there.

"Showtime, baby." Ace produced three ski masks, handing one to Mula and the other to Jonas. "Mula, go stand at the top of the stairs. You see anybody, shout." Mula didn't look happy about being left out of the action, but he didn't argue. Ace reached for the knob, but Jonas stopped him.

"Before we go in, give Mula the strap," Jonas said much to everyone's surprise, including Mula's.

"For what?" Ace didn't like going in without the hammer.

"Mula is too small to do much if somebody tries to rescue this nigga while we're beating his ass. At least with the gun, he can back them down long enough for us to get clear. You really wanna get trapped off up here?" Jonas asked. In truth, he didn't trust Ace not to shoot Black, or worse, Black takes the gun from them as the deliveryman had done with Ace and Cal. It was a weak lie, but enough to get Ace to pass the gun off and take the baseball bat instead.

Ace waited until Mula reached his position at the end of the hall before resting his hand on the doorknob. "For Doug," he extended his fist.

"For Doug," Jonas pounded his fist, and they went in to handle their business.

They entered to find that they hadn't arrived a moment too soon. Black had Jewels pinned to the bed with her skirt hiked above her hips, while he was trying to pry her legs apart with his knee. In his hand was his cock that he was in the process of stroking to an erection.

"Chill; just wait a minute." Jewels was trying to shove him off, but Black's weight was too much.

"Come on with that wait shit, baby. We been playing this game for too long already. Let me just put the head in," Black was trying to convince her while sliding between her legs. When he noticed the door open, he looked up in confusion. "Fuck is this?"

"Room service, nigga!" Jonas cracked Black with the brass knuckles.

Black rolled off of Jewels and onto the floor, dazed but hardly out of the fight. His lip was busted, but other than that, he was unharmed. When he turned his eyes on Jonas, Jonas felt just like he had earlier that day in the hallway with Eight-Ball. It was at that moment that he realized that they might have been in over their heads. "Good one." Black spat blood onto the floor. "My turn now."

Black was on his feet and moving across the room faster than Jonas's brain could register. In the glint of moonlight, Jonas saw the flash of something. It was a knife, no doubt tucked into the pocket of his pants which were around his thighs. Jonas cursed himself for them not thinking to make sure he was unarmed before trying to rush him. Jonas tried to move out of the way, but he wasn't quick enough. Fire shot through his chest as the blade cut through his shirt and the top layer of his skin. The only reason his chest had been cut instead of his face was that Jewels stuck her foot out and tripped Black when he was trying to get to Jonas.

Before Jonas could recover, Ace had joined the battle. He swung the bat in a high arc and brought it down across Black's arm with a resounding crack. The knife went flying to the other side of the room, but losing his weapon didn't deter him from his mission of trying to kill the two young boys. When Ace swung the bat a second time, Black had been expecting it. He swept the cheap lamp up off the nightstand and smashed it against the side of Ace's head. Had it been made from anything stronger than cheap plastic, Ace would've been dead, or at least in a coma. Instead, he was just knocked out.

Black started stomping Ace like he was trying to put out a fire. He probably would've killed him had it not been for Jewels. She had managed to recover the knife Black had been wielding and plunged it into his back. Black roared in pain and backhanded the girl and sent her sprawling across the bed. "You stinking bitch!" He leaped on top of her and drove his fist into her face.

Hearing Jewel's screams washed away the shock of Jonas having just been cut for the first time. His chest burned, and his shirt was damp with blood, but he would live. That was more than he could say for Jewels if he didn't do something—and quick. Just then, he spotted the bat sticking out from under the bed. He wasn't sure what he intended on doing with it. In fact, he wasn't thinking at all when he picked it up. A surge of adrenaline washed through him as he tightened his grip on the handle. He planted his feet and swung it with everything he had. There was a sickening crack, followed by a spray of blood that hit the wall. Black turned to Jonas and looked at him in wide-eyed shock before falling over the edge of the bed.

"Raf . . . Raf, you okay?" he heard Ace calling to him, but his voice sounded as if it were far away.

When Jonas finally came out of his daze, he was standing at the foot of the bed, still holding the blood-stained bat. Jewels was standing near the door, rubbing her neck. It was red and bruised from Black choking her out. Ace looked like shit. His lip was bleeding, and he had the beginnings of a knot forming on his head. On the floor, a few feet away, Black lay facedown. Blood seeped from the opening in the back of his skull along with something white.

"What did you do?" Ace asked, looking down at Black's body.

"He was going to kill her," Jonas said just above a whisper.

"Well, he damn near killed us all. What the fuck was he, a superhero?" Ace half-joked.

"Probably all the powder he's been snorting all night," Jewels explained Black's unusual strength. "He said it was going to make him 'stand up in the pussy.'"

"Well, he ain't gonna be standing up in much of nothing anymore," Ace laughed.

"What's going on in there?" they heard a man's voice in the hall.

"Mind your own business, muthafucka!" came Mula's response.

"We better get the fuck out of here," Ace said. It would only be a matter of time before someone came to investigate the noise, or Mula shot somebody. Neither option would bode well for them. Ace and Jewels made for the door, but Jonas didn't follow. He continued to stand there, looking down at Black.

"C'mon, Raf." Jewels took his hand. Her touch was comforting to him, and he needed it. At that moment, something passed between them. It was nothing that could be put into words, but it was safe to say that was the night when Jonas and Jewels would become more than just friends.

The four of them managed to make it out of the motel and into a taxi without incident. The ride was full of nervous energy. None of the teens were strangers to violence, but none had experienced anything like what Jonas had done. Mula was disappointed that he had missed out on the action and hung on to Ace's every word as he recounted the story. They were all chattering away except Jonas, who was unusually quiet.

They dropped Mula off in his hood and spun back around to 139th. Ace paid the cab, and they all got out. Before sending Jewels into the building, he reinforced to her the importance of keeping quiet about what she had seen, but it wasn't necessary. It was a night that Jewels hoped to forget.

"You good?" Ace asked Jonas once Jewels was gone.

"Yeah, man," Jonas said but didn't sound convincing.

"Listen, bro, you did what you had to do. Don't beat yourself up about it. I'll check you in the morning." Ace gave him dap and slunk off into the darkness.

Jonas continued to stand in front of his building for a time, enjoying the cool night air against his skin. Now that the adrenaline had worn off, he was sore from the fight. When he got upstairs, he would need to soak in the tub for a while. He looked down and realized that he was still holding the bat. He knew he probably should've gotten rid of it, but something about the bat brought him comfort. Ace was worried about Jonas being traumatized about what he had done, but he had it wrong. Jonas felt no grief or guilt for what he had done to Black. In fact, he felt good. For the first time, Jonas had discovered something that he liked more than football . . . violence.

Chapter Twelve

It was three days later when the dominoes of what Jonas and his friends had done would begin to fall. He was awakened early that morning by the sounds of shouting. He was pissed because he had been having trouble sleeping since the events at the motel, and the night before was the first time he had been able to get a good rest. He had been suffering from very violent dreams. They were usually the same, him clubbing someone's head in with the bat. Sometimes, it was Black, but there were others. Always people who had wronged him: Slick, the dude who had tossed his football onto the ice in the park. His mother had even been the victim of his violent outburst in one dream. That was the one that had disturbed him the most. He sometimes disliked his mother, but he didn't hate her enough to hurt her.

Since the motel, rage had become one of his closest companions. It followed him everywhere like a shadow. Little things that he would have normally overlooked now drove him to fits of anger. He had even beaten up a crackhead the previous night when he was hanging out in the park with Ace and Mula. The crackhead had asked Ace to let him borrow a few dollars because he was short of the ten he needed to buy his drugs. When Ace told him to fuck off, the crackhead said something slick. It was a harmless remark, but enough to set Jonas off. He stomped the crackhead out and hit him over the head with a trash can for good measure. Ace was pissed because the fight made the spot hot, and he had to shut down his weed operation for a few dollars. Mula just laughed. He said he liked the new Raf, and Jonas was inclined to agree with him. He was changing, and everyone around him picked up on it, even Sweets. She had asked him about it once, but Jonas downplayed it as him just having a lot on his mind. How could he tell his kindhearted sister that he was now a killer?

Jonas thought about Black often. He wondered what it must've felt like to die in such a violent way. Did he suffer? Or did he pass instantly into the afterlife upon impact? Fuck him! As far as Jonas was concerned, he got what he deserved. It came down to a choice between Black's life and Jewel's, and Black was the odd man out. If Jonas had it to do all over again, the only thing he would've done differently would be to bring the gun into the room so he could've shot him instead. The thought made Jonas giggle.

His thoughts then turned to Jewels. Over the last couple of days, she and Jonas had been hanging out more than usual. When she chose to attend, Jewels went to one of those last-chance schools where you only had to attend classes in the morning, so she was the perfect companion for Jonas to pass the days while Ace and Mula were out grinding, and his sisters weren't at home. Sometimes, late at night when Jewels was having trouble sleeping, or her mother was on one, Jonas would sneak her into his room. At that point, they hadn't done anything more than kiss, though they had come close. Mostly, they would lie in each other's arms like an old married couple, talking and daydreaming about lives outside the ones they were living. Jewels never came out and said it, but what had happened at the motel had done something to her. She had changed. Not like Jonas, but in a way that she couldn't figure out how to put into words. Jonas didn't press her to try. She would speak about it when she was ready or not at all. He was fine either way. The two of them found comfort in each other that they couldn't find with their own families. They were good for each other.

In the other room, the shouting continued. Going back to sleep wasn't an option at that point. He slipped out of bed and pulled on a pair of sweatpants and a hoodie and went to investigate.

He was serving the last day of the suspension from school, so he was the only one of the kids at home that day. This left only two other people who could've been the source of the noise. Sure enough, he found his mother and Slick in the living room engaged in a shouting match. They seemed to be arguing more than usual lately. His mother was still in her housecoat, head wrapped in a scarf, and smoking a cigarette. Slick was dressed in a pair of green pants that looked like that looked like they could stand a good washing and a dingy yellow shirt. His eyes were wide and angry.

"Damn it, Janette. You act like I'm asking you for a lot, and its only ten funky dollars. I need to fix up." Slick was ranting.

"Tough shit. You should've gotten what you needed with the twenty dollars you stole out of my purse last night!" Janette shot back. "I been busting my ass trying to pay off your debt, and you ain't exactly been helpful."

"You act like I ain't been out hustling too!"

"You call boosting shit from the Ninety-Nine-Cent store hustling?" she capped.

"I'm trying to do my part to bring some coins into this damn house!"

"Coins which you smoke, snort, or shoot no sooner than you get your hands on them," Janette accused. "I'm getting a little tired of having to carry both our habits, Slick. Something is gonna have to give."

"Baby, I'm telling you this is just a rough patch. I got a friend of mine from back in the day who's doing good for himself over in Newark. I convinced him to lay a package on me. Once I flip it, we're right back on our feet," he promised.

"Or you're going to fuck it up and have *two* niggas looking to kill you instead of one." Janette blew out a cloud of smoke.

"You know it'd be nice to have a woman who supported my dreams," Slick said sourly.

"It be nicer to have a man who actually pulled his weight! I swear, I gotta look after you more than I do my own kids."

"Then maybe I should leave? You know there ain't no shortage of bitches that would be lined up to take your spot."

"And they would be more than welcome to it! You pimping around this muthafucka like you're some damn prized catch. Contrary to what your ego tells you, I was doing pretty good before you came into my life. Had a good man who loved me," Janette said in a matter-of-fact tone.

"Yup; loved you up to the point where you pushed him to eat a bullet!" Slick sneered. It was a low blow.

Janette slapped fire out of Slick, and he slapped her back. She went spilling onto the floor. The two of them wrestled around on the ground for a while before Jonas decided to intervene.

"Get off of her." Jonas pulled at Slick.

"Mind your damn business, boy! This is *my* woman!" Slick snapped.

"But it's *my* mother!" Jonas continued trying to pull him off. Slick whirled on Jonas and slapped him so hard that he skidded across the living room. He sat on the floor, eyes welling with tears. The tears weren't those of pain but rage.

"What? You gonna cry now?" Slick taunted him. Jonas didn't answer. He picked himself up off the floor and darted back into his room. "That's right, li'l bitch! You better run!"

"You ain't have to do that, Slick!" Janette screamed.

"Fuck that. The li'l nigga act like he's the damn man of the house. I don't see him putting no food on the table." Slick had never cared for Jonas, and it felt good to knock him on his ass finally. "I hope he brings his ass out here so I can give him another dose." Slick's prayers were answered. Jonas did come back into the living room, but he was armed with the baseball bat he'd cracked Black's skull with. "And what you plan on doing with that?" Slick mocked him.

He got his answer when Jonas swung the bat. The only thing that saved Slick's skull was the fact that he had thrown his arm up at the last minute. He howled in pain when the wood connected with the bone of his forearm and broke it. Jonas followed up with a shot to the ribs, folding Slick. He was now on his knees and begging Jonas to stop, but the boy was past the point of mercy. He raised the bat, intent on sending Slick to the hereafter when his mother threw herself across her boyfriend.

"Jonas, don't!" she pleaded.

"He ain't never gonna put his hands on you again. Move, Mama," Jonas ordered, but Janette continued covering him.

"He's sorry, baby. He won't do it no more. Will you, Slick?"

"No," Slick cried.

"This nigga treats you like shit, and you're still protecting him?" Jonas was in total disbelief.

"You just don't understand, baby," she sobbed.

Jonas's eyes were sad. "Yeah, I do. I understand more than you know." He dropped the bat and made hurried steps toward the front door.

Tears were streaming down Jonas's cheeks when he came rushing from his building. He was hurt and angry. He couldn't understand for the life of him how a woman he had always known to be so strong had become so weak and pathetic. Even as an addict, Janette had always been very independent and stood taller than most. She wasn't the ideal mother, but she always made sure that her kids at least had the basics, including love. This all changed when Slick came into the picture. In the years Slick had been around, Janette seemed to slide further and further down the rabbit hole. Watching it was bad, but the fact that he was powerless to do anything about it is what hurt him the most. It was that day that Jonas made a promise to himself that he would rescue his sisters from the madness that his mother had created, no matter the cost.

Something else that troubled him is what Slick had said about his mother driving his father to "swallow a bullet." The details surrounding Zeke's death had always been sketchy, but as far as Jonas or anyone else knew, he had been killed by the husband of one of his lovers. That was the story he had always believed, but now Slick had raised doubts. There were so many things running through Jonas's mind that he felt like he was walking in a daze. He was unsure about where he was going or what he would do next, but the one thing he was sure of was the ball of rage nestled in his gut. He needed a release.

"Yo, yo, what's up, li'l Zeke?" Juan called out to him. He was standing out in front of his store, smoking a cigarette and drinking a beer.

"That ain't my fucking name," Jonas said through clenched teeth.

"Ain't no need for all the hostility, shorty. I was just trying to show you some love," Juan said. He didn't like how Jonas was talking to him. "So, your mom never came through to pay what she owed."

"And?"

"And, I'm running a business, not a charity."

"Look, Juan. You got a beef, take it up with my mother or Slick. I ain't got a nickel in that dollar."

"Sounds like trouble at home." Juan fell in step beside him. "I know how that shit goes. I didn't get along with my parents either when I was growing up. My mom was a fiend too. No offense. I been out on my own since I was about your age. Went out and got it on my own because I knew nobody wasn't going to give it to me. Now, I'm my own boss with my own business."

"Congratulations," Jonas said in an uninterested tone. He wanted Juan to get the hell away from him so that he could brood in peace.

"Look, man, I can see you ain't really trying to be bothered. I just want you to know that I'm here for you if you need anything. I always liked you, Raf." He called him by his nickname. "If things get too crazy for you at home, you could always come crash with me. I got an extra room that I sometimes rent out. I know things are kinda tight for you right now, so I wouldn't charge you anything. Maybe we could work something out." He placed his hand on Jonas's shoulder.

It took Jonas all of two seconds to realize what Juan was insinuating. "Get your fucking hand off me!" he shrugged him off.

"Chill out, kid. I was only trying to—"

"I know just what you were trying to do, you sick bastard!" Jonas spat.

Juan looked around nervously to see if anyone had heard the accusation. What few people knew about him was that so long as the flesh was tender, gender didn't always matter. "Hey, fuck you! I was talking about you maybe helping out around the store in exchange for me giving you a place to stay, but you can forget it now."

"I don't want shit from you, fucking pervert!"

"Pervert? I got bitches throwing pussy at me all day, every day, or haven't you noticed the way your sister looks at me?" Juan said devilishly.

"If I catch you around my sister again, I'll kill you," Jonas threatened.

This made Juan laugh. "You think because you hang around Ace that makes you a tough guy all of a sudden? You ain't shit but a kid. As far as your sister goes, I haven't tried to fuck her yet, but maybe I should. Shit, if she gets down anything like your mom, I'll—"

Juan never got to finish his sentence. Jonas hit him with a two-piece combination to the face, splitting his lip. Juan was a grown man, while Jonas was only a boy, and had it been a fair fight, he probably would've gotten the best of him, but Jonas had the element of surprise on his side. He took all his rage, all his pain, and channeled it through his fists which were raining down on Juan. Tearing into Juan was a better high than any drug, and he imagined it must be what his mother and Slick felt when they were out chasing their highs. The feeling was short-lived, however, as a pair of strong hands grabbed Jonas and pulled him off Juan. He turned, ready to lash out at whoever it was, but paused when he saw it was Fat Moe holding him.

"Easy, boy . . . Take it easy." Fat Moe tried to calm him.

"Get off, Moe. I'm gonna kill him!" Jonas struggled to break free, but Moe was surprisingly strong.

"I can't believe this little muthafucka swung on me." Juan clutched his bloody lip. He took a step toward Jonas, but Fat Moe got between them. "Look out, Moe. This ain't your business."

"Maybe not, but it might become police business if they get a mind to come around asking what happened. Grown man out here trying to fight a child." Fat Moe shook his head. "That might be enough to get them to start snooping around what you got going on out of your store."

"You threatening me?" Juan asked.

"Not at all. Just painting you a picture," Fat Moe said.

For a minute, Juan contemplated beating the hell out of both of them but decided against it. Fat Moe was right. He didn't need that type of heat on him. "I'm gonna see you again, li'l Zeke. When I do, I'm gonna bust your little ass, and it ain't gonna matter who I gotta run through to get to you," he threatened and then went back inside the store.

"You didn't have to do that, Moe. I can protect myself," Jonas said once Juan was gone.

"I believe the proper response would be thank you. And for the record, it wasn't you I was trying to protect," Fat Moe told him. "What's wrong with you, out here swinging on grown people like that? I ain't never known you to disrespect your elders, son."

"Juan is a piece of shit," Jonas said flatly.

"I ain't gonna argue you that, but that still don't change the fact that you may have just made yourself a dangerous enemy. You beat Juan's ass in front of the neighborhood, and he ain't gonna forget it. You watch your back out here, youngster," Fat Moe warned.

"I will and thank you."

"One good turn deserves another. That's actually what I wanted to talk to you about. Jewels told me what happened the other night," Fat Moe revealed.

"Come again?" Jonas wanted to make sure he'd heard him correctly. Jewels had given her word that she wouldn't tell a soul what he had done, and he couldn't believe she'd broken it.

"About the girls who jumped her," Fat Moe explained. "When I saw the bruises on her neck, the first thing I thought was that one of these knuckleheads she's always chasing behind put his hands on her, but then she told me about the fight. I want to thank you for looking out for my niece, Jonas."

"Wasn't about nothing," Jonas shrugged. He wasn't sure how he felt about taking credit for something that never happened.

"Still, I appreciate it. Jewels ain't had the easiest life. That girl is a tough nut and is not easy to trust people because of some of the things she's been through. This is why I was glad to see the two of you spending time together. She speaks very highly of you."

"I like Jewels too. She's cool as hell."

"That she is, but she's also a very fragile young woman. Be mindful of that when dealing with her."

"Oh, you ain't gotta worry about that, Moe. I ain't trying to smash," Jonas assured him.

The term made Fat Moe laugh. "You kids and your slang. Look, I don't know what you are or aren't trying to do. I'm just putting the cards on the table. However you decide to play the hand is on you. One thing I will say is that if you ever do anything to hurt my niece, the next hot dog that goes on my grill will be yours. Do you understand?"

"Sure thing."

"Good, now, since you don't seem to have shit else to do, you can help me set up my grill. I got some burgers to put on today."

This made Jonas's eyes light up. The only thing that Fat Moe did better than hot dogs were burgers. As they were walking back toward Jonas's building to fetch Fat Moe's grill, they noticed two men in off-the-rack suits standing outside. One was black and the other white. You could tell without having to guess that they were cops. For a second, Jonas thought somebody might've called them about the fight that he had with Juan, but uniforms would've been dispatched for that. These were detectives. As they neared the building, one of them looked down at a piece a paper, then back up at Jonas before saying something to his partner. Jonas's stomach suddenly started doing flip-flops.

"You Jonas Rafferty?" one of the detectives asked. He was a white man with short-cropped black hair.

"Who's asking?" Fat Moe answered for him.

"Detectives Rooks and Turner," the black detective made the introductions and flashed his credentials. "You his dad?"

"No, a friend of the family. What's this about?"

"We need to ask him a few questions," Detective Rooks told him.

Jonas silently passed gas out of fear. He wanted to tell himself that the detectives were there for something other than the corpse he had left in the motel room, but in his heart, he knew they were. There was no way they had just randomly shown up less than twenty-four hours after he had committed his first murder. Someone had talked. He wasn't sure who, but it was the only explanation. For the briefest of instances, Jonas thought about running. The black cop, Rooks, must've been reading his mind because he grabbed him by the arm.

"Let's go." Rooks shoved him toward an unmarked car parked at the curb.

"Hold on, now! He's a minor. You can't question him without a parent present or a lawyer!" Fat Moe waddled after them.

"We tried knocking on the door of his apartment. Nobody answered, but we could smell the cigarette smoke coming through the door," Turner, the white cop, said smugly. "When they're finished doing whatever it is they're trying to hide in there, tell them they can pick their kid up from the Thirty-second Precinct."

The two detectives tossed Jonas into the car and took off before Fat Moe could protest any further.

Chapter Thirteen

It was three hours later when Jonas would reemerge from the precinct. It took an hour for Fat Moe to roust his mother and get her to the precinct and nearly another hour of the desk sergeant giving her the runaround. He could tell on sight that she was an addict and decided it would be more fun to give her a hard time instead of doing his job.

After Janette flipped out and threatened to report him to his captain, the sergeant finally showed her to where she could find her son. The detectives had him in a small room, where they were questioning him on the record, which they weren't supposed to be. The first thing Janette noticed when she walked into the room was that it was freezing. It had to be at least ten degrees colder in there than it was outside.

"What the fuck is this? And why is my son chained to the table like some damn prisoner?" Janette whirled into the interrogation room. Jonas was sitting at a table with one of his arms shackled to it. He looked tired, irritated, and a little roughed up, but unharmed. Something else she noticed was the absence of fear. Most teenagers would've been nervous, if not frightened out of their minds from being hauled into a precinct, but not Jonas. He was as cool as a fan. This should've been a red flag, but Janette didn't catch it.

"First of all, I'd advise you to watch your mouth before you find yourself wearing a bracelet too," Detective Rooks warned. "And second, we had to cuff him because we had a bit of an 'incident.'" He nodded toward Detective Turner who was leaning against the wall, scowling at Jonas. There was a Band-Aid on his right hand.

"Little bastard bit me while we were *interrogating* him," Detective Turner filled her in.

"I didn't name him Bastard. I named him Jonas," Janette checked him. "Baby, are you okay?" she reached for him, but Jonas pulled away.

"I'm good," he said with an attitude.

"Would one of you care to explain to me what this is all about?" Janette addressed the detectives.

Detective Rooks went on to explain to Janette why they had brought Jonas in. All she could do is gape at Jonas in shock while the man spoke. She couldn't believe what she was hearing. She knew that Jonas was no angel, but there was no way he could've been capable of the things they were saying . . . Could he?

"Well, you've violated his rights by questioning him without a parent or an attorney present, so you can't use anything you have on that tape," Janette informed them. She might've been an addict, but she was no dummy. She had spent enough time in and out of trouble to know the law like the back of her hand.

"Don't worry on that account. He hasn't said much of anything since we brought him in. I see you've trained him well," Detective Turner said smugly.

"Fuck you. If my son isn't under arrest, I'd like to take him home. Any more questions you have, you can direct them to our attorney. You'll be hearing from him shortly because I plan to sue your asses for what you've done to my son," Janette bluffed.

The detectives exchanged glances before finally taking the cuff off Jonas. Janette hugged her son to her chest, but he didn't hug her back.

"You can take your boy home, but I wouldn't plan on taking any trips out of town if I were you. Your son knows more than what he's telling, and we're gonna find out exactly what went down," Detective Rooks told her.

Janette didn't respond. She just took her son and got out of the precinct as quickly as she could. She was going to need a hit and a stiff drink when she got home.

Jonas breathed deeply when they were finally out of the precinct. He had only been in custody for a few hours, but it felt like days. That was his first taste of captivity, and even a small dose was enough to let him know that it wasn't for him. If that's what a few hours had done to him, then there was no way in hell he'd ever be able to do any real time. This he was sure of.

As he and his mother were standing on the corner trying to catch a taxi, Jonas was overcome with an odd sensation. He felt light-headed, and the hairs on the back of his neck began to stand up. He looked around curiously and didn't see anyone except for a cop leaning against a squad car smoking a cigarette. He was huddled so deep in the shadows that Jonas would've never noticed him, save for the burning ember of his cigarette and his mop of white-blond hair. There was something familiar about him, but Jonas couldn't put his finger on it.

"Boy, bring your ass on!" Janette got Jonas's attention. A cab had finally stopped for them. Jonas spared another glance over his shoulder, expecting to see the cop, but there was nothing except for a few lingering wisps of smoke from a discarded cigarette.

As soon as they were inside the cab, Janette started going off on Jonas. She read him the riot act about him getting caught up in the streets and every road leading to a dead end, but he only half-listened. He was still trying to wrap his mind around what he had learned from the detectives.

Apparently, he hadn't killed Black when he hit him with the bat, but he had put him in a coma. They still weren't sure if he would make it, and even if he did, he would likely suffer from brain damage. Black's fate would be the difference between a murder charge and an attempted murder. Either way, whoever they hung it on was fucked.

The inside-girl they had working at the check-in desk turned out not to be as solid as Mula had given her credit for. All it took was the threat of going to prison, and she gave Ace and Mula up. The only thing that had saved Jonas was the fact that the girl didn't know him by name and hadn't gotten a good enough look at him that night to be able to point him out. The only reason the police even brought Jonas in for questioning is because when they went to the school to get a line on Ace, the bitch of a principal gave Jonas's name as a known associate. They had also paid a visit to Prince's house, but he had an alibi as he had been home with his parents that entire night.

Jonas wasn't sure if he was more relieved at the fact that he hadn't killed Black, as he'd thought, or that he narrowly escaped going to jail for a very long time. Either way, he knew that things in his life were changing. For the better or worse, he was still unsure, but he wouldn't have to wait very long find out.

"Jonas, do you hear me talking to you?" Janette snapped him out of his daze.

"What?" Jonas asked a little sharper than he had meant to.

"You better watch your tone. I said we're almost home," Janette repeated. Jonas had been so lost in his thoughts he hadn't even realized they were nearing his block. "Where is your head these days, boy?"

"I got stuff on my mind," he said dismissively.

"Like what? This shit you've let Ace get you tied up into?"

"I told you and the police, I don't know anything about it," he lied.

"Bullshit! You and that damn Ace are like Mutt and Jeff. One don't move without the other. Now, I would hope that you weren't stupid enough to have had anything to do with this, but if you did, I'd advise you to keep your fucking mouth shut and make sure Ace does the same," Janette told him.

"Ace is solid."

"Listen to you trying to sound like you know some shit about some shit. Boy, you have no idea how big of a pile of shit you have stepped in. This ain't no petty fight in school that Mommy can get you out of. This is attempted murder. Do you have *any idea* what *that* means?" Janette asked. She didn't wait for him to answer. "It means, you could go to prison."

"I didn't do anything," Jonas repeated his lie.

"You didn't have to. If the police can so much as prove that you were in that room, it'd be enough to charge you as an accessory and send you away for a long time. Is that what you want? To spend the next few years of your life in prison?"

"Can't be no worse than where I'm at now," he said.

"Wow! Am I *that* bad of a mother to where you'd prefer jail over being around me?" Janette said in a hurt tone. The remark stung. "I'll admit, I could've probably been better to you kids growing up, but I tried to do the best I could with what I had to work with. Sure, I've got my vices. I'll be the first to admit to that, but not a one of you can ever say you went to bed hungry or to school without clean clothes on your back."

"You think feeding us and clothing us is all it takes to be a parent?" Jonas asked her.

"No, but it's more than what some got. I see kids out here every day get swallowed up by these streets, and I say to myself, *not mine*. My kids will be better. And then something like this happens. Do you remember that day you almost drowned in that lake?"

"Yeah."

"When it happened, I blamed myself," Janette admitted.

"How? You weren't even there."

"I don't mean directly. I mean, what happened to you was a result of how I live. God was punishing me for all the shit I've done in my life by taking the thing I love the most, my precious baby boy," she said emotionally. "When I was on my way to the hospital, I did something that I haven't done in a long time. I prayed. I got on my knees and told God that if he let you live, I would get my shit together."

"Guess your prayers were answered because I'm still here."

"Yes, he held up his end of the bargain, but I didn't hold up mine. I tried to get it together for a little while; staying in the house and trying to keep myself busy, but I slipped. Then I slipped again. Before I knew it, I was right back to it. Because of that, God is trying to take you again."

"Ma, what are you talking about?" Jonas didn't understand.

"I'm talking about the streets," Janette explained. "You think I don't see that look in your eyes lately? The way you're hanging out a little more and coming home a little later."

"I just be chilling with my friends," Jonas said.

"Don't give me that, boy. I'm your mama. I can see the change in you. I know you hear that call, same as I did when I started running around out here all crazy. I don't want my life for you, Jonas. I couldn't take it if I got that call telling me that were dead, or if you had to go away over some bullshit."

"That ain't gonna happen to me," he assured her.

"That's the same thing your father said, but he's gone," Janette replied emotionally.

When Jonas looked over at his mother, he could've sworn he saw tears dancing in the corners of her eyes. This was a side of his mother he wasn't used to seeing. She seemed so . . . vulnerable. Almost frail. He wanted to reach out to her. Everything in him wanted to take his mother in his arms and promise her that he wouldn't die in the streets, but he didn't. Instead, he posed a question. "Is it true?"

"Is what true?" Janette wiped her eyes with the backs of her hands.

"What Slick said earlier, about my father swallowing a bullet? Did he really kill himself?"

Janette studied her son's face for a time as if she were trying to decide how best to answer his question. "Slick is a bitter old man and tends to talk out of his ass when he's in his feelings."

"So, he was lying?"

"Your father was a good man, Jonas, but he was also very troubled. There were things broken inside him that I'm not even sure he knew how to fix. Instead of us, together as a family, facing whatever demons were riding him, he sought help elsewhere, and that was his undoing. It's wrong to speak ill of the dead, so that's all I'll say about that."

Jonas didn't miss out on the fact that she hadn't given him a direct answer. There was obviously more to it, but that was a mystery that he would have to unravel on his own.

"Jonas," she began speaking again, "I know that as a young man, you will have to choose your own path. I should hope that you do the right thing with your life, but at the end of the day, it's your decision. I may not like it, but I understand. The only thing that I ask is that whatever road you decide to follow, it will be on your own terms."

"Ma—"

"I need your word," she cut him off. "I need to know that you will always be your own man and never let someone make you their puppet. Promise me!"

"I promise," he quickly agreed. There was something in his mother's words that made him uneasy. She sounded like she knew something that he didn't, and whatever it was, it scared her.

The last few blocks of their taxi ride were spent in silence, with Jonas weighing the conversation with his mother. She stared out the window, lost in her own world. Occasionally, he noticed her wiping her nose with a crumpled piece of tissue. He knew what that meant. She hadn't had a fix.

When the cab turned onto their block, Jonas noticed a small gathering of people in front of his building. Among them were Jewels, Anette, and Sweets. Sweets was crying, and Drew was trying to console her. Jonas's heart sank as he immediately thought the worst. Was it Yvette? Had something finally happened to his sister? Jonas was out of the car before it had come to a complete stop.

"What's going on?" Jonas rushed to the group. His heart was thudding in his chest. Sweets said something, but she was sobbing so heavily that he couldn't understand her. Had something finally happened to Yvette? "Is it Yvette? Did something happen to my sister?"

"Yvette is fine. She's upstairs with Jo-Jo," Anette spoke up. Her eyes were red, and he could tell she had been crying too.

He breathed a sigh of relief. He didn't think he could've taken it if something had happened to one of his sisters. "If nothing happened to Yvette, why are y'all all out here looking so sad?" Everyone got quiet. None of the girls had the heart to tell him, so Drew accepted the responsibility. With four words, he changed the course of Jonas's life.

"Your friend is gone."

Chapter Fourteen

The days leading up to the funeral were some of the hardest of Jonas's life. When Drew had broken the news to him, he completely blanked out. His mind went elsewhere, and when it finally came back, he was on his knees in the middle of the street wailing like a banshee. It took the combined efforts of his mother, Drew, and both of his sisters to get him up and into the house. His mother had given him something to help him sleep. He woke up the next afternoon, hoping that it had all been a bad dream, but when he went outside to get some air and saw the candles lit in front of the building, he knew that it hadn't been. Doug was indeed dead.

He had a hard time wrapping his mind around it. Doug was one of them, just a kid out having fun and trying to make it in the world. He had never done anything to anybody, but someone had taken his life, and Jonas couldn't understand why. It wouldn't be until later that night when Ace came to see him that the blanks would be filled in.

Jonas had been out on his stoop catching a breeze. He hadn't planned on going outside, but Slick and his mom were in the crib arguing. With the mood Jonas was in, he didn't trust himself to stay out of it, and if it went down, his mother wouldn't be able to stop him from killing Slick this time. For the sake of keeping the peace, he just left and went to sit on the steps.

While he sat there, trying to get his head together, people kept approaching him, offering their condolences. Most of it went in one ear and out the other. None of their empty words nor their pats on the back could take away the sense of loss inside him or bring his friend Doug back. Only death could answer for death.

Ace appeared, seemingly from the shadows. He was garbed in a black hoodie, jeans, and Timbs. He walked close to the buildings, hands tucked in the pocket of his hoodie. A newspaper was tucked under his arm. Jonas hadn't seen much of him since word got out that the police were looking for him in connection with the attack at the motel. The block was too hot, so he moved his operation to Brooklyn. He had been lying low at his cousin's house in Marcy Projects. He hated staying in Brooklyn, but it beat prison.

"Sup?" Ace gave him dap and took a seat on the step next to him. Jonas nodded. "You, a'ight?"

"Not really," Jonas said honestly. "I still can't believe Doug is gone."

"Me either. That's was my nigga . . . gave me a play when nobody else would." Ace recalled Doug plugging him with the weed connect.

"Good dude who died over some bullshit. Who could've done this to him?"

"We did," Ace said sadly, then went on to give Jonas the rundown on what he had discovered. Word of what had happened to Black spread quickly. Everybody was talking about it, including members of Black's crew. They didn't know all the details, but that would change thanks to Brian. Just as Jonas had suspected, Brian betrayed them. He told the crew all about the plan to get back at Black for what he did to Doug but conveniently omitted the part he played. "They caught him coming out of some chick's building and aired him out. Doug never even saw it coming."

"Damn." Jonas put his head in his hands. Mr. Hightower's warning *continuing the cycle of bullshit* came back to haunt him. "If we had left it alone, Doug might still be alive."

"I thought about that too. Been losing a lot of sleep over it, but ain't much we can do about it now. What's gone is done," Ace said.

"I knew that nigga Brian was foul! I wish I knew where to find him. I'd kill that muthafucka!" Jonas fumed.

"Funny thing about Karma. She never leaves debts unpaid." Ace opened the newspaper and handed it to Jonas.

Jonas skimmed over an article about a broad daylight shooting inside of the McDonald's on 125th and Broadway. At first, Jonas didn't understand, but then it hit him. He looked at Ace in wide-eyed shock.

Ace smiled. "We take care of our own."

Earlier that day . . .

When Brian walked into McDonald's, he was tired, sore, and starving. All he'd had to eat in the last few days was a hero sandwich, which had worn off quickly. The bullshit food they offered in the vending machines at the Harlem hospital wasn't worth shit. He had spent the night there, thanks to an unexpected ass whipping he picked up the night before. He had never realized how hard a project hallway floor was until his head bounced off one. He was in bad shape, but it beat the alternative. Instead of hungry with a broken nose, he could've been dead and stinking. The worst part is that he had only himself to blame.

A dark cloud descended over the General Grant housing project when word got back about what had happened to Black. Black wasn't the most well-liked person in the neighborhood, but he was respected. His small corner of the project fed a half-dozen hungry mouths and taking him out of the game threatened how they ate. Whoever was behind removing the food from their plate would have to answer for it. It hadn't taken them long to shake Brian's name loose from a hat. He was the one thread that could connect all the pieces.

He had to admit that when he had given Ace and his boys the information about where to find Black, he had no idea they would go as far as they did. He had never intended on going with them to jump Black, but it sounded good and helped grease the wheel when he tried to talk Ace out of a few extra dollars in exchange for the info. At best, he expected them to jump Black and go back to their block with a story to tell, and he'd have a few dollars, but these kids had gone the extra mile and tried to kill him. He had seriously underestimated the ruthlessness of Doug's friends.

When Brian heard that Flair, who was Black's second in command, was looking to talk to him, he immediately got out of Dodge. He had been hiding out at his dad's apartment in Lincoln Project, only slipping in and out of Grant in the wee hours of the morning when he was sure no one was outside. The only reason he even risked that is because his mother had been sick, and he needed to check in on her from time to time. That was how he had gotten caught.

Brian had just got done checking on his mom, making sure she had her medicine and everything she needed for the day and was about to head back to his dad's. Taking the elevator put him at risk of bumping into one of Black's crew, so he took the stairs, which proved to be a mistake. He ended up running right into Flair.

Black was a big dude, but he looked small standing next to Flair. He was only 18, but already had a full beard and thick arms that were covered in tattoos. Flair didn't see him at first because he had his eyes closed. One of the neighborhood crackheads was in the process of giving him a blow job. Brian swallowed the lump in his throat and tried to ease back the way he came as quietly as possible. He had almost made it—when he stepped on a discarded potato chip bag and gave himself away. When Flair's eyes landed on Brian, a stream of piss squirted down Brian's leg.

"Move, bitch." Flair shoved the fiend off him and yanked his pants up. Brian tried to run, but Flair already had a handful of his shirt. "Where you off to?"

"Come on, man, chill," Brian pleaded.

"Relax. I just wanna talk to you." Flair smiled . . . before punching Brian in the face. He whipped Brian's ass for a good three minutes. In those three minutes, Brian told Flair everything he knew; the revenge plot for what happened to Doug, Ace setting it up. He even told him what he'd had for breakfast that morning. The only thing that stopped Flair from killing Brian was the old woman coming out of her apartment on her way to work. When she threatened to call the police, Flair ran off and left Brian to lick his wounds.

As Brian stood in line waiting for the girl with the blond braids to bring him his order, he couldn't help but think about Doug. A part of him felt bad about how he had to play it. In hindsight, Doug was a pretty decent dude, but he wasn't cut out for the game. He was too trusting. If he hadn't been, then he would've realized that Brian was only doing what was in his nature . . . to cross him. Brian looked up at the dollar menu, thinking about what Flair and his boys would do with the information he had provided. He hoped they caught Ace first and beat his ass. He never liked Ace. But at that point, Brian still had no idea of what he had set in motion. However, he would soon find out.

Brian had just grabbed his two breakfast sausages from the counter and was on his way out . . . when the front door swung open. It took his brain about two seconds to register the gun pointed in his face, but three and a half to recognize the person holding it. "I—" he opened his mouth to say something, and a bullet flew into it and out the back of his head, splattering blood and brain all over the shocked cashier. People screamed and rushed for the doors.

"What you see, bitch?" Mula asked, pointing the Glock .40 at the frightened cashier.

"Nothing," she managed to whimper.

"That's what I thought." Mula shoved the gun into his pants and strolled casually from the eatery.

Long after Ace had gone, Jonas continued sitting on the stoop. He took some comfort in knowing that Mula had murdered Brian. He just wished he could've been there to see it. He had never much cared for Ace's strange little sidekick. Mula was too wild and unpredictable. He was an accident waiting to happen. But one thing that he proved to be was loyal. He had a newfound respect for Mula and intended to tell him as much when next their paths crossed.

It started getting late, so Jonas decided it was time to go back into the house. When he got to his floor, he was surprised to find Jewels sitting on the steps. When she saw him, she flashed an uncertain smile. Jewels had tried to visit him that morning, but Jonas didn't feel like talking, so he had Sweets send her away. Jonas knew that Jewels had become dependent on him, almost like a puppy, so the slight had to have hurt. Jewels had been there for him when he was grieving over Doug, and he felt bad for the way he had treated her.

"Hey." Jonas took a seat on the steps next to her.

"Hey, yourself," Jewels replied. "Thought you might be hungry." She produced a paper plate wrapped in plastic. "My uncle fried some fish, and we had extra."

"Thanks." Jonas accepted the plate and began unwrapping it. Jewels watched him while he tore into the crispy fish. "Look, about earlier . . . I'm sorry I sent you away."

"It's fine. I know me being around all the time is starting to crowd you," Jewels said with a hint of embarrassment.

"Nah, I like having you around. You're always there for me when I need a shoulder to lean on, and I appreciate it."

"Thanks," Jewels beamed. The fact that he had finally acknowledged her made her feel good. "Well, it's getting late. I should be going." She stood to leave.

"You wanna come inside for a few?" Jonas wasn't sure what made him ask other than the fact that he didn't want to be alone.

Jewels studied his face. There was something about the way he was looking at her that was different. For the first time, he wasn't seeing her as one of the gang but as a young woman. "Sure, I'd like that very much."

That night turned out to be one that both Jonas and Jewels would remember for years to come. It was the night their relationship changed, and they became more than just friends. If Jonas had to describe it in a word, it would have to have been "beautiful." As they explored each other on his twin bed, all the troubles in their lives melted away. They were the only two people in the world. Little did either of them know it was the calm before the coming storm.

Chapter Fifteen

The morning of Doug's funeral, Jonas woke up feeling ill, much like he had on the day they attacked Black. He chalked it up to his nerves. He had been to funerals before for relatives and such but never for one of his friends. He wasn't sure if he would be able to go through with it, but he had to go and pay his respects.

Jonas didn't own a suit, so he had to opt for a pair of jeans and a button-up shirt that Sweets had gotten for him from the thrift store. The only thing he was missing was a tie, which he was sure he could find amongst Slick's things. When he came out of his bedroom, he was surprised to find Sweets in the kitchen, still in her pajamas. She was brewing a pot of tea on the stove.

"Why aren't you dressed? I thought you were going with me to Doug's funeral," Jonas questioned. He had been counting on Sweets to be there with him for moral support.

"I can't. Jo-Jo isn't feeling well, and somebody has got to stay here with her," Sweets told him. "Anette and Yvette will be with you, though."

"Shit, I might as well be going by myself," he grumbled.

"Language!" she scolded him.

"Sorry, Sweets. Where's Mama? Why can't she stay with her?" Jonas asked.

"I haven't seen her since this morning. She had to run Slick to the emergency room," Sweets informed him.

"Jesus, what happened to him now?"

"Heck if I know. He came in here all busted up with a cut on his head. Looks like somebody beat him up pretty good," Sweets filled him in.

"I wish they'd kill his ass already so he can get out of our house," Jonas half-joked.

Sweets abandoned the pot of tea and turned to her brother with her arms folded. "How many times am I going to have to tell you about wishing death on people? There is power in words, and you need to watch what kind of energy you send out into the world, lest it come back around to you."

"Whatever." Jonas sucked his teeth. He walked into his mother's room to search for a tie. Janette's bedroom was a pigsty, as usual. There were clothes strewn everywhere, most of them dirty. He was digging through a pile of Slick's clothes in search of a tie when he felt something heavy in one of the pockets of his pants. Curiously, he pulled it out. It was a switchblade with a pearl-white handle. Jonas ejected the blade and studied it in wonder. He didn't give it a second thought before slipping it into his shirt pocket. He doubted Slick would even realize it was missing. Even if he did, he couldn't prove it had been Jonas who took it.

After dressing, he and the twins headed out to the bus stop. As they were passing the corner store, Juan was at his usual position, standing outside and smoking a cigarette. Yvette gave him a friendly wave, to which Juan flicked the cigarette and went back inside the store. Yvette didn't understand the dry response, but Jonas did. He smiled sheepishly to himself.

The bus ride to the funeral home was a short one. In fact, they probably could've walked, but Anette kept complaining about her shoes pinching her feet. The whole ride, the twins cackled back and forth like old hens, while Jonas just stared aimlessly out the window. The closer they got to the funeral home, the sicker he felt. When they got off the bus, he nearly threw up.

"You okay?" Anette asked in a concerned tone. Jonas just nodded.

"Boy, bring your ass on so we can get in and out of here. I got shit to do," Yvette capped and sashayed inside the funeral home.

The first thing Jonas noticed was the scent. The whole place smelled like someone had tried to scrub away the stench of death with a cleanser but couldn't get it all. As they crossed into the room where Doug's body was being viewed, Jonas wished he'd had Ace with him. He had spoken to him the night before and knew that Ace was taking it hard that he couldn't be there. He and Doug were closer than any of them. But the police were still looking for Ace in connection with Black.

Jonas was surprised at how few people showed up. There were a couple of faces from the neighborhood that he recognized, and others that he didn't. The rest, he assumed, were friends of the family. He saw Alex standing off to the side being consoled by Bo, of all people. Seeing them together made Jonas angry, and had it not been for the fact that they were at a funeral, he'd have socked him again. Alex must've felt Jonas staring because she turned around and looked in his direction. Jonas gave her a friendly wave, to which she smiled back dryly before turning her attention back to Bo. What was that all about?

Mr. Hightower was sitting on a bench in the front row, consoling Mrs. Hightower who was a mess. Every time she looked like she was pulling it together, she was hit with another wave of sobs. Jonas felt bad for her. He could imagine what it must've felt like for a mother having to bury her son. He prayed he would never put his mother through such agony.

It was now the moment of truth . . . Jonas's turn to say his goodbyes to his friend. He got halfway down the aisle and suddenly stopped. He tried to will his feet to move but couldn't. He was rooted to the spot. People were now starting to look. He was finally able to force himself the rest of the way down the aisle to say farewell to his friend.

Doug was laid out in a gray casket, trimmed in silver. They had dressed him in all-white silk. When Jonas finally forced himself to look upon his friend, he found that he hardly recognized Doug. His face was swollen, and the makeup hadn't been blended properly with his complexion. There was a raised section on his head, just below his hairline, that was darker than the rest. Upon closer inspection, Jonas realized that it was where they tried to cover the bullet hole in his head with makeup. That was the moment when it became real to Jonas, that his friend was gone.

He felt dizzy, and for a minute, he thought he was going to pass out, then the most unexpected thing happened. He felt a set of fingers snake through his. He turned and was surprised to see his sister Anette. "I got you, little brother. I got you."

Jonas whispered a silent prayer over Doug and then tore himself away from the casket. He noticed that Mr. and Mrs. Hightower were watching him. There was an awkward moment, and he decided that it would be best if he went over and said something. He excused himself from his sister and went to speak to the Hightowers.

Jonas's steps were timid as he approached. Mr. Hightower's face was blank and hard, but Mrs. Hightower's eyes burned into Jonas as he leaned in to whisper. "I just wanted to tell you that I'm sorry about Doug."

Mrs. Hightower nodded . . . before slapping Jonas across the face. "You have no right to be here!"

"But, I—" Jonas was stunned.

"Get out!" Mrs. Hightower's voice echoed throughout the funeral home.

"I think it's best you leave," Mr. Hightower said softly, then went to console his wife.

Jonas looked around the room and realized everyone was looking at him, including Alex. He was both hurt and embarrassed about how Mrs. Hightower had treated him. He hadn't done anything wrong, at least as far as he knew, but she had made it clear that he was unwelcome. He could feel his eyes welling with tears, so he rushed out of the funeral home before anyone could see them fall.

By the time Jonas made it outside, he was crying freely and nearly to the point of hyperventilating. Passersby gave him curious looks, but he was in too bad of a shape to care about what anyone thought of the spectacle. His whole world felt like it was crashing down.

"Jonas," a small voice called from behind him. He turned to find Alex standing in the doorway of the funeral home. She was wearing an expression of pity.

"Don't worry. Tell your mother that I'm leaving." He wiped his eyes with the sleeves of his shirt.

"That's not why I'm here. I wanted to check on you," she told him.

"I'm good," Jonas lied.

"No, you're not. Your friend just died, and you're hurting. You have a right to be hurt."

"But not a right to be here to send him off?" Jonas questioned.

Alex was quiet for a time. "I'm sorry . . . about the way my mom treated you in there. She's taking my brother's death really hard, and I guess seeing you just reminded everybody of why my brother was killed."

"Wait? Y'all think *I* shot Doug?" Jonas was shocked.

"No, nothing like that." Alex hesitated. "Look, I don't have it in me to sugarcoat this, so let me just keep it real. Doug got killed because of what you and Ace did to that boy."

"Alex, I—"

"Jonas, please don't lie to me . . . not today," she cut him off. "Everybody knows Ace was behind it, and I know you and Ace are as thick as thieves. I don't know if you had anything to do with it, but I'm sure you were there."

Alex knew Jonas better than he thought. He could try to lie, but it would be pointless. "Alex, all we were trying to do was look out for Doug. Y'all are like family to us."

Alex laughed. Not because it was funny, but because she couldn't think of any other response. "If this is how you and Ace take care of family, scratch me off the list. You know, I used to think you were smarter than Ace and them, but I guess I was wrong. You're determined to be just another dumb nigga dead or in jail." She shook her head sadly.

"Alex." Mr. Hightower appeared in the doorway of the funeral home.

"I gotta go. I hope one of these days you wake up. I don't think I could take going to your funeral next. See you around, *Raf.*" Alex walked off.

Jonas stood there for a time, weighing what Alex had just laid on him. Her words were sharp and almost cruel, but she wasn't wrong. Alex was mad at him, but when she calmed down, he would make it up to her. He would show her that he wasn't just another dumb nigga. What he didn't know at the time was it would be many years before they would get to have that conversation. A few weeks after they buried Doug, the Hightowers shipped Alex down south to stay with her aunt and uncle. The streets had taken one child from them, and they wouldn't give them another.

Chapter Sixteen

It would be several hours before Jonas went back to his neighborhood. After he left the funeral home, he just walked aimlessly around the city, thinking about his life and the direction it was going in. Seeing Doug in that casket had gotten Jonas to thinking about his own mortality. He didn't want to go out like that, with his mother crying over his corpse. He didn't want to die just another nigga in the streets.

When he got to his building, he found Ace and Mula waiting for him. They were passing a blunt back and forth and sipping something that was hidden inside a brown paper bag. Ace's eyes had bags under them, and his face was drawn. He looked stressed out. Mula was his usual, unreadable self.

"What y'all fools doing?" Jonas greeted them.

"Chasing the pain away," Mula replied and extended the joint to Jonas.

Jonas had smoked weed before, but he wasn't a smoker. That night, he felt like getting numb, though, so he accepted it. He took a deep pull, held it in his chest, and then began to cough. This caused all three of them to laugh. Laughter was definitely something they all could use a dose of at that moment.

"Careful, that's that Purple Haze." Mula took the blunt back.

"Tastes like exhaust fumes." Jonas continued coughing.

"Wash it down with this." Ace handed him the brown paper bag.

Jonas took a deep swing. It burned, but only for a second, and then a soothing sensation passed through him. It was the first time he had ever had a drink, and he had to admit that he rather liked it.

"You just getting back?" Ace asked.

"Yeah, the funeral was over awhile ago, but I needed to clear my head," Jonas told him.

"They do a good job on him?" Ace asked, taking the blunt from Mula.

"Yeah, looked just like Doug," Jonas lied.

"Good," Ace exhaled. "Really wish I could've been there. At least to offer my condolences to his parents, ya know?"

"I know. It's all good, I let them know we were all sorry," Jonas told him. It didn't make sense to tell Ace about how Mrs. Hightower had treated him. He was going through enough as it was.

Eight-Ball came waddling out of Jonas's building, hands cupped around his mouth while he lit a cigarette. When he noticed the boys standing outside, he frowned. "You little niggas is blocking the doorway," he growled. Ace and Jonas moved without saying a word, but Mula lingered for a beat before letting Eight-Ball shoot him a dirty look. Still, Mula held his gaze. "You got a problem, shorty?"

"Nah, boss. No problem at all," Mula grinned. He was clearly taunting Eight-Ball, which meant he had his gun on him. One thing Mula had already proven; it didn't matter to him where he shot a man or who was watching.

"You looking for Slick?" Jonas asked, trying to ease the tension rather than actually wanting to have a conversation with the gangster.

Eight-Ball looked at Jonas, and the faintest hint of a smile touched his lips. "Nah, I ain't looking for Slick. His debt has been wiped. We all squared up," he chuckled and walked off.

"Why you always gotta go antagonizing that dude?" Ace asked Mula once Eight-Ball had gone.

"First of all, I don't even know what antagonize means. Second, fuck Eight-Ball!" Mula said louder than he needed to. He never cared for Eight-Ball, but at that point, he would never tell them why.

"Well, you need to be careful. Eight-Ball runs this neighborhood, and we don't want no problems with a nigga like him," Ace warned.

"Man, I don't give a fuck about Eight-Ball or nobody else. Every man bleeds the same," Mula said defiantly.

"Hey, y'all." Jewels appeared and drained some of the testosterone away. She was coming from the direction of Juan's store, carrying a plastic shopping bag.

"Hope you didn't have to do anything crazy for that," Jonas half-joked.

Jewels ignored the insult and turned her attention to Ace, who was still toking on the blunt. "Let ya girl hit that."

"Your little lungs ain't ready for this high grade," Ace teased her.

"Boy, please." She plucked the blunt from between his fingers. Jewels hit it like a champ, held the smoke, then exhaled it through her nose.

"Damn, baby hit that thang like a vet!" Mula said in adoration.

"Told y'all," Jewels said proudly. "So, what y'all getting into?"

"We about to head to Mula's aunt's crib in Jefferson Projects in a few," Ace told her.

"Yeah, she's gonna be gone all night, so we gonna get smoked out," Mula added.

"You trying to come hang with a nigga?" Ace asked suggestively.

"I don't know. Is Raf going?" Jewels looked at Jonas.

"What, you need his approval before you make a move?" Ace joked.

"Fuck you, Ace!" Jonas said more defensively than he intended to.

Ace looked back and forth between Jonas and Jewels before a light of recognition went off in his head. "Oh, shit! Let me find out my boy's hitting that!"

"And what if he has?" Jewels snaked her neck defiantly.

"My fault. I didn't mean no disrespect." Ace raised his hands in surrender. "So, y'all a couple now or what?"

"We ain't nothing," Jonas said without thinking. A look of hurt flashed across Jewel's face, but the liquor made him act like it didn't matter. "Why you always gotta be up in everybody business anyhow?"

"Damn, why you so sensitive all of a sudden?" Mula questioned.

"Because I just buried one of my closest friends!" Jonas barked. It was only part of the reason he was so up in arms.

"C'mon, man. We all a little fucked-up over Doug. Let's just get back to this bottle and chill," Ace tried to be the peacemaker.

"Nah, I gotta dip. I got school in the morning. I'm about to call it a night."

"Why you leaving, kid? We still got a half bottle left, and Ace is about to roll up some more weed," Mula said. He got on Jonas's nerves, but he genuinely liked him.

"Word, hang out with us. Just for a little while," Ace tried to convince him.

"I'm good. You coming?" Jonas asked Jewels.

"I'm gonna hang out and smoke with Ace for a few. I'll knock on your door later to see if you're still up." Jewels took a seat on the stoop.

Her reply surprised Jonas, but he tried his best not to show it. "Fuck it then." Jonas started into the building. The last thing he saw before going up the stairs was Ace drape his arm around Jewels.

Jonas's mood had gone from mellow to pissed off just that quick. When Jewels chose to hang out with Ace instead of leaving with Jonas, it made him angry, though, technically, he had no right to be. He and Jewels had had sex, but they hadn't officially established what they were. They hadn't expected to sleep together. It was something that had just happened, and neither of them thought past that point. He had said it himself that they weren't anything, but it was said out of embarrassment more than him actually meaning it. He reasoned that to Jewels, it was probably just sex, but to him, it was much more. She was the girl he had given his virginity to. The thought that she could lie with Ace that night hurt, and Jonas cursed himself for being such an emotional sucker.

If he had been mad before, he became even angrier when he found Drew outside his apartment door. He was leaning against the doorway, talking to Sweets. From the way she was smiling from ear to ear, he must've been laying some serious game on her. He was just leaning in for a kiss when Jonas announced himself by clearing his throat.

"Oh, what's good, Raf?" Drew flashed a guilty smile.

"Sup?" Jonas shot him an accusatory look.

"I better get out of here. I got a move to make. See you later, Sweets." Drew winked and trotted down the stairs.

"Bye, Drew." She batted her eyes at his departing back.

"*Bye, Drew,*" Jonas mocked Sweets and pushed past her into the apartment.

"You're such an evil little boy." Sweets gave him a playful shrug. "How was the funeral?"

"A shit show," Jonas said angrily.

"Language!"

"Sorry, I just had a real rough time."

"I saw the twins earlier, and they told me a little bit about it. That woman had no right to put her hands on you. I started to go over there and kick her butt," Sweets said honestly. It was true. When she heard about Mrs. Hightower slapping Jonas, she put on her sneakers, intent on going to her house and punch her in the face. The only thing that stopped her was Yvette and Anette barred the door until she calmed down. Sweets didn't play when it came to any of her siblings, but Jonas and Jo-Jo held special places in her heart.

"Let it go, Sweets," Jonas said, pulling off his button-up shirt.

"You okay?" Sweets asked, noticing that something was troubling him.

"I'm fine," Jonas lied, pulling on a sweatshirt. When he went to throw his dress shirt in the laundry hamper, he felt the switchblade. Keeping his back to Sweets so that she wouldn't see, he slipped it into his pants pocket.

"Don't give me that. I've known you since you were born. I can tell when something is bothering you. What's wrong?"

Jonas was silent for a while. He wanted to talk to somebody about what was going on with him . . . anybody. Sweets was a girl, so she probably wouldn't understand, but she was all he had. "You ever give somebody something that you wish you could take back?"

"All the time," Sweets laughed. "Look at it like this, if it was that valuable to you, then you wouldn't have given it away in the first place."

"But I thought I wanted her to have it."

"Well, Jonas, at least . . ." Her words trailed off. "Wanted *her* to have it? Jonas Rafferty, are you in those streets fucking?"

"Language, Sweets." He ran her own line on her.

"Boy, don't play with me! Are you having sex?" Sweets demanded to know.

"I'm not having anything, but I'm not a virgin anymore," Jonas said with a hint of embarrassment. From the way Sweets was reacting, he wished he hadn't told her.

"Oh my God! My baby brother done got his little thing wet," Sweets teased him.

"I knew I shouldn't have said anything," Jonas said angrily.

"I'm sorry, Jonas. I don't mean to sound like I'm making fun of you. I'm just shocked. I know Yvette is out there having sex, and Anette is curious about it, but I didn't think I'd be having this conversation with you for a very, very long time."

"What? You think I'm too ugly to get a girl to sleep with me?" Jonas asked defensively.

"No, I didn't mean it like that at all. You're handsome as all get out. I'm sure these little girls are out there throwing themselves at you, but I also know you ain't like the rest of these little boys. I always thought that when you finally decided to take that step, the person you took it with would be special."

"I thought she was special," Jonas said, thinking on all the nights he and Jewels had lain in his bed talking about what they would do with their lives when they got older.

Sweets saw sadness in his eyes. Her little brother was suffering from his first heartbreak. "Let me tell you something, Jonas. You are a special child, and you will grow to be an even more special man. You're going to do great things in life. Any woman who you decide to lie with should feel honored, and if she doesn't, then that's her loss. Never let no woman have you walking around with your head down; do you understand me?"

"Yes, Sweets."

"Good, now go set the table. Dinner will be ready in a few."

Jonas felt better after talking to Sweets. Because she was a girl, he thought she wouldn't be able to understand, but she had actually given him a different perspective to look at it from. He really liked Jewels, and if she couldn't see that, then it was on her.

Suddenly, there was a loud banging at the front door. The first thing Jonas thought was that the police had found a way to put him at the motel scene and were coming back to lock him up. He peeked around the corner while Sweets and Anette rushed to the door. There was some murmuring before the door swung open, and Fat Moe came in. He wasn't alone, though. Janette was with him. Her face was bruised on one side, and her lip was split. Her arm was slung over Moe's shoulder for support as if she were unable to walk on her own. There was also blood running down from between her legs and over her feet.

"Ma!" he gasped and rushed down the hall. "What happened? What the fuck happened to my mother?"

"I don't know. I was about to chain my grill up behind the building, in the yard, and I found her out there like this," Moe explained.

"I'm fine; stop making such a big deal," Janette said as if it were nothing. She tried to push off of Moe and stand on her own and almost collapsed.

"You are not fine. Moe, help me get her to the bed." Sweets took control of the situation. Fat Moe helped Anette and Sweets get Janette onto her bed, then excused himself from the room to give the girls some privacy while they attended to their mother.

Jonas was pacing back and forth in the hallway. A million thoughts were running through his mind. He wasn't sure what had happened to his mother, but when he found out, he was going to make all parties involved pay the ultimate price. "Fuck did this happen?" he was thinking out loud.

"I don't know, young blood." Fat Moe assumed Jonas was asking him a question. "Like I said, I found her like that in the backyard when I was going to chain my grill up. Don't you worry, though; we're gonna get all this squared away."

Jonas stopped his pacing. "What did you just say?"

"I said I was chaining up my grill and—"

"No, not that part. The last bit." Jonas's mind had hooked into something, but he hadn't quite reeled it in yet.

"I said we're gonna get all this squared away," Fat Moe repeated.

That was it . . . *squared away*. The pieces of what had happened to Janette and who was behind it now fell into place. "Muthafucka!" Jonas cursed and rammed his fist through the wall. The sudden noise brought Sweets out of the bedroom.

"What the hell is going on out here, and why did you do that to the wall?" Sweets looked from the hole to Jonas.

Jonas was too choked up to respond. When he opened his mouth, the sound that came out was akin to a wounded animal. He pushed past the confused Sweets and ran out the front door.

"Jonas!" she called after him, but he never looked back. "What did you say to him?" she turned angrily on Fat Moe.

"I wish I knew, Sweets . . . I wish I knew."

Chapter Seventeen

The universe must have picked up on how Jonas was feeling at that moment because it had started drizzling when he got outside. Rain was good because the water would wash away the tears that were now flowing freely down his cheeks.

How could this have happened? How could *he* have let it happen? To think, while he was in front of the building getting drunk with his friends, his mother was in the back being violated. To make matters worse, her attacker had strolled right past him.

"We're all squared," was what Eight-Ball had said to him earlier that night. At the time, Jonas wasn't sure what he meant, but then he saw his mother, beaten and broken. His thoughts went back to the night in the hallway Eight-Ball's threat about getting what he was owed *one way or another*. And he had. Slick's debt had been paid with his mother's flesh. Slick was going to die for the evil he had brought down on the Rafferty family, but first, Jonas intended to take care of Eight-Ball.

The gangster wasn't hard to track down. When he wasn't on the block getting money, Eight-Ball frequented a bar called Pops. It was a watering hole on 145th Street that was mostly frequented by killers, thieves, and other underworld types. Jonas was familiar with the place because he'd had to collect his mother from there on more than a few occasions when she had gotten too drunk and became unruly. The owner, Pops, was cool. When

Janette got that way, he would call the kids to come get her instead of having one of his bouncers toss her out on her ass.

There was a homeless man outside, begging for dollars from the people who passed. "Spare some change, young blood?" he asked.

"I ain't got it," Jonas said and kept it moving. Generosity was the last thing on his mind at that moment. He was hunting big game.

Jonas crept up on the bar and peered through the window. It was teaming with people, but he was looking for one in particular. He spotted Eight-Ball at the bar, talking shit and throwing back drinks. It looked like he was celebrating something—likely the conquest of Jonas's mother. His first thoughts were to run inside the bar and attack Eight-Ball, but that was a shitty plan. Even if he managed to make it past security at the door, Eight-Ball's people would likely beat him down before he got within spitting distance of the man. He needed to draw him out, but how? Then it hit him! It was a long shot, but it was all he had.

Jonas walked to 146th Street, near Jimbos, and found what he was looking for. With the invention of cell phones, pay phones were becoming extinct, but that was one of the few in the neighborhood that still worked. He fished around in his pocket until he found a quarter, dropped it in, and punched in a number that he had seen Sweets use awhile back. Drew had given her the number once when he needed Sweets to page Eight-Ball from their house phone when he needed a re-up. She had made the mistake of dialing the number in front of Jonas, and he committed it to memory. The only reason he memorized the number was to pass it along to Ace so that if and when he decided to step up his game from weed into something heavier, he could cop from Eight-Ball. He

had forgotten he even knew it until then. He figured that
Eight-Ball had a cell phone, but hoped that he was too
paranoid about talking business on it. With hope in his
heart, Jonas posted up across the street and waited.

After ten minutes had passed, Jonas was becoming
discouraged and started brainstorming another plan, but
then Eight-Ball emerged from the bar. When Jonas saw
Bruiser come out after him, his heart sank. He wasn't
certain that he would be able to take Eight-Ball by himself, but there was no way he would be able to get both
of them. Then his luck turned. The two men exchanged
a few words before Bruiser went back into the bar and
Eight-Ball started in the direction of the pay phone.

Jonas's heart thudded in his chest as he watched Eight-
Ball draw closer. He thumbed the edge of the bone-han-
dled switchblade in anticipation. He was the spider waiting for the unsuspecting fly to land in the web he'd spun.
Suddenly, a sharp pain shot through his thumb, and he
realized that he had cut himself. Blood dripped over the
knife, soaking into the blade. "Soon," he whispered softly to his weapon.

He waited until Eight-Ball had reached the pay phone
before he started making his way back across the street.
The blade hung loosely at his side, screaming for another
helping of blood. Eight-Ball had his back to him, cradling
the phone to his ear when Jonas stepped on to the curb.
His hands were sweating, and his stomach lurched a bit.
What he had done to Black had been a reaction, but this
was premeditated. There was a moment of uncertainty
about what he was setting out to do . . . commit murder.
He hadn't yet come too far to go back.

And then it was too late.

Eight-Ball turned around and spotted Jonas standing
behind him. He was startled at first, but when he realized
it was just Janette's kid, an amused smirk touched his lips.

The smirk faded when he noticed the knife in the teen's hand. "I see what this is," he nodded in understanding. "Before you try some dumb shit and get yourself hurt, ask yourself a question, Raf. You ready to die because I took something that your whore of a mother sells every night anyhow?"

Jonas didn't answer. Not because he didn't have a million things he had wanted to say to Eight-Ball, but because he couldn't find his voice. Terror had stolen it. If it had been a movie, this would be the part where he gave him some cool line about revenge . . . but this wasn't a movie. It was real life. The moment he had fantasized about was at hand, and all he could manage to do was stand there like a deer in headlights.

"Just what the fuck I thought," Eight-Ball laughed mockingly and started back toward the bar.

Jonas stood there feeling like a total sucker. He was supposed to be the protector of his family, yet when the opportunity presented itself to step up, he had stood there like a scared little girl. Jonas hated Slick because he was weak, but Jonas was worse than weak . . . He was a coward. "*That's right, li'l bitch,*" he heard Slick's mocking voice in his head . . . and then something snapped.

The sound of rubber slapping on concrete caused Eight-Ball to turn around. There was the flash of something shiny under the glare of the streetlight, followed by a sharp pain exploding in his chest. Before he could even register that he had just been stabbed, another pain exploded. This one was on his side.

Jonas stood before Eight-Ball with a crazed look in his eyes. His hand was wet with blood as he shoved the knife as far as it would go, then began to twist. "That whore is still my mother," he growled, before yanking the knife upward and opening Eight-Ball's belly.

Eight-Ball staggered backward, eyes wide with shock. His mouth opened and closed as he gasped for air. One hand dropped to his stomach, trying futilely to stop the blood from pouring out, but it was no use. He took a step toward Jonas, but his legs wouldn't support him, and he ended up falling facedown to the concrete.

Seeing Eight-Ball bleed out into the street filled Jonas with something akin to a high. He thought he had gotten a rush off caving in Black's skull, but it was nothing compared to this. He kicked Eight-Ball over onto his back and straddled him, ignoring the blood soaking into his jeans. He was almost giddy when he placed the knife to Eight-Ball's throat. One stroke of the blade and it was done. His mother would be avenged. When Jonas looked into Eight-Ball's eyes, though, he saw something that gave him pause. It was fear. In all the years he'd known Eight-Ball, he had been a terror in their neighborhood, ruling it with violence, but not now. He was just a scared young man, no different than Jonas.

"You gonna finish him off or what?" A voice scared the hell out of Jonas. He scrambled off Eight-Ball's body, looking around frantically. He missed him on the first pass but saw him on the second. A tall white man appeared from the shadows. He was dressed in a tight black T-shirt under a black leather jacket and jeans tucked into shiny combat boots. His white hair was heavily gelled and spiked, which made him look like a part of a rock band. The shiny gold badge hanging around his neck said that he was no musician. Jonas thought about bolting, but the cop must've been reading his mind. He pushed his jacket back, showing the butt of his gun. "You turn rabbit on me, and I'll put a hole in your fucking back."

There went Jonas's great escape. He stood where he was, trying not to piss himself. He knew he was about to go to jail for a very long time.

"Now, what do we have here?" The detective began pacing a tight circle around Jonas and Eight-Ball, who was now lying in a pool of his own blood. "You really fucked him up. Must've been personal."

"He raped my mother," Jonas said, not sure why he had shared it with the cop. It's not like he cared.

"Your mother, and several other women that I know of. Eight-Ball always did like to play rough," the cop said in a disappointed tone. "I detest rapists, even if their victims of choice are naïve young women and junkies. No offense." The boy gave the cop a hateful look, to which he smiled and patted his gun. "You're upset, not stupid." The cop knelt and checked Eight-Ball's pulse. It was faint, but still there. "How come you didn't finish him?"

"I . . . I don't know," Jonas said honestly. Even if the cop hadn't shown up, he wasn't sure he would have been able to go through with it. "So, you going to arrest me or what?"

The cop measured the question. "Should I? Someone raped my mother, I imagine I'd have had a similar reaction; expect I'd have probably not left the meal half-eaten," he said in a mocking tone.

When the cop stood and turned his cold blue eyes to Jonas, something in them rang familiar. It took him awhile for the pieces to click. "I've seen you before."

"You've seen me a few times. We're old friends, actually. It's thanks to you that I was given this shiny gold badge." The cop brandished the chain around his neck.

"What are you talking about?" Jonas asked in confusion.

"When I pulled your half-dead ass out of that lake I became somewhat of a hero. Even got me a promotion out of the deal," he said proudly.

"The angel!" Jonas remembered when he had first been pulled from the lake and initially thinking the white-haired man was some type of celestial deity.

"Detective Ceaver will do. 'Lou,' to my friends, but whether we become friends remains to be seen. I warned you not to waste your second chance; yet, here you are about to flush it down the toilet." He shook his head sadly. "What's your name, idiot?"

"My name is Jonas, but everybody calls me Raf." He ignored the insult.

"*Wrath*," Detective Ceaver let the name roll around in his mouth. "Yes, I can see that. So much fury in those young eyes of yours. Wrath is a perfect fit, my violent little friend."

"I didn't say *Wrath;* I said—" Jonas tried to correct him, but the cop ignored him.

"So, Wrath, what do you propose we do about this little mess you've made?" Detective Ceaver tapped his chin with one of his slender, white fingers.

"What do you mean?" Jonas was totally confused.

"We can't very well leave him like this. By now, I'm sure his boys are curious about where he's disappeared to. What if they come looking and find him here? He'll surely tell them who did this to him. Or worse, an ambulance could come along and save his worthless life. I'm sure you and your family will be the first people Eight-Ball visits when he gets out of the hospital. No, letting him live will never do."

"What are you saying?"

"What I'm saying is you need to finish what you started," Detective Ceaver said as if the answer should have been obvious.

Jonas couldn't believe what he was hearing. Here was a sworn officer of the law trying to convince him to commit murder. It had to be a setup. "Nah," he whispered.

Detective Ceaver looked at him curiously. "Oh, I get it. You've got trust issues, is that it? Thinking I'm about to pull the old bait and switch?" He gave Jonas a stage wink. Then to Jonas's shock, the detective whipped out his pistol and shot Eight-Ball once in the head. "Problem solved. You and your family are safe."

"And what do you want from me in return? I ain't stupid enough to think you've done this out of the kindness of your heart," Jonas told him.

Detective Ceaver laughed. It was a very sinister sound. "No, kindness has never been one of my strong points. I've done this out of need. The need to correct a mistake that's haunted me for some time now. If we can bring ourselves to trust each other, I can promise you that neither you nor anyone in your family will ever be a victim again."

"And how do you plan on doing that?" Jonas was leery of the grinning detective. There was something about his too-white teeth that reminded him of a shark.

"I'm afraid you've got it wrong," Detective Ceaver draped his arm around Jonas, almost lovingly. The leather of his jacket was ice cold against the teenager's skin. "My work was done with our dearly departed friend, but yours is just beginning, Wrath."

Part III

"For he is the minister of God to you for good. But if you do that which is evil, be afraid; for he bears not the sword in vain: for he is the minister of God, an avenger to execute wrath on him that does evil"

—Romans 13:4 (KJV)

Chapter Eighteen

Jonas sat in the backseat of the Chevy Suburban in front of Popeyes on 125th Street, looking out the window, people watching, as he did whenever he was forced to sit in one spot longer than he was comfortable. It wasn't a conscious thing, just something his brain was trained to do. The man in front of the store drinking his beer, the old woman cursing her kids out at the bus stop . . . Everybody had a story to tell, and he was good at piecing them together. Jonas could look at a person and pick up certain things about them; their lips looking scorched or dark said they preferred blunts to joints, constantly moving eyes meant good liars, if they leaned too heavily to one side when they walked, that meant they were likely packing. There were at least a dozen little quirks that he could zero in on. It was a strange habit that he had picked up over the years, but it had helped him more than it didn't.

The cigarette he had been smoking burned through the filter and singed Jonas's fingers. He sucked whatever life was left from the butt and tossed it out the window before taking another one from the pack. Jonas didn't have many vices, but over the years, he had come to enjoy cigarettes and Hennessey. He wasn't yet old enough to legally partake in either, but it didn't stop him from indulging.

He lit the second cigarette and went back to his watching. Though he made it a point to observe everything and everyone around him at all times, his focus was on a boy named Tavion.

Tavion was a few years younger than Jonas, but in their time together, he had proven to be far more of an adapt hustler than Jonas had been at his age. Tavion was always the first one on the block and the last to call it a night. Sometimes, he would clock a twenty-four-hour shift and still try to get back on the money the next evening. Jonas admired his enthusiasm, which is why he kept him close.

Jonas had been bringing Tavion along gradually, charging him with different menial tasks just to see how he would hold up. So far, he had always managed to rise to the occasion, proving that though he was young and still somewhat green, he was still capable. With this in mind, Jonas had assigned him to a special mission that day. Something that would tell him for certain how high Tavion's star would rise.

There was a dude named Tito who owed a debt to Jonas's crew for some drugs that he had accepted on consignment. Ace had warned Jonas that it was a bad decision to front Tito, but Jonas believed in giving every man a chance to eat. He was kind in that way. For his kindness, Tito had burned him on the package. It wasn't a substantial amount of money and really wouldn't make a dent either way, but the fact that he had been ducking made it a matter of principal at that point. Jonas had charged Tavion with the task of collecting the debt, which had been outstanding for nearly three weeks. When they spotted Tito in front of Popeyes with a few of his boys, Jonas pulled over across the street and gave Tavion his marching orders: *Don't come back without that.* Tavion jumped out and went to do as he was told. He had been on the corner haggling for the last few minutes.

"Bet a hundred he folds," Mula said from behind the wheel of the Suburban. He was so short that he could barely see over the wheel of the SUV, but still, Mula was the best driver in their crew. He didn't have a license, nor had he ever taken a road test, but his years of stealing cars for bread taught him far more than what he could've ever learned at the Department of Motor Vehicles. It was a skill he had picked up when Ace's and his weed business had crashed. Mula and Jonas had become closer over the years. As it turned out, they had more in common than their mutual friendship with Ace. Both the young men excelled at violence. They would often enter into a competition about who could outdo the other when it came to putting in work.

"Nah, he's solid." Jonas exhaled smoke.

"Then put your money where your faith is," Mula challenged, extending his hand.

"That's a bet." Jonas shook his hand. Now that they had agreed to the wager, Jonas rooted even more for Tavion to complete his task.

They continued to watch as Tavion went back and forth with Tito. From Tito's flippant body language and the un-impressed smirk on his face, you could tell that the situation wasn't going in Tavion's favor. Tito barked something at Tavion that Jonas couldn't hear from where they were parked, but when he grabbed Tavion's nuts through his jeans, it gave Jonas an idea of what he had said. Reasoning that Tavion wasn't going to be able to get the job done and he would have to end up paying Mula for losing the bet, Jonas prepared to get out of the car and intervene, but Tavion had one more card to play.

Tito's crew was laughing at Tito's disrespect of Tavion, but their comical moment wouldn't last long. Much to all their surprise, Tavion hauled off and snuffed Tito. It was little more than a glancing blow, but the fact that he'd even had the heart to swing with the numbers being against him made Jonas's heart swell with pride. He'd made the right choice when he pulled the young man in. Tavion had nothing else to prove to him.

Tito and his boys were in the process of kicking Tavion's ass when Jonas stepped onto the curb. The young man was giving as much as he got, and he never stopped fighting. Jonas grabbed the back of the hoodie of the closest person to him, a tall kid with bucked teeth. When he turned to see who had dared lay hands on him, Jonas slammed the butt of his .44 Bulldog into the kid's mouth and knocked out one of his protruding incisors. The second kid, this one wearing cargo pants and a fake chain, took a hostile step toward Jonas, but the Bulldog in his face gave him pause.

"If you need it, I, for sure, got it for you," Jonas warned him. The kid in the cargo pants threw his hands up in surrender and looked at Tito, unsure what to do next.

"Yo, Wrath, what the fuck is this?" Tito asked, trying to sound tough.

Jonas turned the gun on him. "This is me having to remind you niggas the importance of doing good business. Why do I have to run all around town looking for you, T?"

"It ain't like that, Wrath. I just been moving around and making moves trying to get this money right," Tito explained.

"Been a week since my last visit. I'm assuming by now you have what you supposed to have for my peoples," Jonas pressed him.

"Wrath—"

"Tito, anything other than *yes, I have your money,* is unacceptable at this point. Think before you speak," Jonas warned.

Tito felt his bowels shift. The two of them had known each other since peewee football games in Queens. They weren't friends but had a history. He had heard stories about how Jonas handled people who welched on what they owed him, but there were dozens of witnesses about. It was the middle of the afternoon on a crowded city block. Wrath was dangerous, but he wasn't stupid. With this in mind, Tito tried to play it cool. "Jonas," he called him by his government name, "this is me, baby. We played the backfield together. You know I'm good for it."

Jonas looked at Tavion, nursing a busted lip, and watching him to see how he would play it. Jonas knew that whatever he did beyond this point would play a large role in shaping young Tavion's career. "Tito, me and you wreaked a lot of havoc on defense, but this ain't about games; it's about setting an example," he told him before shooting Tito in the face.

The corner of 125th and St. Nicholas was thrown into chaos. People were screaming and running for cover as Jonas pumped two more bullets into Tito's already-still body. The kid in the cargo pants and fake chain took off running down the block. Tavion made to chase him, but Jonas stopped him.

"Yo, Wrath. We need to catch that nigga before he tells somebody what happened," Tavion said.

"Let him," Jonas replied. "I want him to spread the word far and wide. If you owe us, you'll either pay us or see us."

Tavion jogged back across the street to the waiting SUV, but Jonas took his time. He moved at a stroll as if he were nothing more than another shopper on 125th. When he got in the truck, Mula peeled off. When they were safely away from the scene of the crime, Jonas dug into his pocket and counted off fifty dollars, which he handed to Mula.

Mula thumbed through the money and frowned. "What is this? The bet was one hundred."

"He didn't fold; he just didn't get it done," Jonas replied.

Mula shook his head. "Man, you always trying to find a loophole in some shit. You should've been a lawyer instead of a shooter."

"Maybe, but I'm better at death than litigation," Jonas said with a smirk. "Now, slow your ass down before you get us pulled over with these guns in the car."

Chapter Nineteen

Mula eased the big truck through traffic on their way back to the block. It was silent, save for the sounds of The Stylistics humming though the speakers. Jonas wasn't a fan of old school, but Mula loved the throwback music. He played it whenever they were on their way to or from a job. He claimed that it soothed his nerves. It only irritated Jonas. Give him some 2Pac or Biggie, and he was ready to rock.

As they got closer to their neighborhood, the mood in the car lightened. Mula rolled the driver's-side window halfway down so that people could see who was behind the wheel. Certain blocks they passed, people smiled or waved, while others, dudes shot them mean mugs. You either loved Jonas and his crew, or you hated them, but everybody knew them. They had been making quite a name for themselves over the last few years as both hustlers and killers.

Jonas couldn't help but smile as he passed the familiar blocks . . . his blocks. He and his team had come a long way since their days of selling dime bags of weed in the park. This was due largely in part to his relationship with Detective Ceaver.

For the last few years, Jonas served the detective in whichever capacity was required of him. Ceaver used Jonas to carry messages he didn't trust delivered on phones or put people in line who had forgotten their place. Jonas had broken more than a few jaws and various other bones in the name of progress. His status had increased, but in the beginning, he had been little more than a glorified errand boy.

This wasn't to say that having a cop in his pocket hadn't come with perks. Ceaver was always good to give him a heads-up when the block was going to be raided or point him in the direction of easy marks for him and his crew to rip off. The most value came from his *get out of jail free card*. Jonas could pretty much do whatever he wanted, within reason, and Ceaver would smooth over any legal troubles that would arise. That was cool, but he was still waiting for all the bells and whistles he had been promised. This would come later in the way of a tip that would prove to be the turning point for him in his criminal career.

The night Eight-Ball had been killed, the detective promised Jonas that he would change his life. If Jonas had been expecting immediate results, he was disappointed. Months had gone by, and he hadn't seen nor heard from the man. He was beginning to think that it had been an empty promise . . . until the day he came across an article in a newspaper he was reading while riding the subway to school one morning. It detailed the story of a black man who had been shot by a cop, which was nothing new. Police killed black and brown kids every day, especially in the ghetto. Jonas was about to skip over the article and continue to the Sport's page . . . until he spied a picture of the victim. It was an old prison mugshot of a face Jonas was all too familiar with. It was Bruiser.

Jonas had been avoiding Bruiser like the plague since Eight-Ball's death. Word on the streets was that he hadn't taken his best friend's murder too well and was out for blood. There was a $5,000 bounty placed on the head of Eight-Ball's killer. Besides the detective, no one could place Jonas at the scene of the crime, but he reasoned it was still best to keep a low profile for a while. He stayed close to home, going only to school and back. He had even stopped hanging around with Ace and Mula too. He wanted to remain hidden until things blew over, or he graduated high school and left for college. Whichever came first.

According to the newspaper, Roderick Joseph, aka Bruiser, had been gunned down while attempting to rob a liquor store. An off-duty detective happened on the scene and foiled the robbery. While attempting to escape, Bruiser fired on the detective, who returned fire, killing him.

Jonas closed the newspaper, trying to process everything that he had just read. None of it made sense. For one, Bruiser was a thug and a drug dealer, not a robber. When Eight-Ball died, it was Bruiser who took his place at the head of their crew. He wasn't as good a hustler as Eight-Ball, but he managed to hold the crew together enough to where the money didn't stop flowing. With that being said, why would Bruiser be robbing a liquor store? Something even more perplexing was the name of the detective who had gunned Bruiser down: Louis Ceaver. There was no way in hell it was all a coincidence. There had to be more to the story, but Jonas would not receive the final pieces of the puzzle until later that day when school let out.

He and Prince were walking from the train station on 135th Street, discussing a fight they had seen that afternoon when an unmarked white Caprice started coasting alongside them. From the missing hubcaps and long antenna on the back, they knew it was a police car long before the driver hit the siren. Prince took off running. He had a knapsack full of stolen goods and had no intention of getting busted with them. Jonas stayed *where he was. He hadn't done anything and didn't have anything on him. When the window rolled down, he found himself staring into a pair of familiar blue eyes.*

"Well, if it isn't my favorite almost murderer," Detective Ceaver greeted him. "Get in." He pushed the passenger door open.

Jonas didn't move. He just kept looking up and down the block suspiciously. The last thing he needed was anyone from the neighborhood seeing him getting into a police car, and he wasn't under arrest. He'd be branded a snitch, even if he weren't.

"I don't plan on asking you twice," the detective said in an icy tone.

Jonas knew that he would create a bigger problem by not getting in than he would have if he did. "Fuck," he cursed under his breath before jumping in.

"For a minute, I thought I was going to have to make a scene," Detective Ceaver said, peeling away from the curb. "Is that any way to treat a friend?"

"Oh, so we're friends now?" Jonas asked sarcastically.

"I thought so. Friends do favors for friends, right? Last time I checked, I had done you a huge one. Or have you forgotten about our rapist friend?"

"So, you gonna hold that over my head now?"

"No, blackmail isn't my game, Wrath. You don't have to ever worry on that account. Though, I do believe that a word given is a word kept," Detective Ceaver said, running through a red light and almost hitting a woman who was crossing the street with her child. He never even spared them a second look.

"You mean like how you gave me your word that you would change my life but left me hanging?" Jonas questioned.

"Wrath, one thing you will learn about me is, even when I'm late, I'm always right on time. I would've

come to pay a call on you sooner, but I've had my hands a little full. So many moving pieces on the board that it can sometimes get overwhelming. Do you play chess, Wrath?"

"No," Jonas replied.

"You should learn. Chess is a thinking man's game. A game of strategy and anticipation. Every great ruler in government and the streets has had at least a working knowledge of the game. It will help you to stay one step ahead of your enemies."

"I don't have any enemies."

Detective Ceaver laughed. "You were born black. That automatically puts you at odds with the world. Do you know why 2Pac was murdered?"

"Over the East vs. West beef," Jonas replied as if the answer should've been obvious. You had to have been living under a rock if you didn't know the story of the tragic rise and fall of Tupac Shakur.

"So the media would have you to believe. 2Pac getting killed by a rival crew is a far easier explanation for the public to digest rather than the truth. I won't say that his affiliation and antics hadn't put him in a dangerous position, but it isn't why he had to die. 2Pac was assassinated because he represented something that threatened to upset the natural order of things . . . hope. Millions of young eyes watched as he rose from poverty to almost godlike status. In him, kids from the ghetto saw someone who looked just like them beat the odds. One man can inspire thousands, and a thousand men can inspire millions. Had Pac lived long enough to reach his full potential, he could've shifted the balance of power. All it takes is one spark . . . and game over. Those in real positions couldn't have that. There's more money to be made from hopelessness than there is hope."

That was heavy.

"Sorry, I'm going off topic again," the detective continued. "I tend to do that sometimes when I have a lot on my plate, and right now, my plate is full."

"I wish mine was too," Jonas said.

"Aren't you the direct one these days?" Detective Ceaver smirked at him. "That's actually why I've come calling on you today. I'm sure you've heard through the ghetto grapevine by now that Bruiser is no longer a thorn in anyone's side. With him gone, that erases the final stain of Eight-Ball's reign. When conquering, it's never enough to kill whoever is holding on to what you're laying siege to. You have to wipe them from the history books completely. Don't forget that. Now that it's been taken care of, it's time to start your ascension."

This was music to Jonas's ears. He'd been waiting a long time for the detective to make good on his promise. "So, you gonna put me in control of Eight-Ball's old territory?" he asked eagerly.

"Slow down, Scarface. That's been promised to another. You'll get your turn to sit in the big chair, but you'll have to crawl before you walk. I've got a way for you to get some quick start-up, though." Detective Ceaver fished a sheet of paper from his pocket and handed it to Jonas. On it, an address was scribbled. "Be there at 5:45 p.m. tomorrow."

"And what I gotta do when I get there?" Jonas asked.

"Nothing. Just make sure you're on that corner at that exact time. Not a minute later, understand?"

"Yeah," Jonas said with a frown.

"Now get out. I've got something to handle."

Jonas looked up and realized they had ridden fifteen blocks from his neighborhood. "What? Am I supposed to walk?"

"Unless you've sprouted wings since you got in here. Now go—and don't forget to be on time tomorrow."

The next day, Jonas went to the address the detective had given him. When he arrived, he thought he had been the butt of a bad joke. The building was abandoned and looked like it had been for a while. What could be there that could put some money in his pocket? He reasoned that maybe the detective was sending someone to meet him, so he waited. A few minutes had gone by, and he was thinking about leaving when he heard the screeching of tires, followed by the sounds of police sirens. A black car bent the corner so fast that it almost jumped the curb. A blue and white squad car was on its ass. The window rolled down, and a plastic bag came flying out as the car sped past him.

Jonas waited for a few minutes before going to the spot where the bag had landed. He didn't look inside, just tucked it into his book bag and got out of there. When he was a safe enough distance away, he dared to peer inside. A broad smile crossed his face. The bag contained a bunch of small vials of crack. There was at least a thousand dollars' worth. Jonas didn't know much about selling drugs, but he knew someone who did. Ace. With Ace's help, they sold all of the crack. They then took part of what they had made and went to see Drew, who gave them a good deal on an ounce of cocaine. They were officially in business.

Chapter Twenty

"I'm sorry, Wrath." Tavion broke Jonas's train of thought.

Jonas cast his eyes to the youngster. "For what?"

"I let you down back there. You know, by not getting the money off Tito," Tavion said shamefully. It was the first time Jonas had trusted him to do something of such importance, and he had come up short.

"Nah, you did good. Better than some would've, considering you were outnumbered and unarmed," Jonas told him.

"But I didn't get the money, and you ended up catching a body because of it," Tavion pointed out.

"It was never about the money. I knew I was going to kill Tito when I woke up this morning. I just wanted to see how you handled yourself in a delicate situation," Jonas confessed.

"So, this was all just a test?" Tavion asked.

"Isn't it always?"

"You did get your ass whipped, though," Mula laughed. He continued giving Tavion grief for the rest of the ride.

Jonas could tell that Tavion was getting pissed, but he didn't intervene. That was just Mula's way. If he had love for you, he made it a point to pluck your nerves every chance he got. Being a pain in the ass was how he showed affection.

It had been the same way with Jonas when Ace had first started bringing Mula around. It seemed like everything Jonas did or said, Mula found a flaw in or made a joke about. They had gotten into plenty of fights over Mula's constant harassment. It wouldn't be until sometime later that Jonas would come to realize that it was just Mula's way. He hadn't had the traditional upbringing; none of them had, but Mula's situation was different. He didn't know his dad, and his mom was hardly around. He had been raised by his uncle Fish, who spent most of his time in prison, and when he wasn't locked up, he was training Mula to be a soldier. More often than not, he was on his own and had to learn the ways of the world with no proper guidance. Basic things like love and being loved were alien to him, so he tended to fumble when it came to show people that he cared about them. Mula expressed his emotions in either one of two ways: harassing you or trying to hurt you. When he got on your nerves, it was only because he wanted your attention and didn't know any other way to get it.

Jonas and Mula were tight, but there had been a time when he wondered if the two of them would be able to coexist in the same crew without one of them getting hurt. His feelings toward Mula would change when the youngster paid him an unexpected kindness. *It had been a little over a year since his mother was raped. Only his sisters, Ace, and Fat Moe knew what happened to his mother that night. Janette had decided that she didn't want anyone to know and refused to file a police report. She was ashamed of what had happened—as if it had been her fault—which it wasn't. Regardless of whether Janette sold pussy, she still didn't deserve to be violated.*

Another reason she kept quiet was that Eight-Ball had been found dead the same night. To out him as her rapist would've raised some uncomfortable questions about who had killed him. No one could say for sure, but Janette had an idea. She never came out and said it, but something about the way she started looking at her son after that told him that she knew something. So, to protect her son, she was forced to suffer in silence. It was a twisted situation.

Slick had been MIA since it happened. He never came back to the house for any of his clothes or even reached out to check on Janette. He was just gone. Jonas had been looking high and low for him. Ace had even offered up a few dollars to anyone with information on Slick, but so far, it was all quiet. This would soon change.

Jonas was sitting on his stoop talking to Prince one night when Mula pulled up on them. He was pushing a Lincoln Town Car that had seen better days. It looked like he had stolen it from a taxi driver. He double-parked and hopped out, ambling up to the building.

Jonas tensed when he saw him. The night before, the two of them had gotten into a fistfight over something so small he could barely remember what it was about, but Mula was notorious when it came to holding grudges. He eased over on the stoop, closer to the garbage bag Jonas had his gun stashed in.

"What y'all two doing? Jerking each other off?" Mula started in on them.

"Fuck you," Prince laughed.

"Yo, Wrath, I need you to bust a move with me right quick," Mula announced.

"Where we going?" Prince asked.

"Nigga, is your name Wrath?" Mula asked. "I got something I need to talk to Wrath about; it's kind of personal."

"Why can't you talk to me right here?" Jonas asked suspiciously.

"Because I need to provide you with some visual aids," Mula said with a devilish smile. "Just come on. It'll only take about a half hour."

"Cool, you can go to the car. I'll be right behind you," Jonas told him.

"Bet." Mula started back toward the car. "And you can leave that bum-ass gun under the trash. You won't need it," he called over his shoulder.

Five minutes later, they were in the Lincoln and headed uptown. Mula seemed to be in better spirits that usual. In fact, he seemed happy. This worried Jonas. Mula was a sour kid by nature, and the only time you saw him smile is when he was about to do something to somebody. Jonas wasn't sure what he had up his sleeve, but if Mula tried some funny business, he would learn that Jonas was harder to kill than most.

"Yo, Wrath, you remember that night you caved that nigga Black's skull in?" Mula asked, going across the 145th Street Bridge into the Bronx.

"Hell yeah! That dude nearly killed Ace," Jonas laughed, recalling the incident.

"He nearly killed all of y'all. Luckily, you came through with that baseball bat on some Ken Griffey shit. Man, I wish I could've seen you split his shit open! I shot a few cats in my day, but I never beat anybody to death. What was it like?"

Jonas thought about the question. "Honestly, I don't know. Everything happened so fast that I just reacted."

"You still think about it?"

"Sometimes, but not as much as I used to. After a while, the people we do shit to start to become just nameless faces," Jonas said.

"Not for me. I can remember the names of everybody I ever twisted. I keep them written down on the wall inside my bedroom closet," Mula told him.

"Why the hell would you do that?"

"Because when God judges me, I don't want to have to wonder what I did."

Jonas gave a nervous chuckle. "You're one strange dude, Mula."

"We ain't so different, are we? We've both killed people."

"Black didn't die," Jonas corrected him.

"I ain't talking about Black. I think we both know that."

"Mula, where we going with this?" Jonas asked, not liking the direction of the conversation.

"To the end of the rainbow," Mula laughed, making Jonas even more uncomfortable than he already was. Seeing that Jonas was on edge, Mula softened his approach. "You're one cagey dude, Wrath, I'll give you that. You fly under the radar like you're still some square-ass kid off the block, but deep down, you've got a vicious streak in you that, frankly, I'm kind of jealous of."

"Mula, you're tripping. I get busy in the streets, but you know I ain't no killer," Jonas lied.

"You think I don't know my own kind?" Mula questioned. "I can smell the blood on you. It's almost like how a wolf can pick up the scent of its pack mate from a mile away."

"Stop the car," Jonas ordered.

"What?"

"I said, stop the muthafucking car!" Jonas barked.

Mula finally relented and pulled over on a dark block, killing the engine. "Jonas, what's good with you?"

"What's good with me? I ain't sure if I like the direction of this little chat. What? You wired or something?" Jonas started patting Mula down, but he swatted his hands away.

"You know my pedigree. Don't try to play me," Mula
said defensively. *"Look,"* he turned his tone down, *"I'm
trying to tell you something, but ain't sure how to say it."*
He sounded almost like the child that he was.

"Spit it out, or let me out of the ride," Jonas said.

Mula sat there for a while, staring at Jonas, not sure
what to do next. *"I can show you better than I can tell
you."* He jumped out of the car and started for the trunk.
Noticing Jonas wasn't following, he tapped on the
window. *"C'mon, I ain't gonna kill you,"* he half-joked.

Jonas reluctantly got out of the car. Using extreme
caution, he made his way toward the back, where Mula
was standing there with the trunk open. As Jonas neared
it, he caught the scent of something familiar . . . death. He
peered in the trunk, and sure enough, there was a corpse
wrapped in plastic.

*"Mula, I know damn well you ain't had me riding
around all night with no body!"* He was furious.

"This ain't just anybody." Mula produced a pocketknife
and cut a hole in the plastic. The stench grew. He stood
to the side and motioned for Jonas to take a closer look.

When Jonas realized who the dead man in the car
was, his jaw dropped. Half of his face had been blown
off by a high-caliber handgun, but Jonas would know
that face anywhere. It was Slick. He had been searching
for him for months, with no success, and Mula pops up
with him in the trunk of a car. *"What is this?"* He still
didn't understand.

*"You killed the man who broke my family, so I killed
the man who broke yours,"* Mula told him. Seeing Jonas
still didn't understand, Mula explained. *"Me and Eight-
Ball had history."*

Mula and Jonas drove the stolen cab to a field upstate
where they buried what remained of Slick. As they did
so, Mula told Jonas the story of how Eight-Ball and

his mom had once had dealings. It was Eight-Ball who introduced her to drugs, and Eight-Ball who had sold her the batch of bad heroin that had killed her. He had been planning to kill Eight-Ball himself but could never get up the nerve. It was Mula's greatest shame and darkest secret. A secret that Jonas would never share with another soul, including Ace.

Chapter Twenty-one

About an hour after murdering Tito, they arrived back on the block and found Ace posted up in front of Jonas's building waiting for them. He was sitting on the steps chatting away with Prince and two girls who lived in the next building. There was a third man with them. This one, Jonas didn't know, but he looked slightly familiar. A high yellow man with a powerful build. A red bandanna was tied around his head, letting everyone know he was affiliated with the Bloods. The L.A.-based gang had become increasingly stronger in New York over the last decade or so. Gang banding had never been Jonas's thing, but he had some friends who rode under their flag.

The stranger's eyes turned to the car, and a warning went off in Jonas's head. There was something about him that screamed bad news. Jonas didn't like new faces, and he especially didn't like them hanging out where he rested his head. Ace knew better than that, and Jonas was going to check him about it when they were alone.

"Who is that?" Tavion picked up on Jonas's thinking.

"No clue," Jonas said, and got out of the car, intent on finding out.

When Ace noticed Jonas and the others coming his way, he dismissed the girls and straightened up. He was wearing a pair of red sweatpants, white sneakers, and a white T-shirt that looked like it was struggling to contain his thick chest and arms. Over the years, Ace had put on a bit of muscle. This was courtesy of the eleven months he had spent working out on Rikers Island while fighting a case. He had been picked up in connection with a robbery, but while in custody, the assault on Black had come up. Ace had been ducking it for years, and they finally had him. With the attempted murder charge on top of the robbery, Ace was facing at least ten years, and that's if he was lucky. Thankfully, the only witness they had against him, the girl who had been at the desk on the night in question, had suddenly vanished before the trial came up. This was thanks to Jonas tracking her down and sending her on a one-way trip to the afterlife. She had been Jonas's first official murder. Black and Eight-Ball had only been warm-ups, but with the girl, he had gone all the way. He made it clean, though; two to the back of the head, and he left her where she dropped. Without her, they had no case. Ace ended up getting time served and five years of probation for the robbery.

"Look at these degenerate criminals," Prince joked in the way of a greeting.

"Fuck you." Mula gave him dap. "Yo, why you always dressed like you going on a job interview or some shit?"

"A wise man once said dress for the job you want, not the job that you have." Prince popped his collar. He was wearing a Ralph Lauren button-up shirt, straight-legged jeans, and a pair of Prada sneakers. When Prince had taken over Doug's business, it had opened his nose to the other side of the coin. He went all in with the hustle. In addition to the people he had stealing and reselling goods all over the hood, he had also established a small drug operation in Maryland. He was plugged in with some strippers who worked a few of the clubs in the DMV area. He'd supply them with Ecstasy, Xanax, Percocet, or whatever was in demand, and they'd sell them in the clubs for double what he paid. Jonas had fronted him the initial cash to invest, and they were making money hand over fist. Ace and Mula were always low-key hating because they hadn't wanted to get involved when Prince first presented the idea. They had definitely missed the boat.

"Y'all handle that situation?" Ace asked.

"Yeah, everything is everything," Jonas said. He wasn't going to go into details in front of the stranger, who was staring at him.

"Wait? Is that my nigga Raf?" the stranger asked.

Jonas gave him a look. There were very few people who still called him Raf, instead of Wrath. "We know each other?"

"C'mon, man. I know I ain't been gone long enough for you to forget one of your closest running buddies." He spread his arms.

Jonas studied his face, flipping through his mental Rolodex of friends and enemies alike. It took a minute, but then it finally hit him. "Cal?"

"In the flesh." Cal embraced him. He squeezed Jonas so tightly that his back cracked. "Damn, the last time we saw each other, you were a skinny-ass kid trying to follow us to the jux!"

"I remember. I gotta admit, I'm a little surprised to see you on the streets so soon since I heard they were hanging the bodies from that gun on you," Jonas said suspiciously.

"Aw, man, that was a bunch of bullshit." Cal downplayed it. "My mom got me a good lawyer. They couldn't prove that I had anything to do with the murders, so I just had to do a little time on a weapon's possession. I just got paroled."

"Can't keep a good nigga down," Ace cut in. "I was telling Cal that now that he's home, we're gonna bring him in on what we got going on."

"Is that right?" Jonas gave Ace a look.

"Word, I heard y'all out here doing big things out here, especially you, Wrath. Your name is ringing off behind the wall," Cal told him. "I kept hearing stories about some young kid they called Wrath out here laying shit down, but I never made the connection. Wasn't until toward the end of my bid that I figured it out. This kid named Pete came through, bragging about having survived a run with you. He's still got the colostomy bag on his side to prove it. He knew your first name. Sound familiar?"

"Can't say that it does," Jonas lied. He knew just who Pete was . . . The one who got away. Pete was a dude from somewhere in the Bronx that had gone to school with his sister Anette. They had gotten into a trivial argument over something, and Pete had spit on her. The next day, Jonas was waiting for him outside the school. Without saying a word, he shot Pete in the stomach. The only reason he hadn't killed Pete is because he ran and had the good fortune of collapsing in front of a police station. He had always planned on finishing him off one day, but not long after, Pete had gotten locked up for something.

"Niggas gossip like bitches," Mula spoke. Unlike Jonas, who was good at hiding his emotions, Mula wore his on his sleeve. He didn't care for Cal.

"This my partner, Mula," Jonas introduced them.

"What's good?" Cal gave him dap.

"And I'm Tavion." The youngster spoke up without being promoted, which annoyed Jonas. Cal didn't need to know every player on the board until he was sure where his childhood friend stood as a young adult.

"T, do me a solid. Run around the corner and grab me a dub from the Haze dude." Jonas handed him a twenty.

Tavion was naïve, but not so much to where he didn't know he was being dismissed. "I got you, Wrath." He took the money and disappeared.

"Ace, I need to holla at you about something. Pardon us for a minute, Cal," Jonas said.

"Right." Cal took the hint. "I gotta go check in with my PO, so I was about to get out of here anyhow. Yo, but I'm gonna come through and check y'all later on. Good seeing you again, Wrath."

"Likewise," Jonas said in a less-than-sincere tone. He waited until Cal was gone before turning his attention to Ace. "Have you lost your fucking mind?"

"What you mean?" Ace asked.

"I mean you putting an outsider in our business."

Ace sucked his teeth. "Cal ain't no outsider. We've known him since we were kids."

"We ain't seen that dude in years. How do we know he's still the same person?" Jonas questioned.

"Jonas, your ass is too paranoid."

"I ain't paranoid; I'm careful," Jonas shot back. "Keep that nigga at arm's length until we figure out if he's got an agenda or not."

"Whatever," Ace said with an attitude. He fired up a blunt and sat on the stoop sulking.

A few minutes later, Anette came out of the building. She was wearing a pair of pajama pants, and a hoodie with her hair tucked under a bonnet. Over the years, she had really started growing into herself. She had flawlessly smooth skin and bright eyes that were full of promise. Now that she was older, she had started to distinguish herself from her twin, not only in looks but also in the way she carried herself. She didn't hang out partying until all times of the night like her twin, instead, choosing to stay close to home and focus on school. She had graduated high school two years earlier and was about to receive her associate's degree from City College. From there, she planned to go away to school to continue her education. The only reason she had stayed close to home that long was to take care of her family. She had taken Sweets's place as the junior matriarch of the family.

"What's up, fellas?" Anette greeted the boys.

"Hey, 'Nette." Mula was the first to respond. He'd had the biggest crush on her since he was younger.

"What y'all doing out here smoking on the stoop? You know the police be all up and through this strip," Anette warned.

"Police ain't fucking with us. We got a license to ill," Ace said sarcastically, cutting his eyes at Jonas.

"Where you off to?" Jonas asked.

"Nowhere. I came out to meet the bus. Jo-Jo will be home soon," Anette told him.

As if on cue, a yellow school bus pulled up to the curb. A few seconds later, Josette stepped off. She was only in middle school but was already nearly as tall as Sweets. She had inherited her height from her father, the same as Jonas had. She had to use special crutches to walk because her legs no longer worked as well as they once had. They had discovered that the source of Jo-Jo's aches was cancer. It had gone undiagnosed for so long that by the time they caught the disease, it had spread through her legs and into her uterus. She'd had five surgeries so far and had to undergo chemo a few times per week. The doctors were not optimistic about her chances, but so far, Jo-Jo had proven that she was a fighter just like the rest of the Raffertys.

"Put that shit out," Jonas told Ace and went to meet Jo-Jo. "What's up, baby girl?" he smiled at her.

"Hey, Jonas!" Jo-Jo greeted her brother. She tried to rush to him, but one of her crutches slipped, almost toppling her. Jonas went to help her, but she waved him off. "I got it." She righted herself and walked the rest of the way to meet him.

"How was your last day of school?" Jonas asked.

"Long!" she said. "But a funny thing happened. One of the kids in my class got into a fight with the teacher and snatched her wig off," Jo-Jo chuckled.

"Them kids at your school are a mess." Jonas shook his head. When Josette was diagnosed, Jonas wanted the family to put Jo-Jo in a special school, but she refused. She didn't want people to treat her differently because she was sick. She wanted to continue going to a normal school with the rest of her friends. "So long as ain't nobody trying to fight you."

"Nah, ain't nobody stupid enough to mess with Wrath's little sister," Jo-Jo said proudly.

"What did I tell you about calling me that?" Jonas frowned at her.

"But everybody else calls you Wrath. Why can't I?" she wanted to know.

"Because you ain't *everybody else*. You're my *special girl*. Never forget that." Jonas kissed her on the forehead. "C'mon, let's get you upstairs."

"Jonas, I need to bend your ear right quick before you dip," Prince called after him. From the look on his face, you could tell whatever he had to say was serious.

"I'll be up in a second," Jonas told his sisters. Anette gave him a suspicious look before helping Jo-Jo up the stairs. "What's good, Prince?"

"Walk with me." Prince cut his eyes at Ace and Mula, who were trying to see what they were up to. When they got out of earshot, he began speaking again. "Yo, you remember when I used to tell you stories about my cousins over in London?"

"Yeah, them wild Jamaican cats who sell the guns," Jonas recalled.

"Well, they ain't in the life no more. Since all this terrorist shit been happening, firearms have become a very dangerous business. You get caught with enough of them, and they'll fuck around and try to brand you a terrorist. They used the money they had left from the gun profits and started investing it into legitimate businesses.

Their biggest moneymaker turned out to be a T-shirt line they launched."

"These niggas stopped selling guns to sell T-shirts?" Jonas was amused.

"That's the same thing I said . . . until they broke it down to me. Turns out one of those rapper niggas was photographed in one of their pieces, and then the orders started pouring in! They were able to graduate from T-shits to selling actual pieces; pants, women's gear . . . different shit. Last year, they pulled in a million and a half, and this was *before* they opened the boutique."

"Being that you're bringing all this to me, I'm guessing you got an angle?" Jonas knew how Prince thought.

"Indeed, I do. They're looking to expand and started doing things Stateside too. To really do it like they want, they're going to need investors," Prince told him.

"Dawg, you know we ain't getting that kind of paper out here. We doing okay, but I doubt if anything we scrape up will be able to do much," Jonas said.

"Nah, man. I ain't talking about bankrolling it, but we can buy in for a piece and get in on the ground floor. When this shit blow, which I'm sure it will, even as minority investors, we stand to make a nice piece of change."

"How much would we need to go in?" Jonas asked.

"I'm thinking a hundred thousand is enough to get us a nice taste. I got about twenty or so in the stash already. If I really grind, I can probably get up another thirty or so in a few months."

"What little bit of bread I got access to is kinda tied up," Jonas said, thinking of the investment he had made at the suggestion of Lou. It was something that he hadn't yet shared with his crew, but he would in time. "Maybe Ace and Mula can go in with us to put us over the hump."

"I don't think that'll be a good move. I love the homies, but everything ain't for everybody. If you give me everything you can spare, and I put it with what I got, it should be enough for my cousins to hold a place at the table for us until we get the rest. This can be something for just me and you, Wrath."

"Let me think about it," Jonas told him. He was unsure about the move. After dumping the majority of what he had in the stash into his little project, Jonas was running on fumes. He didn't know enough about fashion or the reliability of Prince's cousins to go broke on a whim.

"Well, don't think too long. I'm gonna try to move on this whether or not you're with me. I don't know about you, but I don't plan on risking my freedom over a few thousand here and there. It's time to boss the fuck up."

Chapter Twenty-two

Jonas entered his apartment with Prince's words still fresh in his ears. *It's time to boss the fuck up.* He was right. Jonas and his crew were doing pretty good for themselves, but the fact that he couldn't put his hands on at least $50,000 at will said that he was doing something wrong. Granted, the investment he had made would bring in money once it was up and running, but that would take time, and lately, he had felt like time was something that wasn't on his side.

The first things Jonas noticed in the apartment were two very distinct smells; something cooking and Pine-Sol. The house had been completely scrubbed, and the floors were mopped. These days, the Rafferty house resembled an actual home instead of a den of addicts.

"Go start your homework," Anette told Jo-Jo as she was helping her out of her coat. "I'm going to make you something to eat, and then we gotta get ready to go over to the clinic."

"Another treatment? I hate getting treatments," Jo-Jo whined.

"I know, but you have to get them, so they'll make you feel better," Anette explained.

"They always make me feel like shit!" Jo-Jo cursed.

"You better watch that month," Jonas scolded her.

"Sorry, Jonas." She apologized.

"Now do like Anette says and do your homework so y'all ain't late for the clinic."

Jo-Jo looked like she wanted to argue with him but decided against it "Okay, I'm going." She went into the room she still shared with her sisters.

"I swear, you and Sweets are the only ones who can get that girl to do anything without her giving you lip." Anette shook her head. Now that Jo-Jo was getting older, she was picking up the unmistakable sassiness carried by all the Rafferty women.

"She's just at the age where she's feeling herself a little bit. Much like you and Yvette when you were 11," Jonas reminded her.

"Yvette, maybe, but I was an angel." Anette batted her eyes.

"Bullshit. You were a sour puss, and you know it," Jonas mushed her playfully. "Speaking of your twin, where is she?"

"Probably in the streets somewhere doing something she ain't got no business doing," Anette told him.

Jonas shook his head. While Anette was focused on school and making something of her life, Yvette was doing the exact opposite. All she did was run the streets and hang around people who were no good for her. On those rare occasions when she was home longer than just to change her clothes, she was usually high, drunk, or a combination of both. Jonas had heard rumblings about the kinds of things his big sister was into, and he didn't like it. He'd tried to check her about it a few times, but it would always end in the two of them arguing and her reminding him who the older sibling was. Short of him putting his hands on her, there was nothing he could do but pray she would get it together.

"How're Jo-Jo's treatments coming along?" Jonas changed the subject.

"Well, she ain't getting no worse. I guess that's a blessing," Anette sighed. "Every time we start to get a little hope, she takes another turn."

"Damn," Jonas was frustrated. The doctors had promised that Jo-Jo's cancer would start to go into remission, and for a while it had . . . until it came back. They had assured them that the last operation she had would be the final one, but they had said that about the operation before that one. "I feel like we're just sitting on our hands with this shit."

"We're all doing what we can with what we have to work with. Other than going outside of the Medicaid network, what else can we do? Try not to stress too bad over it."

"Easier said than done," Jonas replied. "I'm about to go see what's up with Mom."

"Wait. I got something to tell you first. I didn't want to bring it up in front of Ace and them. You know how they get," Anette said in a tone that Jonas didn't like.

"What's up? Somebody fucking with you?" Jonas asked. He had already proven he'd get busy for his sisters, but there was always someone who wanted to test the waters.

"Calm down; it's nothing like that." Anette already knew where his head was at. "I saw an old friend of yours today."

"Who? Cal? I already know he's home. I was just with him."

"Not, Cal . . . Alex is back in town," Anette informed him.

This bit of news surprised him. He hadn't seen her since her family had sent her down south after Doug's funeral. They'd exchanged some unkind words, and he never had a chance to make it right with her before her parents shipped her off. He had always regretted the way they left things.

"Where?" he asked.

"See, this is why I didn't want to tell you. I'm sure this isn't the first time she has been home and hasn't bothered to reach out to you, so she probably doesn't want to be bothered," Anette said. She had been afraid that Jonas hearing about Alex being home would stir old feelings in him. Her little brother had been devastated when Alex had gone away. She was his first crush.

"You bugging. I might not even get a chance to check on her. I got mad shit going on right now," Jonas said, as if tracking Alex down wasn't the first thing he planned on doing.

"Fine! I saw her coming out of her parents' building," Anette finally told him. "If she breaks your heart again, don't look for me to help you pick up the pieces this time."

"Whatever," he laughed it off. "Thanks for the tip."

"Thanks, my ass. If I'm going to be responsible for that girl turning your life inside out, then you're gonna have to pay me for my part," Anette told him.

"What you want? Cash?" Jonas reached in his pocket.

"Nah, let me get some weed. I know you're holding." Weed was one of the only vices Anette had. She said it helped her to focus when she was studying.

"I don't have anything on me, but I sent Tavion to the spot a few minutes ago. When I get back outside, I'll grab something for you," Jonas promised, and continued down the hall.

When Jonas arrived in the kitchen, he found his mother over the stove. She was flipping a pork chop while humming softly to herself. Her skin was clear, as were her eyes, and she had gained about twenty pounds. She was coming up on two years sober. Janette was doing much better, and the kids were all so very proud of her. Oddly enough, they had Eight-Ball to thank for it.

The gangster had really done a number on her. Besides raping her, he had beaten Janette up pretty bad. It took about a month to recover from the physical wounds, but emotional ones took even longer. She became withdrawn and skittish, seemingly afraid of her own shadow. She was especially distrustful of men. It was awhile before Jonas was even able to touch her in the smallest of ways without her trembling. The fact that Slick had gone missing didn't help. He was a piece of shit, but he was still *her* piece of shit. When he disappeared, it broke her heart. She blamed herself for him running off, and it was awhile before she was able to get over him.

The only good thing that came out of the whole situation was that Janette had finally decided to get some help for her drug problem. With some help from Fat Moe, they were able to get her into a treatment program. She'd had some relapses, but every time she fell off the horse, she would get right back on it. Eventually, it became easier. Janette still puffed weed from time to time and had the occasional glass of wine, but her days of shooting heroin were over.

"Hey, Ma." Jonas startled her.

"Boy, why don't you make any noise when you walk?" Janette scolded him.

"Sorry. I'm surprised to see you in here cooking. That's usually Sweets's job. Where is she?" Jonas asked.

"I don't know. I haven't seen her since this morning when she came to drop some cash off on me. She said she had some running around to do," Janette told him.

Seems like Sweets was doing a lot of running around lately. She was hardly home anymore since she and Drew had *officially* become an item. The sheepish young girl who had always spent her days in the house attending to her siblings was now going out to dinners at fancy restaurants and attending parties. Jonas was never really comfortable with Drew dating his sister. Not because he was a bad dude or mistreated his sister; in fact, Drew treated her like a princess. Jonas's problem with Drew was that he was a dog. He had other women on the side, but Sweets was wifey, and he made sure they all knew it.

"Let me get a cigarette." Janette wiped her hands on a dish towel. Jonas fished a Newport from his pack and handed it to her. She lit it and took a deep pull. "So, where you just coming from?" She gave him a suspicious look.

"Nowhere. I was out on the stoop talking to Ace," Jonas told her.

"That one there," Janette scoffed. "They should've kept his troublesome ass in jail."

"C'mon, Ma. You know we don't wish death or jail on anybody. How come you don't like any of my friends?"

"That's not true. I love that handsome Prince. Even Mula's little mischievous ass is all right with me. It's just Ace that rubs me the wrong way. Every time you get into something, he's always involved somehow."

"That's not true," Jonas disputed her.

"The hell it ain't! Need I remind you about that business with the boy who got hurt in the motel?"

"That's just one instance."

"Okay, so how about the thing with those boys last summer?" Janette folded her arms.

Jonas had almost forgotten about that. One day, he and Ace had been out on the stoop shooting the breeze when some guys from the Polo Grounds came around looking for Ace. At the time, Jonas didn't know what the beef was over, and it didn't matter to him. Outsiders had come to their neighborhood looking for trouble, and he happily gave it to them. When Jonas pulled his gun and started shooting, the boys took off running. Jonas would find out later that the whole thing had been over Ace sleeping with the girlfriend of one of the guys.

"I'm still amazed that the police never came and carted you off, especially since you were out there shooting that gun in front of the whole damn neighborhood."

Jonas shrugged. "I guess I got lucky."

"You seem to get lucky a lot. Just know that every streak comes to an end. That's a lesson you'll learn firsthand if you don't stop throwing stones at the penitentiary," Janette warned. She was about to say something else when she suddenly went into a fit of coughing. It was so violent that Jonas had to pat her back to clear her airways. She had been coughing a lot lately.

"That cough sounds like it's getting worse. Why don't you let me take you to the doctor?" he asked.

"It's nothing. I'm just getting over a cold, that's all," Janette said as if it were nothing.

Just then, Jonas felt a vibration in his pocket. He pulled out the two cell phones he kept on him at all times. One was one of those expensive smart phones, and the other was a cheaper model. Only one person had that number. He looked at the screen and saw that it was a text message with an address and a time. "Ma, I gotta go take care of something real quick."

"I got some pork chops on. You eating dinner here tonight?" Janette asked.

"I can't make any promises, but I'll try," he said honestly. It would be awhile before he had to tend to the business from the text message, but he wasn't sure how long he would be indisposed afterward.

"Okay, I'll give you a pass today, but tomorrow, I want us all to sit down as a family and have dinner," Janette told him. "Be sure and tell Yvette if you happen to come across her in your dealings."

"I got you, Ma."

"And, Jonas, you be careful out there. The streets ain't nothing nice," Janette warned.

"Neither am I," he winked and left.

When Jonas got back outside, Ace and Mula were gone, but Tavion was sitting on the stoop. He had almost forgotten that he sent the boy on a weed run. He wasn't alone, though. Jewels was with him. She was wearing a pair of tight blue jeans, a short leather jacket, and Tims, untied. Her long, black hair was pulled back into a pony-tail, showing off her pretty face. Jewels looked nothing like the tomboy he used to sneak into his room at night.

"What it do?" Jonas greeted Jewels.

"Whatever I tell it to," she replied, as was their custom. Time and communication had healed their fractured relationship.

"Damn, I thought you forgot about me," Tavion said.

"My fault. Do me a solid. Go up to my crib and give it to Anette," Jonas told him.

"How you gonna send me to the spot and not even let me smoke?" Tavion was disappointed.

"You sound like a real crackhead right now," Jonas teased him. "Here," he handed him another twenty. "Go grab yourself something. I gotta make a run."

"Well, give me a few minutes to drop the weed off, and I'll go with you," Tavion offered.

"Not this time, grasshopper. I'll come check you when I come back."

"A'ight, man." Tavion pouted and went into the build-ing.

"That boy follows you around like a lost puppy," Jewels joked.

"Tavion is a good kid. So, what's up with you?"

"Wondering why you stood me up this morning," Jewels replied.

"My fault. I had something to do that took a little longer than expected. I'll make it up to you," he promised.

"Damn right you will. You better not be out here letting none of these hood rats sample my product." Jewels grabbed his dick through his jeans.

"Stop playing." Jonas shoved her away playfully.

"Ain't nobody playing. I ain't got no problem putting something hot in one of these hoes," Jewels said seriously and flashed the small handgun that was tucked in her jacket pocket.

Jewels was crazy as hell, and that's what Jonas loved about her. For a while, things had been awkward between Jewels and him. He had been holding a grudge over her choosing to hang out with Ace over him that night but never said anything. Jewels had always just assumed that he was just like the rest of the guys and lost interest after he got what he wanted from her. The truth would come out one night at a house party they both ended up at.

Jonas had never been big on parties, but this night, Ace had convinced him to come out. Some girl Ace knew on 129th Street was hosting the party. It seemed like everyone from the neighborhood was there. Jonas had been in the corner nursing a drink when he saw Jewels walk in. He watched her work the room, receiving love from the homies and dirty looks from the girls. Jewels was very well respected in Harlem, especially since she had gotten into the robbery game. She had hooked in with a crew of bandits, and they were jacking everything in the hood that wasn't nailed down. Rumor had it that Jewels had even robbed one of Drew's workers, but it was never confirmed.

He had successfully managed to avoid Jewels for most of the night, but she cornered him in the bathroom. Jonas had dipped off to take a leak but made the mistake of not locking the door. He had just whipped his dick out to relieve himself when she slipped into the bathroom after him.

"What the fuck?" Jonas accidentally sprayed piss on the bathroom floor.

"It ain't nothing I haven't seen before," Jewels said playfully. Her eyes were red and glassy. She had been smoking and drinking all night.

"Can I get a little privacy?" Jonas asked with an attitude. He tried to push Jewels out of the bathroom, but she didn't budge.

"What is your problem lately? For the last few months, you've been avoiding me, and when we do see each other, you act like I did something to you."

"I'm good," Jonas lied. "You might wanna get out of here, though. I don't want Ace to catch us and get the wrong idea."

"Why would you think I give a fuck about what Ace thinks?" Jewels asked confused. And then it hit her. "Wait. You think I'm fucking Ace?"

"Ain't my business who you're fucking." Jonas tried to leave, but she blocked his exit.

"Jonas, I've only slept with two people in my life; the guy I lost my virginity to and you!"

"So, you're telling me that night I left you and Ace on the stoop y'all didn't do anything?" he pressed her.

"Yeah, got sky high! I can't believe you thought I would go out like that. I might be a lot of things, but I'm no whore!" Her eyes flashed hurt.

Jonas suddenly felt like a real asshole. That whole time he had hated Jewels for something she didn't even do. "I'm sorry. I just thought—"

"But you didn't ask!" Tears welled in her eyes. She tried to leave the bathroom, but Jonas grabbed her by the arm. "Get off me." She tried to jerk away, but he held fast.

"I'm sorry, Jewels. I'm really sorry." He hugged her to him.

"Of all people, I would never do you like that. I've been in love with you since we were kids," Jewels sobbed into his chest.

"I didn't know," he said sincerely.

"And that's my problem. Everybody seemed to know except you."

Jonas raised her head so that she was forced to look at him. There was so much pain behind her eyes that he felt it in his soul. That moment was like he was seeing Jewels for the first time, and she was the most beautiful girl in the world. He had no words to express what he was feeling, so he did what came naturally and kissed her. That night, in the bathroom, was the second time he and Jewels had sex. It was also the beginning of what would go on to become a very complicated relationship. They never put a label on it, but they had an understanding.

Jonas eventually accepted Jewels back into the crew. She proved to be quite the asset. Jewels was always down to bust a move, and she never much minded what it was, so long as it paid. Eventually, Jewels taught Jonas about diversifying his income and turned him on to the art of the jux. In turn, he showed Jewels her first dead body. They were a perfect match.

"So, you gonna come through and break me off later?" Jewels asked.

"Of course. I gotta go see somebody right quick," Jonas told her.

"Who? One of these little bitches who are always chasing you and Ace around?" she asked sarcastically.

"Nah, nothing like that. I gotta go see my guy," Jonas told her. It was only partially a lie. He did have to follow up with the text, but he had something else to do first.

"Oh." Jewels knew who he meant without him having to say. She was one of the few people he had ever confided in about his guardian angel. She'd even met him once, and he gave her the creeps. "You be careful, Jonas."

"You sound like my mother," he laughed.

"We both can't be wrong. But seriously, though, watch yourself. I don't trust white people as a rule, and I trust cops even less."

"Don't worry. I'm good," he assured her. "So, what you gonna do for the rest of the day?"

"I gotta go check on my uncle. He's in the hospital again," Jewels told him.

This surprised Jonas. "Is he okay?"

"Yeah, he was complaining about chest pains, so I took him to the emergency room last night. They decided to keep him. I keep telling that fool to watch all that grease and fried shit, but he doesn't listen."

"You know Fat Moe loves to eat. Send him my love and tell him I'll try to get over there to see him. Let me get out of here, so I'm not late. I'll call you when I'm back on the block." He planted a quick peck on her lips and left.

Chapter Twenty-three

Jonas felt like a stalker, sitting across the street from Alex's building. He had been there for nearly two hours.

He wasn't sure why he had decided to go against his sister's advice and came to seek Alex out. It had been years since they had seen or spoken to each other. She had written to him twice from Georgia. Nothing too heavy, just reaching out about where she was and how she was doing. She was clearly trying to open up a dialogue. Jonas never responded. It wasn't for lack of wanting to, but what was he supposed to say? Back then, he had been a kid with a lot of bottled up anger and resentment toward the world. He hadn't looked at it as her parents making her leave, only that she was gone. It wasn't until he was older and had a little more experience with the world that he would come to understand her parents had done the best thing for her by sending her away. He was proof that nothing good came out of their neighborhood.

Jonas was about to call the whole thing off and leave when he saw a car pull to a stop in front of Alex's building. The only reason he even paid any attention to it was because it looked so tacky. The car itself was nice, a pearl-white Lexus, but the gaudy rims the driver had fitted it with totally took away from the quality of the car. The driver had to either be from out of town or just watched too many rap videos.

He spotted Alex in the passenger's seat. It had been years since they had seen each other, but her face was still almost exactly the same. She now wore her hair in a short, natural cut. He had never seen her with short hair, but it looked good on her. He watched from his hiding place as the driver said something to her which made her giggle. Jonas's face immediately flushed. The sight of her with another guy still made him jealous. Maybe Anette had been right, and he should have left it alone. He continued to watch as Alex and the dude behind the wheel exchanged a few last words. When she leaned in, Jonas braced himself to see her kiss him and hoped that he could keep himself from throwing up. Much to his relief, she just hugged him and got out. The driver waited until she had made it safely in the building before pulling off. This was when Jonas made his move.

He hustled across the street, nearly getting hit by a car. Alex was just getting on to the elevator when he entered the lobby. "Hold that!" he called out. The door was closing when he threw his hand out to stop it.

When the elevator door slid open, and their eyes met, time stood still. Alex's face was the same, but the rest of her had changed considerably. Her ironing board flat body had sprouted curves, concentrating on her hips and ass. Looking at her, Jonas finally understood the expression Coke-bottle figure. It was a moment straight out of a movie, even with violins playing in the back of his mind.

"Jonas?" Alex broke the heavy silence.

Jonas studied her, pretending he was trying to place her face and hadn't been stalking her. "Is that Alex? Oh, shit! I didn't expect to bump into you."

"I could say the same." Alex looked at him as if she could see through the lie. "What are you doing in this neighborhood?"

"I got a friend that lives in the building," he lied. "What's up? Give me some love." He spread his arms.

Alex hesitated but only for a moment before walking into his embrace. He smelled of weed and cigarettes, but it felt good for her to be in familiar arms. "Wow, little Jonas Rafferty . . . Well, you ain't so little anymore," she admired him.

"I'm not the only one who's grown up." Jonas gave her the once-over. "That country cooking has been good to you."

"Stop. I'm already self-conscious about the weight I've put on," she blushed.

"Nah, it suits you. So, you back home for good or just the summer?" he asked.

"Just the summer. It's been awhile since I've been back to the old neighborhood."

"You don't come visit your people?" Jonas asked, remembering what Anette had said about her coming home before and not bothering to reach out.

"I've only been here once . . . maybe twice since I moved. Mostly, my folks come down to visit me. They act like they don't want me in the city since . . . what happened," Alex told him. For a minute, there was sadness in her eyes, as if she remembered her brother, but it quickly passed. "So, what have you been up to?"

Jonas shrugged. "Nothing, just trying to stay out of the way."

"I hope you're staying out of trouble in the process."

"I'm a Boy Scout." Jonas raised his hand in mock salute.

"Tell me anything," Alex laughed. "You're developing quite the reputation, Wrath," she said knowingly.

"How did you—" he began.

"My parents," Alex cut him off. "They keep me abreast of current events."

"Didn't realize they still kept tabs," Jonas said, feeling a bit ashamed. Before the incident with Black, the Hightowers had always seen him as the good one of the crew. He could only imagine what they thought of him now.

"Just because you aren't one of my parents' favorite people doesn't mean they're not concerned about you . . . all of you guys. They've watched you grow from kids to what you are now."

The statement hadn't been an accusation or judgment, but it felt like both.

"And what am I?" Jonas asked her, for lack of a better response.

Alex studied his face. At a glance, Jonas was the same kid she used to hang around with and pretend she didn't have the biggest crush on, but there was something different about him. There was a hardness around his eyes that hadn't been there when she had last seen him. "Time changes people. Some of us, it makes better, and others worse. I should hope it has made you better."

"Let's just say I'm a work in progress." He tried to laugh off what she had just laid on him.

The elevator door opened up, and two people got on. It was then that they realized that neither of them had pressed a floor and they were still in the lobby. "Damn, look at us," he chuckled when he realized the blunder.

"You always were easily distracted," Alex teased him. "What floor?" her finger lingered over the buttons.

"Huh?"

"What floor does your friend live on? I don't want to hold you up."

Jonas had completely forgotten his lie, but he recovered quickly. "They can wait."

Jonas and Alex played opposite sides of the elevator as the car went through the floors, dropping off the passengers who had boarded in the lobby. There were no words exchanged, but their eyes silently told a story of longing and regret. The elevator finally reached Alex's floor.

"This is my stop," she told him but hadn't moved for the door.

"I know."

More awkward silence.

"Ah, I guess I'll see you around." Alex made to step off the elevator, and Jonas finally made his move.

He blocked her exit with his arm, holding the door from closing with his back. "Can I see you again? You know . . . not just around? Maybe take you to dinner?"

"I don't know if that's such a good idea," she told him.

"Why not?" Jonas wanted to know.

"Because I get the feeling our lives are going in two different directions," she said frankly.

"I can't tell you where my life is going, but I can help you understand where it's at," Jonas shot back. "Look, I didn't come here with any expectations. I just wanted to see how you were doing."

"Thought you were visiting a friend?" she pointed out his slip.

"Forget it." Jonas moved for her to exit, but she continued standing there.

"You always take the first 'no' for an answer?" Alex questioned.

"I'm not good at begging."

"I'm not asking you to beg. I'm asking you to show me that I'm not making a bad decision by opening a box that's probably best left closed," she said seriously.

"And what's that supposed to mean?"

"It means that I'm focused right now and don't have time to entertain anything that isn't going anywhere."

"And where is this supposed to be going?" Jonas asked.

"I don't know, but I should hope it's beyond a project elevator," Alex smiled.

"You got jokes?"

"Always."

"So, you gonna let me take you out?" Jonas revisited his invitation.

"I don't know yet. I still have to see how much of you is Jonas and how much is Wrath."

"I'm still me," he insisted.

"We'll see. Do you know the assisted living facility on the East Side?"

"No, but I can find it," he said confidently.

"Good. Meet me there tomorrow. I've been volunteering there three days a week while I'm home on break. We're having a friends and family lunch for the residents tomorrow."

"You want me to meet you at your job? Why can't we just go get something to eat?" This wasn't turning out how Jonas had expected.

"Because I still don't know where your head is at. It's been a long time, Jonas, and I don't know if I'm ready to be wined and dined. No pressure, though. If you show up, I'll know you're serious. If you don't, it was good seeing you again. Either way, we're cool." She watched him to see how he would respond.

"I'll be there," Jonas finally agreed. For years, he had been romanticizing about what could have been between them, and he wasn't about to let her slip away again before finding out for sure. He could stand a couple of hours around a bunch of cripples if it meant reigniting the spark between Alex and him.

"Great, and wear something you don't mind ruining," she told him and went inside her apartment.

What did she mean by that?

Chapter Twenty-four

Jonas was walking on air when he came out of Alex's building. The meeting between the two of them had gone far better than he had expected. Alex was giving him a hard time, but the fact that she had even agreed to the meeting said that she was at least open to the idea of them being friends again. If Jonas had it his way, they would be more than friends. All he needed was for her to open the door, and he would do the rest.

He puffed casually on his cigarette, thinking as he strode down the block. He was so deep in his own head that he didn't initially notice the BMW creeping alongside him as he walked down Eighth Avenue. The windows were heavily tinted, and there was no way to tell who was inside. Jonas finally registered it when he stopped at a light to cross the street. Instinctively, his hand slid to where his pistol was tucked. When the light changed, he crossed the street but made sure to keep one eye on the BMW. When the window started to roll down, he drew his gun but kept it behind his back. To his surprise, he knew the driver.

"Sweets?" Jonas put his gun back into its hiding place.

"What's up, baby bro?" Sweets greeted him from behind the wheel. Large Gucci shades covered her eyes, and the diamond studs in her ears twinkled in the afternoon sun.

Jonas approached the car and leaned into the passenger-side window. "Girl, you almost got blasted rolling up on me like that."

"Boy, please." Sweets waved him off. "What are you doing in this neighborhood?"

"Nothing. I was checking up on this chick," Jonas lied. There was no way in the hell he was going to tell her that he had just come from seeing Alex.

"You ain't got no friends in this neighborhood," she replied. There was no mistaking what she meant. After hearing how her little brother had been treated at Doug's funeral, the Hightowers ceased to be any friends of hers. "Where you headed?"

"I gotta shoot downtown to see somebody on 110th," Jonas told her, checking out his sister's ensemble. As usual, she was dressed to the nines in designer wear. That day, it was Louis Vuitton, a nice leather skirt with a matching jacket. Beneath, she wore a shirt that was sheer at the top, just showing off a bit of cleavage. Not too much; just enough to let you know that she was stacked. Since she had lost her baby fat, she became more daring with how she dressed. She never crossed the line, like Yvette did, but she had no problem showing off what God had blessed her with.

"I'm going that way too. Jump in. I'll give you a ride," she offered. Jonas opened the door and made to get in, but she stopped him. "Now you know you ain't getting up in this ride puffing that cancer stick."

"C'mon, Sweets. I'll smoke it out the window."

"No, you'll toss it or walk," she told him.

"Fine." Jonas plucked out the cigarette and got in.

"I don't know why y'all smoke. It's a disgusting habit," Sweets started in.

"Cigarettes keep me calm."

"That's the lie you tell yourself. Those damn things are going to kill you one of these days."

"Cigarettes are the last thing I have to worry about dying from," he joked.

"I'm glad you think your health is a joke. You need to quit, for real, Jonas."

"Okay, I'll try, Sweets," he promised. Jonas took a minute to admire the interior of the car. It was totally tricked out: plush leather seats, sound system, GPS, and wood paneling. It smelled brand-new. "This yours?" he changed the subject.

"No, it's Drew's. I just dropped him off at the Metro North Station. He had to go out of town until tomorrow."

"Your boyfriend is doing big things these days, huh?" Jonas asked. Since Eight-Ball had gotten knocked off, Drew was now running the neighborhood.

"A little something-something," she smiled.

"Well, you make sure you're careful riding around in this car. This Beamer will attract a lot of attention," Jonas warned. He noticed the heads that were turning on every block they passed.

"You know this isn't my style. I'm going to park it in the garage when I drop you off," she told him. "I heard your boy Cal is home," she changed the subject.

"Damn, news travels fast in the hood, huh?"

"You know I keep my ear to the streets." She winked at him from behind her shades. "So, are you happy he's home?"

"Honestly? I don't know yet."

His response took Sweets by surprise. "That's funny. Back in the day, you, him, and Ace were inseparable. I thought you and Cal were friends?"

"We were. I mean we are . . . Aw, man, I don't know what I mean. It just doesn't feel right," he told her.

"How do you mean?"

"Who gets locked up for a murder and comes home in less than five years?" Jonas asked.

"Wow. That does sound suspect. Anybody check his paperwork?"

"Don't you have to be a lawyer to do that?"

"Not at all. It's just a matter of going down to the county clerk's office and filling out the right paperwork. Drew put me up on it. If you want, I can go down there and see what I can find out," she offered.

"No, I don't want you to get wrapped up in this. If the boy ain't who he claims to be, I don't want you anywhere near the situation," he said. He had known Cal since they were kids, but if he was up to no good, then he was as good as dead.

"Let me know if you change your mind. You know I'm ten toes down when it comes to fam," Sweets capped.

Jonas laughed. "I don't think I'll ever get used to hearing you talk like that. You used to be all quiet and shy, and now look at you . . . talking in Ebonics and dripping in jewels. The caterpillar done turned into a butterfly."

"I'm not the only one who's changed." She nodded toward the imprint of the gun under his shirt. "You're making quite the name for yourself out here."

"What you talking about, Sweets?" Jonas faked ignorance.

"I told you, I keep my ear to the streets. They're out here telling stories about you like you're some kind of boogeyman."

"Niggas is just talking. Don't go believing everything you hear." Jonas downplayed it.

"I believe none of what I hear and half of what I see. You don't think I know you're out here playing grown-up games, selling drugs and shit."

Drugs I buy from your boyfriend, he wanted to say, but instead, he just let Sweets keep talking.

"I never wanted this life for you, Jonas, but you're in it nonetheless. You're too old for me to tell you what to do anymore, but I still love you and want you to be safe. These people are afraid of you out here."

"I'd rather be feared than loved," Jonas said slyly.

"A scared person will kill you the quickest, smart-ass. But seriously, Jonas. I know you've got this big bad reputation going for yourself, but it hasn't stopped me from worrying about you. The rules of the game are changing, and these younger guys don't value human life. Just earlier, I heard about a guy around your age getting killed in front of Popeyes. Happened in broad daylight."

"Wow, that's terrible!" Jonas tried his best to keep a straight face. She had no idea that he had been the shooter.

"So, you can understand why I worry about you. I'm not stupid enough to think if I tell you to stop hustling that you'll actually listen. I just hope you're moving smart."

"I am," he assured her.

They continued driving for a time but quietly, each in their own thoughts. Sweets's cell phone, which was resting in the center console, vibrated to let her know she had a message. She waited until they were stopped at a red light to check it. She frowned, typed a quick response, and tossed it back down. She was clearly annoyed at whatever she had seen but did her best not to show it.

"You good?" Jonas asked, noticing her mood had shifted a bit.

"I'm always good," Sweets said and pulled through the light, which had just turned green.

It was at that moment that Jonas had a revelation about his sister. This wasn't the same chubby girl who wore hand-me-down clothes from the church and bribed her siblings with candy to get them to behave. There was an *edge* to her, for lack of a better word. After all the years she had spent putting the needs of everyone else before her own, she was finally putting herself first. Sweets was finally coming into her own. The wallflower was blossoming.

"Why're you looking at me like that?" Sweets caught him staring.

"No reason," he told her. He was silent for a beat. "Sweets, can I ask you something?"

"Sure."

"Are you happy? I mean with Drew?"

Sweets thought about the question. "Drew is a good man."

"That's not what I asked. Does he make you happy?"

"I wouldn't be with him if he didn't. Drew treats me well and takes care of me."

"With drug money. You were always the first one to say you'd never let a man feed you with dirty money," Jonas reminded her.

"Times get hard enough, and you start to realize the money doesn't know where it comes from or cares where it's going." Sweets told him. "I don't agree with his lifestyle, but I've come to accept it. Some people are just destined to play the hand that life deals them. Sure, it's blood money, but that blood money is going to pay my tuition. I've decided to go back to college."

This was news to Jonas. Sweets had done a year at Rutgers, and then never went back. She claimed the commute from Harlem to New Jersey every day was too much, but Jonas thought it was a bullshit excuse. She had become more interested in chasing Drew than graduating.

"I'm proud of you, Sweets!"

"Thanks, baby brother. You're the only one I've told so far. I'll tell Mom and the girls when the time is right."

"How about tomorrow night? Mom is cooking, and she wants all of us to be there," Jonas told her.

"Drew is coming back tomorrow, and I have to pick him up."

"C'mon, Sweets. He can take a taxi. Come have dinner with us and tell Mama the good news."

"I'll make a deal with you. I'll be there if *you* will."
Sweets extended her hand.

"That's a bet." Jonas shook it.

Sweets pulled up in front of St. Luke's Hospital on
114th. "I've got an appointment to keep, and I don't want
to be late. You don't mind walking the rest of the way, do
you?"

"Nah, that's cool," Jonas said. He was actually glad
that Sweets was dropping him off a few blocks away. He
confided a lot in Sweets but didn't want her too deep in
his business. "You okay?"

"I'm fine. Just need to get a quick checkup. I haven't
been feeling well lately," Sweets told him.

"I could hang out and wait if you need me to," Jonas
offered. There was something about the look in her eyes
as she stared at the hospital that gave him pause.

"No, I'm okay. You go do what you gotta do, and I'll see
you tomorrow for dinner."

"Okay, but if you change your mind and need me to sit
with you, just hit my phone." Jonas slid out of the car.

"I love you, Jonas," Sweets called out the window
before pulling off.

Jonas continued to stand there for a few minutes,
watching the taillights of the BMW blend in with traffic.
It wasn't unusual for Sweets to say that she loved him,
but there was something about the way she said it. It felt
so . . . final.

Chapter Twenty-five

When Jonas arrived at the address where he was directed to come in the text message, he had to double-check it to make sure he was in the right place. Sure enough, 1047 Amsterdam Avenue. Why he was told that they would meet at St. John the Divine Church was beyond Jonas, but he had learned a long time ago not to ask unnecessary questions.

On the steps of the church sat a homeless man. He was huddled within the folds of a tattered blanket. It had so many holes in it that it probably did little to fight off the chill at night. As Jonas drew closer, the beggar began shaking his cup of loose change. "Spare a few coins for a veteran?" he asked in an accent that marked him as a southerner.

Jonas was about to tell him to fuck off and keep walking, but he suddenly had a change of heart. He fished a five-dollar bill from the cash in his pocket and dropped it into the cup.

The man peered into the cup. When he saw the bill's denomination, he looked up and smiled at Jonas. Jonas was only able to catch a glimpse of his face in the shadows of the blanket, but he could see a black hole where his left eye once rested. "Appreciate it, young blood. This city ain't got a lot of love for those of us who are down on their luck."

"Then maybe you should go back to wherever you're from," Jonas suggested.

"I go where I'm needed and stay where I'm wanted," the homeless man replied. "Hopefully, one day, I'll find myself in the position to do you a good turn."

"I doubt it. Don't smoke that up, old head," Jonas capped and proceeded inside the church.

When Jonas crossed the threshold, a strange sensation washed over him. It was hard to describe, but it felt wrong. It was like he wasn't welcome, and the feeling was mutual. After all he had been through in his young life, he reasoned that God had no use for him, and he had no use for God.

There was hardly anyone in the church at that hour of the day, on a weekday, so Detective Ceaver wasn't hard to spot. He was down at the front, near the altar, on his knees with his head bowed and his hands clasped in front of him. Was he praying? Jonas had never taken the detective for the religious type, but over his years of dealing with him, he had learned that he was full of surprises. Jonas made his way down the aisle and sat on one of the benches in the front while he waited for him to finish.

"I was raised in the house of God. Have I ever told you that?" Detective Ceaver asked over his shoulder. Jonas didn't even realize he knew he was there.

"No," Jonas said.

"Sure was." The detective rose and took a seat on the bench next to Jonas. "When my father would minister the Word, I was the faithful son right there at his side. My father was my hero. I took everything he said as the gospel—until I realized that it was all bullshit. There's nothing more hurtful for a son than to find out that his father wasn't who he thought him to be."

"I know a thing or two about that," Jonas said, thinking of his father and the conflicting stories about how he died.

"Of course, you do," Detective Ceaver nodded in agreement. "So, how's my little avenging angel doing today?"

Jonas shrugged. "I can't complain. If I did, who would listen?"

"I would. You can always come to me if you have a problem. It doesn't matter how big or small. Never forget that."

Jonas nodded.

"Enough about all the sentimental shit. On to business. I spoke to my guys a few days ago at the lawyer's office. All the paperwork is done. The only thing left to do is have your friend go down to the office and sign off. Before we do all that, I need to ask . . . Are you sure you can trust her?"

Jonas shrugged. "I don't trust anyone, but she'll do what needs to be done."

Ceaver nodded. "I just wanted to make sure you're certain. This is a big step for you."

"Can't play street corner games forever. I need to boss up." He repeated Prince's words.

"And boss up you shall, my young friend. That's one of the reasons I've called you here. I know you've had a busy day, so I won't keep you long," Detective Ceaver said with a hint of a smirk. "I have a problem that I need a little help with it."

"Tell me what you need, and it's done," Jonas said without hesitation. The detective had helped him out of more than a few jams. He owed him.

"That's why I like you, Wrath. You understand the importance of loyalty and are always willing to help a friend in need. You're a good soldier, but you'll be a better general when your time comes. Anyhow, a few years ago, I helped out another wayward soul. Much like you, I took him out of the gutter and put him on the path to greatness. He's been doing quite well for himself over the last few years, and I'm afraid it's starting to go to his head. I need him humbled . . . for good."

This was unexpected. Since the night they met when
Jonas had stabbed Eight-Ball, Ceaver had never asked
him to murder anyone. At least not outright. Jonas
had blasted a few people in the line of handling the
detective's business, but that was collateral damage. This
was a request.

"Wrath?" Detective Ceaver was waiting for an answer.

"I got you. Just give me his résumé, and he's gone."

"That's the type of enthusiasm I like in my guys."
Detective Ceaver clapped his hands gleefully. "Now, let
me be up front with you. This guy is no pushover. He's
got no problem with killing, and neither do the guys he
surrounds himself with."

"I'll get Ace to handle it with me."

"No, not him. I know he's your friend, but I don't trust
Ace. There's something about the set of his eyes that
I don't like," Detective Ceaver said. "Not Mula either.
Besides, they're all too close to this."

"And what's that supposed to mean?" Jonas asked.

"We'll get to that," the detective assured him. "This is
a sensitive matter, and one that I'm sure you'll find well
worth your time and trouble."

"How much?"

Detective Ceaver chuckled. "You always with the
money. One thing that you should've learned from all
the time you've spent around me is that some things are
more valuable than cash."

"Like what?"

"Revenge," the detective said. "Not that money isn't
always a factor. I happen to have it on good authority that
at the time of his untimely demise, he'll just happen to
be sitting on a good amount of cash and probably drugs.
All you find . . . all you keep, same as usual. This includes
all territories previously promised to your victim. He has
command over three buildings which he runs drugs out

of. That added to your already-growing territories will make you quite the power player. I want you to not only take him out but erase all memory of him. Anyone who happens to be there goes along for the ride too."

"This guy must've really pissed you off." Jonas had never seen the detective quite so animate about getting rid of someone.

"My beef with him is over money. Yours is over blood," Detective Ceaver told him.

"You lost me," Jonas said.

"Wrath, what would you say if I told you that doing this for me could kill two birds with one bullet? That by killing this man, you can not only send a message on my behalf but also settle an old score?"

"I'd say, give me a name."

The detective smiled. Wrath's reaction had been no less than what he had expected. "His mother named him Robert, but on the streets, he's known as Flair."

Chapter Twenty-six

Jonas left St. John's Church with quite a bit to think about. In the years since Doug was gone, they had never known who his killer was. Mula had dispatched Brian before they could pry the secret loose. They had to charge it to the game, but it had never sat well with Jonas. That was the one name he had always wanted to add to his list of corpses. Thanks to the detective, he finally could.

It was ironic in a way, the timing of it all. The same day Jonas got back in touch with Alex, the name of her brother's killer had suddenly fallen into his lap. It had to have been the universe sending Jonas a sign that he was moving in the right direction.

When Jonas got back to the hood, the first thing he did was check in at the trap house. It was an apartment inside of a building on 138th and Eighth. That was the strip Drew gave them to hustle on when they started. Since then, they had claimed six other blocks as their own, but 138th was their hub. Everything they did flowed through that apartment.

Jonas climbed the stairs to the third floor and knocked on the door of the trap house in a coded pattern. A few minutes later, the locks on the other side came undone. A smoker, Paula, opened the door. The apartment belonged to her. She was in her early thirties but looked closer to forty. She was wearing a floral housecoat and slippers. Erect nipples poked through the fabric. Though she was an addict, Paula still had a nice body. A few of the homies had smashed, but Jonas never did.

"Sup, Wrath?" Paula greeted him with a yellow-toothed smile.

"Chilling. Who all up in there?" he asked.

"The usual suspects. Everybody in the living room."

Jonas brushed past her and walked down the hall toward the living room. Under his feet the floor was sticky, so it made a funny noise when he walked. He could smell the heavy stench of weed coming from the living room. When he bent the corner, he frowned. At least half a dozen people were hanging out, smoking, and drinking beer. Jonas didn't like anybody in the spot who wasn't serving a purpose. Too much traffic would make the spot hot. If they lost Paula's crib, they wouldn't have anywhere else to conduct their business.

Mula and Tavion sat at the table, stuffing baggies with crack rocks. Jonas took a mental assessment of the drugs on the table and reasoned they would have to re-up soon, which was a good thing. Business had started picking up, but it still wasn't enough to mark them as anything other than small-time hustlers. Hopefully, when he took care of Flair for the detective, things would change.

Ace sat in an armchair near the window. A fat blunt dangled between his lips and a beer was clutched in his mitt. On his lap was a young girl that Jonas had seen around the neighborhood. He knew that Ace had been trying to fuck her for a while, and from the way she was smiling, it probably wouldn't be too much longer before he got into her pants. It seemed like all Ace did was smoke weed and chase pussy.

When Jonas's eyes drifted to the couch, his mood darkened. Two girls sat there; one was rolling up weed, while the other was pouring Hennessey into a plastic cup. The girl pouring the liquor was Stacey. She was brown-skinned and a bit on the chubby side, with hair that she always wore in a tight bun atop her head. With her pink glasses resting on the bridge of her thick nose, she had a bookish look about her. She was Paula's niece. She used to come by after school and help them bag up drugs for extra money, but when Jonas peeped how smart she was, he realized her talents were being wasted. She was now a part of upper management. Stacey kept the books and handled whatever clerical tasks Jonas had needed. It had been her idea to always set aside a small part of their monthly income in a reserve in case the boys needed lawyers or bail money. She was almost as valuable to Jonas as Ace was, sometimes more.

The other girl Jonas hadn't ever recalled seeing in the spot. She was light-skinned, wearing a too-tight dress, and a face full of makeup. Her eyes had been locked on Jonas since he walked in the house.

Sandwiched between the two girls, and looking like he was having the time of his life, was Cal. Jonas had specifically told Ace to keep him at a distance, but here he was smack in the middle of their operation, taking it all in. It was officially time for Jonas and Ace to have a serious conversation about protocols.

"What's good, Wrath?" Ace greeted him.

"You tell me," Jonas said sharply, looking from Ace to Cal.

"Ain't nothing. We in here getting to this money," Ace said coolly.

"Look like y'all in here partying to me. What I tell you about having a hundred niggas in the spot?"

"Man, calm your paranoid ass down. Everybody here is solid. I got this shit under control," Ace replied like it wasn't a big deal. He didn't like the fact that Jonas had checked him in front of people.

"Sometime I wonder," Jonas mumbled.

"What's up, Wrath? You too big to speak now?" the girl with the face full of makeup got his attention.

Jonas was trying to figure out why she was speaking to him, but when he studied her face, he realized that they had met before. It was the girl who had come to the house the day Yvette and his mom had gotten into it, Shauna. "Oh, what's good? Been a minute."

"Yeah, last time I saw you, you were a little kid. You ain't so little anymore," Shauna said, openly eyeing him. He returned her gaze.

"What's up, Wrath? No love for your boy," Cal announced himself as if Jonas hadn't seen him sitting there.

"What's good?" Jonas replied dryly. "I see you've made yourself at home."

"Yeah, Ace invited me up to enjoy some friendly hospitality." Cal draped his arm around Shauna, marking his territory. "Y'all got a nice little setup going. Real nice. I was telling Ace that I got a homeboy who's getting a lot of money down in Richmond. The shit y'all are selling for twenty goes for fifty out there. I thought maybe y'all can do something together. It's nothing for me to set up a meeting."

"Fo'sho," Jonas said. He had no intentions on doing business with anybody Cal brought to the table.

"You want me to pour you a drink, Wrath?" Stacey offered.

"No, thanks. I ain't staying long. I got somewhere to be," he told her.

"My man, Wrath. Always on the move," Ace said sarcastically.

"Let me holla at you for a second, Ace." Jonas started toward the bedroom without waiting to see if he was following.

Ace purposely waited for a few beats before sliding the girl off his lap and getting up. "I'll be back," he told his company.

In the bedroom, Paula was sitting on the edge of the bed. She had a small glass tube, stuffed with crack, to her lips. She was about to fire it up when Jonas walked in.

"Give us the room for a sec, Paula," he told her.

"Sure thing, Wrath." She tucked the tube into the pocket of her housecoat and left the room.

"So, what's so important that you dragged me away from the little party we got going on?" Ace asked.

"That's just it. You're in here partying when you're supposed to be handling business. You know better than that, Ace," Jonas scolded him.

"I told you, everybody is solid." Ace sucked his teeth.

"Nigga, besides Mula and Tavion, you can't vouch for nobody else in that room! Ace, we gotta move smarter than this, man. All it takes is somebody chatting about what they've seen in this apartment, and either the police or the stickup boys are gonna kick this door in. I ain't trying to fuck my shit up over a good time."

"Don't you mean *our* shit?" Ace questioned. "I know you're the one who got the ball rolling, Wrath, but sometimes you act like we didn't build this shit together. It's like we're your workers instead of your crew."

"It ain't like that, Ace. You know I'd never put myself above the team, but somebody has to be the voice of reason around here. I got something lined up that could potentially take us to the next level, but I gotta know that the people around me are ready to take that step."

"You know I'm ten toes down for whatever, whenever. All you gotta do is tell me what the play is," Ace said.

Jonas considered telling him about the conversation he'd had with the detective, about him finding out the name of Doug's killer. Ace had just as much a right to the man's blood as Jonas, if not more. Doug had been the one to put Ace on his feet. Had he not blessed Ace with the weed connect, maybe none of them would have gotten into the game. Or worse, they could all be working for Drew on the block. Jonas decided it would be a bad idea. It wasn't that he didn't trust Ace. Ace was a pain in the ass, but he was still the closest thing Jonas had to a brother. He just didn't want to run the risk of it getting back to Ceaver that he had talked. The detective seemed to know everything. "I'll fill you in later. Right now, I need you to get all of these people out of the spot. Especially Cal."

"Why you going so hard with this Cal business? He just came home from a bid, and he's already trying to put food on our table. I think we should look into his people in Richmond."

"And I think you're speeding," Jonas shot back. "Where the fuck we know these niggas from? Shit, we don't even know how well we know Cal just yet. Let's not jump the gun and fuck ourselves up."

"But this is Cal, not some stranger. He's one of ours, and we look out for our own," Ace reminded him.

"I hear you, Ace, and I'm not disagreeing with you. All I'm saying is slow down," Jonas cautioned. "Look, if you wanna put Cal on, I ain't gonna stop you. Give him a package . . . Hell, give him a whole block if you want to; just be mindful you don't feed him too much too soon."

"I'm telling you, Cal is solid," Ace insisted.

"You willing to stake your life on it?"

There was a brief pause before he answered. "Yeah."

"Good, because you just did."

Chapter Twenty-seven

After Jonas left the trap house, he headed home. He was dead tired and wanted nothing more than to lie down and catch a quick nap, but he still had things to do. The first would be to shower and then change his clothes. He stank of gunpowder, drugs, and cigarettes.

The sun had gone down, which was a good thing. It would be a lot easier for him to slip in and out of his building undetected under the cover of night. This would make it harder for Jewels to spot him. He had been ducking her since earlier that day. She had been blowing his phone up, but Jonas had chosen not to answer. He didn't know what to say to her. Seeing Alex had stirred old feelings Jonas thought long dead, and he was still trying to sort them out. Jewels had been his right hand and lover for years. She was loyal, street smart, and fine as hell, but she wasn't Alex. It wasn't that he loved her any less; he just loved her in a different way.

Jonas managed to slip into his building without bumping into Jewels, which was a blessing. He felt like a crab for ducking her, but it was what it was. He would deal with Jewels in his own time. He had bigger problems that needed his attention. This would become more apparent when he walked into his apartment. He found his mother and his sister Anette sitting in the living room, watching TV and eating ice cream. "Hey, y'all," Jonas greeted them.

"Hi, baby," Janette greeted him. Anette just nodded. They both looked exhausted.

"You seen Jewels? She came by here looking for you twice," Anette told him.

"I'll catch up with her," Jonas said. Jewels was the last thing on his mind at that moment. "Where's Jo-Jo?" he asked, noticing that his baby sister was missing. The two things she loved most were television and ice cream, so for her to be skipping out on both was strange.

"She's lying down. Wasn't feeling too hot this evening," Anette told him.

"The chemo?" Jonas asked. He knew how much of a toll the treatments took on his sister. Sometimes, she'd be fine for a day or so after getting treatment, and then she would slip into a lethargic state that made it hard for her to do anything other than lie in bed.

"I swear, it's hard to watch my baby suffer like this," Janette said.

"I know, Ma, but the treatments are for her own good. They're the only thing that's going to make her better," he said.

"So they say," Anette cut in. "You know they make more money off the treatment than they do the actual cure. People with money don't have to go through all this shit."

"Well, we don't have no money, so ain't much we can do except endure and put our faith in God," Janette said sadly.

"We've been waiting on God for years, and he ain't came through for us yet," Jonas capped.

"Don't be talking like that, Jonas. We need to keep the faith, all of us," Janette insisted.

"Whatever. I'm going to check on Jo-Jo," Jonas said and headed toward the back. He wished he had as much faith as his mom did, but he had suffered through too much to believe in miracles.

He tapped on the door before letting himself in. Jo-Jo was nestled in her bed, watching cartoons on the nineteen-inch television that sat atop the tall dresser. She looked paler than usual in the light of the television. The few strands of hair that hadn't fallen out due to the treatment hung from beneath the scarf wrapped around her head. Her glassy eyes turned to Jonas, and she mustered a weak smile.

"Hi, Jonas."

"How's my special girl?" Jonas sat on the edge of the bed and kissed her on the forehead. "I got something for you." He pulled a Snicker bar from his pocket. They were Jo-Jo's favorite.

"Thanks, I'll eat it later," she told him. She never turned down chocolate . . . ever.

"Okay, well, I'll leave you alone and let you rest." Jonas got up and made to leave when her small voice stopped him.

"Am I going to die?"

The question gripped Jonas around the heart and squeezed. "No, of course not. You're going to be fine, Jo-Jo."

"You don't have to lie to me, Jonas. I'm not a baby anymore," she said. She was trying to be strong.

Jonas went and knelt beside the bed. He took her small hands in his and noticed that they were cold. "Josette, you're going to be fine."

"Sometimes it hurts so much that I think death might be better," Jo-Jo admitted. "Death wouldn't be so bad. I'd get to see Daddy again, and the pain would be gone."

"You hush that dying talk, you hear me? You are going to be fine. Your big brother is going to make sure that you beat this thing, Jo-Jo. You just gotta trust me. Do you trust me?"

"Yes, I trust you, Jonas."

"Good, then you just keep fighting, and everything is going to be okay." He kissed her on the cheek.

He had barely made it out of the room before the tears started falling. He hated seeing his little sister in such agony and being powerless to do anything about it. His mom and Sweets had faith that God would come through and perform some miracle, but Jonas did not. He had been waiting for God to show up his entire life, and he had yet to show his face. If Jo-Jo was going to get the help she needed, it would be up to him to make it happen.

Jonas never made it back outside that night. He was so drained, emotionally and physically, that after he took a shower, he ended up lying across his bed and passing out. He had never been a sound sleeper. That night was more fitful than most. Dreams of death plagued him.

In one dream, he was standing trial for murder. The courtroom was full of people he knew from the neighborhood: Ace, Prince, Mula, and Fat Moe. Even Doug was there to bear witness. Doug was still wearing the gray suit he had been buried in.

Presiding over the trial was Detective Louis Ceaver. A long, black robe had replaced his usual leather and denim, and a colonial-style wig covered his spiked blond hair. He invited the prosecutor, Juan, to call his first witness. A woman took the stand, dressed in silk pajamas like she had been pulled out of bed to give her testimony. She was quite attractive, save for the leaking bullet wound at her temple.

The jury, which was comprised of his mother and all his sisters, watched Jonas with accusatory eyes while the victim of the crime sat on the stand recounting the details of how she had been added to Wrath's list of kills. Jonas had never seen her a day in his life; yet, here was this woman trying to convince a jury of his family that he had been the one responsible for her murder.

There was no need for deliberation. The guilty verdict was instant. In the eyes of the Rafferty women, he was indeed the monster the victim on the stand had painted him out to be. The verdict came swiftly, and the sentence just as swiftly.

"For your crimes, I sentence you to a life of doing what you do best," Detective Ceaver said with a maniacal laugh.

A scythe appeared in Jonas's hands. It was a sinister-looking tool with a long, black shaft and a curved blade that shone so brightly that Jonas almost couldn't look at it. Before he realized what was happening, he was stalking toward the jury box where his family sat. He was powerless to stop himself as he raised the scythe above his head and cut his mother down. Sweets was next, and the twins got it with the next stroke. He then moved to little Josette, who was staring up at him with questioning eyes.

"Am I going to die, Wrath?" Jo-Jo repeated the question she had asked him earlier. Only this time when she called him Wrath, he didn't correct her.

Jonas looked at her. Tears burned his eyes and a lump formed in his throat that was threatening to choke him. "Yes," he sobbed before bringing the blade down and taking off her head.

Jonas woke, kneeling beside his bed and gasping for air. His heart thudded so hard in his chest that he feared it would burst. Clutched in his hands was a baseball bat. The wood was old and starting to rot, but you could still make out deep red stains at the end of it from when he had bashed Black's skull in years before. The bat was one of the few things that could link Jonas to that crime, and it would've probably been best to get rid of it, but something about it brought him comfort.

Just then, he remembered Jo-Jo. Tossing the bat, he hustled down the hall to the girl's room and pushed the door in. What he saw almost made him faint. The room was empty. Jo-Jo's bed was mussed, and there was a large bloodstain on her pillow. "God, no!" he gasped, fearing the worse.

"Jonas?" a small voice called from down the hall. He turned and saw Jo-Jo coming out of the bathroom. There was a wad of tissue stuck in her nose.

"Oh, my sweet sister!" Jonas rushed to her. He snatched Jo-Jo off her feet and spun her around joyfully. "I thought something had happened to you."

"Relax, it was just a nosebleed," Jo-Jo assured him.

"What's all this noise out here?" Janette came out of her room.

"Nothing, Ma. Nothing at all," Jonas said, still clutching Jo-Jo in his arms.

Chapter Twenty-eight

Jonas took another shower before dressing and hitting the streets. He was glad that his family was well, but the dream still had him on edge. Jonas wasn't much of a believer in God, but he did believe in the universe and the signs it sent. The dream had been an omen. One which he fully intended to take heed to. He needed to start doing things differently.

The streets were his bread and butter, but so far, the risks were outweighing the rewards. If going down in a blaze of glory was how his story would end, he was fine with that, but he'd be damned if he would go out and leave his family living from hand to mouth. His best bet was to get up the money to get in on Prince's London deal. He wasn't sure how he would get the money up but was determined to figure it out.

He still had some time before he had to go and meet Alex, so he decided to stop by the trap house. He wanted to follow up and make sure everything was good, and besides that, he needed to holla at Stacey. He needed her to go to the lawyer's office to sign off on the final paperwork. He'd wanted to run things down to her the day before but had gotten sidetracked by the business with Ace and Cal. They needed to start moving things along, so he couldn't put it off any longer.

Ceaver had been against the idea of using Stacey because he didn't trust anyone outside of Jonas, and even that was sometimes up for question, but Jonas had faith.

Since Jonas had put her on, Stacey did everything he required of her without question. She was a good soldier, but her real test was yet to come.

As Jonas neared the corner, he slowed and surveyed the location of where Juan's store once stood. The neighborhood grocery store where his family, as well as the rest of the neighborhood, had shopped since he was a kid was now gone. In its place was a burned down husk. Soon, the contractors would come in and start construction on what would replace the store, a social club. It was an unexpected series of events that had been orchestrated by none other than Jonas.

For years, Jonas walked around carrying resentment toward Juan. He would sit on his stoop and watch in disgust as the store owner lured unsuspecting young girls in and out of the store to trade sexual favors for groceries and other gifts. Juan was a parasite, and something needed to be done about him, but just what he was still unsure. Killing him outright was always an option, but Jonas wanted to make a statement. For weeks, months, he plotted on ways deal with the man, and then an opportunity finally presented itself.

The word was that Juan was the latest to fall victim to the drug epidemic that was spreading like wildfire through the American ghettos. He started, as most addicts do, just chipping, and the next thing he knew, Juan had a monkey on his back. Jonas would sometimes see him skulking around, buying drugs from some of his workers. Jonas always told them that whenever they saw Juan, give him more drugs than he actually paid for. This was all a part of his grand scheme.

It wasn't long before Juan's habit started affecting his business. He was burning through his line of credit with his suppliers, and eventually, started falling behind in the rent on the property. It wouldn't be long before he lost the store. This was when Jonas stepped in. Through Lou, he'd had an investor approach Juan about saving the store, which by some was considered a landmark. It had been in his family for three generations. For the promise of a quick cash infusion, Juan was to sign over the majority stake in his grocery store. He took the deal without giving it so much as a second thought. This was when the other shoe dropped.

While Juan's business was being stolen out from under him, he had been too concerned with pussy and powder even to notice. Jonas felt it his civic duty to bring it to his attention. He waited until late one night when he knew only Juan would be in the store. Jonas waited until he had seen the last customer leave and Juan flip the closed sign before he approached. Getting inside wasn't a problem. He had stolen a copy of the keys from José one night while they had been drinking beers and debating sports. José was a good guy, but his trusting nature and low tolerance for alcohol would prove to be his undoing. While he was in the back throwing up, Jonas had snatched the key.

Using his stolen key, he let himself into the store. He was wearing a hood, gloves, and carrying a backpack that contained Juan's going-away present. When he got inside the store, he didn't see any sign of Juan behind the counter, so he walked to the back room. It was there that he found the store owner, with a girl of about 14. Juan was in the process of working the girl's panties down when he realized that he wasn't alone.

"Yo, muthafucka, we're closed!" Juan said, snatching his pants up.

"Just came to see if my mom could get a loaf of bread on credit," Jonas said, pulling his hood off.

"Raf?" Juan was surprised to see him.

"These days, it's Wrath, but we'll get to that," Jonas said with ice in his tone. He turned to the girl, who looked scared. "Good little girls should get home before the streetlights come on. Monsters are hiding in the dark."

The girl didn't need much more of a warning than that. She collected her things and got out of the store as fast as she could.

"I see you're still out here fucking with babies," Jonas said.

"Hey, she said she was 18!" Juan lied. "Look, if this is about your sister, you don't have to worry. I listened to what you said and stayed away from her. I never touched her."

"You may as well have because it isn't going to change the ending of your movie." Jonas slid the knapsack off his back and placed it on the floor. There was the clang of something metal inside. "Have a seat, Juan." He motioned toward an empty folding chair. Juan was hesitant. Jonas pulled his gun and pointed it at him. "I'm not going to ask you twice."

Nervously, Juan took the seat. He watched as Jonas began removing the items from the knapsack. There was a roll of duct tape, a pair of handcuffs, and a canister of gasoline. "Put these on." He tossed the handcuffs to Juan.

"Wrath, before you do anything stupid, just know that I've got cameras all over this place," Juan warned.

"Cameras that haven't worked properly in years. Your brother gets awful chatty once he's had a few drinks," Jonas laughed. "Now, either you can cuff yourself to the chair, or I can shoot you in the head. It's your call."

Juan did as he was told. "Wrath, if you just tell me what this is about, I'm sure we can work it out."

"This is about me getting you the help you so desperately need." Jonas began pacing a circle around Juan.

"For years, I've watched you usher young girls in and out of this place, doing only God knows what with them here in this back room. I had always hated you for it until I began to see the bigger picture. You can't help yourself, Juan. What you have is a sickness, and I am the cure."

There was a sharp pinch in Juan's neck, followed by something being pumped into his vein.

"What the fuck was that?" he asked, fearing that Jonas had poisoned him.

"Some of the best heroin money can buy." Jonas showed him the empty hypodermic needle. "No sense in making this unpleasant. I'm not a complete animal."

"C'mon, Wrath. You ain't gotta do this," Juan pleaded. His words were beginning to slur as the high-powered dope began to take effect.

"I know I don't have to, but I want to." Jonas picked up the gas can and stood before Juan, who was going into a nod. "You and this store have stood as a beacon of what's wrong with this community. Tonight, I will cleanse this neighborhood of your taint once and for all. Your death will signal the coming of a new day . . . the day of reckoning."

Juan was finding it hard to focus. His head lolled up, and he could see Jonas lighting a cigarette. "Jonas," he said weakly.

"I am Wrath!" Jonas declared before tossing the cigarette onto Juan's lap and sending him up in a ball of flame.

Jonas stood across the street watching as Juan's store burned to the ground with him inside it. He found himself suddenly filled with something that he couldn't quite put his finger on. Then he realized what it was that he was feeling . . . relief.

It took nearly forty minutes for the fire department to finally show up and put the fire out. By the time they got it under control, there was nothing left of the store except a melted counter and the remains of the owner. When they investigated the fire, they would discover that Juan had been high in the back, smoking, and fell asleep. It was officially ruled an accident, thanks to Lou's contacts within the fire inspectors. Once again, the detective had come through for him. The neighborhood residents would have to find somewhere else to shop, but it was a small price to pay to ensure the safety of their children. He was proud knowing that the mothers in his community would be able to sleep well that night, knowing that he had slain the beast.

Jonas had scraped together almost every dime he had to pay the contractors who would restore the property. To him, it was worth it. For the first time in his life, he would actually own something of value besides clothes and guns. The social club probably wouldn't be much in the beginning, but over time, he would grow it, and, hopefully, it would birth other more profitable businesses. Businesses that would feed his family for generations to come. *Boss the fuck up.*

"Crazy, ain't it?" A voice brought Jonas out of his daydream. An older man who lived in the building had come to stand beside him and was looking at what remained of Juan's. "A damn cigarette did all this."

"Crazy, indeed," Jonas agreed.

"What do you think they'll build in its place?" the man asked.

Jonas smiled. "Something that isn't tainted."

Jonas pushed thoughts of murder from his mind and continued to the trap house. With the way things were going with Jo-Jo's condition, he had to get the ball rolling sooner than later. Between his sister's sickness and what he had talked about with Prince, Jonas had quite a lot on his mind, namely, stepping his game up.

Jonas had to admit that he hadn't anticipated it taking so long for him to blow up when he first started hustling. He saw guys like Drew, and some of the other big-time dealers, in their fancy cars and expensive jewelry, and he wanted that. He'd always thought getting would be as simple as putting drugs on the street and watching the money roll in. He had been wrong. He was making enough money to keep himself and his family above the poverty line, but they were still in the hood. If he wanted to ensure that the people he loved were taken care of long after he was gone, then he would have to rise above the street shit he was doing and start making power moves. This is why it was so important for him to get Stacey on board. She would be the key to everything.

Ace and Mula thought Jonas kept Stacey around just to crunch numbers, which was partially true, but they had no idea that she was a pivotal piece to his endgame. No matter how much cash Jonas scraped together, there wouldn't be much he could do with it on his own. He wasn't old enough to even buy alcohol, had never owned anything that he didn't pay for in cash, and didn't even have a high school diploma. He was a walking question mark that no sensible establishment would do legitimate business with, but Stacey was clean. She didn't have a criminal history, and her credit score was good. Aside from a few bullshit parking tickets, Stacey was an otherwise law-abiding citizen. With those credentials, she could walk into any bank and get a loan or get some property in her name without so much as a second look. She would make the perfect front.

Chapter Twenty-nine

When Jonas arrived at Paula's apartment, he was pleased to find it not teeming with a bunch of people who didn't belong there. What he had walked in on the last time he checked in had really bothered him, so much to the point where he had started putting out feelers to find a new traphouse. They had been pumping out of Paula's crib for a long time and hadn't had any problems, but that was before Ace adapted an open-door policy. Too many eyes had seen what they should not have, and Jonas had a bad feeling about it. He could very well be paranoid and overreacting to the whole situation, but he would rather be safe than sorry.

Mula was seated at his usual position at the table. He was counting out money, which he would wrap with rubber bands and toss into shoe boxes. They would be picked up later on and taken to a second apartment, which they used exclusively to keep money in. Jonas never liked to keep his cash in the same place he stashed his drugs. That was a lesson he had learned from Drew. One of his spots had gotten raided, and the police ended up getting him for his money as well as the drugs. Drew was sick over it for a week.

Tavion sat on the couch with Stacey, watching a movie. He had been trying to get next to her since she started hanging around regularly, and so far, hadn't had much success. It wasn't for lack of effort on his part. Tavion had been going out of his way to woo the young woman but couldn't seem to make his way out of the friend zone. Young girls loved Tavion, but Stacey was unmoved. Poor Tavion's ego was becoming bruised. Jonas didn't have the heart to tell him that Stacey wasn't shooting him down because he wasn't attractive; she just wasn't into men. It was something that she had confided to Jonas, and he wouldn't break her trust.

Ace was at his usual post, sitting in the armchair near the window. That was his spot, and no one was allowed to sit there when Ace was in the traphouse. He liked that spot because it gave him a view of the street, and he could see whoever was coming and going at all times. Ace always had control issues, and they seemed to get worse as he got older. As Jonas studied Ace's face, he noticed something was off. Nothing obvious, just something about the set of his eyes that seemed strange.

"Didn't expect to see you around here so early," Ace said, blowing out a cloud of smoke. He had noticed Jonas examining him.

"I got a lot to do today; just needed to pop by here real quick to make sure y'all were good and to handle something," Jonas told him.

"I keep telling you we don't need a fucking babysitter." Ace stormed off into the bedroom.

"What the fuck is his problem?" Jonas asked Mula after Ace had gone.

"You know that nigga is always on his period." Mula shrugged it off.

"Whatever, yo. I need to holla at Stacey real quick." Jonas gave him a look. Mula took the hint.

"I gotta hit the store anyhow." Mula pushed himself from the table. "Take a walk with me, Tavion."

"But the movie isn't over." Tavion didn't want to leave Stacey's side.

Mula snatched the power cord from the television. "It is now. Come the fuck on."

Tavion sucked his teeth and mumbled something under his breath before following Mula out the door.

"What's up, Wrath? Everything okay?" Stacey asked, noticing the serious expression on his face.

"Everything is right as rain, baby girl," Jonas smiled. "Do you remember that thing I needed you to do? With the papers?"

"Yes, I remember."

"It's time."

Stacey looked unsure. "Jonas, I've been having second thoughts. I mean, I want to help out, but I don't want to get into trouble."

"I keep telling you that you don't have to worry about it. This transaction will be totally legit. All you'll be doing is starting up a new business under the LLC that I set up in your name. The lawyers are going to do all the heavy lifting. All you have to do is sign off on the papers."

Stacey still looked unsure. What Jonas was asking her to do was far bigger and far riskier than getting rental cars in her name or signing off on bail for one of the boys. She didn't know all the details about the deal, but what she did know was that he had acquired the property under questionable circumstances. If it all blew back, it would land squarely on her.

"Stacey," Jonas began, "when you first started hanging around us, neither Ace nor any of the others wanted to let you get down. They all said that you were too young and too square. Who was it that let you rock out?"

"You."

"And when you had that *other* problem, who took care of it?" Jonas was speaking of an incident with her mother's boyfriend. He couldn't seem to keep his hands to himself, which is why she was always at Paula's. One night, he had come into her room and forced her to suck his dick. When she told Jonas about it, he had gone to pay the man a visit. When he was done, he made sure that her mother's boyfriend would never force his dick anywhere else. Jonas had never told another living soul about what had happened to Stacey.

"You." Stacey's voice cracked as she relived the abuse in her head.

"Exactly! I've always taken care of you, Stacey, and I always will. Whether or not you do this thing for me, that'll never change. I love you like one of my own sisters. But I'm not gonna sit here and act like I really don't need this favor from you. It's important to me . . . important to us."

Stacey was silent for a time. There was an internal struggling going on in her mind about doing what she felt was right versus not wanting to disappoint Jonas. He was one of the few men in her life who had always been kind to her and had never asked for anything in return. What kind of person would that make her if she couldn't do him this one small favor? "Okay, I'll do it."

"That's my girl!" Jonas scooped her in his arms and spun her around happily. "Look, I need you to go to one of those stores you girls like so much and buy yourself a nice outfit. Something dressy like what you might wear to a job interview. Then jump in a cab and head to the lawyer's office ASAP."

"Why do I have to change my clothes if all I'm doing is signing papers?" Stacey was comfortable in her sneakers and jeans and didn't feel like changing.

"Because we have to keep up appearances. If you're going to play the role of a shrewd businesswoman, I'm going to need you to look the part."

After Stacey had gone, Jonas went to the bedroom to check on Ace. Paula was stretched out across the bed, high as a kite, while Ace sat on a folding chair. He was smoking a blunt and sipping from a bottle of Hennessey. When his eyes turned to Jonas, Jonas finally realized what it was about them that he had missed earlier . . . sadness.

"You good?" Jonas asked.

"Yeah, I'm straight. You don't have to worry about me slacking on the job," Ace said sarcastically.

"Yo, what's good with you? You've been acting real funny lately, Ace. If you've got something to get off your chest, let's get to it instead of dancing around it."

Ace stared at Jonas with uncertainty. It was as if he were weighing whether to confide in his friend. "I fucked up," he finally admitted.

"What do you mean?" Jonas asked, fearing the worst. His first thoughts were that his suspicions were confirmed, and Cal turned out to be foul.

"Remember Tisha?"

"Of course I do," Jonas said. Ace was a pussy hound and had girls all over the city, but Tisha was different. Tisha didn't drink, smoke, hang out, or go for Ace's bullshit. He had met her when he was hiding out in Brooklyn when the police were looking for him in connection with the assault on Black. They had been dealing off and on for the last few years. She was the closest thing to a girlfriend he had.

"She's pregnant," Ace confessed.

Jonas breathed a sigh of relief. "Is that what you're walking around in a funk for? Shit, that ain't about nothing. If anything, you should be happy. Tisha is a good girl."

"Yes, she is. That girl loves me even when I do shit to make her hate me. She's been down for me since I was selling nickel bags in the park. That's what's got me so fucked up about this."

"I don't understand," Jonas said, trying to see where Ace was going.

"She ain't the only one that's pregnant. I fucked around and put one in this bitch Shauna," Ace said in frustration.

This threw Jonas for a loop. Shauna was a hood rat and offered her pussy up to the highest bidder. He hadn't missed the looks she had been giving him while being pawed by Cal and apparently pregnant by Ace. Shauna gave new meaning to the title "Scandalous Bitch."

"You sure it's yours?"

"With that ho, ain't no telling. I knew I shouldn't have run up in her raw, but I was drunk and on a bean," Ace said as if that were a good enough excuse. "All I know is that she's threatening to blow the shit up unless I break her off with some bread for an abortion and to keep quiet."

"Then pay the bitch and be done with it," Jonas said as if it were that simple.

"With what? You know I blow money faster than we make it," Ace said honestly. Almost nightly, you could find him in whichever spot was hot, popping bottles and tricking off on women. Prince was always warning all of them about their spending, but Ace wasn't trying to hear it. He was too busy living in the moment to worry about what the next day might bring.

"So, what you gonna do?" Jonas asked. Ace gave him a look that said the answer should've been obvious. "Ace, you can't kill a pregnant broad, man."

"You fuck with the bull, and you get the horns," Ace said, taking another swig from his bottle.

"Look, I got a few dollars I can kick in. I hope it helps, but you gotta get your finances under control," Jonas told him.

"I know, man. That's why I've been giving some serious thought to going out of town with Cal."

"Here we go with this again," Jonas sighed.

"I already know, you don't trust Cal. I hear you, but I need to pick up some extra bread. We're doing all right with the few blocks we're holding, but with Drew right next door, there ain't so far we can stretch our legs," Ace pointed out.

"Ace, I got some shit in the works. It's going to take time to get it up and running, but we're gonna be okay. I just need y'all to hold your heads while I sort it out," Jonas said.

"Well, run the play down for me. You know I'm ten toes for whatever," Ace assured him.

"I can't really say right now. I just need you to trust me."

"You've been saying that a lot lately, Wrath. You know, there was a time when we confided everything in each other, but now you're playing your hand close to your chest. It's like you don't trust a nigga," Ace accused.

"Of course I trust you, Ace. It's just that—"

"Just that what? C'mon, man. I'm getting tired of you with all this secret squirrel shit. You're keeping your crew at a distance, and I'm not the only one who's noticing your funny moves."

"And what's that supposed to mean?"

"It means there are some of us who are starting to question your motives. Maybe you've got your own agenda outside of us, like that white boy you're plugged in with." Ace gave him a look. "I know you don't think I'm the smartest muthafucka, but I peep shit. I know you've got some type of side hustle going that you've been keeping from us."

"It isn't what you think," Jonas told him.

"Then stop having me guess and just tell me what it is."

Jonas was silent.

"Just what I thought," Ace continued. "You keep talking about how we can't trust Cal, but it's you who are out here making suspect moves."

"As much as I've sacrificed for this team, how dare you come at me sideways like I ain't about my shit!" Jonas snapped. He was on his feet and standing over Ace menacingly. "Now, I'm sorry that I don't share your dreams of being a corner nigga for the rest of my life, but I've got bigger plans. I'm gonna take what the fuck this world owes me, and then some. Those who are with me will eat, and those who ain't will get eaten. We clear on that, nigga?"

"Yeah, we clear." Ace looked up at him with larceny in his eyes.

"I got moves to make." Jonas started toward the door.

"So, you still gonna lend me the money?" Ace called after him. Jonas never even broke his stride.

Chapter Thirty

By the time Jonas left the trap house, he was in a foul mood. This was thanks to Ace. Here he was trying to be a friend and a brother, and Ace had the nerve to come at him sideways. It wasn't his fault that he had two girls pregnant at the same time and found himself in the middle of a love triangle as well as an extortion plot. Even so, he tried to help, and what did he get in return? Ace was an ungrateful bastard, and it was starting to wear on Jonas. Ace was content to get rich, while Jonas was chasing wealth. There was a big difference, but his friend hadn't seemed to have figured it out yet.

The friction between them had started to affect not only their relationship but also the hierarchy of their crew. No one had come out and said anything, but Jonas could feel it. The funny looks he would get from some of the newer recruits, who were loyal to Ace, hadn't gone unnoticed. Likely because Ace was probably poisoning them against him. None of them were stupid enough to move against Jonas, but the tension was there and steadily building. Jonas knew that he would have to confront Ace sooner than later to put it to bed or risk a civil war within their organization.

Another thing that troubled Jonas was the fact that Ace knew about his relationship with the detective. Their arrangement was something that Jonas kept close to his chest, not only to protect his arrangement with Ceaver but also to protect his crew as well. Detective Ceaver had made no secret of the fact that he didn't care for nor trust the members of Jonas's crew, and if he had begun to see them as a problem, Jonas couldn't say for sure what steps he would take to resolve it. He had seen what the man was capable of with the way he had dealt with Eight-Ball and Bruiser and didn't want to risk Ace or Mula becoming the next headlines in the paper.

He jumped in a taxi and took it across town to the assisted living home where Alex volunteered. He had to admit that it looked nothing like what he expected. When someone said "assisted living," visions of hospitals and clinics immediately sprang to mind, but this wasn't that. It looked like a regular apartment building.

As he was walking inside, his phone went off. It was Jewels. Again, he didn't answer. There would only be so long that he could avoid her. Jonas would get with Jewels in his own time and talk with her, but he needed to find out where he stood with Alex first.

Jonas went into the facility, where he found a thick man dressed in all white sitting behind a desk. He seemed more preoccupied with his cell phone than he did Jonas. Jonas stood there for a full thirty seconds before he finally cleared his throat and got the man's attention.

"Name, ID, and the name of the resident you're visiting." The man slapped a clipboard on the desk in front of Jonas.

"I'm not here to see a resident. I'm here to see an employee . . . well, a volunteer," Jonas explained.

"Still need your name and a copy of your ID," the man insisted.

Jonas hadn't expected this. As a rule, he never carried ID. This was so that if he ever got caught committing a crime by the police, he could be anyone he told them he was. He had never been officially arrested, and the only time he had ever been fingerprinted was when he had gotten picked up by the two detectives who were asking about Black. Even then, that had been illegal, so the prints had to be destroyed, or so Lou had told him. He was about to change his mind and leave when Alex came through a door in the back.

"It's okay, Frank. He's with me," she told the man.

"Why didn't he say so? You know I don't mind breaking the rules for you, Lex." Frank winked.

Lex?

"Hi, Jonas, I'm glad you decided to come." Alex hugged him.

"I told you I would," he beamed.

"Come on; I'll take you in the back where the residents will be having lunch." She took him by the hand and whisked him away.

Jonas wasn't sure what to expect when Alex led him into the community room, but he was quite surprised by what he saw. The whole ride there he had been preparing himself for the worst: a room full of people suffering from terminal illnesses or being ushered around with machines hooked to them like in hospitals, but it was quite the opposite. There were people there who were clearly suffering from different conditions, but for the most part, it looked like a regular party. Residents were enjoying themselves playing games with their families or sitting at tables eating. There was also some kind of dance battle going on between two people in wheelchairs. This wasn't anything like he imagined it would be.

"What did you think? I was inviting you to hang out with a bunch of people knocking on death's door?" Alex joked as if she had been reading his mind.

"Nah, nothing like that," he lied.

"Hey, Alex, is this your friend?" A beefy woman wearing a white apron approached them.

"Yes, Mrs. Windle. This is my friend, Jonas Rafferty. Jonas, this is Mrs. Windle. She runs this facility." Alex made the introductions.

"Well, it's a pleasure to meet you, Jonas." Mrs. Windle shook his hand vigorously. "I've heard quite a bit about you."

"Good things, I hope," he joked.

"Of course. If I'd heard anything else, I'd have never agreed to have you around our residents," Mrs. Windle said seriously. "These are God's special children, at least that's what I call them. They're just like us; they just need a little more patience and love than most folk."

"Jonas knows all about being patient. Don't you, Jonas?" Alex winked at him.

"Mrs. Windle?" One of the staff called over to her.

"Well, duty calls." Mrs. Windle smiled. It was a warm, motherly smile. "It was nice meeting you, Jonas. Hopefully, we can talk again soon. Oh, and thank you so much for agreeing to help out."

"Help out?"

As Jonas had planned, he got to spend some quality time with Alex, but it wasn't in the way he had thought. He spent the next couple of hours shoulder to shoulder with her serving food to the residents of the assisted living facility. At first, it was awkward for him. Jonas had never spent much time around the handicapped and wasn't sure if he was supposed to act a certain way or not. Some of them were a handful, like the woman who had thrown a fit and tossed her plate at Mrs. Windle, but for the most part, they were just like regular folks. After a while, he got comfortable and even began to enjoy himself talking to some of the residents and hearing their stories. It was as Mrs. Windle had said, all some of them needed was a little extra love and patience.

"You did great today, Jonas. Thank you," Alex told him once they were done serving the residents and cleaning up.

"It's all good, Lex," he winked. "But seriously, I'm kind of glad that I came. It *was* fun."

"No greater joy than service," Alex replied.

"I could think of a few things." Jonas smiled at her.

Alex shook her head. "I see you're still the same horny-ass little boy from when we were little."

"You must have me confused with Ace."

"It wasn't Ace who was always trying to look up my skirt in school when we would be walking up the stairs."

"Damn. I didn't know you peeped that." Jonas flashed embarrassment.

"I peeped everything. That's why I stopped wearing shorts under my skirts," Alex revealed.

"I see I ain't the only one who was a little on the nasty side," he teased her. "So, what's up? You think we can go do something after this?"

Alex thought about it. "I guess you have earned a little bit of my time. But I can't stay out long. My parents are expecting me home for dinner."

The mention of dinner made Jonas remember the promise he had made his mother. "That's fine."

"But before we get, I have someone I want you to meet."

"Another one of your coworkers?" Jonas asked, hoping not. The entire morning, he had been fielding questions from Alex's coworkers about his background and his relationship to Alex. He wasn't looking forward to another round.

"No," she said and walked off. Jonas waited a moment before following.

They found themselves at the end of the community room where a television was set up. Some of the residents were sitting around it watching a game show. They all took a moment to greet Alex. Jonas could tell she was well liked at the facility by both the staff and residents. A man in a wheelchair sat in the corner, facing the window. His back was to Jonas so he couldn't see his face. Alex knelt beside him and said a few soft words before waving Jonas over. Now that Jonas was up close, he could get a better look. The man was shriveled, with bony limbs and dark skin. His face was sunken to the point where he looked emaciated. There was a machine latched on to the side of his wheelchair with a tube that ran to his neck. It was to help him breathe. His hair was a matted black Afro, but you could see a long surgical scar beneath that stretched the length of his skull. He was in far worse shape than any of the other residents.

"Jonas, I would like you to meet Stanley. He's one of our residents here." Alex introduced him.

"Hi." Jonas extended his hand, but Stanley didn't move to shake it. He just stared at Jonas with vacant eyes.

"Stanley has lost the use of 75 percent of his motor functions. He can't do much for himself these days without the help of a caretaker," Alex said sadly.

"I'm sorry." Jonas felt for the man. He couldn't imagine what he would do if he were in such a state. It couldn't have been much of a life. "What happened to him?"

"A couple of years ago, Stanley was attacked. His attacker beat him so badly that he suffered permanent brain damage and has been reduced to what you see here."

"Damn, that's fucked up. Who would do some shit like that?" Jonas wondered.

"I think we both know the answer to that," Alex said in an accusatory tone.

"What the hell are you talking about?" Jonas was clueless.

"His name is Stanley, but when he was in the streets, they called him Black," Alex revealed.

Jonas moved in for a closer look. He was slightly older and had lost a lot of weight, but it was indeed Black! "What is this shit? You trying to be funny?"

"No, I assure you that there is nothing funny about stealing away a man's life," Alex said seriously. "I wanted you to see firsthand how your actions can affect the lives of others. Black was a young man who could've gone on to be anything he wanted if he had only been allowed the chance to change. But you stole that from him, Jonas. You've left a mother without a son and children without their father."

"Black had kids?" this came as a shock to Jonas.

"A boy and a girl," she informed him. "Their grandmother brings them to see him from time to time. I was hoping they would come today so you guys could have met."

"For what? I ain't got shit to say to them, and they ain't got shit to say to me. Look, if you're trying to get me to feel sorry for him, I can't, Alex. Too much has happened . . . too much has been taken. If it hadn't been for Black, maybe Doug would still be alive."

"Doug was still alive after you did what you did to Black. It was the aftermath that caused my brother's death," Alex reminded him. "It wasn't easy, but I've managed to forgive Black, as well as whoever else, was responsible for my brother's murder. I'm not asking you to forgive him, Jonas. I know that's not in your nature, but I know that what you did that night is something that you've been carrying around for a long time. It's time to set that burden down."

"Alex—"

"I'm not putting any pressure on you, Jonas. I was only making a suggestion. Whether you make peace with the man you put in this chair is your decision. One thing I can tell you, though, is that you don't want to go through the rest of your life with regrets about things that you could've made right but chose not to."

"Alex, can you help me for a second?" Mrs. Windle called over.

"Be right there," Alex replied. "I'll be back in a few. Hopefully, when I walk out of here, it'll be with Jonas and not Wrath," she said and excused herself.

Jonas stood there for a long while looking down at Black. Back in the days, he had been a terrorizing character, but now, he was just a withered old soul who was waiting to die. It was almost sad when he thought about it.

"Anybody home?" Jonas waved his hand in front of Black's face. His eyes followed, but other than that, he was nonresponsive. "You know, you were the last person I expected to run into today. In fact, I never thought I'd see you again. I sometimes wondered what happened to you that night, whether you ever pulled through or bit the dust. To be honest with you, I'm not sure I even cared."

Jonas paused as if he were waiting for Black to say something. He was still silent, accusatory eyes staring up at Jonas.

"I don't think you'll ever understand the affect that night had on my life. Everything changed after what I did to you. Whether it was for better or worse, I still don't know, but shit is definitely different now," Jonas said. "Alex was right, you know? We shouldn't go through life with regrets, and I've got more than my fair share. Do you know what I regret the most, though, Black? I regret hitting you in the head with that bat. I should've taken Ace's gun and blew your stinking brains out. I should've left you dead in that motel room and then went and tracked the rest of your crew down and put them in the ground too. That was a mistake on my part, but don't worry. I'll be making it right real soon when I pay a visit to your friend Flair."

There was a flicker of movement in Black's eyes.

"Oh, since you ain't a player in the game you must not have heard. Your boy Flair called himself avenging you and killed Doug," he filled him in. "Snuffed that boy's life like he wasn't shit, but I intend to return the favor. Killing your boy ain't good enough, though. I'm going to wipe him and anybody else who was loyal to you off the board. I'm going erase any memory of you or crew ever having existed. Wanna know the best part? Nobody is going to miss y'all. You were nothing when you were on the streets, Black, and you're less than nothing now. Who knows? Maybe when I'm done with Flair, I'll come back here and finish what I started with you. Just something to think on while they're changing your diapers this evening. Until we meet again, my friend." He patted Black's cheek way harder than he needed to.

When Jonas rejoined Alex, he was smiling from ear to ear.

"I take it everything went well with Black?" she asked.

"Yes, and I wanted to thank you and tell you that you're right. I feel a lot better now that I've gotten it off my chest."

Jonas and Alex didn't go to a restaurant on their first real date or even a movie. They went for a walk and got reacquainted. Their journey took them to Central Park, where they took the winding paths and enjoyed the scenery.

Alex mostly talked, while Jonas listened. She told him about her life as it had been down south and school. She had completed high school by the time she was 16 because she had skipped a grade. She always was a whiz academically. She was currently in her third year at Spellman. She went on and on about all the amazing things she had going on in her life, but Jonas had very little to offer to the conversation. He didn't think she would be interested in hearing about how many men he had killed or the fact that he had burned Juan's store down so that he could take it over.

"Am I talking too much?" Alex asked when she noticed Jonas had gone silent. "I'm sorry. I know sometimes I can get to rambling."

"No, it's cool. I like hearing you talk," he said.

"That isn't what you used to tell me. It seemed like every time I opened my mouth to say something, either you or my brother were telling me to shut up."

"That's because you had a smart-ass mouth. You were vicious with your shit." Jonas recalled some of Alex's antics.

"That was only because I was trying to impress you."

"Me?" Jonas was surprised.

"Yes, you. I used to see how you and Ace would always be chasing around after the trump-mouthed hood rats, and I thought that's what you were into. I tried to dumb myself down to get you to notice me."

"You didn't have to do all that, Alex. I always noticed you." Jonas took her hand as they were strolling. "Can I ask you something?"

"Sure."

"How come you never just came out and told me that you liked me?"

Alex thought about the question. "I dunno. I guess I was just afraid of you shooting me down. It's like I said, I saw the kinds of girls who got attention from you and Ace, and I didn't fit the mold."

"Fit the mold? Alex, you *were* the mold."

"Stop gassing me, Jonas." Alex blushed.

"I'm serious, Alex. I know we were young and didn't know shit, but from the first time we played together on the school yard, I didn't want to spend a minute not being around. I used to pray that the weekends would hurry up and pass so that Monday could come and I would see you in school again. Sounds dumb, right?"

"Not at all. I'd be lying if I said I didn't think about you a lot," Alex admitted.

"Then why did you leave me?" he asked. It was an unexpected question, one that he wasn't even sure why he asked.

"I didn't want to," Alex answered after a time. "After Doug was killed, things in my family changed. There was a lot of strain, not just in my relationship with my parents, but with me too. I started acting out and doing things that I normally wouldn't have, like getting into fights and talking back. I was angry at the world and probably on my way to ruin, just like Doug. My parents decided that I needed a fresh start, so they sent me away. I didn't want to go; in fact, I stopped speaking to them for a while. It wasn't until I got a little older that I began to realize that they had done it for my own good, and I'm thankful for it. They made sure I at least had a shot at becoming something."

"And you didn't disappoint," he said.

"Yeah, I'm grateful for everything that I've accomplished, but there is still so much more that I need to do. I've got big dreams. Do you dream, Jonas?"

He wasn't quite sure how to answer the question. "Like at night?"

"No. I mean, like, do you dream about where you see yourself in life in say five years?" she clarified.

"I used to. These days, I just take life as it comes from one day to the next. If you don't get your hopes up, then you don't have far to fall when people let you down," he said honestly.

Alex gave him a pitiful look. The light that she used to
see whenever she looked into his eyes had begun to dim.
It was still there, but faint. "I'm sorry, Jonas. Sorry for
whatever you've gone through in life that has made you
this way."

"What way?"

"Hopeless." It may not have been the right word to use,
but it conveyed what she felt when she looked at him. He
was a hopeless soul.

"So, what's next for you?" Jonas changed the subject.
"I guess at the end of the summer you'll be going back to
school?"

"Yes, one more year of this, and then I'm over it. On to
bigger and better things.

"You dropping out?"

"No, not dropping out. I'm graduating. Then I'm off to
study abroad as a part of an exchange program."

"Abroad?" Jonas didn't understand the word.

"It means overseas. I'll be studying in London."

This made Jonas laugh.

"What's so funny?" she asked defensively.

"I'm not laughing at you; I'm laughing at the irony of
the universe," Jonas said. He was thinking about the deal
Prince was putting together. If he hadn't been sure about
going through with it before, he was now. All he needed
was the money to invest, and, hopefully, it would come
soon.

"Speaking of irony . . ." Alex motioned behind Jonas.
When he turned, he realized that they were at the lake he
had nearly drowned in years before.

"Damn, I haven't been here since that day." Jonas
walked to the edge of the water and stared into it. His
reflection stared back at him. Then he was joined by Alex.

"What did you see? You know, when you drowned," she
asked. It was the first time anyone had ever posed the
question to him.

"I don't know," he said honestly.

"I'm glad you didn't drown."

"Me too. I'd hate to have died before doing the things that I should've."

"Like what?"

"This." Jonas took Alex in his arms and kissed her. It wasn't like when he kissed Jewels. This was deep, passionate, and full of love.

"What brought that on?" Alex asked surprised.

"It's like you said, can't live life with regrets, right?"

"Right," she agreed. "So, what now?"

"We do what we should've done back then and be together."

"Jonas," she began, "I care about you; I really do, but our lives are going in two different directions. I can't afford to allow anything into my space that isn't positive. I've got too much to lose."

"Alex, I can read between the lines. You don't want to fuck with me because I'm a dope boy, right?"

"It isn't just that, Jonas. You live a very dangerous lifestyle. I can't allow myself to fall for you, knowing that every time you walk out the door, there's a good chance that you won't be coming back. I can't carry that around with me, and I won't."

"And you won't have to. Listen, I've got some things in the works that I can't talk about, but if all goes according to plan, I'll be able to take a backseat and let Ace and Mula run the operation."

"Jonas, we both know there's no such thing as one foot in and one foot out. I owe it to myself to expect more out of the man I choose to be with, and you should expect more out of life than what you're settling for. What? You gonna sell crack with Ace until you stack enough bread to get out of the life? That's not a realistic expectation. Me even pretending I'd entertain it is not being real with you, and you're someone I always have and always will keep it one hundred with, because I care. This has been nice, but things could never really work between us because we're not on the same page as far as what we want out of life."

"But, Alex—"

"Don't ruin it with words or promises you can't keep. God willing, tomorrow and whatever it holds will be there, but for now," she slipped her hands around his, "let's just live in the moment."

Chapter Thirty-one

Jonas and Alex shared a taxi back uptown. He dropped her off at her building, with a promise to see her again the following day; then he continued back to his block. It was still early, so he had time before he had to be home for dinner. He had quite a bit to think about until then.

It was just as Anette had warned, Alex had gotten into Jonas's head and now had him all over the place. This time, though, it wasn't a case of him being love struck. It was more like determined. What she had said about him having one foot in and one foot out had been true. Jonas knew that the only way to break free of the game was to get out of the game, but how? And did he even really want to? He had been Wrath for so long that sometimes Jonas got lost in the mix, but Alex had brought it out of him. Even though they had only spent a few hours together, in that time, he was able to be Jonas and not Wrath. He had almost forgotten how good it felt to do the simple things, like enjoy a walk in the park.

He and Jewels did things, like catch the occasional movie or go out to eat, but the majority of the time they spent together either involved fucking, getting high, or scheming. Sometimes, all three. It was nice, but it wasn't the same.

Then there was his crew. He, Ace, and Mula had come up together. They had shed both blood and tears. What would they do if he pulled away? Ace was perfectly capable of running the crew, but it was Jonas's connection to the detective that gave them their real power. He had no illusions about whether Ceaver would deal with Ace directly. He didn't half like him, so there was no way he was going to trust him. If Jonas stepped off, then, their veil of protection would be lifted, and where would that leave his boys? There had to be an angle he could play that would allow him to have his cake and eat it too.

Jonas hopped out of the taxi in front of his building. No sooner than his foot hit the curb did he find himself overcome with an eerie feeling. A quick sweep of the block revealed the source of his uneasiness. A man was sitting on a car out in front of his building. He wore his hair cut low, but his beard long and shaggy. He was dressed in a fatigue army suit and black combat boots. When he saw Jonas approaching, he stood at attention.

Jonas let his hand drop to where he had his gun tucked as he neared the man. He had seen him somewhere before but wasn't sure if he was a friend or a foe. Either way, he wasn't about to risk someone getting the drop on him.

"What's good, Wrath?" the man in the army fatigues greeted him.

"You know me?" Jonas now had the gun out and hanging at his side. Now that he was close up on the man, he could see that one of his eyes was missing. In its place was a black sphere that looked like it had a gold pentagram etched into it. The glass eye seemed to bore into Jonas's soul and sent a chill down his spine. He knew without question that this was a dangerous man.

"In a way, but we've never been introduced formally. They call me One-Eye Willie." He extended his hand, but Jonas didn't shake it. This made Willie smirk, showing off the gold cap over one of his teeth. "I'd heard you were a cautious one. That's a good thing. Lou sent me."

"What can I do for you?" Jonas asked suspiciously.

"Ain't about what you can do for me, but what *I* can do for *you*." Willie turned to reach for something in the car.

"Not so fast." Jonas leveled his gun at him.

"Be easy. I'm just getting the information you're supposed to be getting familiar with," Willie told him. He very carefully retrieved the folder from the passenger seat of the car and handed it to Jonas. "Everything you need to know about the guy we're gonna hit is in there."

"*We?*" Jonas raised an eyebrow.

"Lou thinks it's best if you had someone experienced with this type of thing go along with you," Willie explained.

"I told Ceaver I'd get somebody to handle it," Jonas told him.

"I hear you, but it don't change the fact that it will be just the two of us on this. One thing you'll learn about Lou Ceaver is, he's not someone you want to disappoint when he asks you to do something," Willie said seriously.

"A'ight. When does he want this to go down?" Jonas asked.

"Now," Willie said quite unexpectedly. "Been an unexpected change, so we have to push the timeline up."

"Damn. Lou doesn't waste time when he wants you gone."

"Never, and you should always keep that in mind," Willie warned. "I got clean guns for us, masks, and gloves in the trunk. Let's make a move." He walked around to the driver's side.

Jonas didn't want to get into the car with the stranger. The setup felt wrong and rushed. Every inch of him said that it was a bad idea, but he didn't feel like he had a choice. Reluctantly, he slid into the passenger's seat. He didn't bother with his seat belt because he wanted to be able to get to his gun if Willie had ill intentions.

Willie fired up the car, then rested his hand on the wheel. As an afterthought, he dug into his pocket and pulled out a five-dollar bill, which he gave to Jonas.

"What's this?" Jonas asked, looking curiously at the bill.

"Me doing you a good turn." Willie winked his good eye before pulling out into traffic.

It took a few seconds before it dawned on Jonas why One-Eye Willie looked so familiar. He had seen him before—three times, actually. Once, years ago when Mula had slapped the cup from his hand outside the motel. Again, when he was scheming on Eight-Ball, and more recently, outside the church that day. Every time Jonas's life was about to take an unexpected turn, Willie had been there.

Willie gave Jonas a knowing nod when he saw the light of recognition finally turn on in Jonas's head.

Jonas knew without question that his meeting the detective hadn't been one of chance but design. How long had he been on the detective's radar? More importantly . . . Why?

As they were leaving his block, Jonas spotted Jewels. She was coming out of the neighborhood liquor store. When the car he was in passed Jewels, their eyes met momentarily.

Was she crying?

Chapter Thirty-two

Jonas rode quietly in the passenger seat while Willie expertly navigated the evening traffic. To have one eye, Jonas had to admit that he was an excellent driver. He discretely studied the black marble in Willie's head. The gold pentagram on it made the eye appear sinister.

"Go on, ask," Willie spoke up unexpectedly.

"Ask what?" Jonas faked ignorance.

"The eye. Everyone always wants to know the story about the eye and how I lost it. So go ahead and get it out of your system."

"Fine, how did you lose your eye?" Jonas *had* been curious.

"There are a few stories, but I'll tell you my favorite. Rumor had it that when I was a kid, I used to see ghosts. They would haunt me day and night, so much so that it was even getting hard to think. So, I went and grabbed my mama's favorite chicken fork and plucked it out."

Jonas looked at him in disbelief. "You shitting me?"

"Maybe . . . Maybe not," Willie smirked.

"You still see ghosts?" Jonas asked sarcastically.

"Sure, I see plenty of dead folks these days. Mostly on the wrong side of my gun," he said seriously.

Jonas never asked about the eye again.

For the rest of the ride, he busied himself with the folder. There was quite a bit of information about Flair. It contained his name, address, where he hustled, and a list of known associates. There was even a note in the file about where his grandmother attended church. Detective Ceaver had really done his homework. This made him wonder if the detective may have had a file on him tucked away somewhere. He'd be a fool to believe he didn't. Men like Ceaver operated with control, and information on someone was control over them. It was that moment that Jonas decided to launch an investigation of his own and would put Stacey on the job. *Who was Detective Louis Ceaver?*

"Where are we going?" Jonas noticed they had just driven past Grant Projects. According to the file, that's where Flair hustled. Jonas naturally assumed they would hit him there.

"We don't want the eggs; we want the chicken. Best place to find one of those is in its coop," Willie told him.

They rolled further south and hit Central Park West. When they rode past the park on 100th Street, Jonas was taken back to the afternoon that he had almost drowned. Back then, he had no idea that it would be the turning point in his life. The day everything would change. When they hit Eighty-eighth, One-Eye Willie turned into the block. It was a tree-lined street in a nice neighborhood. Willie parked the car near a hydrant in front of a brownstone.

"He lives here?" Jonas asked, looking at the brownstone. He assumed Flair lived in the same neighborhood that he sold drugs in, same as everybody else. Nope. He had stepped up his game. Jonas couldn't help but feel a tinge of jealousy seeing the differences in how he and Flair lived.

Willie got out of the car and opened up the trunk. There was an assortment of firearms inside: automatic pistols, revolvers, etc. There was even a beat-up shotgun that looked like it had seen better days, which he handed to Jonas.

"What the fuck am I supposed to do with this? It doesn't even look like it'll fire without blowing a man's hand off," Jonas complained.

"I've killed men in three different cities with that old pump. It's never failed me, and you treat it right, it may do you some justice. Now, stop fucking around, and let's go kill this nigga." Willie slammed the trunk and marched toward the building. Jonas followed him down the steps that led to the lower level of the brownstone. He watched curiously while Willie picked the lock on what looked like a big fuse box. Once he got it open, he pulled out a penlight and shone it around inside until he found it. "C'mere, kid," he called to Jonas.

Jonas peered over his shoulder at a series of fuses that were different colors.

"When I tell you to, hit *this* one." Willie tapped a red switch marked power. It appeared Willie was going to knock out the power and use the element of surprise. Jonas only saw one problem with that.

"How are you gonna see in the dark?"

Willie tapped his glass eye and went to take up a crouching position outside the door, two big guns gripped in his gloved hands. When Willie gave the signal, Jonas threw the switch. There was a loud *pop;* then, the entire building went dark. Inside, confused voices could be heard. A few seconds later, an armed man came out the side door Willie was hiding behind. He never even saw it coming. Willie hit him twice in the back of the head.

"I'm going in. Count to ten before you follow me in and shoot everybody who ain't me! If you find yourself getting cold feet, just remember that it's you or them," Willie ordered and disappeared inside the house.

As Jonas was counting, he could hear screams, follow by the double bangs of Willie's two guns. When he reached ten, he went inside. He was startled to hear a whirling sound, followed by a faint red light bathing him. The brownstone must've had a generator in the event of a power outage. The first thing he noticed was a body on the floor just inside the entrance. A few feet away, another lay facedown. There was a scream from the next room, followed by a gunshot and the sound of something heavy hitting the floor. Willie was a one-man wrecking crew. It was a wonder if even needed Jonas along on the job.

He heard footsteps above him. Cautiously, Jonas crept up the stairs to the next floor. His shotgun rested across his arm, swiveling back and forth, ready to bark at a moment's notice. He was nervous, admittedly so. He'd been in shootouts and killed people before, but never on a tactical hit. "Them or me," he whispered to himself. There was movement to his left. Jonas didn't think twice. He whirled and fired. On the floor, near the archway of the kitchen, lay a boy who didn't look to be much older than Jonas. Lying next to him was the .45 he'd meant to use to end Jonas's life. "Them or me."

Jonas found no resistance as he moved up another level to the top floor. There were two bedrooms on either side, one at the top of the stairs and another one down the hall. Jonas peered into both bedrooms, the one on the right first, and then the left. One was a child's room, decorated in shades of pink with stuffed animals lining the bed. Jonas wondered what the child who occupied the room would say when she came home and found the mess that they had made of her home.

He whirled when he heard a noise at the end of the hall. It was coming from the bedroom. Jonas considered waiting for Willie to catch up but reasoned whoever it was might escape out of one of the windows by then. This was his mission, and he had to take control of it. He had to boss the fuck up.

Jonas made his way to the last bedroom, careful to keep his back to the wall so he couldn't be ambushed from behind. He placed his ear to the door and heard movement inside. Someone was definitely hiding in there. He placed his hand on the doorknob, just about to rush the room when he heard something behind him. He spun in time to see someone bounding up the stairs. Instinctively, Jonas went down to one knee so that he could fire the shotgun from the hip. No sooner than he went down, a bullet pierced the bedroom door where his head had been seconds before. Someone inside was shooting at him.

Jonas dropped onto his back and fired the shotgun through his legs. The man who had been coming up the stairs took a spray to the face. If he wasn't dead, he probably wished that he were. Still on his back, Jonas kicked the door open. The shooter was still standing, fired high, and missed him. Jonas jerked the trigger once more and tore the man's stomach out with the shotgun.

Pulling himself to his feet, Jonas carefully made his way into the bedroom. The guy he had shot was on the floor, clutching his gut, rolling around and moaning in pain. Jonas kicked the gun out of his reach, then planted his foot on his chest. He looked down at his frightened face and recognized it from the picture. "You must be Flair," he sneered down at him.

"Don't kill me . . . I ain't got nothing in the house," Flair pleaded with him.

"See, you already starting off on the wrong foot . . . No pun intended." Jonas stomped him in the face. "I been waiting for this for so long that I don't know whether to shoot you or just bash your fucking skull in like I did your homeboy."

"What are you talking about?" Flair was confused.

"I'm talking about our sins coming back to haunt us,"
Jonas laughed maniacally. He wished Ace could be there
to see what was about to happen.

"I ain't never seen you a day in my life. You got the
wrong man," Flair insisted.

"Oh, I've got the right man," Jonas told him. "Your sins
have come back to haunt you, homie."

Flair studied Jonas for a moment and then nodded his
head as if he had just figured something out. "He sent
you, didn't he? You Ceaver's new boy, huh?"

"I ain't nobody's boy," Jonas checked him.

Flair tried to laugh, but pain shot through his stomach,
and instead, a cough came out. "That's the same thing I
used to say until I realized that I couldn't wipe my ass
without him telling me what kind of toilet paper to use.
How much is he paying you?"

"This isn't about money."

"It's *always* about the money, shorty. That's how he
gets us, by promising things we could never get on our
own. Take a poor kid who ain't never had nothing and
give him something, and he'll do whatever you want,
including kill." Flair looked at the shotgun barrel.

"You think you know my story?" Jonas asked angrily.
He felt like Flair was trying to get into his head.

"Your story . . . my story . . . They'll all play out the same.
There will come a time when you think you've made it.
Everything Ceaver has promised will finally be yours.
You will weigh what you've sacrificed versus what you've
gained and figure it was all worth it—and then it'll turn
to shit. It's at that moment when you'll finally realize the
nature of the monster you're dealing with," Flair warned.

"We done?"

"I don't suppose me offering you the hundred grand
I've got in the stash will get you to let me walk out of
here?" Flair offered. Jonas gave him a look that said: "not
happening." "Guess not," he chuckled. "Well, when you

gotta go, you gotta go." He lunged for the shotgun. Flair never even felt it when Jonas blew his head off.

"For Doug," Jonas whispered. It was an emotional moment; one that he had been dreaming about for years. He only wished that Ace and Mula could've been there to share it with him.

"That Flair always was a smooth talker." Willie's voice startled him. He had been standing in the doorway of the bedroom watching the whole exchange. "For a minute, I thought you were going to take the money."

"Some things are worth more than money," Jonas told him. He wiped a lone tear from his face with his finger.

Jonas and Willie spent the next forty minutes searching the house for whatever they could find to loot. It was mostly drugs, a kilo stashed here, a few ounces in the freezer. All told, they had unearthed maybe two and a half kilos. That wasn't all they found. Flair had been lying about having a hundred thousand stashed. It was closer to two hundred thousand. The idiot hadn't even had the good sense to keep his cash in a safe. The money was stuffed into shoe boxes that lined the closet in the pink room. Even after giving Lou his cut, and the rest split between the two killers, Jonas would still clear about sixty grand for himself. That was more than enough to seriously entertain Prince's offer.

Jonas and Willie were making a last sweep of the room Flair's body was in. Willie was going through the drawers looking for jewelry, while Jonas checked under the bed. It was just then that Jonas realized they had never checked the small closet in that room. Having found the money in one closet, he was anxious to see what they would find in this one. He wasn't sure what to expect but definitely didn't expect what he discovered.

There was a woman huddled on the floor of the closet. She was dressed only in a pair of satin pajamas, as if she had been in bed when the men stormed their brownstone. "Out!" He grabbed her by the arm and pulled her from the closet. She stumbled and spilled on the floor. When she turned, Jonas was able to get a good look at her face, and he had to do a double take. It was the woman from his dream—either that or a dead ringer.

"Please, don't kill me!" she pleaded.

"I'm not going to kill you," Jonas assured her. Flair and the men guarding him knew the rules of engagement. They were soldiers, and therefore, fair game. This was different. When he reached down to help her to her feet is when he saw the flash of something tucked into her pajama pants. By the time he realized that it was a gun, she had already drawn and fired.

Jonas managed to stumble out of the line of fire, but not before a bullet creased his cheek. Searing pain shot through his face. He pulled the trigger on the shotgun— and to his dismay, it clicked empty. As he stared down the barrel of the woman's gun, the woman he had tried to help, he couldn't help but think of Jo-Jo and the promise he had broken. "I'm sorry," he whispered and closed his eyes.

There was a thunderous bang. Jonas braced himself for the impact of the bullet . . . but after a few beats, he realized that he hadn't been hit. He opened his eyes in time to see the woman stumble to one side. Blood was gushing from her shoulder. There was a second bang. This time, the side of her head exploded. The woman crashed to the floor, dead eyes staring up at the ceiling. A few seconds later, One-Eye Willie stepped into view. Both of his guns were breathing smoke. He had saved Jonas from a terrible fate.

"Thanks," Jonas said weakly. His heart was beating so hard and so fast that it sent blood rushing to his head, and he was feeling dizzy.

Willie reached down and grabbed Jonas by the front of his shirt. He lifted him as if he weighed nothing and pinned him against the wall. Willie sneered at Jonas, pushing the hot barrel of one of his guns into the soft flesh of Jonas's neck. "You stupid, fucking kid; you almost got yourself killed!"

"I—"

"Shut up . . . Don't you say another fucking word!" Willie shook Jonas like a rag doll. "I don't know what kind of hopscotch shit you and your boys play on them crack-corners, but this ain't it. When we erase a mutha-fucka, *everybody* goes. I don't give a shit if it's the nigga's granny. They get caught out of bounds, they're dead—or we are! Now, Lou may think that you're hot shit, but I ain't convinced. If you ain't got the stomach to dance with a man like Lou Ceaver, then I suggest you get off the floor before the record stops spinning. If not, you're sure as shit going to wish you had before it's all said and done."

Chapter Thirty-three

The hit at Flair's had rattled Jonas. Probably more so than he had let on. Jonas had shot men before, but the game of extermination was something different. He could still see Willie moving through the brownstone shooting people like fish in a barrel. Then there was the girl, the one from his dream. Willie blew her wig off without so much as a second thought. Jonas had always fancied himself a seasoned killer, but he was small potatoes when compared to One-Eye Willie.

Willie drove him to an apartment where he made Jonas shower and change. He took the clothes they'd been wearing and the pistols and packed them up to be properly disposed of. He hardly said two words to Jonas on the ride back home. Willie was pissed, and rightfully so. Jonas's sense of morality had caused him to hesitate, and it had almost gotten him killed.

"I'll explain to Lou what happened," Jonas said when Willie dropped him on the corner of his block. He knew the detective wouldn't be happy about how he had conducted himself on his first paid contract, but it was better that he heard it from him instead of Willie.

For a minute, Willie didn't respond. He just sat there, both hands locked tightly on the steering wheel like he was trying to compose himself. "Leave it be, kid. What happens on the field stays on the field."

"Thanks."

"Don't thank me now. Thank me in five years if you find that you haven't found that swallowing a bullet is a better option than doing what will be required of you in the service of Lou Ceaver. If you can hold it together that long, thank me then." Willie peeled off.

When Jonas got upstairs to his floor, he was surprised to find Jewels sitting on the steps. He took one look at her and knew something was wrong. She looked tired, and dark circles were around her eyes. She held a bottle of Hennessy in one hand and a Newport in the other. Jewels didn't smoke cigarettes.

"What it do?" he greeted her.

"Does it still matter to you?" she replied, instead of giving the customary response.

"Damn, you're acting like I kicked your dog or something. Fuck is your problem?" Jonas didn't feel like getting into it with her.

"My problem is that I've been trying to reach you, and you're looping me like I'm some chickenhead trying to find out why you never called after fucking me," she snapped.

"Well, I've been busy."

"So, I've heard," Jewels said. Jonas knew from that, that she had been talking to Ace.

"A'ight, so what's so important that you been blowing my phone up?" he asked, wanting to cut straight to the chase. He didn't have time for Jewels and her emotional shit. He'd almost lost his life, so whatever was eating at her failed in comparison.

"My uncle died yesterday," she said with a heavy heart.

"Moe?" Jonas immediately felt like shit for the way he had been treating her. "What happened?"

"He's gone, Wrath," Jewels said with a heavy heart. "He had a heart attack. Shit took him out."

"Damn, I'm sorry, Jewels." Jonas hugged her to him. He was truly sad to hear about Fat Moe. He had been a good man. "You okay?"

"No, I'm fucked up. My uncle was all I had in this world. Now that he's gone, I'm all alone," she sobbed.

"You're not alone, Jewels. You still got me," Jonas told her.

"Yeah, when you have time to pencil me in. I really needed you, Wrath, and you ducked me. That shit is foul."

"Jewels, I wasn't ducking you. I was just . . . never mind. It's not even important. You look like shit. Have you eaten anything?"

"No, been me and the dog for the last two days." Jewels hoisted the bottle of Hennessey.

"Well, how about you give the dog a rest for a minute and put something on your stomach?" Jonas plucked the bottle from her hand. "My mom is cooking. Come eat with us."

"Nah, y'all don't need my depressed ass around right now. Go be with your family," she told him.

"You *are* my family, Jewels. Come have dinner with us; then I'll help you start putting things in order for Fat Moe."

When Jonas walked in with Jewels, he found Anette and Jo-Jo setting the table. Janette was in the kitchen finishing up dinner, but she wasn't alone. Sweets was helping her. She had made good on her promise and showed up. Her eyes lit up when she saw Jewels.

"Hey, stranger!" Sweets hugged Jewels. They had always been close. They spent a lot of time together back when Sweets was learning how to cook from Fat Moe.

"Hi, Sweets." Jewels did a poor job of hiding the sadness in her voice.

"What's wrong?" Sweets asked.

"I lost my uncle yesterday."

"Oh my God!" Sweets gasped. "I'm so sorry to hear it. I didn't even know Moe was sick."

"None of us did. I guess he'd been sick for a while but hid it," Jewels said.

"Well, you know if you need help with anything, I'm here for you. Money to pay for the funeral, support . . . Whatever you need, I got you," Sweets told her.

"Thanks." Jewels mustered a weak smile.

"Ma, is it okay if Jewels eats with us?" Jonas asked.

"Of course. Just have Josette set another place at the table," Janette said. "Now, the two of you go wash your hands. Knowing y'all, ain't no telling where they've been."

Dinner at the Rafferty house turned out to be quite memorable. Not just because Janette had put her foot in the food . . . fried chicken, baked macaroni and cheese, collard greens, and corn bread, but because, for once, they seemed like a real family. Everybody was there . . . except for Yvette. As usual, she was out somewhere running the streets. It saddened Janette that she hadn't bothered to show up, but she tried not to let it dampen the mood.

Jo-Jo told them all about her adventures in school that day, including the wig-snatching incident with the teacher. Jewels roared with laughter when Jo-Jo got up and did the reenactment. Jonas was glad to see her smiling.

As they ate, they talked. Everybody went around the table and shared their blessings and good things that they had going on in their lives. Jo-Jo was doing well in school, as was Anette. She had raised her GPA to a 3.7 and stood a good chance at getting a scholarship to a four-year school of her choice. She had been seriously considering UCLA. Janette didn't want her going so far away to school, but she understood her daughter's need to spread her wings. Jonas kept waiting for Sweets to break the news about her deciding to go back to school, but she hadn't yet. He figured she was just waiting for the right time.

"So, Jewels, when are you and my brother gonna get married?" Jo-Jo asked, quite unexpectedly.

The question caught Jonas so off guard that he almost spit his Kool-Aid out. "Girl, stop talking crazy."

"I'm not talking crazy. When people love each other, they usually get married. I know you two love each other because of how you're always looking at each other. Been a long time since I've seen Jonas look at a girl like that," Jo-Jo said with a knowing smirk.

An awkward silence fell over the table. Anette was cutting her eyes at Jonas, and for a minute, he wondered if she had revealed the secret of Alex being back in town. If she had, he would kill her for blowing up his spot.

"Josette, stay out of grown folks' business," Janette stepped in. She too had seen the look on Jonas's face at the mention of Alex and knew something was up.

"I don't think your brother is the marrying type. He's got too much going on in his life for a committed relationship," Jewels said. She too had seen the look.

"Well, he needs to stop and smell the roses. Running them streets from sun up to sun up ain't gonna do nothing but burn you out," Janette said.

"You tell him, Ms. Janette," Jewels cosigned.

"That goes for you too, Jewels. Just because I ain't out there no more doesn't mean I don't know what's going on." Janette gave her a look. "I think both of you need to take some time to enjoy being kids for a while, instead of being in such a rush to grow up. Adulthood will be there when you're ready."

"Personally, I wouldn't mind seeing Jonas and Jewels together. Nothing like having a good girl in your corner who you know isn't going to leave you when things get rough," Sweets capped.

"I see you're a comedian this evening, *Claudette*." Jonas called her by her birth name just to irk her. "While you're over there trying to play matchmaker when is Drew going to put a ring on *your* finger?"

"He's proposed to her twice, but Sweets keeps shooting him down," Anette volunteered. This shocked everyone at the table.

"Why is this my first time hearing about this?" Janette asked.

"Ma, it's no big deal," Sweets downplayed it.

"The hell it isn't. Anytime a man proposes to one of my daughters, it's a *big* deal," Janette insisted. "Drew is doing good for himself. Why did you say no?"

Sweets shrugged. "I dunno. I'm too young. I don't think I'm ready to be anybody's wife."

"But you're ready to be his live-in girlfriend?" Jonas asked smugly.

"Me and Drew don't live together. I just spend the night over there sometimes," Sweets corrected him.

"You spend more time over there than you do here," Jo-Jo added.

"Mind your own business!" Sweets snapped.

"Personally, I'm glad you said no. Drew is cool, but I don't think he's right for you," Jonas said.

"And why not?" Sweets questioned.

"Do you really want me to answer that?"

"Enough, you two," Janette interjected. "You know we don't pass judgment in this house. Aside from Josette, I don't think any of us are innocent." Her gaze fell on Jonas. "Sweets, whatever you choose to do, we will support you as a family. Ain't that right, Jonas?"

"Yes, ma'am," he mumbled.

Chapter Thirty-four

After they ate dinner, Sweets and Jewels cleared the table while Anette put Jo-Jo to bed. She wasn't feeling well. Jonas worried about his little sister. The treatments she was getting helped ensure that she didn't get sicker, but they didn't seem to be improving her condition. He had looked into getting her some specialized help, but most of the places he found didn't accept Medicaid and charged a small fortune just to get her in the door. Jonas needed a come-up in a major way. This made him think back to Prince's deal. If the brand blew up like Prince was predicting, then he would be able to get Jo-Jo the best of care.

"You okay?" Janette brought him out of his thoughts. She was smoking a cigarette and sipping a glass of water.

"I'm fine. Just got a lot on my mind," he said.

"Heavy is the head," Janette said. She took a seat on the couch next to him. "I wanna thank you for making time for us, Jonas."

"You don't have to thank me, Ma. I wanted to be here," he told her.

"I wish all my children felt that way," Janette said, thinking about Yvette.

"Don't stress yourself over her, Ma," Jonas said as if he could read her mind.

"Let's see how easy it'll be for you to say that when you have children of your own."

"That's something you're never gonna have to worry about. I ain't having no kids. I'd never curse them to this fucked-up world."

"It ain't the world, Jonas. It's the people in it. You know, sometimes I look back on all the time I wasted running in the streets instead of spending it with my kids, and it breaks my heart. There is so much that I wanted to do for you all, and so many things I wanted you to experience. All that damn time wasted." She shook her head sadly.

"You did what you could, Ma. Don't worry about it. We've got plenty of time to do all that stuff still," he assured her.

"Life ain't forever, Jonas. We're given very little time in this world, so we should make the most out of every precious moment," Janette replied. There was a far-off look in her eyes.

"Ma, you're starting to scare me."

"I'm sorry, baby. Don't worry about me. I just get lost in nostalgia sometimes." Janette smiled. "So, how is she?"

"Who, Jewels?"

"We both know I'm not talking about Jewels. I mean Alex. I'm sure you've seen her by now," Janette said knowingly.

Jonas thought about lying but decided against it. "Yeah, I was with her earlier," he admitted.

Janette shook her head. "You always were like a dog on a bone when it came to her. She's always had power over you."

"And what makes you think she has power over me?" he asked.

"Because as soon as she comes back around, you're suddenly blind to what you have and chasing what you want," Janette said. "That girl Jewels loves you, Jonas. You know that, right?"

"It ain't that serious." Jonas downplayed it.

"For you maybe, but for her, it's real. You can see it in her eyes when she looks at you; that longing in them. I know Jewels might not have the pedigree of Alex, but she's a genuine soul. I hope you don't break that girl's heart, Jonas."

"As my mother, you're supposed to be on *my* side," he pointed out.

"I'm your mother, but I'm a woman first. You're old enough to where I can't tell you where to stick your little thing, but what I will tell you is to be careful when you're playing games of the heart."

"Me and anybody I deal with have an understanding. They all know what it is," Jonas said proudly.

Janette laughed. "You sound just like your dad when you say that. He thought he had all his hoes in line too, but we see how *that* played out."

"How come you never talk about him?" Jonas asked.

"I guess sometimes it's just too painful," Janette admitted. "Zeke was a good man, but he also brought a lot of grief into this house."

"You mean because he slept around on you?" Jonas asked. He had heard the stories about how big of a womanizer his father had been.

"A man is going to be a man, I guess. Zeke's wandering dick was only part of the problem. He played with fire and got burned, almost burning the rest of us in the process," Janette said angrily.

Jonas was quiet for a time. He had so many questions about his father but wasn't quite sure how deep he wanted to dig. "What really happened to my father?" he finally asked.

Janette studied her son for what felt like an eternity. She had been dreading this day but knew it would come eventually. She didn't want to tell him the truth but knew that she needed to. She wanted to spare her son the pain of committing the sins of his father. "I will speak about it just this once. You are never to ask me again or tell your sisters what I'm about to tell you. Do you understand?"

Jonas nodded.

Janette took a sip of her water and lit another cigarette. She needed to compose herself for the tale she was about to tell. "Well, it's no secret that your father was in the streets. Never too heavy, but from time to time, he did what he had to do to keep food on our table. In the course of Zeke's wheeling and dealing, he found himself hooked in with a very dangerous man. It started with Zeke doing little stuff for him here and there, but as time went on, the favors he was asking got bigger. I tried to get Zeke to cut ties with him, but by the time I understood what he was involved with, he was already in too deep. Eventually, Zeke did try to break away, but the man wouldn't let him. Zeke started trying to duck him, but it never worked. The man always seemed to be able to find him, no matter which hole he crawled into. Eventually, Zeke saw only one way to break the hold the man had over him, so he ended his life."

"Why lie to us all these years about him being killed?" Jonas asked emotionally.

"I never lied to you; I just never told you all the details. That part is true. Zeke had a nice-sized life insurance policy, but we wouldn't have been paid a dime if he committed suicide. So he figured another way. He knew what would happen if he was ever caught with her, which is exactly why he kept going back."

"He intentionally got the man to murder him so that you could cash in the policy?" Jonas said, with the pieces finally starting to fit.

Janette nodded. "That was Zeke for you. He could find a loophole in even the most airtight agreements. I always told him he should've been a lawyer," she half-joked.

By the time his mother finished her story, Jonas was numb. All these years, he had thought his father had been killed over some bullshit, only to find out that he had orchestrated his own murder for the good of his family. He wasn't sure if he hated him for taking the coward's way out or respected him for putting his woman and kids above his own life. "What happened to the man? The one Daddy was in debt to?"

"I have no clue. If there's really a God, then that bastard is rotting in hell by now," Janette spat. Just then, she was hit by a wave of coughing. This time, it was bad, so bad that she had trouble catching her breath.

"I got you!" Jonas patted her back until the fit of coughing passed. When she removed her hand from her mouth, specks of blood were in her palm. "Ma, you need to go to the hospital."

"I keep telling you I'm fine," Janette insisted. She pulled a napkin from her pocket and wiped her palm on it.

"You okay?" Sweets came out of the kitchen with Jewels on her heels.

"Yes."

"No, she isn't. She's coughing up blood," Jonas told his sister.

"Ma, I'm taking you to the E.R. Get your coat," Sweets ordered her.

"I wish you all would stop fussing over me. It's nothing," Janette protested.

"Coughing blood is not nothing. We're taking you to the hospital," Jonas said.

"I'm not going to sit up in no emergency room all night, just for them to prescribe me antibiotics or some other shit that I don't need. I'm supposed to be going for a checkup in a few days anyhow. I'll see about my cough then," Janette promised.

Jonas wanted to argue with her, but he knew it wouldn't do any good. You couldn't force one of the Rafferty women to do anything they didn't want to. One thing was for sure, though. He would make sure that he was around to see that she kept her appointment.

Once things had settled down, they all sat in the living room to watch television. Reruns of *The Cosby Show* were on. Jonas had always loved that show. He would sometimes dream about what it might've been like to be a Huxtable instead of a Rafferty. While everyone else's attention was on Bill Cosby, Jonas was thinking about his father and the man who had driven him to his death.

In the middle of their show, they heard the front door open and slam loudly. A few seconds later, Yvette appeared in the living room. She was wearing leggings, heels, and a T-shirt that was a size too small. Her hair was slightly mussed, and her eye shadow was partially wiped off one eye. She looked a hot mess. With her was a shifty-looking, light-skinned dude who Jonas had seen around before. Jonas didn't know his name, but he knew his game. He was a stickup kid.

"I hope you didn't wake Jo-Jo up when you slammed that door," Anette said with an attitude. When they were younger, the twins were very close, but as they got older and Yvette got wilder, they had grown apart.

"Sorry," Yvette said in a less-than-sincere tone. From the slight slur of her words, you could tell she had been drinking.

"We missed you at dinner," Janette said.

"My bad. I guess I lost track of time. Is there any food left?" she asked.

"I left a plate in the oven for you. Make sure you wash your hands before you go in my kitchen," Janette told her.

Noticing that all eyes were on her guest, Yvette finally made the introductions. "Oh, this is my friend, Steve. Steve, this is everybody."

"What up?" Steve offered in the way of a greeting.

"Oh, Sweets, I'm glad you're here. I need a favor," Yvette said to her sister.

"No," Sweets said flatly.

"But you don't even know what the favor is."

"Knowing you, it's probably money, so the answer is no," Sweets said firmly.

"C'mon, Sweets. I don't need but twenty dollars. I'll pay you back when I get paid Friday," Yvette whined.

"You must think I'm stupid. I spoke to Mr. Lewis at the supermarket the other day, and he told me they fired you two weeks ago. Said you kept showing up late and high," Sweets informed her. "Besides, you still owe me $100 from the last time I loaned you money."

"You acting like you ain't got it. All the coke your man is pumping in the hood, I know you ain't hurting for no bread." Yvette folded her arms.

"What my man does or what's in my pockets ain't none of your business." Sweets rolled her eyes.

"I can't stand a bitch that gets a little come-up and think they better than everybody else," Yvette spat.

"You know I don't play with people calling me out of my name. Watch your mouth," Sweets warned.

"How about you, Mama? You got twenty dollars?" Yvette asked.

"Yeah, but I ain't about to give it to you to shove up your nose. Why don't you ask your new friend?" Janette eyed Steve.

"Because I'm asking you!" Yvette got loud.

"Yvette, if you're hungry, I'll feed you. If you're tired, I'll give you somewhere to lay your head, but I can't contribute to you hurting yourself," Janette told her. It broke her heart to see her daughter like that.

"Ain't this some shit?" Yvette snorted. "All I'm asking for is twenty damn dollars, and I can't get it? It's the least you can do, considering you ain't never did shit else for us."

"I'm gonna let that slide because I know it's the drugs talking, but don't push your luck," Janette warned her.

"What? You gonna go upside my head again like you used to do?" Yvette challenged. "I ain't a little girl no more, Mama. I'm grown."

"If you're grown, then you shouldn't have a problem getting your own money," Janette replied. "Why don't you let me get you some help, Yvette?"

"If that ain't the damn pot calling the kettle black! You spent my entire childhood banging smack and selling pussy, and now you wanna try to tell me something?" Yvette was becoming belligerent.

"Yvette, you bugging. That's still our mother," Jonas spoke up. He could feel the tension mounting and knew the situation was about to take a turn for the worse.

"Ha! Now you wanna try to play the good son?" Yvette laughed. "You ain't shit either, *Wrath*. You think I don't know what you out here doing?"

Jonas got up off the couch and addressed Steve. "Fam, I think it'd probably be a good idea if you and my sister go back to wherever it is y'all just came from. At least, until she comes back to her senses."

"Don't talk to him like he's one of your little friends!" Yvette barked. "Ain't nobody scared of you, Jonas."

"Yvette, I'm warning you." Jonas's voice dripped ice.

"What? You gonna shoot me too? Or maybe you're just gonna bash my skull in like you did Black? I know all your dirty little secrets, Wrath. The streets are talking," Yvette sneered.

Jonas hadn't even realized that he had moved until his sister bounced off the living room wall. He had slapped her so hard that it sounded like a gunshot. He grabbed her by her throat and lifted her damn near off the ground.

"You disrespectful little bitch! Who the fuck do you think you're talking to?"

"Jonas, let her go!" Jewels tried to pry his hands from around Yvette's neck, but he shoved her away.

"If you weren't my sister, I'd put your junkie ass in the fucking ground!" Jonas rained spittle in her face. He was choking her so hard that Yvette's eyes had begun to bulge.

Steve finally got over the shock of what was unfolding and decided to do something. He ran up on Jonas and sucker punched him.

Jonas released Yvette, letting her fall to the ground. He then turned his rage-filled eyes toward Steve. "She's family, so I can't kill her, but you?" he cracked his knuckles. "You're about to meet God."

Jonas attacked Steve with a fury that none of them had ever seen him display before. He rained punches all over his head and face. Steve tried to defend himself, but he was no match for Jonas. All five of the women in the living room tried to pull Jonas off him, but they couldn't. He was in an insane rage. Long after Steve was on the floor, unconscious, Jonas was still hitting him and screaming curses. The only thing that stopped Jonas from killing him was Jo-Jo.

"Jonas?" Jo-Jo appeared at the end of the hall.

When Jonas looked up and saw the terrified expression on his sister's face, he stopped his pummeling of Steve. He could only imagine how he must've appeared to her, fists slick with blood and his shirt torn. "Jo-Jo, I . . ." He couldn't find the words. With terror in her eyes, the girl ducked back into her room and slammed the door.

"I'll go check on her." Anette rushed past him.

Jonas pushed himself to his feet and took stock of what he had done. Steve was sprawled on the floor. His face looked like hamburger, and the only sign that he was still alive were the gurgles of bloody bubbles coming from his mouth. When he turned to face the women in the living room, they all looked terrified of him, even Jewels. She had heard the stories about Jonas when he became Wrath, but this was her first time seeing it firsthand.

"I'm so sorry," Jonas whispered to his mother before rushing from the apartment.

Jonas was on fire when he got outside. He could feel the anger clawing at his insides like an animal fighting to get out of a cage. He began screaming like a madman, punching out the windows of parked cars. He had knocked out three of them before Jewels came out behind him.

"Jonas," she called after him.

"Leave me alone, Jewels," he growled and started stalking down the block. With the mood he was in, he didn't trust himself.

"No." She caught up with him. Jewels grabbed him by the arm and spun him around. Jonas tried to turn his face away, but she held it in her hands and forced him to face her. "Look at me," she commanded. His eyes were full of anger and tears. "I got you. Do you hear me? I got you."

Jonas felt some of the rage begin to drain away, but it still lingered beneath the surface of his skin like worms. "I'm sorry you had to see me like this," he sobbed.

"Don't you dare apologize to me for being you. You've seen me at my lowest and never judged me. Me and you against everybody else, right?"

"I can't, Jewels . . . I can't bring you into this madness. I'm poison," Jonas said sadly.

"Then let me be your antidote," she replied. "Don't you understand that I am here for you? Where you lead, I will follow."

"You don't want to go where I'm going," Jonas said, thinking about the murders of Flair and his lady.

"What part of *I will follow* don't you understand? I want to help you, with whatever is going on with you, but you have to let me in. I will do any and everything in my power to make sure your heart is always protected."

"Even kill for me?" Jonas asked. He had been trying to turn Jewels off, anything he could think of to get the girl to wash her hands of him.

Jewels looked at him with great seriousness and said, "Without question."

Chapter Thirty-five

Jonas didn't return home that night. Instead, he and Jewels checked into a motel in the Bronx. She suggested that they stay at Fat Moe's since there was nobody there, but Jonas declined. It was too close to home for his taste. He was ashamed of what he had done. Not because Yvette and Steve didn't have it coming, but because he had let his control slip, and Jo-Jo had been there to witness it. The poor girl would probably have nightmares over it.

A pair of warm hands brought Jonas out of his daze. Jewels eased up behind him and began massaging his shoulders. "You're tense," she breathed into his ear. He could smell the faint trace of Hennessy on her breath from the bottle they had been sipping from for half the night.

"You would be too if you had so much weighing on you," he said over his shoulder.

"I told you, you don't have to carry it alone." She kissed his earlobe, sending a wave through his body. "I got you." Jewels eased from behind him and straddled his lap. She was naked. Her perky breasts brushed against his chest. She had a flat stomach, and her erect nipples reminded him of Hershey's kisses. Jewels spent so much time in jeans and baggy shirts that he sometimes forgot how nice her body was. She began grinding back and forth on his lap, causing his dick to rise through his jeans.

"Damn," Jonas rasped, feeling like he was about to burst through his zipper.

"Let him come out to play," she whispered while undoing his pants.

Jonas didn't resist when she pushed him back on the bed and began sliding his pants and underwear over his hips. His penis stood tall and hard. She gripped it with one hand and began tugging on it firmly. She was taking him there. When she made to slide down between his legs, he stopped her. "You don't have to." He knew that Jewels didn't like giving head. It had something to do with the boy she had lost her virginity to forcing her to go down on him. Jonas enjoyed a good blow job. He'd had a few but never stressed her about it.

"I want to," she said and took him into her mouth.

Her lips were warm when they wrapped around the head of his dick. She took him, a little bit at a time, making it halfway down his shaft before he hit the back of her throat. When she first began the task, he winced as her teeth scraped him, but he didn't complain. He was glad that she was inexperienced at sucking dick. He often found that he looked at girls funny who were too skilled. Ace called it "mileage mouth," which she didn't have. He let his mind drift as she serviced him, forgetting the problems of the world and enjoying what she was doing.

"You like that?" Jewels paused long enough to ask.

"I love that," he replied.

Jewels went back to giving him oral, slow, and then fast, and slow again. She could feel his body tense like he was about to blow. "You better not." She popped his dick out of her mouth. She knew him all too well.

She slid up his body, causing him to shiver. Her skin was so warm against his. She straddled him, running her clit up and down his throbbing shaft. Jewels reached back and began slipping him inside her, but Jonas stopped her. "Chill; let me get a condom."

"Not tonight. I want to feel you, Wrath." She kissed him.

Sweets had always warned Jonas about having sex without a condom, and except for the night he had lost his virginity to Jewels, he always did. There was something about the pleading look in her eyes that moved him. Against his better judgment, he honored her request and hit it raw.

To say that her pussy felt much better without a condom than it did with one would've been an understatement. She was tight, wet, and . . . oh so inviting. It was like God had carved out her pussy for the sole purpose of receiving his dick. He lasted through about fifteen minutes of her riding him before he felt himself about to bust. He tried to lift her off him, but Jewels pushed all her weight down on him and locked her legs around his.

"Give it to me, Wrath . . . Fill me up . . . Fill me up!" she moaned. Before he could even stop himself, Jonas let off inside her. Even after he had spilled his seed, she kept going, making sure that she had drained him.

"Why did you do that?" Jonas shoved her off him.

"Why you tripping?" Jewels asked as if it were no big deal.

"I'm tripping because I don't want kids. You know that." Jonas got up and went to retrieve his pack of cigarettes from the motel room desk.

"Maybe it's just that you don't want to have a kid with *me*," Jewels accused.

"What are you talking about?"

"I'm talking about Alex!" she replied. "You think I don't know why you've been so preoccupied the last couple of days? As soon as I heard she was back in town, I knew you'd be off chasing her."

"It isn't like that, Jewels," Jonas tried to explain. "Me and Alex just have a history."

"And *we* don't?" she fired back. "I don't recall her being by your side when shit got thick, stashing your drugs, holding your guns, tending to your wounds whenever you got hurt. Where was *she* for all that?"

"I'm out." Jonas started gathering his things.

"That's right, run from the truth like you always do," Jewels taunted him.

"What do you want from me, Jewels?"

"I want you to stop selling me false hope!" she said passionately. Tears ran down her cheeks.

"Please don't cry over me, Jewels. I'm not worth it." Jonas felt bad. What she was saying were all the things he felt but didn't have the heart to put into words.

"That's what girls do when they're hurt. They cry." Jewels wiped her eyes.

"It was never my intention to hurt you." Jonas embraced her.

"I know. I did this to myself. I knew I could never have all of you and instead of moving on, I settled for whatever pieces of you I could get. I was a fool for loving you, Jonas."

Her words stung because they were full of truth. He hadn't realized it until that moment, but all those years he had been running around with Jewels he had just been passing the time until Alex came back to him. Seeing her all broken up over him made him think of what his mother had probably gone through with his father. He wasn't sure what else to do, so he kissed her.

Jonas made love to Jewels for the second time that night. This time, it was slow and passionate. She cried the whole time. Whether they were tears of joy or pain, he was unsure. He just didn't want her to hurt anymore. When they were done, they rolled over to their respective sides of the bed, both lost in their own thoughts. As Jonas drifted off to sleep, he heard Jewels whisper softly, "You'll never know how much a bitch loves you until she kills for you."

Part IV

"Then said Jesus unto him, Put up again your sword into his place: for all they that take the sword shall perish with the sword."

—Matthew 26:52 (KJV)

Chapter Thirty-six

The last year or so of Jonas's life had been a bittersweet one. He had gained quite a bit but measured against what he'd lost, he wasn't sure that it had been worth it. He took the money he had ripped off from the hit on Flair and gave every dime to Prince. They finally had enough to buy into the company his cousins were getting up and running. Prince had made the trip to London to oversee the deal personally. Jonas wanted to go with him, but he didn't have a passport yet. Prince had been right in his prediction about it blowing up. They were selling pieces out of the boutique and the online store, and they had also secured contracts to supply merchandise to several major retailers in the States. Jonas beamed every time he saw someone in the streets wearing the pieces. Granted, they were only stockholders, but they were still making money.

After what seemed like forever, construction was nearly complete on his social club. Between the weather causing work stoppages, and problems they kept running into with acquiring the necessary permits, Jonas was beginning to think that it would never get done. Thanks to Detective Ceaver pulling a few strings, and Jonas paying extra to the right people, they had finally managed to push through. They would be ready to have their grand opening by his birthday, which was in a little over a month.

The night of the grand opening was going to be a special one. Not just because it was Jonas's birthday, but because it would signal the end of summer and Alex's time in New York. She was done with Spellman, and it was time for her to leave for the exchange program in London. He had known for a long time that it was coming, but now that the moment was almost on them, it had started to become real. He was still having trouble wrapping his mind around the fact that they would be apart for months. Of course, there was a standing invitation for Jonas to come and visit, but this wasn't like the short flight to Atlanta. London was on the other side of the world. It was going to be tough on him, and he still wasn't sure how he was going to make it through the coming nights without her.

In the meantime, he had thrown himself into his work. Jonas had recently discovered a trade where he could make as much for a few hours of work as he could playing the block all week. *Murder for Hire.* It was Detective Ceaver who had planted the idea in his head. When he'd first approached Jonas with the idea, he had been against it. He was trying to master one hustle at a time, and right then, all his energy was going into keeping the drug business going. Lou was able to sway him by running through the list of people he had killed and never received a dime for. "If you're going to be out here killing anyhow, you may as well get paid for it," the detective had pointed out. He was right. On Jonas's first job, he had been paid $5,000 and ten on the next. With each hit, the bag went up, and he got better at it.

Jonas had even managed to earn the respect of One-Eye Willie. Jonas had become somewhat of a protégé to him. Willie taught him that killing wasn't just about shooting things up. There was an art to it. Jonas had proved to be an adapt pupil, and their shared love for death and money had brought them closer together. It had gotten to a point where he was able to confide as much in Willie as he could members of his inner circle. The older man was quite wise and seemed to have a solution to any problem Jonas brought to him. He grew to love Willie because Willie never judged him and had never broken his confidence. He was a good friend.

His drug business was booming as well. With Flair out of the way, the Broadway side of Grant Projects was wide open. There was some opposition at first. Those who had been loyal to Flair hadn't taken too kindly to the newcomers trying to lay claim to their hood. They didn't want to give up what they felt was theirs, so Jonas sent Mula and Tavion through there every day with machine guns until they got the message. Thanks to Mula, Tavion had finally popped his cherry. He couldn't have had a better teacher than Mula when it came to laying down the murder game. As a reward for their hard work, Jonas made a gift of that territory to the two youngest members of his team. It was Mula's hood, but Tavion was his right hand. Ace didn't like it, wanting, instead, for the position to go to Cal, but he didn't have a say in the matter. It was Jonas's call, and his word was law.

Jonas's business wasn't the only thing that was going well. He and Alex had been growing increasingly closer. They spent the entire summer that she was up from school together, and he had even gone to visit her in Atlanta when classes started back that fall. It was Jonas's first time traveling outside of New York. He was so afraid to get on the plane by himself that he had begged Sweets to go with him. He was surprised that it hadn't taken much convincing. Sweets had been going out of her way to spend time with all her siblings lately. She had even moved back into the apartment. There was obliviously trouble in paradise between Drew and her, but whenever one of them asked, she would simply say they were taking a break. Jonas knew that there had to be more to it than that, and if he found out Drew had hurt his sister, he planned on killing him. He had become very good at killing.

Visiting Atlanta had been like traveling to another planet for Jonas. He had never in his life seen so many well-to-do black folks gathered in one city. Alex was a gracious hostess. She showed them all around the city and even introduced them to some of the kids she went to school with. Jonas had expected them to be uppity or look down their noses at him due to his lack of a proper education, but Alex's friends were cool. They were kids, just like him. Jonas had had so much fun that he had even given some thought about going back to school. He had dropped out in the tenth grade, and being around other kids his age that were living the college life made him realize how much he had missed out on. Not just with school, but with life, period. He had been in the streets so long that he didn't know what it was like to be a teenager. One day, he would take his mother's advice and stop to smell the flowers . . . one day.

A life filled with joy wasn't without pain, and Jonas had come to know a great deal of it. He had gained a lot, but also lost a lot, including two people he loved. As it turned out, his mother's coughing hadn't come from the lingering effects of a cold. She had lung cancer. By the time she was diagnosed, there wasn't much the doctors could do but make sure that she was comfortable for the remainder of her time on earth. Jonas made sure that those were the happiest forty-two days of her life. He made sure that his mother was able to tackle everything that she had wanted to do but never had time to when she was chasing drugs. They were even supposed to fly to Africa together because she had always wanted to see the place where they came from, but, unfortunately, she passed before they were scheduled to leave. He missed his mother dearly but took solace in the fact that he was able to give her flowers while she was living.

All of the Rafferty children took Janette's death hard, but none harder than Yvette. None of the children had been easy to deal with, but Yvette had treated her mother the worst. She was a rotten kid, and her punishment was her mother dying without her ever having a chance to say a proper goodbye because she was out chasing a fix. For a long while, Jonas resented her for that. It would be a long time after his mother had passed before they were able to hold a conversation without him wanting to kill her. In the end, Jonas realized that life was too short to hold grudges. None of them were promised tomorrow, and he would've hated for something to happen to him or one of his sisters with bad blood still lingering. He eventually accepted her back into his life and even got her into a treatment program. He had done his part, and the rest would be up to her.

Jonas sat in the back of the limo, smoking a cigarette and nursing a nip of scotch. There had been five of them stocked in the minibar when he got in. The one in his hand was the last one. Hennessey was his drink of choice, but the scotch had proved to be a more-than-adequate substitute. He needed to numb himself, and it was working.

His eyes drifted out the window to the funeral home. He hadn't been back there since Doug had passed and hadn't expected to be back so soon, especially not under those circumstances. Sweets stood outside, chatting with Tavion and Anette. She was wearing shades, but her face was flushed. You could tell she had been crying. Sweets had never taken death well, even less so when it hit that close to home. It seemed like every time Jonas turned around, he was putting someone in the ground. He was tired of burying people he cared about. Tired of death stealing away his joy. It seemed like a tragedy followed every blessing. They'd all hurt, but none quite like this one.

"Are you ready to go inside?" Alex asked. She was sitting on the seat next to him. She had been so quiet that Jonas had forgotten she was there.

"In a minute," Jonas told her. He was trying to find the strength to say his farewells but couldn't.

"You can't hide in the limo forever, Jonas. Let's go in and get it over with. I'll be there with you every step of the way," Alex promised, taking his hand in hers.

Jonas allowed her to help him out of the limo. His legs felt unsteady, like they wouldn't hold him up. Tavion saw him about to buckle and rushed to his aid, but Jonas waved him off. He would not show signs of weakness, not that day. With his woman and two of his sisters flanking him, Jonas walked inside of the funeral home to say his goodbyes.

The first thing he noticed was how empty the viewing room was. Aside from the stranger sitting on the front row, there were only his sisters and a sprinkling of homies in attendance. You would think that for all the people Jonas helped and all the lives the deceased had enriched, there would've been a grander showing to see his family off. He wanted to spaz out at the lack of respect. Alex must've been reading his mind because she squeezed his hand.

"It's not important," she whispered to him. She was right. Those who were important were in attendance, and those who weren't, Jonas would settle up with at a later date.

It was a closed casket funeral. The body was so damaged that there wasn't much the mortician could do with it. The casket was made from hickory wood that had been polished to a high shine. Brass handles ran along the side of it. The casket seemed small, but then again, so was the person resting inside of it. The lack of height of the deceased had always been the running joke, but no one was laughing now. It was an incredibly solemn moment. The closer he got, the more his stomach lurched. It was a wonder he didn't throw up. With Alex's help, he had finally made it to the front of the aisle. He placed his hand timidly on the casket and felt a wave of sadness wash over him. He couldn't believe Mula was gone.

When Jonas first received word of Mula's death, he had been having dinner with Alex's family. After years of hating Jonas, they were less than pleased to find out that their daughter had been creeping around with him. By this time, the two of them were madly in love, and there wasn't much anyone could do about it. They hadn't accepted him with open arms once they realized that he had the best intentions for their daughter, but the Hightowers eventually began to come around, and agreeing to have dinner with him had been a start.

Stacey had been the one to deliver the news. She was so distraught that he had trouble understanding her at first, but he knew right away that something was wrong. He immediately thought that something had gone down with Ace. He had been moving very recklessly lately, and Jonas knew it would only be a matter of time before he got the call that somebody had whacked him. He finally got her to calm down enough to make sense of what she was saying. He couldn't have heard her right. Mula? *Dead?* It didn't even seem possible. Mula was of the toughest sons of bitches Jonas had ever met. He'd been shot three times that Jonas knew of by the time he was 14 and was still running around giving the streets hell. He had refused to believe it until he had to identify the body. It was Mula, at least what was left of him.

The details of his death wouldn't come out until later. Against Jonas's warning, Ace had entertained Cal and his offer to plug them in with his people in Richmond. He'd even pulled Mula into it with him. To Cal's credit, it had been a sweet setup. The drugs they brought down from New York had the fiends on tilt. Smokers were coming from as far as D.C. to sample their wares. They had been bubbling down there for about six months . . . before everything went wrong. With more money came more problems. Some of the locals hadn't taken kindly to the New Yorkers coming into town and cutting their throats. When they stepped to them, Mula had beaten the brakes off one of the guys. Instead of retaliating like soldiers, they pulled a sucker move and called the police.

The day after the fight, the police rushed the spot. Ace had been off fucking with a chick instead of handling business. Cal went down without a struggle, but not Mula. There were enough guns and drugs in the place to put him away forever, so he went out as he had always lived—by the gun. They put so many holes in Mula that the only way Jonas had been able to identify him was by his tattoos. To Mula's credit, he took three of the cops with him before he went down.

Jonas blamed Ace for what had happened. Had he listened to Jonas, then Mula would still be alive, and Ace wouldn't be a fugitive. Word had it that Cal had dropped a dime on Ace. Jonas had planned to murder Cal, but no one had seen him since. He wanted to kill Ace too, but Alex talked him out of it. He and Ace were like brothers and had too much history for Jonas to kill him over something that he hadn't meant to happen. Ace loved Mula as much as Jonas did, but he was too blinded by the money to see the writing on the wall. They still did business together but from a distance. Whenever Ace was around, Jonas made sure that he wasn't. When they needed to talk, it was through Tavion. Ace could keep his life, but his relationship with Jonas was damaged, possibly to a point beyond repair.

Jonas hadn't realized that he was crying until a tear hit the back of his hand. It was crazy because he hadn't even cried when his mother died. It hadn't been because he didn't love her, but he had to be strong for the girls.

"Are you okay?" Alex asked.

"I'm fine; just give me a minute." Jonas wiped his eyes. Alex lingered for a moment longer before heading to the back of the funeral home to talk to Sweets. Jonas had his head bowed saying a silent prayer over the casket. When he felt someone standing next to him, he looked to see it was the man who had been sitting in the front row. He was an older dude with a salt-and-pepper goatee and a hairline that had begun to abandon him. Jonas didn't appreciate the man invading his space, and his face said as much.

"Didn't mean to disturb you. You're Wrath, right?" The older man extended his hand.

"We know each other?" Jonas asked in an unfriendly tone, not bothering to shake the man's hand.

"No, but my nephew has told me so much about you that I feel like I do. I'm Mula's uncle, Fish." He introduced himself. Fish had been a legend in the streets when he was running with the Red-T boys. He had been locked up during Jonas's and Mula's rise to power.

"Sorry about that." Jonas shook his hand. "My head is elsewhere right now."

"I can dig it. Mine too." Fish's eyes went to the casket. "Fucked me up when I heard what happened to Clyde."

Clyde? Jonas had been running with Mula for years and never knew his government name.

"I want to thank you for taking care of the service," Fish continued. "I've been trying to get back on my feet since I been home, but it hasn't been easy."

K'WAN

"No need to thank me. Mula was my brother. It was the least I could do. Listen, if you ever need anything, all you have to do is reach out. I even got a position for you, if you're up to it?"

"Thanks, but no thanks. I just did an asshole full of time, and I'm in no great rush to go back. At my age, I ain't got no more years left in me to give the state of New York," Fish told him.

"I can respect that. Well, if you need a couple of dollars to fill some of those holes in your pockets, I'll take care of it," Jonas told him. He looked toward the front of the funeral home and saw a familiar face walk in. "Excuse me for a second."

Jonas had almost forgotten how nice Jewels cleaned up when she wasn't decked out in thug gear. She was wearing a black skirt, white blouse, and a pair of black heels. Her hair was straightened and hanging around her shoulders. Jonas and Jewels hadn't seen much of each other after that night at the motel. For a while, they would still hook up from time to time for capers or a quick roll in the sack, but those rendezvous had become fewer between as he got in deeper with Alex. After a while, they stopped messing around altogether. Jonas and Jewels were still cool, but not like they had been.

"What it do?" Jonas greeted her.

"Whatever I tell it to," she replied. There was an awkward pause.

"What's up? You ain't got no love for the kid anymore?" Jonas spread his arms.

Jewels smiled and hugged him. It felt good to be in his arms again. It felt like it had been forever since she'd known his touch. The embrace started to feel too good, so Jewels broke it. "You better be careful. I don't want your girlfriend getting mad at you."

"Knock it off. Alex knows we have history," Jonas said and immediately regretted it. That was the same thing he had told Jewels about Alex that night at the motel.

"So, how you holding up?" Jewels asked.

Jonas shrugged. "Fine, I guess. This shit is rough. You know how close me and Mula were."

"Yeah, besides, Ace that was your closest friend. Speaking of Ace, y'all still beefing?"

"We ain't beefing; we just ain't fucking with each other like that right now," Jonas corrected her.

"Jonas, you need to let that shit go. We both know Ace didn't mean for that shit to happen to Mula. He loved him."

"If he really loved him, he wouldn't have put him in harm's way," Jonas shot back. "I ain't trying to give him no energy right now. How are you doing these days?"

"I'm doing a'ight. Still out here getting this paper," Jewels told him.

"So I've heard. I heard you're the man out in Queens," Jonas teased her.

"We moving and shaking a little bit." Jewels downplayed it. She was actually doing well for herself, selling pills thanks to Prince cutting her in on his pill operation. He had been so busy with putting the London deal together that he hadn't had time to be in the streets.

"Well, I'm glad to see you're out here getting it for yourself," Jonas said.

"Ain't like anybody was going to do it for me. Ain't no happy endings in the hood, at least not for *all* of us," Jewels said. Jonas knew it was a dig at him.

"Listen, Jewels, I was thinking that one day we could meet up for lunch and talk."

"About what? I appreciate the offer, but I came here to pay my respects to Mula, and then I'm gone. Let the past stay where it is," Jewels said. She was nowhere near over Jonas and didn't want to risk opening a box that she wouldn't be able to close again.

"I respect that," Jonas said, feeling slighted. "It was good seeing you, Jewels." He hugged her. It was a tight, intimate hug. He wanted to let her know that there was a part of him that still cared.

"Take care of yourself, Wrath." Jewels walked off to pay her respects.

Jonas stood there for a while, watching her walk down the aisle to the casket. He had to admit that she was looking good. He loved Alex but had to admit that if the opportunity ever arose for him to sleep with Jewels again, he wasn't so sure he would turn it down. With a smirk on his face, he turned around to find Alex standing in the doorway watching him.

Chapter Thirty-seven

"What was that all about?" Alex asked.

"What was what about?" Jonas faked ignorance. He knew she had seen the exchange between Jewels and him.

"Don't play stupid," Alex said. She knew what Jewels represented in his life.

"Alex, don't start that. Not today. Me and Jewels are ancient history." Jonas fished a cigarette from his pack and fired it up.

"So long as history isn't trying to repeat itself," she warned.

As they were standing there talking, a car pulled up. Jonas's eyes immediately went to it. Though they were at a funeral, he was still strapped. It wasn't the most respectful thing, but Jonas believed in being prepared at all times. It wasn't like he had never shot up a funeral before. He continued to watch the car as it double-parked and the driver got out. His jaw clinched when he realized that it was Ace. He was wearing a black suit and dark sunglasses. He had also let his facial hair grow out into a thin beard so that he wasn't so easy to recognize. Jonas kept his eyes locked on him as he approached.

"Hey, Alex," Ace greeted her.

"How you doing, Ace? Sorry for your loss." She hugged him.

"Thank you. They took one of the greatest ever to do it," Ace said, recalling some of Mula's exploits. His eyes then went to Jonas. "Sup, Wrath?"

Jonas just frowned and walked over to where Sweets was standing.

"That was foul," Sweets told him. She had seen the exchange.

"I ain't fucking with him," Jonas said.

"Jonas, after all you and Ace have been through, you at least owe him a conversation," Sweets told him.

"I let him keep his life. I don't owe him shit beyond that."

"Boy, you sure do know how to hold a grudge." Sweets shook her head. "Was that Jewels I saw walk in."

"Yeah, that was her."

"She's looking good these days." Sweets gave him a mischievous smirk.

"Knock it off. You know I only got eyes for Alex," Jonas assured her.

"I know. I just always hoped you and Jewels would end up together. We all did."

"And you talk about me knowing how to hold a grudge. Are you going to accept Alex as your future sister-in-law?"

"We'll cross that bridge when we come to it. Don't get me wrong. I think Alex is a nice girl who has a lot going for herself. I just don't trust her to be there for you when the chips are down," Sweets said honestly. "Did you get a chance to talk to Anette?"

"Yeah, we talked," Jonas confirmed.

"So, how do you feel about it?"

Jonas shrugged. "I'm okay with it, I guess."

"I think California will be good for Jo-Jo. I was doing some research, and they've made some serious strides in cancer treatments on the West Coast. I read about clinical trials they're conducting at the University of California San Francisco. If we move on it soon, Jo-Jo stands a good chance of getting in. Besides, ain't shit out here for her now that Mom is gone."

"Yeah, she was the glue that held us all together. Now that she's gone, it's like we're all going our separate ways."

"Well, none of y'all ain't babies anymore. It's time to grow up and start living life, while we can," Sweets said.

"What about you? You going with them?" Jonas asked.

"Nah. There's nothing for me in California. I'm going to stay my ass right here."

"Probably so you can keep tabs on me," Jonas joked.

"You don't need me chasing you down anymore, Jonas. You're a grown man. The only thing I want for you is to get out of these streets. That deal you and Prince got going is going to put you in a position to where you don't have to hustle anymore. I don't want to see you end up like Mula."

"That ain't gonna happen to me," Jonas assured her.

"I'm sure he said the same thing, and now we're laying him to rest. Life is too short to spend it fucking off, Jonas. Don't wait until it's too late. If you've got dreams, now is the time to start chasing them," Sweets said.

"Like you did?" Jonas asked sarcastically. "Whatever happened to you going back to school?"

"That's a long story. One that I'll tell you at another time," Sweets said. She looked like she was about to say something else, but suddenly she turned pale. She wobbled a bit and had to lean on a car to steady herself.

"You okay?" Jonas asked, seeing that she didn't look well at all.

"I'm fine. I've just been a little under the weather."

"Seems like you've been sick a lot lately. I hope you ain't pregnant," he joked.

"Now, that's something you don't have to worry about. I've spent so many years of my life raising y'all troublesome asses that I have no desire to have kids of my own."

"Well, when me and Alex have babies, you can help us with ours. I know their Auntie Sweets is going to spoil them to death, same as she did their daddy."

"Lord willing, Jonas . . . Lord willing."

They stood around talking for a while longer. Ace reemerged from the funeral home. He had removed his shades, and you could see that his eyes were red from crying. He and Mula had been very close, and Jonas knew that he was taking it hard. A part of Jonas wanted to go to him and comfort him, but he just couldn't bring himself to do it. Ace noticed Jonas watching him and came over.

"You okay?" Sweets asked him.

"No, but I will be," Ace sighed. "Wrath, can I talk to you for a second?"

"Let me give you boys some privacy." Sweets excused herself.

The two of them stood there for a time without saying anything. It was Ace who would break the silence. "How long are we going to do this?"

"Do what?" Jonas asked as if he had no idea what Ace was talking about.

"This." Ace motioned to the space between them. "Me and you are supposed to be brothers. We look out for our own, remember?"

"You mean like you looked out for Mula?" Jonas asked angrily.

"Jonas, you don't have to keep reminding me. I'm going to have to carry that boy's death with me for the rest of my life. I loved him."

"Ace, miss me with that shit. You don't love anybody but yourself. Since we were kids, all you've done was look out for number one—you!" Jonas pointed at him.

"You act like I'm the only one who was trying to secure his future. I know all about the deal you and Prince got going. The deal you didn't want me to be a part of."

"Man, don't try to use that shit to absolve yourself of this."

"I'm not. All I'm saying is we're all out there trying to get it by any means necessary. You can't blame me for doing the same shit you did, which was try to come up."

"I ain't got time for this shit." Jonas tried to walk away, but Ace grabbed him by the arm.

"You're going to stop giving me your back like I'm your bitch!" Ace shouted.

"Ace, you better get your hand off me before we have a problem," Jonas warned.

"What you gonna do, Wrath? Don't forget, it was *me* who used to watch your back when you was a punk kid, running around, afraid of your own shadow!"

That was the last straw. Jonas socked Ace in the jaw. It staggered him but didn't drop him. Ace followed up with a combination to the face, busting Jonas's lip. The mourners watched in horror as two men who were once friends were outside beating the hell out of each other.

"Isn't anyone going to stop this?" Sweets made to break it up, but Tavion stopped her.

"This is long overdue. Let them get it out of their system," he said, watching the fight.

Ace held his own down for a while, but eventually, Jonas started getting the better of him. For every punch Ace landed, Jonas landed two. Ace went down to one knee, and that's when Jonas really started raining on him. He was in a blind rage. "You killed him, you bastard! You killed him!" Jonas raged as he pummeled Ace. Ace just lay on the ground while Jonas choked him. It was as if all the fight were drained from him. It was then that Jonas realized what was happening. He wanted to die.

"Don't stop now," Ace said when Jonas stopped hitting him. "Kill me. I deserve it!"

Jonas pushed himself off Ace and looked down at the ruin he had made of his face. His nose was gushing blood, and one of his eyes was closed. It was then that all the memories he had shared with his childhood friend came rushing back. Jonas wanted to hate Ace, but he couldn't. Ace had been his best friend and sometimes protector for as long as he could remember. There was bad blood between them, but Jonas still loved him.

"Kill me, Wrath." Ace got to his feet. He grabbed the front of Jonas's shirt and tugged while sobbing uncontrollably. "I know you hate me, but not more than I hate myself for what I let happen to Mula."

"I don't hate you, Ace," Jonas was choked up. "I could never hate you." He pulled Ace close and hugged him. Standing there in front of mourners, friends, and strangers, Jonas released the tears he had been trying so desperately to hold back. He wasn't just crying for Ace; he cried for Doug, Mula, his mother, and every other soul that he had pushed from the world. He was tired.

Chapter Thirty-eight

Things had finally started to get back to normal, if that were a word you would choose to describe a thriving drug organization. It took some time, but eventually, Ace and Jonas were able to bury the hatchet. Their fight had been a brutal one but a necessary evil. It was blood which their relationship had always been built on, and blood that would reinforce their bond.

Of everyone, Stacey was probably the happiest that Ace and Jonas had squashed their beef. She and Jonas were like brother and sister, but Ace was her big homie. He'd sometimes get on her nerves, but she had love for him and didn't wish him harm, which was what Jonas was planning. Aside from Alex, Jonas spent more time with Stacey than any other woman. They had been working closely on his legitimate investments. Stacey found herself the keeper of a lot of his secrets, with the darkest being his plan to kill Ace. She breathed a deep sigh of relief when she heard that he had called it off. Stacey was glad to have him back. The same couldn't be said for Tavion.

With Mula off on his secret excursion down south with Ace, and Jonas focusing on his social club and the London deal, Tavion found himself shouldering a good deal of new responsibilities that came with running their drug business. When Jonas was away, Tavion was his voice on the streets. If Jonas was the king, then Tavion was the prince, and it was a role he had taken to. With

Ace back in the fold, he was stripped of some of his power. Tavion still held sway over the territories they had conquered in Grant, but Ace was once again Jonas's number two man in the organization. For a while, he had suffered in silence, but the tension between them came to a head a few weeks after Mula's funeral.

By that time, Jonas had let the rest of them in on the fact that he had assumed ownership of Juan's old spot and what he was building in its place. Tavion was to spearhead the grand opening. He had become quite the social butterfly over the years, becoming a regular in all the happening spots around the city. He had a unique insight into what it would take to get Jonas's spot up and running, starting with a name, which they didn't have yet. That was the gist of the conversation they were having that day in the shadow of their new trap house.

When Cal turned rat, Jonas immediately shut down Paula's apartment and moved everything into an apartment two blocks away. This one didn't belong to a fiend but a young dude who had inherited the apartment from his grandmother when she passed and needed a way to earn some extra cash to keep on with the rent. Sure enough, two weeks after they moved, the police kicked in Paula's door. They had moved all the drugs out of the crib, but the cops did find a gun in the toilet tank that Mula had stashed in there in case it ever went down while he was in the bathroom. He believed in being prepared for any and all occasions. Even from beyond the grave, he was still playing twisted pranks on the team. Paula would have to sit down on the gun charge, and to her credit, she wore it like a G and never mentioned Jonas or anybody else in the crew. For her silence, Jonas made sure that she lived like a queen while she did her time.

The weather was fair that evening. Not too hot and not too cold. It was just the right temperature to sit outside and enjoy the company you were in. They were all out in front of the new trap house building, smoking and drinking liquor in five-cent plastic cups. There were no drugs in the house at present, only money, which is why Jonas had been willing to bend on his rule about loitering where they hustled. There was a folding table erected on the sidewalk, where an intense game of Spades was being played. Jonas and Ace had beaten Stacey and Tavion two games in a row, and frustrations were starting to mount.

"How many times do I have to tell you young mutha-fuckas?" Ace threw down a Queen of Hearts, trumping the weak Jack Tavion had just played. "You gotta watch the board, so you'll know what was played."

"Man, stop bumping your gums and play cards," Tavion fumed.

"Spoken like a nigga who knows he's about to get ran." Ace slapped the little Joker on the table. That too was boss. "Wrath, how much is the little fella and his girlfriend into us for so far?"

Jonas peeked at the score sheet, which Stacey was keeping. "About five hundred."

"Oh, that ain't shit. I can't even start to get excited until we in they asses for at least a grand!" Ace played the big Joker he had been holding.

"Fuck!" Tavion slammed his Ace of Spades on the table, losing it to Ace's big Joker. He hit the table with so much force that Ace's cup waddled, but it didn't fall. That had been the story of Tavion's life since Ace was back . . . always movement but never follow through.

"So, you figure out what you're going to call this place yet?" Stacey asked Jonas. She was trying to deflect from some of the tension building between Ace and Tavion.

"Not yet." Jonas collected the cards so that he could shuffle them. It was his turn to deal.

"You the only dude I know that will build a whole club and not give it a name," Ace teased Jonas.

"Whatever I decide to call it, it has to be a name that means something. A name that's impactful. C'mon, I'm about to be the only dude from our neighborhood that actually owns something in the neighborhood," Jonas pointed out.

"I say we call it A. J.'s," Ace suggested. "How many years me and you been running up credit in Juan's or stealing when we couldn't get it on the arm?"

"Word! Yo, do you remember that time Mula dipped out of there with two cases of Coors?" Jonas recalled.

"Yooooo, that shit was hilarious! His little ass was in flight with those two boxes under his arms," Ace laughed. It was the funniest thing they had seen in a while. "I really miss my li'l man."

"Me too, Ace . . . me too. But everything we do from here on out will be for Mula," Jonas declared, raising his Hennessey-filled plastic cup.

"Straight like that." Ace raised his cup in salute. "We lost our brother, so now we're two the hard way, but the goal hasn't changed. We gonna take this city one block at a time, my nigga, and sit as kings of this bitch. Me and you against every-fucking-body else, Wrath!"

"What about the rest of us?" Tavion spoke up. He was tired of hearing Ace's mouth.

"What about you?" Ace shot back. Tavion was pissing on his moment, and he wasn't feeling it.

"I'm saying, I know you and Wrath started this shit but don't forget the little people when you're accepting your award," Tavion said.

"C'mon, fresh fish. I know you've put in work in your short time here, but watch how you talking when speaking to one of the founding fathers. I was putting food on the table when Wrath was sending you on weed runs," Ace checked him.

"And I was holding down the fort when you were inviting snitches to the table," Tavion shot back.

"Y'all be easy." Jonas sipped from his cup. He was feeling good and didn't feel like dealing with the bullshit.

"Nah, Wrath. He's acting like he's got something on his chest. Let him get it off. You got something you need to say to me, shorty?" Ace challenged Tavion.

"First of all, my name ain't *shorty*. It's Tavion, and you're the only one here acting like he doesn't know it," Tavion told him.

"Maybe I know it and just don't give a fuck," Ace replied. "Who you shot, stabbed, or fought in the last forty-eight hours that makes you even feel like you can hold a hostile conversation with a nigga like me?" He let his hand drop to his lap where his gun was tucked in his jeans.

Tavion peeped his move and responded in kind. Only he wasn't as subtle as Ace. "You act like yours was the only one manufactured." He placed his pistol on the table. This was unlike Tavion, and had he not been tipsy, it may not have played out that way. Tavion looked at Jonas, whose face was unreadable. All it would have taken was a certain look from Jonas, and Tavion would've ended Ace.

"Show some respect in front of the lady," Jonas finally spoke up. "Y'all wanna kill each other? I'm okay with that, just not in front of civilians."

With just a word from Jonas, the tension faded just as quickly as it had gathered.

In the distance was the sound of gunfire. Tavion was the first to his feet, with Ace a beat behind. They formed a protective wall in front of Stacey and Jonas, who hadn't moved. He continued sipping from his cup as if he hadn't heard a thing. After a few seconds, they realized that the shots had been coming from a few blocks away and posed no immediate threat to their benefactor.

"These niggas always out here tripping," Stacey said in frustration. It was getting to the point where not a night went by that they didn't hear gunshots.

"Soon, all this will be a not-so-fond memory." Jonas dropped his cards on the table and downed his plastic cup. "That is my cue to leave, though."

"What, Alex got you on a short leash tonight?" Ace teased.

"Never that. She's staying with her parents tonight. I gotta get up early to get with Prince," Jonas told him.

"Speaking of Prince, I need to holla at you right quick," Ace told him. The look on his face said that it wasn't a conversation for prying ears.

"Walk with me." Jonas stood. "Stacey, you good?"

"Yeah, I'm parked up the street. I'm fine," she assured him.

"Don't worry. I'll walk with her, Wrath," Tavion volunteered.

Jonas and Ace walked the few blocks back to 139th Street, sharing a joint. They stopped on the corner where Juan's store had once been, and Jonas's social club would stand. The site was almost complete, but there was still a plywood barrier around it. All you could see of the place was the black glass door and green awning. The front of it, where the name would go, was still blank.

"I still can't believe it." Ace looked over the site. "We went front splitting orders of chicken wings to this. Who knew?"

"You did," Jonas replied. "Even when you were still trying to make ends meet with the bullshit connect Doug had plugged you with, you were always looking for more . . . knew there was more. You set the bar."

"But it was you who rose to the occasion, Wrath. I was the mastermind behind a lot of our shit, but it was you and Mula who always had the balls to go out and do what needed to be done."

"Ace, you act like you weren't on the front lines with us," Jonas reminded him.

"I put in my share of work, but it was y'all who were out here laying shit down left and right," Ace told him. "Do you remember that night when I was giving you shit about being scared to ride out with us on Black?"

"Yeah, I remember. Had it not been for you putting the battery in me, I may not have gone," Jonas admitted.

"And that's why I did it," Ace confessed. "I know back then, I talked a lot of gangster shit, but I knew that I didn't have it in me to do what needed to be done to Black, but I had already put my foot in my mouth. I was counting on either you or Mula stepping up so that I could save face."

Jonas laughed. "Same old Ace, getting people to do his dirt for him. What would you have done if neither of us stepped up?"

Ace shrugged. "I can't say for sure. I'm glad I didn't have to find out, though. The point I'm making is, you may not have realized it, but you have always been my crutch. No matter what the situation was, I could always count on Wrath to see it through with me. This is why I don't know what I'm going to do when you leave us."

"Leave y'all? What would make you think that?" Jonas asked, wondering if Ace was psychic.

"I can see the writing on the wall, man. We all started at the bottom together, me, you, Doug, Mula, and Prince; yet, you and Prince were the only ones who could see the bigger picture. I know this London deal y'all put together is going to be huge! With that kind of bread rolling in, why would you still be throwing stones at the penitentiary with us?"

"Ace—"

"Let me finish, bro," Ace cut him off. "For a long time, I was acting funny because I resented the fact that you had a backup plan, and I didn't. It was petty, I know, but

I'm just being real about how I felt. Looking back on all we lost . . . on all you lost, I see that I was wrong. You've given so much to this life that only a sucker would hold it against you for wanting to get out. These last few years, I haven't been a good friend and an even worse brother. I apologize for that."

In all the years Jonas had known Ace, he couldn't recall ever hearing him use the word *apologize*. Ace could be as wrong as two left shoes and still wouldn't accept responsibility for his actions. Mula's death had changed him . . . It had changed all of them, but it was most apparent with Ace. He had grown from it. Maybe he was finally ready for Jonas to let him in . . .

Chapter Thirty-nine

When Jonas entered his apartment, he nearly tripped over a duffle bag. There was luggage lining the hallway. Among them was the pink roll-on with a picture of Ariana Grande printed on the side. He had bought it for Jo-Jo last Christmas. He knew how much she loved the singer. Jo-Jo took that roll-on everywhere with her. The following morning, it would travel with her to California.

It had been a tough decision, agreeing to let Anette take Jo-Jo with her to Los Angeles when she left for school. She had been the last cog in the wheel that kept their family spinning and Jonas's motivation to get rich. Not seeing her annoying little face every night when he came in from the hustle was going to be an adjustment. Though he would miss her dearly, he realized it was for the best. It was as Sweets had said, there was nothing left for the girl in New York but bitter memories of what was, and it was time for her to spread her wings to see what would be.

When he entered the living room and flicked on the light, he was surprised to find Sweets sitting on the couch. She was sipping a glass of dark liquor. Drinking was a habit she had adopted only recently, as she had never touched drugs or alcohol in her life. That was another sign that something was going on with her.

"What you doing sitting here in the dark?" Jonas asked.

"Drinking and thinking." She hoisted the glass. "I was worried. I heard gunshots, and I was afraid something might have happened to you."

"I'm good, Sweets," he assured her and took a seat on the couch.

Her eyes were tired, and he couldn't be sure, but she looked to have lost weight since the funeral. Even when Sweets dropped the baby fat, she was still thick. Over the last few weeks, she had shrunken to a shell. You could even see the bones in her cheeks. She didn't look well, and he was concerned.

Jonas picked up her cup and took a sip. "Hennessey?" He recognized the familiar taste. He drank it damn near every day, so he knew it immediately.

"Don't nothing numb the pain like the dog." Sweets took the cup back. She drained it and poured herself another drink from the fifth sitting on the table. From the dent in it, he could tell she had been at it for a while.

"Sweets, I'm starting to worry about you," Jonas said after a brief silence.

"That makes two of us," she smirked. "I'm good, Jonas. If I don't know anything else, I know that God has got me now as he always has. My main concern right now is y'all, you and the girls."

"So, they're really going, huh?" Jonas looked back at the bags in the hallway.

"Yeah, by this time tomorrow, Jo-Jo will be some-where pretty with the sun shining on her face. Thanks for making sure they'll be set up when they get there," Sweets said. Jonas had Stacey rent them a small house not far from the campus, and dropped $15,000 into a bank account in Anette's name. That would be enough to get them up and running, and Jonas would send them money every month.

"You don't have to thank me. Y'all are my sisters. I'm always gonna look out for you guys," Jonas promised.

"When are you going to start looking out for yourself? The game is changing, Jonas, and the risks are starting to outweigh the rewards."

"Tell me about it," he said, thinking of Mula.

"Have you given any thought to what we talked about? You know, about getting out?" Sweets asked.

"I thought about it, but to be honest, this life is all I know. I wouldn't even know what to do with myself if I came in out of the cold," he said honestly.

"You can do anything you want. You'll be 20 soon. You're still a very young man with his whole life ahead of him. Take your money and get out of this city before it destroys you like it destroys everything else. I don't want to bury you, little brother," Sweets said emotionally.

"How come all you talk about is death lately?"

"Because it's the only thing in this life that we're guaranteed. Doesn't matter how much money we have or how good we live. Death will visit us all. Some of us sooner than later," she said. She was quiet for a time, but her next words would be ones that he would never forget. "Acquired immune deficiency syndrome."

"Huh?" Jonas was unfamiliar with the term.

"AIDS," she clarified. "You asked me at Mula's funeral why I never went back to school like I said I would. It's because I'm sick."

Jonas was stunned. He knew about AIDS. It had taken out a few people in their hood, mostly addicts that he knew of. "Nah, that can't be right. AIDS only affects faggots and junkies, and you ain't either one of those things."

"AIDS doesn't just affect homosexuals and addicts, Jonas. It also strikes people who aren't careful who they have sex with. Why do you think I'm always on your back about condoms? I may not be a junkie, but it doesn't mean I didn't have an addiction. My drug of choice was love, and it's ultimately what's going to kill me."

"Drew?" Jonas asked, putting the pieces together.

Sweets nodded. "I always knew he had a wandering dick, but I accepted it because he took care of me. Those bitches could have his body as long as I had his heart. Drew was a lot of things, but I never took him for irresponsible. My diagnosis has taught me otherwise. This is a hard lesson I'm learning, but what am I going to do?"

"I'll kill that muthafucka!" Jonas said with tears staining his cheeks.

"For what? Taking him out isn't going to change the fact that I have this disease."

"So, that's why you didn't want to go to California with Anette and Jo-Jo?" he asked.

"It's bad enough they had to watch Mama die. I don't want to subject them to this."

"Do they know?"

"No. You're the only one I've told. This is something that will stay between us."

"We can get you help. I have money now. We can find a doctor for you like we found for Jo-Jo."

"Unfortunately, this is something that not even the doctor can get rid of. There are treatments for the virus, but no cure. Don't waste your money because the outcome will be the same no matter what we do. I am going to die."

"Stop saying that shit! You aren't going to die! You can't!" Jonas was going to pieces. "I don't want to lose you, Sweets . . . I can't," he sobbed.

"Hush that crying, Jonas." Sweets hugged him. "I've made my peace with it, and you should too. I'm just glad I got to live long enough to see you all grow into strong, beautiful individuals. When I'm gone, it'll be up to you to take care of the family. You'll be all they have left."

"We can fight this, Sweets. Promise me you'll at least try." Jonas wept.

"I promise, little brother." Sweets rubbed his back.

That was the first time in Jonas's life that he could ever remember Sweets lying to him. Two weeks after Anette and Jo-Jo arrived in California, Jonas got the call about Sweets. They found her body in a hotel room. There was an empty bottle of Hennessey on the table along with what remained of the pills she had used it to wash down. Rather than live with the terminal disease, she chose to end it. She was only 22 years old.

Chapter Forty

The loss of Sweets devastated Jonas. He found himself dragged into a very dark place. Sweets had been more of a mother to him than Janette. She was his world, and his world was brought crashing down all because she had chosen to love the wrong man. Jonas had every intention of killing Drew for giving his sister the virus, but karma beat him to the punch. Another girl that Drew had infected with his lethal dick caught him coming out of his apartment building and blew his brains out.

The majority of Jonas's days were spent drinking, smoking, and crying in his bedroom. Not even Jo-Jo could bring him out of it. She and Anette had flown home for the funeral, and they tried to get Jonas to come back with them to California for a few weeks. They were worried and didn't want to leave him alone, but Jonas refused. If it wasn't at the bottom of a bottle, he wasn't interested. It crushed them to see their brother like that, but at the end of the day, they had lives to lead, so they reluctantly left him to his suffering.

Jonas had become a recluse, staying boarded up in his apartment and only coming out to go to the liquor store. Ace and Tavion handled the drug business while Stacey and Prince tended to everything else. His friends had tried to bring him out of it, but he was not receptive. He refused to see anyone, including Alex. He wouldn't take her phone calls, and when she came by the apartment, he refused to answer the door. There were times Jonas wanted to reach out to her; he wanted to pour his heart out about everything he was going through and beg her to help drag him from the darkness, but he couldn't bring himself to. It was as he had told Jewels years before, he was poison, and he didn't want to risk infecting her. So, he did everything in his power to push her away. Eventually, it worked, and she stopped coming around.

In Jonas's absence, Ace and Tavion made sure that the business didn't suffer. They did what they could to keep things going, but Jonas had always been the real power behind their organization, and without him, the foundation had begun to crack gradually. Usurpers had started coming out of the woodwork to try to lay claim to what they had built. There had been at least six shootouts on blocks they held, and they had lost two buildings so far. Things were getting ugly, but Jonas was numb to it. He didn't care about the drugs, the business in London, or even himself. He just wanted to fade into nothingness.

Jonas rolled over on his twin bed and picked up the bottle of Hennessy he had been nursing. He turned it to his lips and frowned when he realized that it was empty. He didn't feel like going outside, but the liquor store didn't deliver. That was something he was going to have to discuss with the owner when the opportunity presented itself.

Jonas pulled on a pair of sweatpants and a hoodie, preparing to make his daily liquor store run. As an afterthought, he grabbed his gun. He was depressed but not stupid. There was a chill in the air, and it helped to sober him up. With his hands tucked in his pockets and the hood pulled snugly over his head, he began walking.

He paused briefly on the corner to take in what he had spent so much time building. Across the once blank awning, the word *Sweets* was printed in cursive. He had decided to name it in honor of his sister. Though she was gone, her name would live on. The grand opening was in two days, a day before his birthday and a week before Alex was scheduled to head to London. Tavion was still planning on going through with the grand opening, but he couldn't say for sure if he would even attend. He was in no mood to celebrate. After all that he had gone through to make it happen, you'd have thought he would be happy, but he felt nothing . . . only the emptiness of all the loses he had suffered over the last few years.

As Jonas was about to walk to the liquor store, he thought he heard someone calling his name. He ignored it and continued on to the store. Behind him, he heard feet slapping against the ground rapidly. Moving off instinct, he spun, gun raised and ready to fire. His finger had just caressed the trigger when he realized who it was.

"Mr. Hightower?" Jonas asked in surprise. Alex's dad was the last person he had expected to see.

"I'd heard this was the best place to catch up with you." Mr. Hightower's eyes went to the liquor store. "You wanna put that pistol away so we can talk?"

"My fault." Jonas tucked the gun. "What can I do for you?"

"Truthfully, not a muthafucking thing. I'm only here because I love my daughter."

"Alex? Did something happen?" Jonas asked frantically.

"No, but she's worried about you. As much as I hate to admit it, we all are a bit concerned. What are you doing to yourself?" Mr. Hightower looked over his slovenly appearance.

"I'll be fine. I'm just going through a little something."

"Looks like more than a little something. My condolences on the loss of your sister, by the way," Mr. Hightower said sincerely.

Jonas nodded. "Appreciate that. And thank you for the flowers you sent. They were beautiful."

"Sweets was a good girl," Mr. Hightower said.

An addict walked up and interrupted their conversation. "Say, Wrath . . . You holding?"

"Get the fuck away from me before I murder you, junkie!" Jonas spat and sent the fiend slinking off. When he turned back to Mr. Hightower, the man was giving him a pitiful look. "What?"

"Nothing, man. I just can't believe how far you've allowed yourself to fall," Mr. Hightower said. It wasn't a dig at Jonas; just an observation.

"Well, you don't have to worry about my hood stink rubbing off on your daughter. We ain't exactly rocking like that right now," Jonas informed him.

"She told me. I wish I could say that I didn't see this coming. She's been crying for days over the way you've been treating her, and, frankly, I don't appreciate it," Mr. Hightower told him.

"So what? You wanna kick my ass because I broke your little girl's heart?"

"For as much as I would like to fuck you up, it won't do either of us any good. I've come to see if I can talk some sense into that hard-ass head of yours."

"I'm good on lectures, but thanks," Jonas said dismissively.

"I'm not here to lecture you, Jonas. I've come to pull your coat to some shit. Now, you looked me in my eyes like a man and promised that you would always do right by my daughter, and like a fool, I believed you. I thought that if anything else, you were a stand-up dude, but, apparently, I was wrong."

"Sorry to disappoint you, but I've been doing a lot of that lately," Jonas laughed.

"You think this shit is funny?" Mr. Hightower asked angrily. "Well, let me tell you something that might put things into prospective for you, Wrath. While you're over here wallowing in your own sorrow and stink, my daughter is preparing to bring your child into the world."

Jonas was now completely sober. He couldn't have possibly heard Mr. Hightower correctly.

"Thought that might get your attention. She didn't want you to know because she isn't sure if she's going to keep it or not. Frankly, I don't even know why I'm even telling you outside of the fact that despite everything you've shown me to the contrary, I still feel like there's good in you, and you deserve the chance to at least try to do the right thing."

"Mr. Hightower, I didn't know. I'd never have let Alex go through this alone. Whatever she needs, I'll pay for it. I'm not going to be no deadbeat."

"Fool-ass boy, this ain't about money. We've got that. What Alex needs right now is to know that you're ready to step up to the plate and do what needs to be done. Now, it's up to you to do whatever you feel with the information, but know this . . . With or without you, Alex is going to be okay. We'll see to that."

"Mr. Hightower—"

"I've said what I needed to, Jonas. What happens from here is up to you. Now, if you want to keep playing in these streets until you eventually die in them, I'm okay with that, but you won't take my daughter down with you. Alex doesn't need a dope boy; she needs a grown man. If you're the man that I think you are, you'll step up; if not . . . I'll kill you myself if I ever catch you around my daughter again," he said. He didn't wait for Jonas to reply before he jumped into his car and left.

Jonas stood there for a long while after Mr. Hightower had gone, weighing his words. He couldn't believe that he was about to bring a life into the world. It was surreal! Jonas had never had to take care of anyone but himself and had no idea how to be a father, but he knew where he needed to start. His mother and father fed the Rafferty children with dirty money, and it had been that which had cursed them. This was a curse that he had no intentions of passing on to his unborn child. He knew at that moment that he was done.

Alex was up and out early the next morning. She had been suffering from a terrible case of morning sickness and desperately needed a ginger ale to settle her stomach. When she came out of her building, she was shocked to find Jonas sitting on a bench. His eyes were clear and sober, and he had finally changed his clothes. He was starting to resemble his old self again.

"Hey," Jonas greeted her.

"What the fuck do you want?" she asked angrily.

"Alex, I know I have been a real asshole lately, but—"

"Asshole is an understatement. Do you know how worried about you I've been? You haven't been taking my calls, and you ignore me when I come to the house."

"I know, and I'm sorry. I've been going through something," he told her.

"And I haven't?" she shot back.

"Your dad told me about the baby. Why didn't you tell me?"

"Maybe I would've if you hadn't shut me out. Besides, I still don't know what I'm going to do. I'm leaving for London next week to start this next chapter in my life, and I don't know if a child has a place in it."

"What do you mean? Alex, you're going to have this baby . . . *We're* going to have this baby," he insisted.

"Jonas, I told you from the beginning that I didn't want to be involved with a man who was in the streets, but the heart wants what the heart wants. I allowed myself to love you, even knowing you weren't good for me. Us running around and living on the edge is one thing, but bringing a baby into this . . ." She shook her head sadly.

"You don't have to worry. I'll be there for you," Jonas promised.

"Be there for me? You can't even be there for yourself! Look at the way you live, Jonas. Gun in one hand, a bottle in the other. I love you so much that I couldn't even begin to imagine a life without you, but this isn't about us. It's about what's best for this child. Whatever world I create for him or her, Wrath will have no part in it. Now, if you'll excuse me . . ." She began walking off.

"I'm done," he called after her.

"Spare me the bullshit, Jonas." She continued walking.

"I'm serious." He caught up with her. "If it's a choice between the people I love and the streets, I choose love."

Alex stopped walking. "Jonas, I appreciate that, but we both know you're in way too deep. You think Ace is just going to let you walk away like that?"

"Fuck, Ace. Shit, he'll probably be glad I'm stepping down. He's been wanting to be the boss for years, and I'm going to grant his wish happily."

"I want to believe you, Jonas, but it's going to take more than words this time," she told him.

"Then I'll show you! When you leave for London, I'll go with you. I have a passport now, and I've been saying I wanted to go check out our operation in person for a while. No better time than now."

"Jonas, that's a big move, and I know how much you love New York."

"But I love you more," he told her. "My mother and Sweets are dead, and Anette and Jo-Jo are on the West Coast. When Yvette is done with rehab, she'll be joining them in California. There is nothing else to hold me here. We don't even have to wait until your exchange programs starts. We can leave right after the grand opening and do some sightseeing before your classes start."

Alex studied him for a time. She was searching for signs of hesitation or uncertainty on his part but found none. He was serious. "Are you sure about this?"

"Surer than I've ever been about anything in my life," he said as he embraced her. "I love you, Alex. I always have and always will. Let me prove to you just how much. Me and you against the world, baby. What do you say?"

"I say that if you make me regret this, I'm going to kill you," she smiled. As she was leaning against him, she felt something in his pocket vibrate. He pulled out a small, prepaid phone, and when he looked at it, his face darkened. "See, this is the shit I'm talking about." She pushed away from him.

"It ain't even like that. Look, I got something to do right quick, but I'll be back to check on you later, and we can talk some more about our big move."

"I love you, Wrath." Alex kissed him.

"Wrath is dead. It's time for Jonas to start living."

Chapter Forty-one

After leaving Alex, Jonas headed to the address that had been sent to him in a text message. It was a steak house in midtown packed with the people who had come in for the lunch rush. Even through the sea of people, the man who he had come to meet wasn't hard to spot. He was seated at a table in the back, bleached blond hair standing up like a beacon. When he saw Jonas, he waved him over.

"I see you've learned the benefits of being punctual," Detective Ceaver said, cutting into a thick steak. "Please, sit."

Jonas took the seat opposite him.

Detective Ceaver took the piece of steak he had just cut off and popped it into his mouth. He chewed slowly, savoring it before swallowing. "How do you take your steak, Wrath?"

"Huh?"

"Meaning, how do you like it prepared?"

"Well done, I guess. Same as everybody else."

"Ah, and this is where you are wrong. Real connoisseurs of fine beef understand the joy of a good, rare piece of meat. There's an art to preparing a good steak; no more than two minutes on each side. This way, you preserve the tenderness and its natural juices. Care for a taste?" he offered his steak to Jonas.

Jonas looked at the blood pooling on the plate. "No, thanks."

"More for me, then." The detective went back to his meal. He continued eating as if he had forgotten Jonas was even sitting there.

"I don't mean to be rude, but I've got a lot to do today, so if we could move this along?"

"Right. You're planning a trip, aren't you?" the detective asked, much to Jonas's surprise. "No, I haven't been having you followed or tapped your phones." He read Jonas's mind. "Your girl crossed paths with a friend of mine when she was making your passport application. I'm glad you've decided to broaden your horizons. I had seen so many different countries by the time I was your age, touched so many different cultures. I was especially partial to Macedonia. Now, those were a lot who knew how to have a good time. Things got a little stale when that business with Persia happened, but I assume you aren't here for a history lesson."

Just then, One-Eye Willie appeared. He was carrying a wooden box under his arm. When he saw Jonas, he nodded in greeting, but there was a coldness to him that Jonas hadn't experienced since they first met. Willie was usually warm and smiling whenever they were around each other, but today, his face was like stone.

"Right on time, as always, Willie." The detective smiled. He then motioned for him to set the box down in front of Jonas.

"What's this?" Jonas asked suspiciously.

"Only one way to find out." The detective paused his eating long enough to watch Jonas.

Cautiously, Jonas opened the box. Inside, he found the most beautiful gun he had ever seen lying on a bed of velvet. Its barrel was made of chrome, but it had a rose-colored hue to it, and the handle was wrapped in a black rubber grip. Jonas slid his hand around the grip, and it curved to his fingers perfectly.

"And early birthday gift," the detective answered the question on his face. "There are only two others like it in existence. These are only entrusted to the most gifted killers. This one originally belonged to me, but now it's yours."

"I can't accept this." Jonas pushed the box away.

"Of course, you can, Wrath. You've earned this. When we first started working together, there were some among us who were afraid you wouldn't live up to your full potential," he glanced at Willie, "but I'd say you've exceeded our wildest expectations. You are as loyal as a dog but as dangerous as a viper. My own personal hybrid, so to speak. We have done some amazing things together, but the best is yet to come. Has Willie told you yet?"

"Told me what?" Jonas asked, looking back and forth between the detective and Willie.

"Of course, he hasn't. Someone who owes me a debt has recently had a bump in political power in a third world country that most people wouldn't bother to stop long enough to take a leak in were it not for one very valuable export that comes through there. Can you take a guess what that is?"

Jonas shrugged.

"Cocaine, Wrath! Pure, uncut booger sugar!" the detective said excitedly. "Now that my friend is calling the shots over there, we can run as much cocaine up the pipeline as we like, and it'll cost us little more than a song and a dance. In six months, I'm going to be the biggest importer of cocaine since Ronald Reagan. Would you like to know the best part about all this? I've chosen *you* as the person to run the whole thing."

"Wow," Jonas said unenthusiastically.

"I've just told you that I am about to make you a god in the drug game, and all you can say is *wow*?" The detective gave him a disbelieving look. "Excuse me, but I had expected a little more fanfare for keeping good on my promise to change your life."

"I'm sorry, Lou. I don't mean to sound ungrateful at all. I'm honored that you have such confidence in me, but maybe I'm not the right man for this job," Jonas told him.

"Not the right man? Who better than my Wrath? My angel of death?" The detective couldn't understand it. His eyes narrowed to slits, and he looked over Jonas as if he had x-ray vision. "Something is different about you. Are you in some trouble? I've always told you that if you had a problem, then bring it to me, and I'd fix it."

"I don't have a problem, Lou. It's just that, after all that I've been through lately, I feel like I need a break," Jonas confessed.

The detective's eyes softened. "Of course, you do. You've lost damn near your entire family and have barely had a chance to mourn your recently deceased sister, and here I am trying to dump more work in your lap. Forgive me for being insensitive, Wrath."

Every time the detective called him that, it seemed to grate on his nerves.

"We all get a little tired sometimes," Willie spoke up. "Take some time for yourself."

"Yes, Willie's right. You need time," the detective agreed. "You've got your passport now, so do a bit of traveling. Take that little girlfriend of yours on a trip. A week or two in Cabo will do wonders for your spirit."

"I think a week or two may not be enough. Lou, I—"

"Don't say it," the detective cut him off. "Whatever you were about to let fall out of that depressed mouth of yours, keep it to yourself. I don't want to hear it."

"Hear what? That living the way I have for so many years is beating me down?" Jonas challenged. "Listen, Lou. You've done a lot for me over the years, and I am truly thankful for it, but this shit is becoming too much for me. If you were worried about me leaving you high and dry, don't. Ace can run the drug side of things, and Tavion can continue the arrangement that you and I have. He's ready."

"I like Tavion, a lot, and though he might be ready, it isn't him who I made the deal with. I made you an offer, Wrath. You didn't have to take it, but you did. I've done my part, and now you're telling me you can't keep up your end of the bargain? I'm sure you know that this will never do. I can't let you walk away."

"What you trying to say?" Jonas's hand slid to his gun.

"Calm down; nobody's threatening you, and we both know Willie would cut your fucking head off long before you were able to clear that pistol," the detective warned. "What I'm saying is that you aren't thinking clearly. You're so weighed down by your past that you can't see your future clearly. I can help you with that." He slid a piece of paper across the table.

Jonas opened it and read over the address. "What's this?"

"That, my friend, is the map that will lead you down memory lane. An old friend of yours will be waiting for you at the end of it. I'm sure Mula would've wanted you to go see him sooner than later."

Jonas knew just who he would find at that address. "Thanks, Lou."

"Of course. That's what friends are for. So long as you look out for me, then I'll always look out for you. After you've handled your business, come back and see me, and we'll discuss our futures further."

"Right." Jonas got up from the table.

"You're forgetting your present." The detective pointed to the box.

"Hold on to it for me until I come back to discuss the future," Jonas told him and left. He had no intention of ever seeing the detective again. Once he handled one last piece of business, he was gone. Lou had been an important fixture in his life, but not more important than Alex or the life she had growing inside her. Regardless of whether he had Lou's blessing, the game was over.

Chapter Forty-two

The sun had just set when he and Ace hit the New Jersey Turnpike. He had denied him his revenge with Flair, but on this, he wouldn't. Ace had just as much right to this as anyone. This would not only be his opportunity to make things right for Mula but between Ace and Jonas as well. This trip was to be Ace's baptism of fire.

During the ride, he told Ace everything . . . about Juan, about him seeing Black at the assisted living home, and what he had done to Flair right after. He even told Ace about his relationship with the detective. After hearing Jonas's story, Ace felt like his head was going to explode. There was so much to process!

"Wrath, I had always known you were keeping secrets, but this shit . . ." Ace shook his head in disbelief. "Why didn't you ever tell us about this cop?"

"Because I wanted to protect you. One thing I've learned about Lou Ceaver is that he is dangerous and suspicious. I couldn't risk him thinking one of you would open your mouths; then he'd do something to you or one of your families. I'm sure that dude has files on all of us."

"Well, I guess it's a good thing I got one on him too." Ace went on to tell Jonas about how he had spied him with the detective one night and followed them. After Jonas had left, he continued following the detective to his apartment. "I thought I had a line on your plug and was planning on robbing him, but when I found out he was a cop, I fell back."

"And you call *me* sneaky," Jonas joked.

"Hey, man, we all thought you were about to get ghost on us, and I wanted to make sure if you did leave, we'd still land on our feet," Ace admitted. "So, now what?"

"My plans haven't changed. We're going to do this thing, and that will be my last official act as the leader of this team. Once I leave for London, all this shit is yours," Jonas told him.

"So, you just gonna up and move to London?" Ace asked.

"For a little while. At least until I figure things out. I don't know what I'm going to do with the rest of my life, but it won't be this," Jonas vowed.

"And what about the detective? You said yourself that he don't wanna let you walk," Ace reminded him.

"To a man like Lou, a nigga like me ain't nothing but a tool. Lou damn near raised me, so he knows how far I'm willing to go. He ain't trying to go to war over this. It'd be bad for business. I've offered him a capable replacement that he can either give my position to or go fuck himself. I've always lived life by my own rules, and nobody is going to change that. Not even Lou," Jonas said confidently.

"If you like it, I love it. I'm gonna ride out with you regardless. We take care of our own, right?"

Jonas looked at his crime partner. "Right."

A few hours later, they were coasting through the streets of West Baltimore. That was where the address he'd gotten from Lou had brought him. When Cal disappeared, they had all assumed he was in a witness protection program. As it turned out, after he had dropped a dime on Ace, he turned rabbit on the police and ran off instead of showing up at court to put the final nail in the coffin. If he had been smart, he'd have at least moved to a different coast. Maybe then, he'd at least have had a fighting chance. Hiding in Baltimore might've put him out of reach of the Richmond police—but not Wrath. He would root him out no matter how deep he tried to bury himself. He owed Mula that.

"I know this place," Ace said once they had pulled up on the street of row houses. It was a run-down-looking house, with only a few of the buildings not being burned down or condemned. "Cal brought me out here to cop some guns before from this kid he was dealing with."

"That's good to know. I hope he's strapped when we run down. I want him to fight. It's always better when they fight," Jonas said and slipped from the car.

Together, he and Ace crept up along the side of the house. It was located at the far end of the block. Both of the buildings next to it were abandoned. The house was cloaked in shadow. Jonas peered through the living room window. The television was tuned into a game show. Beyond, he could see shadows moving about in the kitchen. He wasn't sure how many people were in the house. It didn't matter. Everything was food.

"Remember, everybody goes along for the ride," Jonas told Ace, repeating what Willie had once told him. This time he wouldn't hesitate.

Ace chambered a round into his gun. "Nigga, this is for Mula. Let's get it popping."

When Jonas's booted foot hit the thin wooden door, it caved in with little resistance, sending splinters of wood flying. He let off a spray of his machine gun in the air. He wanted to get the roaches scattering so he could stomp them out. A young man of about 16 appeared at the top of the stairs. When he saw the gun-wielding men in his doorway, he turned to run. He never made it far. Jonas let the machine gun spit, tearing open his back and legs. The boy crashed down the stairs and landed at his feet.

"Daddy's home!" Jonas yelled, stepping over the corpse. He directed Ace to take the downstairs, while he went up.

He had just reached the second floor when he heard the
sounds of gunfire coming from the kitchen. He smiled,
knowing Ace was taking care of business. There were
two bedrooms on the second floor. Jonas shoved one
door open. A young man and a woman were having sex.
They had the music turned up so loud that they hadn't
even heard the shots. "Knock, knock," Jonas announced
himself. He never even allowed the boy to pull himself
out of the girl before he sprayed them both. They died in
a bloody embrace.

Jonas moved to the final room. He had learned his
lesson from Flair, so he made sure he stood clear when he
opened the door. At a glance, the room was empty. The
bed hadn't been made, and men and women's clothes
were strewn on the floor. He checked the closet and found
it empty. He was about to leave the room when he saw a
discarded order of Chinese food sitting on a snack tray.
Jonas touched his fingers to the rice. It was still warm. He
stood on the bed and pointed his machine gun down at
it. "You got until the count of three before I see how this
memory foam holds a bullet. One . . . two—"

"Okay," a voice called out. A brown-skinned girl crawled
from under the bed, holding her hands in the air, and her
eyes were filled with terror. "Don't shoot."

"Where's Cal?" Jonas asked.

"I don't know no Cal," the girl lied.

"I see." Jonas grabbed a fistful of her hair and slammed
her face into the television, shattering the glass. "Bitch,
don't make me ask you again."

"There!" she pointed to the bed, squinting from the
glass in her eye.

"Funky bitch!" Cal cursed. He scrambled out from
under the bed and tried to break for the door. Jonas let
off a spray that peppered the door frame, and Cal froze.

"Next ones won't miss," Jonas assured him.

"You got who you came for. Can I go?" the girl asked hopefully.

"Sure, baby. You can go—straight to fucking hell!" Jonas ate her up with the machine gun. He then turned to Cal, who was standing there trembling. Piss ran down his leg and pooled on the floor. "That how you greet all your day-one homies?"

"Wrath, let me explain—" Cal began.

"Explain what? How you got one of my brothers killed and tried to cross the other one into the penitentiary?"

"Jonas, that shit that happened with Mula wasn't my fault. He drew down on the cops. There was nothing I could do," Cal tried to explain.

"And what about Ace? You gave him up," Jonas reminded him.

"I didn't have a choice in that, man. The police had me. I was already on parole for the bid I did on the guns. In a commonwealth state, they'd have given me the damn electric chair. Besides, Ace was foul anyhow. That nigga was plotting on you. He was always jealous and wanted what you had. I know the whole plan."

"Good, because I can't wait to hear it." Ace suddenly appeared. His gun was in his hand, and his hoodie was bloody.

"Don't try to deny it, Ace. Tell Jonas how you planned to take over the block and how you were going to rob his connect!" Cal accused. He figured if he could expose Ace to Wrath, he might be grateful enough to let him walk out of there.

"Everything he's saying is true, Jonas," Ace admitted.

"See! He's not even trying to deny it!" Cal said. This was going better than he thought.

"I appreciate your putting me up on the game, Cal. I might even find myself grateful if Ace hadn't already come clean to me," Jonas told him.

Cal's head whipped back and forth from Ace to Jonas. He was sandwiched between them. There would be no escape. "But I'm one of y'all . . . We look out for our own, remember?"

"Cal, you were *never* one of us," Jonas told him before opening fire.

Cal's body did a sick dance as bullets tore into him from both Ace and Jonas. He was dead long before he hit the ground. Jonas and Ace stood around the body in silence. It was as if a great weight had been lifted off them.

"For Mula." Ace extended his fist.

"For Mula." Jonas pounded it.

Jonas and Ace were making their way down the stairs. The police were surely on their way after hearing all the shots, and they didn't plan on being there when they arrived. They still had to get the gas cans from the car to torch the place before they left. Jonas had learned that when you erased somebody, you not only erased all traces of them, but also all traces of yourself from the crime scene. Nothing did the trick quite like fire.

As Jonas was passing the living room, he stopped in his tracks. He saw an old woman, gagged and tied to a chair with telephone wire. In front of her, *Wheel of Fortune* played on the television. "What the fuck?" He looked at Ace.

"My fault. I forgot about her. Found her in the living room when I hit the muthafuckas in the kitchen. I tied her up because I figured we were gonna let her live," Ace explained.

Jonas thought about it. If nothing else, he had learned from the mistakes he had made in the past. "Everybody goes."

"But, Jonas, she's just an old woman," Ace said.

"You want to be the king or not?" Jonas asked.

Ace was hesitant but only for a second. "Fuck it." He stepped forward and shot the old woman in her head.

Jonas and Ace proceeded to douse the place from top to bottom with gasoline. They lit it and watched from across the street to make sure that the fire caught. The building was made of cheap material, so it didn't take long for it to go up.

Long after they had made it to the highway, Jonas still had visions of the burning building in his head. Mula's killer had finally found justice. Cal and every trace of him went up in that fire, but the crime scene wasn't the only thing Jonas was leaving behind. The slaughter of all those innocent people, except for Cal, was the last act of a once-feared man. Wrath had burned up in that fire, along with Cal. Jonas was finally free.

Chapter Forty-three

Present day . . .

The muzzle flashed a split second before Jonas spun. He was fast, but not faster than a bullet. Pain shot through his face. "Bitch!" he roared, clutching his cheek.

"What kind of way is that to talk to somebody you claimed to love? Shame on you." Jewels got out of the car. She was wearing black leggings, black boots, and a black hoodie. She looked like a shadow. Her hair was pulled back into a ponytail, and there was a crazed look in her eyes.

Tavion tried to creep up and get the drop on her, which proved to be a mistake. He had almost reached her when the insane woman spun and shot him in the chest.

Jonas watched in horror as his protégé fell onto his back. Tavion's eyes were open, rolling around in his head, and he was breathing in short gasps. "Jewels, what the fuck are you doing?" Jonas shouted.

"I came to wish you a happy birthday . . . or should this be bon voyage?" Jewels cackled. "You were just going to leave and not say goodbye? I thought we were better than that."

"Jewels, you better put that fucking gun down before—"

"Before what? What, you gonna make me another promise that you can't keep? Nigga, your word means shit!" she spat. "You know, I accepted it when you broke my heart to go chasing a broad who wouldn't piss on you if you were on fire . . . I even sucked it up when you cut me off so that you could keep your nose shoved up her uppity ass. I told you, as long as I could always have a piece of you, it was enough to hold on to the hope that you would one day come to your senses. And then I have to hear through the grapevine that you're about to chase this bitch all the way to the other side of the world? You're gonna leave me, Wrath? Don't you love me anymore?"

Jonas knew he had to handle this situation with kid gloves. Jewels was distraught, but she wasn't stupid. The most effective weapon he had at his disposal was the truth. "I do love you, Jewels, but I'm not in love with you. That's never been a secret between us."

Her eye twitched like the admission had hurt her physically. "But you never tried to learn," she said sadly. "I could've been a good woman to you . . . I *was* a good woman to you. Why was it so easy for you to toss me out like trash? Was her pussy that much better than mine?" She jabbed the gun in Alex's direction.

"Don't! She's pregnant!" Stacey blurted out. She was trying to help the situation but only made it worse.

A deep look of hurt settled over Jewels's face. "She's pregnant?" her voice trembled. "You told me that you didn't want kids."

"It's just something that happened," Jonas admitted.

"What about when it happened with *me?*" Jewels asked.

Jonas was clueless.

"That night in the motel," Jewels explained. Her eyes began to water. "I never told you because you had made it clear that you didn't want kids, and as your ride-or-die chick, I respected your wishes and did what I had to do. I killed the part of you that was growing inside me, and you expect me to sit by and take it while you go play house with another bitch?" Her hand trembled. "Fuck you for making me think that I was really worth something. And fuck her for being enough for you when I wasn't."

Jonas knew what would happen long before it unfolded. It was like slow motion. He saw the gun jump, fire belching from the barrel. The shell casing ejected, flipping end over end. The bullet seemed to be dripping toward Alex instead of streaking. Jonas moved as if in a dream on an intercept course. He managed to throw himself across Alex just before the bullet made contact. It felt like someone had hit him in the back with a sledgehammer. Jonas could feel his strength fading, but he managed to roll over onto his back. His shirt and overcoat were both slick with blood, and he was having a hard time catching his breath. Jonas's vision was beginning to double, but he could make out Jewels stalking toward them. He pushed himself up so that he was still covering Alex. No matter what, he would protect her with his last breath.

Jewels pointed the pistol at Jonas, and for the first time, he was able to get a good look at it. It was a Glock—a custom job with a rose-chrome barrel and black rubber grip. There were only three like them in existence. It was then that it all made sense. Jewels had already been on edge. All she needed was a little push. "Farewell, my love." Jewels prepared to finish him.

"Bye, bitch!" Ace stepped into view. He then proceeded to blow Jewels's brains out the side of her head.

The last thing Jonas recalled seeing was Jewels lying on the ground a few feet away from him. Part of her head was missing and her eyes . . . those eyes. Even in death, they still stared at him lovingly. Then, everything went black.

The first thing Jonas noticed when he woke up was the smell. It was a peculiar scent that reminded him of the first day of school when the janitor would hit the hallway floors with that fresh mop and wax. This was before the unruly kids would tear through his handiwork, spilling snacks and urinating on the newly cleaned floors. It smelled like the time between the initial cleaning and that when the doors opened—that hour or two when everything was sterile.

At first, he thought that he was in a hospital . . . until he saw the large print poster of Spike Lee's "*Do The Right Thing*." Hospitals usually didn't brandish those. The room he was in was familiar to him. He had been there several times when the tenant who resided there was still alive. He was in Mula's apartment. How he had gotten there was anyone's guess.

Flashes of what had happened began to come to him. He couldn't believe Jewels had shot him. He should've seen it coming. His mother had warned him about how fragile a woman's heart could be, but he hadn't taken heed. Because of it, he had almost gotten himself and the woman he loved killed.

Just then it hit him. Where was Alex? The last time he had seen her, he was acting as a human shield while Jewels had been trying to kill her. Had she survived the assassination attempt too, or had he failed. Jonas tried to sit up but was racked by a throbbing pain in his left shoulder. It was like someone had popped it out of the socket, popped it back in, and then repeated the process. Spots danced before his eyes, and he was forced to lie back down before he passed out.

"Easy, Wrath." Ace appeared at his bedside.

"Fuck happened?" Jonas asked as if he didn't already know.

"That nut-ass bitch Jewels tried to off you, and I domed her traitorous ass!" Ace fumed. Jewels was supposed to be like family, and he couldn't believe she had turned on them. It hurt him to kill her, but it would've hurt more if she had killed Jonas.

"It wasn't all on her, Ace. I brought this on myself," Jonas said, thinking of how their relationship had unfolded over the years. He had been as much to blame for what had happened as Jewels was. He had strung her along, never quite committing but not totally pushing her away, either. He'd always known that she was fragile. Fat Moe had even told him as much, but Jonas was determined to have his cake and eat it too.

"Tavion didn't make it. By the time the ambulance finally showed up, he was gone," Ace said sadly. He had never cared for Tavion. He was a kiss-ass and too big for his britches, but he was as dedicated to their cause as any of them. Ace might not have liked Tavion, but he was growing to respect him.

"Damn." Jonas lowered his head in shame. He'd known Tavion since he was a kid, raised him up to a man, and promised to show him the right way. Jonas should've put a book in his hand, but instead, he put a pistol in it. "I'll reach out to his mom and let her know. Of course, we'll cover the cost of his services. Prince ever turn up?"

"Yeah, in the trunk of his car. A day after you got shot, Stacey got a call to come down to the impound to pick the car up, since it was in her name. They noticed something leaking from the trunk and found Prince inside. Somebody poked him full of holes and left him to bleed out."

Jonas was sad to hear that Prince had been killed. Much like Doug, Prince had been a dude who stayed out of the way and got his money quietly. Also, like Doug, he had died as a result of some shit he really didn't have anything to do with.

As Jonas lay there listening to Ace fill him in, something occurred to him. Ace said Prince was found *the day after* he had gotten shot. How was that possible? It felt like only the span of a nap between his memories of the grand opening and him waking up in the hospital. "How long have I been here?"

"Two days, going on three," Ace told him. "I didn't want you in no hospital where you couldn't be guarded or would have to answer a bunch of questions for the police, so I brought you here. We had Doc patch you up and leave us with some meds for the pain. We were all worried because you hadn't lost enough blood to be in a coma, but you just wouldn't wake up. None of us could figure it out."

"Two days," Jonas thought aloud. Two days since the attempt on his life. Two days head start for his enemies to prepare for what they had to know was coming.

"Two funky days to cripple our organization," Ace added. "It's like we're being picked off."

"Not picked off. Erased," Jonas corrected him. He wasn't sure who had been the one who actually snubbed out Prince's life, but he knew who was behind it. The same person who had been the maestro over Jonas's symphony death throughout the years. He had known from the moment he saw the gun Jewels shot him with. The birthday present he had left on the table.

"And Alex?" Jonas asked, not sure if he was ready for the answer to the question.

Ace was silent.

"Don't go mute on me now. I asked you a question. Where's Alex?" Jonas demanded.

"Gone," Ace told him.

"Is she . . . ?"

"Nah, man. You saved her from Jewels," Ace said, much to his relief. Jonas was hopeful . . . until he finished his statement. "She was pretty bruised up, but otherwise, okay. Her and the baby."

"Then what do you mean, she's gone?"

"As in, out of here. She stuck around long enough to make sure you were going to pull through, and then she hopped the first flight she could book to London. She left this for you." Ace placed a small velvet box into Jonas's hand and closed his fingers around it.

Jonas didn't need to open it to know what was in it. Before the grand opening kicked off, he had pulled her into a quiet corner. He got down on one knee and asked that she be his forever. This would seal the pledge he had made to her about getting out of the streets and helping her to raise the baby. She had accepted his proposal, and they were to have a small ceremony once they were settled in London. All that had changed now. It was like Sweets had warned . . . When the chips were down, she was gone.

"I'm sorry, Wrath," Ace said, seeing the devastated look in Jonas's eyes. He hadn't seen his friend so broken since Sweets died.

"Don't be. I brought this on myself," Jonas told him. He could chase Alex down and try convincing her that this hadn't been his fault, but it was. He had known what would happen. Had been all but told that there would be consequences for his actions, but he hadn't listened. It was just as Flair had predicted: When you think you've got it all, that's when it'll turn to shit, and you'll realize what kind of monster you're dealing with. "Help me out of this bed."

"Wrath, you're banged up and only got one good arm. Where the hell are you going?" Ace watched as Jonas struggle to his feet.

"To discuss my future."

Chapter Forty-four

As it turned out, Ace's scheming on Jonas turned out to work to his advantage. He had something that in all Jonas's years of working with the detective he had never managed to uncover . . . a home address.

Ace wanted to mount up and ride in a small army, but Jonas shut that plan down. He didn't know what he could potentially be walking into, and if things went wrong, someone would have to remain alive to continue the legacy of what they had built. He didn't want it all to have been for nothing.

The detective lived in a one-story house out on Staten Island. It was a modest-looking place with manicured lawns and a small white fence around the front yard. It appeared very ordinary, hardly where he had expected someone as eccentric as Lou Ceaver to call home.

Jonas made a quick survey of the property. He looked for cameras, motion detectors, and anything else that might announce his arrival before he was ready. He found nothing, not even so much as an ADT sticker on any of the windows. What was more peculiar was that when he went to pick the lock, he found the door already open. It felt like a setup, but he had come too far to go back.

He crept inside the house, 9 mm held firmly in his right hand. His left arm hung awkwardly at his side. He had popped enough pills to numb the pain, but the arm still wasn't much good to him. It was no matter, so long as his shooting arm worked. As he made his way through the darkened house, he heard music coming from a room at the end of the hall. He eased up and peered through the door.

There was Detective Ceaver. The room was dark, save for the light from the fire burning in the fireplace. He had his back to him, hunched over a black piano. His fingers moved expertly over the keys as he played a tune that struck a familiar cord in Jonas. He wasn't sure, but it sounded like "Crossroad Blues."

"Are you going to stand there gawking at me or come in?" Detective Ceaver called over his shoulder. Jonas had no idea how he even knew he was there.

Jonas looked around the room cautiously, as if he expected someone to jump out of the shadows and ambush him.

"No need to worry. I can assure you that we're alone. I gave Willie instructions to stay away for the day, not that he would've come even if I had asked him to. He is genuinely quite fond of you."

This made Jonas feel slightly better. He had naturally assumed that Willie had been in on the attempted hit and planned to track him down and settle up as soon as he was done with Ceaver. Jonas entered the room. He kept his gun at the ready and eyes still sweeping back and forth for signs of danger.

"You know, this has always been one of my favorite songs," the detective continued. "From the first time I heard it in that backwater dive down in Mississippi, I knew that I loved it. It was so special that it deserved to be shared with the world, and so I pulled a few strings and made sure that it was. Did I ever tell you that I was once in the music business, Wrath?"

"And explain to me why I should give a fuck," Jonas replied. Then the detective did stop his playing.

When the detective turned to face him, he looked different. The flames from the fireplace played tricks with his cold blue eyes. They almost seemed to glow. His stare went from Jonas's angry face to the gun in his hand. "Is this what we've come to?" he asked almost sadly.

"This is what you made it, Lou," Jonas shot back. "You couldn't just let me go, could you?"

"Of course not, and I told you as much, but you didn't listen. You just had to go and fuck everything up, all because of that bitch who had your nose so open. And where is she now?" The detective stood. "I never liked that girl. She was always messing with your head for her own personal gain. I'm glad she's gone. Now, Jewels, she was a keeper. She was ambitious, dedicated . . . A perfect princess for my young prince. I would've loved to see what you two could've accomplished, but I guess that will never be, thanks to Ace."

"That girl's blood is on your hands!" Jonas shot back. "What did you offer Jewels to turn her against me? Money? Power?"

"We both know that none of those things interested Jewels. I simply offered her what her heart had always desired . . . you. I knew that you still held love in your heart for Jewels, and all it would take was removing a small obstacle so the love could blossom. I was saddened to hear that Jewels had been killed, but even more upset to hear that she had failed to take that bitch Alex with her."

"Watch your fucking mouth!" Jonas pointed the gun at him threateningly.

"What? Your little feelings hurt that I called your beloved Alex out of her name? She *is* a bitch; a manipulative bitch who only wanted to control you. She was threatening to upset our plans. Now that she's gone, we can get back to business."

Jonas laughed. "If you think I'm going to continue working for you after what you've done, you're crazier than I thought."

"That's where you're wrong. We had an agreement, and where I come from, a deal is a deal," the detective told him.

"And where I come from, if a muthafucka shoots at you and misses, you don't give him a second chance," Jonas told him and opened fire. The first two bullets took the detective high in the chest, knocking him back into the piano. Jonas stood over him and placed his gun against the detective's forehead. "Consider our contract voided," he snarled before blowing the detective's brains all over the piano.

Then Jonas collapsed onto the couch. He was so tired that he felt like he couldn't stand. He was only 20 but felt 40. He was tired . . . so very tired. The game was over, and for the first time, he had actually won. Jonas had closed his eyes for a second—but they immediately snapped open again when he heard the sounds of clapping. He turned white as a ghost when he saw the detective pulling himself to his feet.

"Bravo, Wrath . . . bravo!" the detective clapped his hands gleefully.

"What the fuck?" Jonas rolled off the couch, crashing onto his shoulder, sending pain up the side of his body. His eyes *had* to be playing tricks on him. He had put two bullets in the detective's chest, and half of his head had been blown off. How in God's name was he still standing?

"You don't look so good, Wrath. Let me help you up." The detective moved toward Jonas. Jonas opened fire again. The bullets tore through the detective, knocking him this way and that, but he kept coming. By the time he reached Jonas, his 9 mm had clicked empty. "Are you done?"

"How in God's name . . . ?"

"God has nothing to do with this, or haven't you figured it out yet?" the detective smiled. His once straight, white teeth were now pointed and crooked. A forked tongue danced in his mouth. "When we first met, I told you that in you I would right a wrong from my past. You were my fresh start, and my chance to avoid some of the pitfalls of that idiot Zeke."

"What does my father have to do with it?" Jonas asked.

"Wrath, you can't be that dense. Do you think that I just came upon you by chance? No. You were promised to me. I watched you grow, waiting for the opportunity to collect on the debt Zeke owed me."

"*You* were the man my father was in debt to?"

"Bingo! A lifetime of servitude in exchange for riches. Zeke was smart, smart enough to find a way to break our agreement, and there wouldn't have been shit I could've done about it. Luckily, he didn't read the fine print . . . There are very few escape clauses in my deals, but they're in there if you know what you're looking for. Death can be a deal breaker, but it's not as simple as you would think. Not about when you go, but how. The devil is in the details. No pun intended. Death would do it, but it had to be a certain kind of death. He thought he was slick by getting that woman's boyfriend to kill him, but all that did was pass the debt to his children. This is what brought you to me, my Wrath."

"Who are you?" Jonas asked, fearing he already knew the answer.

"I told you what my name was when we met. Weren't you listening?"

"You said you were Detective Lou Ceaver." Jonas repeated what he'd been told when they first met.

"Right, now say it a little faster and as one word."

"Lou Ceaver," Jonas repeated. "Louceaver . . . *Lucifer*." Jonas's eyes were wide with shock.

"Smart boy gets a cookie!" The detective kicked Jonas in his gut, sending him sliding across the floor. "Now, I tried going about this the reasonable way, but you want to make things hard, so we'll play it your way. I *own* you, boy. For the rest of your days, *your* black ass will be at *my* beck and call. One of these days, we'll even put your unborn child to work. Would you like that, Wrath? Working side by side with your kid?"

"Nooooo!" Jonas charged the detective and punched him in the face over and over with his good hand, which only seemed to amuse the detective.

The detective grabbed Jonas by his injured arm, digging his nails into it. Jonas howled in pain. "I love it when they scream," he laughed and tossed Jonas across the room as if he weighed nothing.

Jonas violently slammed into the grate of the fireplace. Hot embers burned his back. He had pulled himself into a kneeling position. The detective was standing over him looking down triumphantly. "I'll do it . . . I'll come back to work for you. Just leave Alex and the baby out of this."

"I'm afraid not. Thanks to you and your daddy, they come as a package deal with this blood debt. For as long as you live, you belong to me. And when the time comes that you are too old to hunt and that trigger finger of yours is too arthritic to work, that bastard Alex is carrying around will take your place."

Jonas had never felt more helpless in his life. He had allowed the detective to make him think he was in control, but he had been the one pulling the string the whole time. In Jonas's foolish quest for power, he had damned himself and his unborn child, and there was nothing he could do about it.

Or was there?

The detective watched with an amused look on his face as Jonas grabbed one of the fireplace pokers. They were made from pure iron. "Here we go again. You can't kill the devil, Wrath. Have you learned nothing during our little chat?"

"I've learned quite a bit, Lou, like you don't know when to shut the fuck up. Thanks to your big-ass mouth, I know where my dad went wrong and how to void our deal," Jonas sneered at him. "By your own admission, death is a deal breaker, but it had to be a certain kind of death. My father was murdered, and his debt was passed on, so this got me to thinking."

"Now, wait a second, Wrath. Let's not be hasty." The detective was suddenly very nervous watching Wrath handle the iron poker. "We can work something out. I was only kidding. You don't think I'd ever go after your kid, do you?"

"That's not a gamble I'm willing to take!" Jonas braced the poker against his chest and fell forward, impaling himself.

"Noooooooooo!" the detective roared, his voice shaking the entire house.

"Game over, Lou," Jonas laughed, coughing blood. As he passed into the next life, his final thoughts were of how he couldn't wait to tell his dad how he had beaten the devil at his own game.

Epilogue

Ten years later . . .

Seven months after Jonas's death, Alex gave birth at a hospital in London to a beautiful baby boy. She named him Jonas, after his father. When news of his death reached her, Alex took it extremely hard. Contrary to what everyone may have said about the way she left Jonas, she truly loved him. She also knew that the chances of him changing were slim. He had lived too long as Wrath. It was as much a part of him as Jonas had been.

Ace made sure that the proceeds from Jonas's and Prince's venture went into a trust that baby Jonas would have access to when he turned 21. It was the least he could do for his friend. Jonas had always been there for him, so Ace felt like it was his duty to be there for Jonas's kid. He played the role of the good uncle . . . but it was short-lived. Ace was gunned down one night while coming out of Sweets. They said the killer was little more than a kid. The description given to the police was that he had a badly burned face and one milky-white eye.

With her new baby also came a new lease on life. Alex was doing so well for herself in London that she decided to stay. Her parents had recently died when a fire broke out in their apartment. They never even got a chance to see her new son. They were the only ties she had left to New York, and with them gone, there was no reason to go back.

For the first few years of Jonas Jr.'s life, Alex had been an excellent mother. Then tragedy struck on the boy's fifth birthday. They had been riding in a car, coming from the bakery picking up the birthday cake when they were involved in a head-on collision with a drunk driver. Jonas Jr. survived, but Alex had not. With no other family, Jonas Jr. ended up in the foster care system where he would remain for the next five years.

"Today is your big day, J. J.," Mrs. Tully said, fixing Jonas Jr.'s tie. She was the woman who ran the home he had been living in. "You're finally going to be adopted. Isn't that special?"

Jonas Jr. didn't respond. He hadn't said more than a few words here and there since his mother died.

"Come on; let's go meet your new family." She took him by the hand and led him from the room. Mrs. Tully took the child into the office where the woman who was to be his new mother was waiting. She was a white woman with red hair and kind eyes. "Sorry to keep you waiting for so long, Mrs. Jones. This is little Jonas; we all call him J. J."

"My, but aren't you a darling little one," Mrs. Jones smiled.

"I thought your husband would be joining us," Mrs. Tully said.

"He should be along shortly. He stopped to pick something up for Jonas from the gift shop," Mrs. Jones said. As if on cue, a man walked in. He was tall and white with a shaved head. Atop it, he bore a scar that looked like it had come from major surgery. "Look at him, honey! Isn't he just perfect?"

Mr. Jones knelt in front of Jonas. It was then that you could see his cold blue eyes. "Yes, perfect indeed. I've been looking for you for a very long time."